To

Missy!

DEATH OF THE INNOCENTS,

A DETECTIVE MURPH MYSTERY

Enjoy Murph's First
adventure!

Bill Rockwell

2018
HMB

Bill Rockwell

Copyright 2016 William Rockwell
ISBN 13: 978-1507688526
ISBN 10: 1507688520

BOOKS BY BILL ROCKWELL

DEATH OF THE INNOCENTS, A DETECTIVE MURPH MYSTERY

NOT PRIVILEGED TO KNOW

Corinne's psychically connected twin is murdered in Washington, DC. Corinne is alone in her mind for the first time in her life, but must adjust to this, solve the murder, and survive the political conspirators' attacks on her life. She learns the future of American freedom depends on her success.

HEAVEN'S CONFLICT, THE RISE AND FALL OF ANGELS

God tries to redeem Lucifer with the help of His Archangels before He must condemn Lucifer to Hell.

GENERATION Z, BIRTH OF THE ZOMPIRE

Damon is bitten by both a Vampire and a Zombie, and becomes a new creature, a *Zompire*. He must convince his girlfriend, Gabby, that he still loves her, and the police that he does not represent a danger to society, all while tracking down the Vampire who bit him to discover his motive and destroy him.

Future Novels

NEED TO KNOW
(aka *PRIVILEGED INFORMATION*)
(The sequel to *Not Privileged to Know*)

Corinne returns to New York City, and is immediately arrested for murder. All the evidence points to her; so, she again hunts the real killer, putting the killer into action again. As she tries to prove her innocence, she is also thrust into the New York mob's machinations. She searches for what she has no "need to know."

ZOMPIRE WAR

Damon and Gabby pursue the Vampire Council, but this time the Vampire fiends are prepared for the Zompires. They have learned their weaknesses, and have set a trap. Will the Zompires fall prey to the Vampires and their Zombie horde, leaving all humanity at risk, or will they rally, and prevail?

McALLISTER,
DEATH AT WHISPERING PINES

A locked room mystery

HEAVEN'S CONFLICT,
THE FALL OF MAN

Satan makes good on his promise to temp Adam and Eve to Evil.

THE MYSTERY OF THE GILDED EAGLE

Jackie Kant's investigation of an unusual mystery at an elegant, romantic restaurant with her new boyfriend leads to mayhem.

DEDICATION

To all the unborn babies who were never given a chance to experience life and contribute to society, and to all the women and men who have been touched by abortion.

ACKNOWLEDGEMENTS

I would like to thank Carol Zukowski, Dr. Anthony Vento, Clarissa Cincotta, Eileen Bianchini, and Lairen Vogan for their help and encouragement with this story.

I also need to thank Theresa Burke, PhD, founder of Rachel's Vineyard, whose books and work helped inspire me to write this novel.

I would also like to express my indebtedness to all my family and friends, too numerous to list, for all their help and support in bringing this novel to fruition.

Who can ascend the mountain of the Lord?
or who may stand in His holy place?
He whose hands are sinless, whose heart is clean
who desires not worthless things,
nor swears deceitfully to his neighbor

Psalm 24: 3,4

CHAPTER 1

The rapping on Eve St. Marie's door awoke her with a jolt. She yanked her head from the desk, her hand striking her half-full coffee mug, sliding it toward the edge, nearly spilling its cold contents. She grabbed the teetering mug as the drink within it scrambled up one side, then the other, and finally settled into a swirling pattern. Without thought, she slid the mug closer to the center of her work area. She wiped the sleep from her eyes, the pressure causing several short-lived spots to flash across her vision. Sniffling, she shook her head to clear her mind. It didn't work.

What was that? Where am I? Oh, yeah, living room... desk... diary. I guess I fell asleep. Her eyes searched the room. *Nothing out of place!* She checked the time: almost midnight.

A second series of knocks, louder this time, rattled the door. *Who could that be at this hour?*

She had been hovering above her diary all day, trying to find the words to express her innermost feelings. They had eluded her. As the night wore on, her mind had become weary, the words blurred. Her hand had shaken with each thought that had succeeded in transferring to the page, causing her handwriting to become that of a drunk, although she hadn't had a drink in weeks. At the end of each sentence, her bawling had forced her to pause. She had gone through three mugs of black coffee since dinner and two boxes of tissues. Neither brought her comfort, nor closer to solving her problems.

With tears again streaming from her bloodshot eyes, she forced her wobbly legs to carry her to the door. *I don't want company. I can't possibly talk to anyone right now. Why would anyone want to bother me at this time of night? They're going to be sent away. I don't care who they are, or what they're selling.*

She tore open her apartment door, her anger causing her to grip the door handle harder than necessary. She froze, eyes springing open at the sight before her. She stared down the barrel of a cocked pistol. Her sobs ceased. She gasped. Her mouth fell open. Her mind raced, struggling to determine if the caller represented the answer to her prayers, the end of her life, or both, deciding, in an instant of self-induced insanity, it really didn't matter. She couldn't tear her eyes from the weapon, held less than a foot from her torso. The gun's barrel loomed much larger than it's actual size, and she swore she could see her name embossed in large, red letters along its entire length.

The hand holding the gun trembled, as if its owner had consumed too much caffeine. This multiplied the movement at the end of the barrel several fold, making its deadly tip appear blurred and surreal.

Eve's body now shook almost as much as her assailant's hand. "No," was the only thing Eve could blurt out before the two bullets, fired in quick succession, slammed into her chest, rupturing her twenty-six year-old heart like sharp pins puncturing a hyper-inflated balloon. Death had been so swift that she didn't even have a chance to raise her arms in defense of her life, nor to grasp her chest that, for a brief moment, filled with excruciating pain.

Eve collapsed in the doorway. Her pale-green nightgown billowed like a parachute, finally deflating only after Eve thumped to the floor. When her body finished its unceremonious collapse, her wide-open eyes starred at her assailant, as if looking for an explanation for the unprovoked attack.

Smiling, the killer squatted down, and checked for a pulse in Eve's thin neck with the index and middle finger of a gloved hand: none. A quick glance down the hallway for potential witnesses assured the killer that no one had seen the execution. Being careful to avoid any contact with Eve's blood, the killer placed a business card in Eve's open hand, forcing her fingers closed around it. The killer, whose hands still shook, then stood, pocketed the gun, and rushed down the front steps of the apartment.

Halfway down the stairs, the killer's cell phone's signature song, *"America the Beautiful"* sung by Frank Sinatra, shattered the stillness of the night. Answering the call while on the run, the killer blasted through the front door, and charged toward an awaiting car without ever looking back.

Tears coursed down Doug's face as he lowered his head. "…but we really need information about this abortion thing before we let anyone know about…" The thought caught in his throat. He groaned.

Molly placed a gentle hand on his shoulder. "I know it's not much consolation, but you're not the first couple to be in…well, this…situation…I mean…Betty Ann's…pregnancy, of course."

"It's Okay, Molly," Betty Ann said. "You can be upfront with us. Call it what it is, my unplanned pregnancy." She lowered her head in concert with Doug.

Molly struggled to find the right words, the right emotion to comfort her friends. "But it's not the end of the world. I mean, you're both still young. Others have been through this, and have come out okay. I mean, you shouldn't feel like you're the first, or that you're all alone, or there's no ultimate answer to all this." She paused, raised her eyes toward Doug. "There simply has to be." She smiled, trying to radiate encouragement. "After all, I'm here for you. What more can you ask?" The smile faded. "But I'm not sure having the information will make it any easier, or make the problem go away." Her voice dropped to barely above a whisper. "I'm afraid the clinic won't make the final choice…I mean, about having…an abortion…or…having the baby. I don't know how they work."

Doug raised his tearful eyes toward Molly, the sadness within him chiseled into the deep furrows now surrounding his lips. "After all, that's why we're going there, to gather as much information as we can. I think it'll be easier then. Won't it, Betty Ann?" His gaze drifted toward her.

"If…if you say so." She lowered her head as she spoke, her long brown hair tumbling off her shoulders to cover her face. Her lips trembled. "This is so…so hard."

Both girls had spent much of the day in the back seat of Doug's car, crying, hugging, and praying for God's guidance. They both felt that God had offered neither help, nor consolation.

Molly leaned closer to Betty Ann, struggling to view her friend's face, to make eye contact, to console her, but her friend's eyes remained scrunched closed behind the veil of her hair. Betty Ann's makeup had smeared, and accumulated into the sobbing-induced, deep creases in her normally smooth skin. The image made Molly wince.

Doug forced a small, but fleeting smile. "Maybe we should call it a spy mission. You know, like the missions 007 goes on, all serious and secret."

"Oh, God," Molly said, "let's hope it's not that exciting! After all that's happened, I'm not sure I'm up to that much adventure or danger."

"Don't worry," Betty Ann said, her expression still sullen as she raised her head, her tearful gaze bouncing from Molly to Doug and back. "I'm sure all you have to do is meet with the doctor, and get some information…about ending the pregnancy." She tried to smile, but couldn't complete the gesture. She lowered her head again, and sobbed softly.

Molly sniffled once. "I'm still not sure about all this. Are we sure you should even be considering an abortion? I mean, shouldn't you be talking about a beautiful baby, a bundle of joy, you know, all the good things that come along with a new baby instead of…destroying it?"

A hush gripped the interior of the car, the only sound the gentle hum of its engine. Betty Ann and Doug hung their heads as their hands interlocked.

Betty Ann finally cleared her throat. "I'm not sure of anything at this point." She sniffled, preferring not to blow her nose. "All I know for sure is that we can't confide in anyone right now, but I am afraid of one thing. The doctor might try to convince us…maybe *coerce* is a better word…into jumping into the abortion right away, maybe even today. Who knows how they work?" She lifted her head, exposing now reddened cheeks, dripping with tears.

"I'm afraid you have to go in alone, Molly, convince them you're there only to get information for a friend, nothing more. Don't agree to anything, no examination, no information on health insurance, nothing! Give them as little information as you can. It's the only way, I'm afraid. I promise we'll be waiting right here for you. We're here to back you up."

"That's right," Doug said. "If anything goes wrong, call us, and we'll come for you."

"And do what, drag me out of the clinic?"

Doug shrugged his shoulders. "Whatever it takes."

Betty Ann gripped Molly's shoulders, squeezing harder than she had intended. "But make sure you get the information you're going in for. Otherwise, this trip will have been a waste of time."

Molly smiled at her friend, and placed a gentle hand on her knee. "Of course I'll get the information you want." She sucked in a deep breath, blew it out forcefully. "But let's get to the clinic before I change my mind, or I'm late for that appointment." She lowered her head once more, and shook it slowly. She took another deep breath. "Okay, here goes nothing, or should I say *everything?* I'm still not sure about...any of this, but, okay, I'll do whatever I have to...whatever you want me to...whatever you think you need." A shudder spread through her body despite the warmth of the car. Her voice became hushed, almost inaudible. "Let's do this...and soon...before I lose my nerve. May God forgive me!"

CHAPTER 2

Dr. John Rebak, chief medical examiner for Adams, Connecticut, had been kneeling over Eve St. Marie's body for only a few minutes when he spotted Senior Detective William Murphy, affectionately known as "Murph," approaching from within Eve's apartment. Rebak had been the medical examiner for over twenty-eight years, and had worked multiple cases with Murph. Rebak wore a sullen expression, his long, drawn face toughened by years of dealing with death in all its forms. He frowned, adding more wrinkles to his already time-wrinkled appearance. He wore thick glasses that were a progressive bifocal that still made him dizzy. He pushed them up his nose, trying to adjust the tilt of his head to get them focused. *I wonder if I'll ever get used to them.* Frustrated, he ran his fingers through his frizzy, jet-black hair, and then shook his head. With a gloved hand, he removed a probe from the girl's liver as Murph stepped behind him.

"Any preliminary findings, Doc?"

Rebak smiled. "I thought you'd never ask. We've got to stop meeting like this, Murph. Our wives will start wondering what we're doing together."

"Maybe your wife, Doc, not mine. Jen trusts me, and I've never given her reason to think otherwise. You, on the other hand..." Murph returned the smile, letting the words hang in the air.

Rebak threw an angry stare at Murph. "You know me better than that."

Murph laughed, "I was just..."

"Joking with me, I know."

"It's too late at night to spar, though, Doc. What've we got?"

Rebak sighed, shook his head again, and closed his eyes briefly. *Too late is right!* He turned away from Murph, fixing his gaze upon the probe, moving it away, and then closer to get its digital readout in focus. "I get it. You only want the facts. Okay, by her liver temperature, I'd say she died between eleven PM and two AM. These two obvious gun shot wounds in her chest are the presumed cause of death. She's got gunpowder residue on her nightgown. So, she was shot at point-blank range, probably less than two to three feet, but certainly no farther than four."

Murph stood, but remained silent, sensing Doc hadn't finished.

"There aren't any exit wounds," Rebak continued, lifting the body to expose her back. "My guess is some small caliber weapon, maybe a .32 or a .38 hand gun, but I'll get you the exact caliber when I retrieve the bullets. Death was probably instantaneous. There are no obvious cuts or bruises on her body. I'll get you a complete report, including the rape kit result, as soon as I get the young lady back to the morgue." The doctor re-checked the time on his wristwatch. "Should be later this morning. I've got no back up of cases right now. It's a miracle of miracles in my line of work."

"Thanks Doc." Murph turned back toward the interior of the apartment. Over his shoulder he added, "Tell your wife we met on police business, not funny business."

"Will you sign a sworn affidavit to that effect?"

"If it comes down to either that, or going to your funeral, I'll consider it. Let me know."

Deciding not to continue the banter, Rebak resumed his exam.

"Johnson, what'd you find?"

Tom Johnson, Murphy's partner of twelve years, had been busy writing in his notebook. He smiled widely as he walked toward Murph. "You mean besides the grouchy ME bending over the victim?" He clipped his pen to the notebook cover, lost the smile, and began reading from the first page. "The initial call came in at 11:35 PM from a neighbor, one Margaret Hanabee, a senior who lives next door with her husband. She heard the shots a few minutes before. Claims it sounded like two loud bangs or a car backfiring."

"No silencer then."

"Apparently not. It's surprising more people didn't hear the shots. At that time of night, it would have been very quiet in the building. You would think someone else would have awoken, but the neighbors all claimed to be sound asleep, asserting they never heard anything. Mrs. Hanabee was watching the 11 o'clock news. Claims that's all she knows."

"Don't suppose she caught the plates of the shooter's car," Murph said, already knowing the disappointing answer. Murph scrunched up his face, and looked at Johnson with eyes trained by twenty-two years on the force, dotted with a few unsolved cases, but many more commendations for his successes. Murph's previous partner, Joe Smithson, had retired, having taught Murph his doggedly tenacious approach to solving crimes. Joe's work motto had been that the criminals always, *always* left clues to their crimes, whether they realized it, or not. He preached that the detective's job was really an easy one: identify those hidden clues before the perp fled to a country without extradition, or committed another crime. He spent one hundred percent of his time on a case, studying all the events surrounding the crime, and trying to separate the clues from the "red herrings." During his career, Smithson had proved to be more successful than any other detective in the Northeast, a service record Murph strove to not only emulate, but to exceed. Even Smithson, however, couldn't overcome a reluctant witness. That reticence often complicated his investigations, forcing him to work harder, give more attention and importance to every detail of an investigation, and ultimately helped sculpture Smithson's work motto and his career.

Before Murph could verbalize his thoughts, Johnson smiled, nodding in agreement, as if reading Murph's mind through Murph's Smithson-trained eyes. Johnson shook his head. "Never even saw the car. When she heard the shots, she went into the hallway, found the door open, and discovered the victim. Her screams woke most of the other neighbors. A lot of them called 911 after that." He paused, and, when Murph said nothing, continued, "Even if some neighbor did hear those shots, or spotted the car, they're not talking, probably afraid the perp will come after them." He sighed in frustration, his shoulders drooping as he spoke. "We'll keep grilling them, but I guess we're going to have to solve this case the old

Bill Rockwell

fashioned way: with sweat and hard work! It's never easy, Murph, is it?"

"No, but that's what makes the job interesting."

"Interesting, but difficult. Anyway, we've got Mrs. Hanabee next door if you want to talk to her. She's pretty shaken up, but very cooperative. Apparently, she liked the victim."

"Okay, I'll go talk to her while the CSI team works in here. I'll be back to go over this place with you when I'm done."

Johnson nodded, and then pointed down the hallway, indicating the direction of Mrs. Hanabee's apartment.

Without saying a word, Murph stepped around Doc Rebak and into hallway, giving a fleeting look at the beautiful victim, seemingly staring up at him for some consolation and an explanation for her murder. He shook his head. *So young! What a waste! I'll try to get you that explanation, Miss St. Marie, so you can truly rest in peace.*

CHAPTER 3

The chocolate brown paint of the hallway, along with the darkly painted banister, gave the hallway a somber feel. A dim, hanging lantern, located halfway down the hallway provided the only lighting. *It needs a brighter bulb, if not an entirely modern replacement.* As he approached Mrs. Hanabee's door, he flashed his badge to the officer standing there. "Is she up to some questioning?"

The officer nodded, and smiled broadly. "She's a tough old lady. I think she can handle it."

Murph entered the apartment through the already open door, making sure he knocked on it hard to announce his entry. "Mrs. Hanabee? It's detective Murphy. Can I see you for a couple of minutes?"

"In the living room," a female voice said to his left. "We're in here."

Murph followed the short hallway, and entered the living room to find an elderly woman in a green floral housedress, sitting on a wooden rocking chair. Across a metal tray table, set up in front of her, sat a droopy-eyed man of similar age that Murph presumed to be her husband. He sat on a rickety-looking, rusted, metal chair that squeaked with each movement of his corpulent body. A solid-blue couch stood along the wall adjacent to her chair with two rusted, folded, metal chairs leaning against it. Dozens of photographs framed in black covered the dull beige walls. From their resemblance to the Hanabees, Murph guessed these to be close relatives. Two table lamps decorated with a floral design, and brandishing tall, white lampshades provided all the lighting.

Murph flashed his badge again. "I'm Detective Murphy. I know you already talked to my partner, but do you mind if I ask you to go over what happened one more time for me? Sometimes when people repeat a story, they remember new things, and that would be a great help to us."

"No, don't mind at all," she said, bolting upright in the rocker as if she had just been startled from an unplanned catnap. "Grab a seat. Can we offer you a cup of coffee? It's fresh brewed in the kitchen." She pointed to a doorway to Murph's left. Her voice resonated, and swayed with a slight Irish brogue.

Murph guessed her age as mid-seventies. *She probably came to America as a youth, and has been trying ever since to overcome the accent...with limited success.* "Thanks, no." Murph took a seat in one of the chairs he retrieved from those resting against the couch. He placed it at the side of the tray table so he could observe both Hanabees.

Mrs. Hanabee raised her coffee mug toward her husband. "This be my husband, Brian. He didn't hear nothin'. He sleeps like a hibernatin' bear. An atom bomb wouldn't wake him. Matter of fact, I'm not sure he's awake now. You with us, Brian?"

"Yeah," Brian said, taking another large gulp of his coffee, taking the opportunity to glare over the cup at Murph, and snarl as if Murph were a dangerous home invader.

Murph ignored him. "Detective Johnson said you were watching television when you heard the shots. Is that how it happened, Mrs. Hanabee?"

"Yeah." She lowered her eyes, and stared into her coffee as she rotated the mug slowly. Her accent grew thicker as she spoke, her voice lower, forcing Murph to lean forward to catch every word. Releasing her mug, she patted the arms of the rocker, her hands barely touching the aged wood, as if any hard banging would shatter them like fragile glass. "I be sittin' right here in me favorite chair, watching the eleven o'clock news." She pointed to the television, as if Murph wouldn't recognize its use. The older, nineteen-inch television rested on a well-aged, wooden table against the wall opposite her seat. On the muted screen, a movie Murph didn't recognize had just been interrupted for a series of easily identifiable commercials. "The weather report had just started when I heard two bangs." She pointed in the direction of her front doorway. "Sounded like a car backfiring, but the sounds seemed to be coming from the hallway instead of outside." She stared deep into Murph's eyes. "Made me jump, I tell you."

"You only heard two bangs?" Murph wrote the essentials of the narrative into his notebook.

She held up two fingers in Murph's face. "Only two."

"How close? I mean, were they bang, bang, real close together? Or were they more separated, bang" …Murph paused for a few seconds…"bang, for example?"

"Oh, they be very close. Bang, bang. Real close together they be."

"And then what happened?"

"I muted my TV, and got up to see what be making the noise." Mrs. Hanabee patted the top of her legs. "I hobbled these painful legs up to our front door there…it's always locked, you know…and put me ear against it, and listened for a few seconds. I didn't want to go out if there be a ruckus going on, you know."

"Did you hear any noise at all from the hallway while you walked to the door, or maybe after you got there?"

"Not a bloomin' thing!" Mrs. Hanabee shook her head, and stared at her husband.

Murph noted an almost imperceptible rise in her husband's eyebrows, and a very small, slow movement of his head from side-to-side.

Mrs. Hanabee frowned, drooped her head, and stared into her mug again.

Murph turned toward her husband, smiled, and said, "You know, I think I will take a cup of coffee. It's been a long night, and I'm beginning to feel the lateness of the hour. Can I bother you, Mr. Hanabee, to get it for me while I finish with your wife? I've only got a few more questions. I sure would appreciate it."

Brian Hanabee didn't move, other than to shift his squinted eyes toward Murph as if to say: "And whom do you think you are to order me around anyway?"

"Go on, Brian," Mrs. Hanabee said, as she shook her hand, its fingers bent and deformed by arthritis, in front of her husband's face. "Be polite to our guest, and get him a mug o' coffee right away."

Brian snarled, but stood, and lumbered toward the kitchen. "Fine," he barked over his shoulder, his snarl cemented in place, "but she don't know nothin' else 'cause she didn't see, or hear nothin' else. Understand?"

"I take my coffee black. Thanks, I really appreciate your getting it for me."

CHAPTER 4

As soon as Mr. Hanabee exited the room, Murph leaned toward Mrs. Hanabee, and whispered, "Please, Mrs. Hanabee, anything, anything at all, that you remember might be of extreme importance to our case. It might make the difference between catching your neighbor's killer, and having him get away with murder." He glanced toward the kitchen. "Please, before your husband returns, tell me what really happened."

Mrs. Hanabee also checked the kitchen doorway before speaking. "Well," she said, matching Murph's whisper, and adding a sly smile and a wink, "when I listened at the door, I heard someone runnin' down the hallway stairs very fast, indeed."

"Were the sounds of the footsteps on the stairs loud, or soft?"

Mrs. Hanabee paused for a moment to relive the scene in her mind. "Well, they sounded soft, but the stairs are carpeted, you know. So even a heavy person's steps might sound soft, especially listenin' through the door the way I be, but, if you were asking me to guess, I'd guess he be a light one on his feet that one be, like maybe he be a leprechaun." She paused, checked for her husband again, and then added, "I also heard some music."

Murph's eyes widened. "Music? What kind of music?"

"Music like a cell phone plays when it rings. I recognized the song. "America the Beautiful," sung by non other than Frank Sinatry…you know, the one they used to call, 'Ol' Blue Eyes.' Then, before the song finished, that old front door of this decrepit building opened, and then slammed shut. Bang!" She started to clap the palms of her hands together, being sure to keep her hands at right angles to prevent the fingers of one hand from striking the other. However, she stopped before they connected, realizing that her husband would hear the clap, wonder what she had done, and possibly return faster from the kitchen, preventing her from finishing her story. She glanced toward the kitchen, actually wondering why Brian had not returned.

As if answering her inquisitive stare, four beeps sounded from the kitchen. Mrs. Hanabee smiled, realizing her husband had been using the microwave to heat the detective's coffee.

"Did you happen to hear a car speed away?"

"Actually, yes." Mrs. Hanabee lowered her head, her eyes continuing to search for her husband. "Brian doesn't want me to get any more involved than I already am. He'll be real mad at me when he finds out I told you what I heard, but I want to see Eve's killer caught. Humph! So, the heck with him!" She leaned even closer, her voice barely a whisper. "It sounded like a big engine...maybe a Corvette or a Cadillac...you know, a big gas-guzzler, but smooth as Irish blarney, if you're knowin' what I mean."

Murph didn't, despite his Irish ancestry, but nodded, and smiled anyway.

She winked at Murph's projected understanding, and then continued, "Didn't hear any tires squealing the way they show on TV, though." She leaned back in her chair as her husband re-entered the room.

"Hope this coffee is to your liking. I heated it in the microwave. That old coffee brewer doesn't keep the coffee hot enough for me."

"I'm sure it'll be fine," Murph said, accepting the mug that actually felt cold despite the steaming coffee it contained. He sipped the coffee. Besides being boiling hot, he found it toe-curling strong. "I've only got a couple of questions more, then we'll be done. I really do appreciate all your help."

"Don't mention it," Mrs. Hanabee said, smiling at Murph.

"Did Miss St. Marie have a boyfriend?"

"Sure enough did," Mrs. Hanabee said. "Only met him a couple o' times in the hallway. We never visited with them. He came over to visit Eve every now and again. They'd go out, and then return a few hours later. Where they'd get off to I have no idea. Maybe they would go to a movie, or out to dinner. Always home early though, like a good girl, she be."

"Do you know his name, or where he lives?"

"Bob was his first name," Mrs. Hanabee said. "Kil...something was the last name...like Killjoy or Kilroy. No, that's not right." Her gaze shot to her husband, now sipping his coffee. "Do you remember Bob's last name, Brian?"

Brian's gaze swung from his drink to his wife and back. He shook his head. "No idea. Never said much to me anyway."

"That's okay," Murph said. "We'll get his name and address some other way. Did she throw many parties?"

Brian's head snapped up. "No, never...no parties, ever."

"That's right," Mrs. Hanabee said. "Eve wasn't into no shenanigans at her place. She kept it real quiet over there. Like I said, she be a good girl that one be. We're going to miss her." She lowered her head, and again studied her coffee grounds.

Murph stood, carefully placed the still steaming coffee mug on the tray table, and returned his folding chair to its original position against the couch. "That'll be all for now. Another officer will be over in a few minutes to complete your statements, and give you our phone numbers in case you remember something later on. Thanks again for helping. I'll show myself out."

"You make sure you catch Eve's killer," Mrs. Hanabee said. "What happened to her shouldn't happen to anyone, especially anyone as nice as she be."

"We will, Mrs. Hanabee," Murph assured her. "We will."

As Murph exited the apartment, the officer standing outside nodded. "Was she any help?"

Murph smiled widely. "Sure was. Keep your eyes open for a patriotic, smooth talking, light-footed leprechaun with a gun, who's driving a luxury car that's just been tuned up." They shared a laugh that kept Murph amused until he entered the victim's apartment, and paused over Doc Rebak who still knelt over Eve St. Marie's body.

CHAPTER 5

Murph turned toward his partner who had just taken a picture of the victim's face with his cell phone to use until official photos became available. "So, what else do we know?"

Johnson flipped open his notebook. "No forced entry that we could detect. She opened the door, so maybe she knew the perp. There's a dead bolt and a chain in addition to the keyed handle."

Murph inspected the locks after donning gloves. The bolt retracted with ease.

"There are plenty of fingerprints on the doorknobs and bolt lever. They'll probably all match the victim. We think she sat at that desk writing in her diary before she was murdered." Johnson pointed to an older, maple, roll-top desk that looked like Ben Franklin could have used it as the Deputy Postmaster General of the colonies in 1753. The top stood retracted, revealing a neat desktop with a cup of coffee, an open diary, a fountain pen, and a stack of blank writing paper.

Murph tried to imagine the victim sitting, writing in the diary, and then jotting a quick note to a friend about whatever tidbit she had entered into the diary, and mailing it the next day. *I wonder if she could be one of those disappearing breed who still preferred snail mail to email.*

Johnson walked toward the desk with Murph at his heals. "The chair is in the pulled out position at an angle from the desk as if she slid it out to answer the door." Johnson gaze drifted up from his notebook to Murph, who listened attentively to his rhetoric. "The kitchen is in the other direction." Johnson pointed to an open doorway behind the chair. "She must have swung the chair to answer the door. She never finished her last diary entry."

"What's in it?"

Johnson leaned over the desk, being careful not to disturb anything. "Friday, June 20th, Eleven PM. Had a terrible day. Home all day. Cried a lot. Tried praying, but couldn't. God doesn't want to hear from me! Called the clinic this afternoon. Talked to Barbara. She tried to assure me I did the right thing. I'm not so sure. Told me to come down tomorrow for another counseling session. Not sure the first one did any good. I don't deserve counseling! I don't deserve forgiveness! I am evil, but I am truly sorry! I regret so much what I did. I regret…." Johnson turned toward Murph. "That's where it ends. There are some round wet marks on the same page. My guess is that they're tears, but forensics will confirm that later today. I guess we'll have to figure out what she regretted doing."

"I may be able to help with that," Rebak said, still bending over the victim. "She has a business card crumpled in her hand." He forced open the woman's hand to grasp the corner of the card between his fingers. He dropped it into a clear plastic evidence bag. Without reading the card, he handed it to Murph who had hustled back to the body at the mere mention of another clue.

"Adams' Pro-Life League, "Be One with the Lord and Respect All Life…Including the Unborn," Katherine McDonahue, President." Address is on First Street, downtown."

"Killers don't usually leave their calling cards," Johnson said. "Nice of the perp to help us."

"Might not be the killer's," Murph said. "She could have been holding it while writing in her diary, and carried it with her to answer the door. Her hand may have clamped down around it when the killer shot her." He shook the bag. "Maybe this Pro-Life movement is the clinic she referred to in her note."

"My guess is an abortion clinic," Rebak said. "The Pro-lifers don't have clinics. As a matter of fact, they're usually trying to close the abortion clinics, or at least interfere with their business."

Johnson took the evidence bag from Murph, and examined the card. "You mean performing abortions, right?"

Rebak stood, and waved his assistants over to remove the body. "Basically; the Pro-Lifers believe life begins at conception, and anything that's done to deliberately end a pregnancy is wrong. It goes against their religious beliefs."

Johnson handed the evidence bag back to Murph. "But it's legal, right?"

"In this state, yes," Rebak said, "but they still consider it morally wrong."

"But haven't those same Pro-lifers bombed some of those clinics, killing doctors, nurses and anyone else there? Isn't that murder too?" Murph asked.

"Yes," Rebak said, "some members of the Pro-Life movement across the country have done some really violent things, but those are the acts of only a few radical extremists. You get those in any large group of people, especially large religious groups, and, to them, anything, including murder, is acceptable to achieve their goals. That doesn't mean the whole organization thinks that way, though."

Johnson shook his head. "The ends justify the means, eh? Doesn't make any sense to me; but, then again, I'm a detective. So, I'm prejudiced toward the victims of violence…any violence…at any age."

"Maybe I'm wrong, " Murph said, ignoring Johnson's comments, and shrugging his shoulders, "maybe the killer did bring a card to the murder. Maybe it enticed the victim to open the door."

"Then, wouldn't the killer have retrieved the card before leaving the scene?" Johnson asked.

"Maybe he or she panicked, and forgot to take it, or maybe I guessed right the first time, and the victim had the card in her hand when she answered the door. In either case, we need to talk to Katherine McDonahue of the Pro-Life League."

Rebak watched his assistants push the gurney out the door. "I'll be able to tell you if she had a recent abortion after I examine her later this morning."

"Thanks, Doc," Murph said, nodding his head and turning back toward the victim's desk. As he walked slowly toward it, Murph's eyes examined the floor, looking for anything that could aid his investigation, but found nothing of consequence. He sat in the wooden chair, wondering if its thin, delicate-looking legs would support his weight. They did. The seat felt small for his six-foot, two hundred pound muscular frame, his hips rubbing on the fine, ornately carved arms. As he examined the desk's surface, he tried to imagine the victim, sitting and writing words she thought would remain private, never to be seen by another human being. *How wrong she was!* "Has forensics finished in here?" He reached for the fountain pen lying alongside the diary, silently awaiting its owner's delicate hand to convert its ink into precious, personal thoughts.

"Yes. The CSI team almost finished before you arrived. They've photographed and fingerprinted the whole place, and I've got an inventory of the things they took to the lab. They shouldn't be too much longer. They're making sure they didn't miss anything the first time around. I asked them to leave the desk for you to examine before they packed up its contents."

"Anything interesting in what they found?" Murph lifted the green pen. Lighter than he had guessed from its large size, it had the words: "SEASIDE VACATION RESORTS" printed in gold leaf on its side. "Looks like she stayed in a resort hotel recently. Do we know if she's been in the apartment long?"

Johnson checked his notebook. "According to the 'Super,' she moved in six months ago. She signed a two-year lease...told him she originally lived in Cincinnati, but transferred here because of her employment. Maybe she took a vacation at that resort before starting her new job. She's an executive for a small beer brewing company in northern Ohio called, 'Rockson Brewing.' She told the 'Super' they were interested in setting up a distribution center here to promote the beer. I guess they wanted to turn their micro-brewery into a larger, profit-making company by expanding their base out here, first here in Connecticut, then New York City, and then up and down the whole East Coast."

Johnson had lowered his voice almost to a whisper. Murph looked up from the desk to see what had caused the sudden somber timbre in his partner's voice.

Johnson now stood slouched, his expression matching the melancholy in his voice. "I checked the fridge," Johnson muttered, without moving a muscle, "no samples of the beer, I'm afraid."

Murph smiled. "If there had been, I'm sure you would have tasted them even though it's only around 5 AM. Right?"

Johnson returned the smile, bringing his hands up so he could once more read his notebook. "It's all part of good detective's work. Try the brew, get to know the victim as best as one can to figure out what thoughts might have gone through her mind right before being murdered."

"Even if those thoughts are clouded by alcohol?"

Johnson saluted, and then performed an exaggerated bow. "It's a sacrifice I would have made for the department, Detective Murphy."

Murph's smile grew as he pulled open one of the desk drawers to find it empty. "You're so dedicated, Detective Johnson. I may even recommend you for a commendation for your intended efforts on advancing this case."

Johnson lost the smile, his voice becoming serious. "The CSI team didn't find much else, no men's clothes or toiletries anywhere in the apartment. So, if she did have that abortion, the father wasn't her live-in boyfriend."

Murph rummaged through the travel brochures, empty notepads and other papers he found in one of the other drawers and the desk's open cubbyholes. "Or he left when he found she had become pregnant. Of course, if what she regretted related to an abortion, maybe he encouraged her to have the procedure, and she threw him out afterward as part of her grieving process. That could also lead to another suspect if they were having an affair, and her pregnancy got back to a wife. That wife might be furious enough to kill. Whoa! Look here, a brochure from the "Adams' Women's Medical Clinic." It's on Clinton Avenue downtown. Medical Director is one Elliot Svensen MD, and the assistant is Barbara Schine, presumably the same Barbara mentioned in the diary. I wonder if it's a clinic that performs abortions."

"I believe they're called 'Pro-Choice' clinics," Rebak said as he collected his equipment bag, and left the apartment.

"I guess that's our next stop then," Johnson said.

"Almost correct," Murph said, piling all the papers alongside the diary for the CSI team to collect. He stood with difficulty as the arms of the small chair caught on his hips, forcing him to push down on them to extricate himself. "First, we stop at the diner for some breakfast. I'm starved, and I don't think well on an empty stomach. Besides, I presume the clinic won't be open for at least a few more hours, if it's open on Saturday at all. By the way, were there any usable prints on the brochure, like maybe from her absent boyfriend?"

Johnson frowned. "None, I'm afraid, and there were no usable prints on the outside door handle or the railing going downstairs. It started to rain hard around eleven last night, so, the street got washed real good by Mother Nature. Any oil drippings or other clues that might have been left from the escape vehicle are gone, I'm afraid."

Murph sighed. "Figures. Let's go. The rest of the team can finish the clean up." As he walked toward the door, he yelled to no one in particular, "You can reach me on my cell if anything interesting turns up."

CHAPTER 6

Breakfast consisted of eggs, rye toast, pancakes, orange juice and several cups of coffee that the waitress assured them contained extra caffeine.

Murph stared into his cup. *This doesn't even come close to the strength of Mrs. Hanabee's.*

They left the waitress a large tip despite the weak coffee, and drove to the address of the Women's Clinic. Located in a storefront, it had a small sign over the door: "Adams' Women's Medical Clinic." Beneath the name, in tiny print were the words: "Adams' Women's Reproductive Health Center (WRHC): 24-Hour Phone Service: 1-800-555-0367."

Bordering the clinic on its right stood a store offering "Everything for a Dollar Plus." A convenience store with a rack of newspapers stacked neatly outside its front door stood to its left.

Johnson parked the unmarked black Dodge Charger directly in front of the clinic in a clearly marked "No Parking Zone." He placed a placard in the window that read: "Official Police Business," with the Police Commissioner's name in smaller letters in the lower right corner.

As he exited the car, stepping onto the six-foot wide sidewalk, Murph checked his watch: a few minutes after nine. Only a few people strolled by, most sporting either suits or smart dresses, as if heading for office jobs. There were a few women dressed in casual clothes, window-shopping in no particular rush, stopping briefly at each window to inspect the wares within, and pointing at things of interest. All acted as if the policemen didn't exist, and were simply part of the normal background of this downtown area.

The city of Adams, a midsize community in central Connecticut, had made an effort recently to rid the downtown of the homeless and derelicts that tended, by their mere presence, to drive away would-be customers of the merchants. These citizens had been relocated to low-to-no-income housing, and the town's social service department had made a valiant effort to get them gainfully employed. However, despite what the public thought, these unfortunate people usually were not responsible for most of the violent crime in the area. Instead, it had been driven in large part by the relentlessly illegal activities of drug addicts, pursuing the money needed for their habits, and the illegal gambling activities and prostitution being run by organized crime. Increased police patrols in the area had cut down on, but had not totally eliminated, these criminal groups and their activities.

An officer on a bicycle, wearing dark blue shorts and a light blue uniform shirt rounded the corner, spotted the illegally parked car, and headed in their direction. Both Murph and Johnson drew their police shields, and flashed them as the officer approached.

Spotting both the shields and the placard in window of the car, the officer smiled, slowed his bike, and parked on the curb in front of the police car. The mountain bike had riser handlebars, grip shifters, red and blue lights powered by a battery pack beneath the upper tube, and a complex gear mechanism capable of at least 27 speeds. Its thick black tires shined, as if they had been recently polished, complimenting its spotless, silver metal spokes. It came equipped with a red metal water bottle attached to the down tube that gleamed in the morning sun. It also sported a black leather trunk bag behind the seat, secured with Velcro straps, held closed with a double zipper. A two-inch wide strip of silver reflective material on the side of the bag shone brightly in the early morning sunlight. Below the strip, the word "POLICE," printed in large white letters, announced its ownership.

"Good morning, Sirs," the officer said, as he dismounted the bicycle, and removed his helmet. He ran his hand through his short, thick black hair, as he hooked his helmet, via the chinstrap, on one of the bike's handles. He snapped the kickstand down with a loud "click," and balanced the bike on it, turning the front wheel in the direction of the kickstand before removing his hand. Tall, lean and clean-shaven, he had an exaggerated angular jaw that gave him the rugged appearance of a movie actor arriving fresh from shooting an action-adventure movie. He wore no rings.

"I'm Detective Murphy and this is Detective Johnson."

"I'm Officer Joe Martinelli, badge 308, Community Patrol Division. Can I be of any assistance to you in your investigation, Detectives?" He wore shining black sneakers with low cut, black socks. His uniform shirt and shorts were smartly pressed. Around his slim waist hung a black leather belt, securing his holstered 9 mm automatic, a canister of mace, a nightstick, a two-way radio with a microphone clipped to the lapel of his shirt, and a pair of shiny handcuffs, snapped to the belt via a short, leather loop.

Murph smiled as he returned his ID to his jacket pocket. *All in all, this young man's appearance is the exact image the department has been trying to project in the downtown area: friendly, helpful, but prepared for any emergency.* "Actually, yes, we're investigating the murder of a young woman named Eve St. Marie uptown in her apartment last night. Ever heard of her?"

"I don't think so." Martinelli paused briefly to search his memory. He pointed to the clinic door. "Is she connected to the clinic here?"

"We're not sure," Murph said, as Johnson joined him at his side. "She may have been a patient there. Have there been any disturbances or problems recently at the clinic?"

"Oh, yes, definitely, just yesterday morning, a group of about ten Pro-Lifers, as they call themselves, from the Pro-Life League, were here protesting the abortions that are performed in there. One of the neighbors, who lives above the stores, called it in when they first arrived, and I was sent to investigate. They were very polite, and, after I talked to the person in charge, they agreed not to block anyone's access to the clinic. They had brochures that they tried to hand to anyone who would take them, both men and women. Some took them, others didn't. The group just said prayers, Rosaries, I think, over and over again."

Johnson raised an eyebrow. "You mean to tell me that men go in there too?"

Martinelli nodded a few times. "Oh, yes, Sir, usually they're accompanying a woman, of course. Don't know that I've ever seen a man go in alone, now that I think about it."

"Do you happen to remember the name of the person in charge by any chance?" Murph asked.

"Wrote it down, just in case." Martinelli reached for the notepad in his back pocket. He flipped through a few pages, and then nodded. "Here it is, Michael McDonahue. He told me that his wife, Katherine McDonahue, is the actual president of their organization, but she wasn't at the prayer service or protest, whatever they called it."

"Is that unusual," Murph asked, "I mean, for the person in charge of a group not to be present?"

"Actually, it is a bit unusual. Most of the time, the person leading the group is present for the entire period of the protest; however, Mr. McDonahue claimed his wife had become ill that morning, and decided to stay home. I've got their address and phone number, if you'd like them. They've protested in front of this clinic before, as have other groups."

"Yes, please. Give it to Johnson, and thank you for all your help, Officer Martinelli."

"You're welcome, Sir." Martinelli held his notebook so Johnson could copy the information. His handwriting was as neat as his outfit, and very easy to read. "If you need any further assistance, the Station can reach me on my two-way radio, if I'm on patrol. If you ever need me when I'm not working, the Station has my cell. This is my beat, and I like keeping up on whatever happens here. I love the downtown area and its people. So, don't hesitate to call me." He returned the notebook to his pocket after Johnson indicated that he had finished.

"We will," Murph said, appreciating the young man's genuine and sincere enthusiasm. "Thank you."

"Would you like me to accompany you into the clinic?"

"No. I don't think that will be necessary. We'll give you a call if we need anything."

"Okay." In one fluid motion, Martinelli raised the kickstand, and mounted his bike. "Please keep me in the loop, if it turns out someone in there had anything to do with the murder. I'd like to squelch any problems, including bad feelings or repercussions between the groups before anything blows out of control. Sometimes a simple word from someone like me who cares about the neighborhood and its residents can prevent violence or misunderstandings before they have a chance of even starting."

"Understood," Murph said, "and the sentiment is appreciated. We'll call you with anything we find. Please keep your eyes and ears open for us also."

"Will do." Martinelli pushed his bike, mounted it, and peddled down the street, waiving at the people he passed in a friendly, smile-filled manner.

"Seems like a nice fellow," Johnson said.

"And a good officer, I suspect," Murph agreed, as he watched the officer disappear around a corner. Turning toward the clinic, he said, "Now, let's go meet the staff."

CHAPTER 7

The Double glass doors to the clinic were etched with the clinic name, but did not list any of the physicians or other medical personnel who worked there.

Murph pointed to the door. "I guess they don't want their employees' names advertised to the public."

"Guess not," Johnson agreed, shrugging, and pulling open one of the doors.

Murph grabbed his badge as he approached the front desk. The woman there, who Murph judged to be in her mid twenties, wore a yellow flowered blouse with a squared-off neckline and three-quarter length sleeves. A silver necklace with a heart-shaped slide dangled above the top of her blouse. She wore her short, blond hair pulled back behind both ears, and sported hoop earrings. She looked up, and smiled as the men entered the light brown, carpeted entranceway.

"Good morning, Gentlemen. How can I help you?"

"I'm Detective Murphy, and this is my partner, Detective Johnson. We'd like to see Dr. Elliot Svensen and Barbara Schine." He read the names from his notes, and wrote the receptionist's name, Linda Summerset, into his notebook, copying it from the nameplate on her desk.

"Certainly," Linda said, reaching for the white phone on her desk. "May I tell Dr. Svensen what this concerns?" She held the phone inches from her ear, awaiting a reply.

"Just tell him it's official police business," Murph said.

"Certainly!" She punched a four-digit extension, and waited for a few seconds. "Dr. Svensen, there are two detectives, named Murphy and Johnson, here, asking to see you." She paused, listening for a short time. "No, they won't tell me what it's about, just that it's official police business." Another pause. "Certainly,

Doctor." She smiled. "Dr. Svensen will see you in a few minutes. He's finishing up with a client interview at the moment. Won't you please take a seat? It won't be long."

"We'll stand," Murph said with as stern a look as he could generate. *Official police business should trump all other business, including a doctor interview with a client.* Murph could feel his face redden. He recognized the beginnings of one of his classic headaches. He rubbed his temples. *I wonder why they refer to their patients as clients? Didn't they see them as patients? Lawyers and real estate agents have clients. Doctors have patients. There's a big difference, and "clients" just sounds cold.* He shook his head, increasing his headache.

Three minutes later by Murph's watch, the receptionist's phone buzzed.

With the smile still plastered on her like a clown, she answered it. "Certainly, Doctor." She replaced the phone slowly.

"Well," Murph said, "can we go in now?"

"Yes, the doctor will see you now, Detectives. Go through that door, and then straight down the hall. Dr. Svensen's office is the fourth door on the right. He's expecting you. I'd take you, but someone has to stay at the desk to answer the phone."

Murph growled at the receptionist's blasé attitude as he left the reception area with its serene, light-blue paintings and photographs of Caribbean ports that he was never likely to see. His headache had worsened despite the serene paintings. He snarled at both the walls and the receptionist.

For some reason that he could not immediately put his finger on, Murph shuddered as he opened the door, and entered the long, light-green hallway, illuminated with several sconces. *I would have expected the fluorescent lighting that seemed standard in every doctor's office I've ever visited. This dim lighting reminds me of the brothels I raided during my stint in vice so long ago. The women who worked those brothels knew how to protect themselves, at least from the burden of an unwanted pregnancy, unlike those who end up walking down this passageway.*

They passed two adjacent hallways and several closed doors with numbers on them. They found Dr. Svensen's door open with no number on its wood-paneled surface. The doctor stood behind his desk, tumbling a pencil, end over end, switching it from hand to hand like a juggler practicing his trade in slow motion.

Murph stared at the doctor, and frowned. *You look worried, maybe even defensive, Doctor. What are you worried about? Are you hiding something? If so, what?* "Dr. Svensen?" Murph took a step into the small, blue-carpeted office that had been painted the same beige color as the reception area. Two leather chairs and a pink loveseat stood against one wall. The lone window behind the couch had its blinds closed. A painting of the American flag, unfurling in a brisk breeze in front of white clouds flanked it on one side. A picture of Dr. Svensen, accepting a commendation from a high-ranking military officer occupied the other. In large letters, the inscription beneath the photo thanked the doctor for his service in the US Air Force. Shelves filled with medical textbooks and journals covered the opposite wall. A coat rack, holding a black raincoat, stood inside the door to the right. As they passed, Johnson ran his hand over the coat's surface.

"Yes, I'm Dr. Elliot Svensen. Please come in. Take a seat." He gestured to the chairs.

As he sat, Murph flashed his badge. The doctor stared at the badge, as if trying to burn the name into his memory. His frown deepened. He checked his watch, and then stared into Murph's face, ignoring Johnson altogether. Murph took a quick inventory of the desk's surface: a white phone, a closed appointment book, a penholder attached to a pad of paper, and one thin chart turned face down, presumably so the patient's name couldn't be seen.

"I'm Detective Murphy, and this is Detective Johnson. Do you have a client," Murph hesitated at using the word "client," cleared his throat before continuing, "named Eve St. Marie?" Murph thought he saw a slight upturn to the edges of the doctor's mouth, changing his frown into a minute smile.

Dr. Svensen's smile grew. "I'm afraid any information about our clients is confidential. We're prevented from even speaking about them by HIPAA; that's the Health Information Portability and Accountability Act. I'm sorry."

"We're aware of the HIPAA regulations, Dr. Svensen," Murph said, knowing this always represented the first hurdle they had to overcome in any medical facility, "however, in this case, Miss St. Marie died last night, and we have reason to believe she came here as one of your clients." This time the word 'client' came out with ease. "Since your client is dead, privilege no longer applies, and we would appreciate your complete cooperation."

"Oh, my," Dr. Svensen said, his frown returning, as he leaned back in his chair, so far that Murph thought he might fall backward onto the floor. "Oh, my! This is terrible news, terrible for the clinic." He shook his head, as if trying to clear the upsetting news from it. "Of course we'll cooperate, Detectives." He shook his head a few more times. "Oh, my," he repeated. "When did it happen? And how did she...?"

"Shot, I'm afraid," Johnson said, "last night."

"Now, if we could see her chart, doctor," Murph said, glancing sideways at his partner, and shaking his head. *Too much information, Johnson! You should know better. We try to give out the least amount of information to the people who may become suspects in a case.*

"Of course," Dr. Svensen said, returning his chair to upright, and picking up the phone "but I'm afraid there's not much in it."

"Any information will be helpful," Johnson said, nodding his head, acknowledging Murph's silent warning.

"Yes, of course," Dr. Svensen said, as he dialed the four digits to the reception area. "Linda, could you bring me Eve St. Marie's chart right away?" A slight pause ensued. "Thanks." He again shook his head in disbelief. "This is terrible news. Do you really think it may be connected to our clinic?"

"Possibly," Murph said. "When did she first come to your clinic?"

"About a month ago, if I remember right." Dr. Svensen stroked his chin, as if that would help his memory. "I can give you the exact date when the chart arrives."

"Did she seek an abortion?" Johnson asked.

"That's why most women come here," Dr. Svensen said, folding his hands together on the desk, as if praying. "Most didn't want to get pregnant in the first place. Some took precautions that failed...condoms that ripped, or they forgot to take their birth control pill...that sort of thing. We get a few rape victims. Most of our clients are single, but some are married also."

"Any repeat customers?" Johnson asked.

"Some, but not as many as most people think. There are much easier and less expensive ways to prevent live births than interrupting an active pregnancy. All of our clients get counseling both before and after their procedure. We pride ourselves on making sure they know how to prevent another unwanted pregnancy. That may be why we get so few repeat customers, as you so crudely put it."

After a loud knock, Linda entered before Dr. Svensen could say: "Enter." She handed a chart to the doctor, leaving without a word, and without even glancing at the two detectives.

"Thank you," Dr. Svensen said as Linda closed the door behind her. He opened the chart, pausing to read before speaking.

CHAPTER 8

"To answer your first question, Miss St. Marie was originally seen here on June 1st this year. She was ten weeks pregnant. Termination occurred one week later." He flipped through a few loose pages, taking only a few moments to read the content of each. "Let's see, my assistant, Barbara Schine, took Miss St. Marie's intake information, and Janet Robertson had been assigned as counselor." He looked up from the chart, his gaze jumping from one detective to the other, as if he didn't know which to address. "As a routine, I don't meet with the clients before the surgery whether it is on their first clinic visit or later, as in Miss St. Marie's case, but every client must meet with one of our counselors before a termination of pregnancy is performed. Unfortunately, Janet is off today. I can get her address and phone number, if you want to meet with her later today or tomorrow; otherwise, she'll be back on Monday."

"We'll need to speak to her as soon as possible," Murph said. "So, we'll need her contact information today."

"Sure," Doctor Svensen said, his eyes returning to the chart. As he turned the next page, the doctor's eyes opened wide. His mouth fell open. He stared.

Murph's eyes narrowed at Dr. Svensen's sudden silence. When the doctor appeared to be making no effort to speak but, instead, continued to scrutinize one particular page, Murph asked, "Is something wrong, doctor?"

"Huh?" the startled doctor asked, as if he had forgotten about the detectives. Regaining his composure, he said, "Oh, it's nothing, really. It's just that Miss St. Marie apparently phoned our clinic yesterday. She talked to my assistant, Barbara. Barbara wrote the content of the conversation on one of our office visit sheets, and put it in the chart. We're in the process of converting all our files to electronic records, but haven't gotten all entered yet. Miss St. Marie's is one of those."

"Is that unusual?" Johnson asked. "I mean to write phone conversations down in a client's chart."

"Oh, no," Dr. Svensen said, as he handed the chart to Murph, "just the opposite."

Murph grabbed the chart, literally yanking it from the Doctor. *About time you relinquished it! Had to assure yourself everything was in order first, didn't you?*

"The clinic's normal practice," Dr. Svensen said, addressing himself to Johnson almost exclusively, "is to record any conversation, regardless of how it occurred, phone or face-to-face, with a client in their chart." He leaned back in his chair again, emphasizing his comments with a hands-up, plaintiff gesture. "I mean, the clinic has to protect itself from a repentant client who might call and, well, regret their actions after the fact, and make threats toward the clinic or my staff."

"Is that what she did?" Murph asked, wondering about the doctor's use of the words "repentant" and "regret." Murph thought back to the victim's diary: "I am truly sorry, I regret so much what I did. I regret..." *What did she regret? Did she truly regret her abortion? Did she regret killing the child growing inside her? Is that what she discussed with Barbara? What, exactly, had Barbara discussed with her, and why, if it is routine to enter conversations in a chart, is Dr. Svensen so surprised at his assistant's entry?*

Murph read aloud. "June 16th, 3:10 P.M. Client called. Said she regretted having the abortion. She read some literature she had been handed the first day she visited the clinic by the Pro-Life group demonstrating outside. It stated that God loved her, and would forgive her whatever choice she made, but that she should consider alternatives to killing her baby. She is sure God could never forgive her actions, and that she had not only ruined her life here on Earth, but also had condemned her "immortal soul" to everlasting punishment in Hell. I assured her that the group that gave her the brochure represents a radical, God-lover group, whose members have no concept of reality, and are so consumed with worrying about the next life that all the problems and suffering caused by an unwanted baby didn't exist in their warped minds."

Murph glared at the Doctor. "Warped minds? Is that really what your staff thinks of the groups who oppose the abortions you perform?"

"Of course not," Dr. Svensen said, repeating his plaintiff gesture, this time accompanied by closed eyes and a lowered head, "but we're prepared to fight fire with fire. If they're going to call us murderers and other nasty names, then we can return the gesture."

Murph didn't respond. He couldn't respond. *I feel as if I'm talking to a group of five-year-olds, calling each other awful names, rather than adult professionals who should know better, and behave accordingly, like thoughtful adults.*

"Well," the doctor said, picking up on Murph's staring invitation to explain further, "if they're going to call us atheists, devil worshipers, and who knows what else, we can certainly imply from such comments that they have warped minds, but your objection is noted. I'll talk to Barbara about it to ensure her future notes are less," he paused, searching his mind for an appropriate word, "let's say, 'caustic.'"

Murph shook his head, noting, as he did so, that Johnson was jotting down the essentials of their interview in his notebook. *Good job, Johnson! Get it all down. These people are sick. Don't know if they're capable of Miss St. Marie's murder, but they're sick, nonetheless. We may not be able to trust anything they say. We need to check them all out carefully, very, very carefully.*

CHAPTER 9

"We need to talk to your assistant as soon as we're finished with you, if you don't mind, Doctor," Johnson said, "preferably before you talk to her about what she wrote in that chart. Wouldn't want you to say the wrong thing to her, and maybe influence what she might say to us now, would we?"

"Oh," Dr. Svensen said, putting both hands up in front of him in a defensive posture, "I wouldn't want to interfere with your investigation, and of course you can speak to her first. I'm only saying I will talk to her to make sure she uses more appropriate language for her entries into a patient's chart in the future, that's all."

"It looks like your assistant did invite her to come into the clinic today," Murph said, continuing to read from the chart. "'I told her to come into the clinic for counseling, and that what she's experiencing is normal. I assured her that we've seen it before, and know how to help her. She refused to make an appointment now, but said she would consider calling later.' The note is signed 'Barbara Schine, Assistant Director.'" Murph flipped through the rest of the chart as he asked, "How long has Ms. Schine worked here?"

"Five years," Dr. Svensen said without hesitation. "She moved here from Buffalo, New York. She said she got too cold there. She's originally from New York City. Came to us with glowing recommendations from a clinic in Buffalo where she also held the job of assistant director. They really were sorry to see her go."

"Did you check her references, by any chance?" Johnson asked.

"Of course! I called them personally, and spoke to her superior there. He said he had even offered her more money to stay, but one final brutal winter with tons of snow apparently became the final straw that forced her to look elsewhere. She couldn't find any positions in the lower states. We just happen to be looking because my original assistant director retired due to illness on short notice. But you can't possibly imagine Barbara is involved in this affair, can you?"

"Not necessarily," Murph said. "We just like to know the people we interview, that's all." Murph held up one sheet of paper. "Along those same lines, what can you tell us about this counselor, Janet Robertson? It seems her note is a lot shorter than Ms. Schine's. It reads: 'Counseled Miss St. Marie on her choices. Explained that termination is the best option for her to get her life back. Client agreed, and didn't seek further discussion, but wanted to wait a while before termination. Told her I am always available for any questions or problems she may have, although I assured her most women don't have any problems after the procedure. Client seemed to understand, and scheduled the termination after the visit.'"

"Seems a little short for a counseling session," Johnson said.

"Well," Dr. Svensen said, shrugging his shoulders, "some clients need longer and deeper counseling sessions than others. Apparently, Miss St. Marie didn't express any doubt about her decision to undergo a termination. So, she didn't need a prolonged counseling session. Janet Robertson is one of our best counselors. She rarely misses a client's needs, and has gotten many letters of thanks from grateful clients."

"How long has she worked here?" Murph asked.

"Just over one year," Dr. Svensen said. "She also came highly recommended. She worked in a clinic in Hartford, but lived closer to Adams. She liked where she lived, and didn't want to move. So, she looked for a position here. When I saw her résumé, and interviewed her, I hired her almost on the spot." He smiled, rubbing the top of his desk, as if he were petting a favorite animal. "We really didn't need another counselor, but her credentials were so impressive, we couldn't pass her up. As it turned out, we had a counselor quit several months later. So, in retrospect, it became a great move on our part."

"We?" Murph asked. "Who are the *we* you mentioned?"

"Oh, I'm sorry." Dr. Svensen's smile disappeared, as he placed both hands on his lap. "The four physicians who run the

41

clinic make all the hiring and firing decisions."

"Based on your recommendation in this case," Johnson said. "Am I right?"

"Why, yes, she really impressed me! Nothing wrong with that, especially when the clinic gets such a good employee."

"Maybe she'll impress us when we interview her," Murph said. "We'll let you know." He held up another sheet of paper. "You signed the operative note. Do you remember Miss St. Marie?"

"I remember all my clients." Dr. Svensen leaned forward, placing all his weight on his forearms. "Yes, I do remember her. She appeared as a young, pretty girl, as are most of our clients." He reached across the desk. "May I see the chart a minute, please?"

Murph placed the op-note back into the chart, and handed the chart to the doctor.

"Yes, I remember her case. No pre-surgical complicating factors. Procedure went easy, no complications during or after the procedure either. She was eleven weeks pregnant. Here's my final note on discharge. I wrote: 'No complaints from client. Advised to call if any bleeding or anything else unexpected occurs.' I never heard from her again. Barbara didn't tell me about yesterday's phone call, though."

"Is that unusual?" Johnson asked.

"Oh, no, that's one of the reasons I hired her. I can't possibly screen all the calls we receive. We do have a clinic meeting every morning to discuss the clients who are on our appointment book for that day. We also discuss any procedures we are going to perform in order to ensure we're ready for any contingencies. We then go over any lingering problems from the day before, but I wouldn't expect Barbara to discuss, or even mention, that phone call until the morning of Miss St. Marie's return visit. We'd want to plan the type of counseling we might recommend for her before she arrived. In Miss St. Marie's case, Janet Robertson would propose the type of counseling, and actually meet with the client."

"Then, there are different types of counseling you offer," Murph said.

"Oh, yes, the type of counseling depends on the problem. Some we can handle here, for example if the Pro-Lifers are bothering the client...and that's what sounds like may have occurred here...our staff is trained to effectively deal with the situation. More

42

deeply rooted problems like severe depression, suicidal thoughts, or severe anxiety, whether linked to the client's procedure, or not, we refer out to a clinical psychologist for their expertise. Of course, in Miss St. Marie's case, we never got the chance to do either."

Murph placed his fingertips together just below his chin, forming a tent. "We'd like to talk to Ms. Schine now. Could you arrange it?"

"Sure," Dr. Svensen said, reaching for the phone.

"Barbara, could you step into my office for a minute. There are some detectives here who want a few minutes of your time." He returned the phone to its cradle with such gentleness that it produced no sound.

"We do need the phone number and address of that counselor involved in Miss St. Marie's case, and we especially need to speak to your assistant *alone*," Murph said, opening and closing his tented fingers several times.

"Oh," Dr. Svensen said, as if the idea had never occurred to him, "of course you do. You mentioned that already. Let me do the introductions, and then Barbara can take you into her office for privacy. Before you leave, I'll have our receptionist give you Janet's contact information." He handed Eve's chart to Murph. "You may need this to jar Barbara's memory. She handles many phone calls and clinic problems, so, like me, she may not remember every aspect of Miss St. Marie's case without the chart."

"Of course," Murph said.

Murph glanced at Johnson. Both knew that the initial interaction between the doctor and his assistant might speak volumes about the case. If it did, it might elevate the doctor from clinic director to prime suspect. Murph nodded toward the door. Understanding, Johnson turned his attention there. Murph then stared at Dr. Svensen.

Bill Rockwell

CHAPTER 10

With a light knock on the door and a quick, rather too loud "come in" from Dr. Svensen, Barbara Schine entered the office. She sported a large smile, the brightness of her teeth contrasting drastically with the deep tan of her skin and the bright red lipstick on her puffy lips. She was short, about five feet tall, and took a few tentative, diminutive steps into the room. The doctor stood, and rushed to meet his middle-aged assistant. He reached for Barbara's hand and, with his back to the two detectives, silently mouthed something to her.

Murph's position effectively shielded him from the Doctor's subterfuge; however, Johnson noted the whisper. The smile disappeared from Barbara's face for a brief second, and then returned as fast as it had disappeared.

The doctor then turned, and led his assistant into the room by the elbow. Her bright green eyes scanned both detectives' faces. Although tanned, her skin looked weathered and dry. In contrast, her hand felt soft to Murph.

"Detectives Murphy and Johnson, this is my incomparable assistant, Barbara Schine."

She nodded to both detectives, but said nothing.

"They want to talk to you about one of our clients, Miss Eve St. Marie."

"Oh?" she said, her smile again disappearing, but this time failing to return. The resulting frown caused even more lines to appear at the corners of her mouth. She tucked a loose strand of her bright-red hair behind her right ear.

"Doctor Svensen said we might be able to use your office," Murph said.

"Yes, of course, please follow me." With a wave of her hand, she invited both men to accompany her. "Doctor, I need to talk to you about one of our other clients when you can spare a minute."

"Fine, Barbara." Dr. Svensen reached for the thin chart on his desk. "When you're through with the detectives, join me back here. I've got an appointment with a new client for an initial interview, but I'm sure I'll be able to give you the time you need after that."

"Yes, Doctor." Barbara followed the detectives, giving one final, small wave and nod to her boss.

Murph studied her as she closed the door. She had a nice shape, emphasized by a tight fitting, purple sweater that she had tucked into her tan pants. A two-inch wide, black belt with a highly polished brass buckle emphasized her tiny waist. Only her orthopedic shoes blemished her fashion statement. *I wonder if she has orthopedic problems, or wears them to prevent future trouble. In either case, it doesn't seem to bother her gait, which appears totally normal except for those exaggerated hip movements.* His mind summarized the assistant's appearance as a complicated mix of attractive woman hidden inside a proven career professional. *I wonder which persona wins out at the end of the day, and, more importantly, if there's more than a professional relationship between her and the doctor. That wave she gave the doctor as well as the twinkle in her eye that seemed to appear when she first came into his office seems inappropriate between a male boss and his female employee. If there is more to their relationship, we will have to find out what it represents, and determine if it has any relevance to our murder investigation.*

"This way, please," she said, walking down the hallway, leading them with another wave of her hand.

As they walked Johnson held up his notebook for Murph to read, never taking his eyes off her ponytail, wagging in time to her gait like the mesmerizing watch of a carnival hypnotist. The note read: "The Doc mouthed something to her when she first came in. Conspiracy? Raincoat wet. Rain stopped at 4 AM. How did it get wet? Doc must have been out in rain last night? Was she with him? Must find out where they were. Conspiracy!"

Murph's eyebrows rose. *Johnson always has suspicions of*

conspiracies, but, this time, he might be right. Conspiracies are rare, but they do occur. Maybe Johnson stumbled onto something. We'll see.

After two turns, they came to an open doorway with a silver number "9" above the entrance.

"Please go in, and take a seat, gentlemen. I need to talk to our receptionist for a minute. It's right around the corner. I'll be right back." Before either detective could object, she disappeared down the corridor, turning the corner like a sprinter headed for the finish line. In the distance, they could hear a door open as she entered the waiting area.

The detectives entered her light blue-carpeted office, and were immediately struck by the similarities to the one they had just left. Painted the same yellow, it had one window that, similar to Dr. Svensen's, also had its blinds closed. *I wonder if these people don't want to see whatever the view contained, presumably the street or adjacent building, or if concern for client privacy and anonymity lay behind the closed blinds.*

Murph noted the same American flag picture hanging to the left of the lone window; however, on the other side stood an enlarged photo of Barbara seated in a small sailboat with an elderly man. *Probably her father by their facial similarities!* Both were waving to the camera, and sported broad smiles. A couch, the clone of the one in Dr. Svensen's office as well as two chairs faced her desk. By the door, stood a similar wooden coat rack as Dr. Svenson's; however, no coat hung there for their examination.

Murph and Johnson stood behind the two chairs, awaiting Barbara's return. In less than one minute, she re-entered the room, wearing a large smile that exactly matched the one in the photo.

"I do apologize for that delay," she said, hurrying around her desk to her chair, also a duplicate of Dr. Svensen's, "but I had an important message to give to our receptionist about a patient that couldn't wait. I also asked her not to disturb us during this interview. So, we shouldn't be interrupted. Please sit. Now, how can I help our police department?"

Murph handed her Eve St. Marie's chart as they sat. "Do you remember this woman by any chance?" Murph asked.

"Eve St. Marie," she said without opening the chart. "Of course I remember her. As a matter of fact, she called yesterday afternoon. I took the call, and wrote a note. So, I reviewed this chart then." She placed the chart on the desk, folding her hands on top of it, reminding both detectives of Dr. Svensen's similar hand position only moments before. "Did she call you? I hope she didn't file a complaint about our clinic." She squinted, a look of deep concern crossing her face, her mouth deepening into a frown.

"Did she have reason to complain?" Johnson asked, retrieving his notebook and pen. "Is that why she called you?"

"Oh, no," Barbara said, almost too quickly for Murph's taste. "No, no!" She shook her head three times, shaking it so hard that her ponytail struck her face like a whip attached to the back of her head. "Don't get me wrong. She never had any reason to complain about our service." She jabbed her index finger down on the chart to emphasize her statement. "I even offered to arrange counseling for her, as you probably already know since you've reviewed her chart. No, she was very happy with our clinic. I fully expected her to call this morning to make an appointment for that counseling. As far as I know, however, she hasn't."

"She won't be calling," Johnson said flatly.

"Oh?" Barbara asked, leaning back in her chair. "And why not?"

"She was murdered last night," Murph said.

Barbara leaned forward across her desk, her forearms acting like pilings, propping up the rest of her body. She stared right through Murph for a few seconds, and then spoke fast, not giving either detective a chance to comment. "Murdered? Oh, My God! When? Where? I can't believe it. You can't possibly think her murder has anything to do with our clinic. You mustn't!"

"Oh?" Murph asked, mimicking her earlier questions. "And why not?"

"Oh..." She hesitated, organizing her thoughts before speaking. "I told you she was happy with our services. Her...murder..." She seemed repulsed by the word, snarling as she said it. She tried to repeat the word, but couldn't. She swallowed once, very hard, and then flopped back into her chair, the leather screaming in protest. "Well, her...death...just can't be connected with this medical facility, that's all." She closed her eyes, as if trying to block out the awful news.

Neither detective spoke, choosing instead to let her digest the information, and then, hopefully, pick up her comments after she had composed herself.

CHAPTER 11

A loud, shrill ring broke the ensuing silence. Barbara jumped, and reached for her cell phone, ringing in her pants pocket. She pulled out the device, checked the caller ID, and pressed the "off" button. "Sorry about that, Detectives. I forgot to turn it off. The call's not urgent. I'll just let it go to voice mail, and retrieve it later. I've turned it off now. Again, I'm sorry." She placed the phone on top of Eve St. Marie's chart. "Where were we?"

"You said Eve St. Marie's murder couldn't possibly be connected to your medical facility," Johnson said, referring to his notes for accuracy. *Of course, that was the first reference to this clinic as a medical facility. Was that supposed to elevate what she and her boss had, up to now, referred to as a "clinic" to something more respectable, something akin to a hospital? Or was this a defensive move on her part, thought out in advance to protect the clinic, her job, or maybe her boss, or possibly all three?*

"That simply has to be true," she insisted. "This medical facility is here to provide comfort and medical aid to these women, not to harm them in any way."

Ignoring her comment, Murph asked, "What can you tell us about Eve St. Marie? Anything you remember might help us in our investigation."

"Yes, yes," she said, gripping the arms of her chair so tight that her knuckles turned white. "It's such a shock to me. Please excuse my outburst. I do understand that you must look into all possibilities. Let me think." She stared at the white paneled ceiling, as if the information would suddenly appear there. "Eve St. Marie...she struck me as a nice girl. I only knew her briefly, but I liked her a lot." She moved her cell phone to the side, and flipped open the chart, but didn't pick it up. "Let's see. I did her intake. She was unmarried and pregnant, of course."

"Was her boyfriend with her when she first came in?" Murph asked.

"No, as far as I know, he never accompanied her. It's a common occurrence. Most men in these cases are only interested in the women for the sexual pleasure they can provide, but if the woman gets pregnant, and the man sees the pregnancy as a burden to him, he often abandons her. These men tend to run, never looking back at the problems they caused. It's a sad commentary. Unfortunately, it's one that happens all too often."

"Isn't that a bit cynical?" Murph asked.

"Yes, it probably is," she said after only a brief pause, "but you have to remember we see the failures of these relationships. The successes…those relationships that grow stronger, or where there is a very supportive family…are never seen in our clinic. As I said, we mostly see women who have been abandoned, or have no other option open to them…and not having the man stick around is still the number one cause of women seeking our services, at least at this clinic."

"Is that what happened with Miss St. Marie?" Murph asked.

"No, not exactly. Eve moved here, and met this man at a local bar called Kilmore's, I believe, when she first got here, and they began dating. She had no intention of getting pregnant." She paused, looked at Murph with her big, mournful eyes, reminiscent of a beagle puppy, and shook her head slowly. "They never do, you realize."

"Otherwise they wouldn't need your services, would they?" Johnson offered.

"No, of course not. Anyway, Eve decided to terminate the pregnancy because of her new position with the company she worked for…a beer brewing company, I think. She feared it would compromise her upward mobility, I guess."

Neither detective said anything.

"Anyway, the man involved…I won't call him her boyfriend because she never referred to him as that…didn't really care what she did with the pregnancy or the baby, as far as I could tell. So, she came here for advice."

"For advice on what to do, or advice on how to…how did you put it…terminate the pregnancy?" Johnson asked.

"Both, really," she said without hesitation. "By the time most women walk through our doors, almost all have decided to terminate the pregnancy. We simply carry out their wishes, some on the same day, others later. It depends on the woman."

"Simply?" Murph asked, an angry expression flashing across his face, his stare unmerciful and seemingly unrelenting.

Johnson leaned toward Murph, and gripped his shoulder to calm him. Shaking his head, he whispered, "No, Murph."

"Did I say something wrong?" she asked.

"No," Johnson said. "Please go on, Ms. Schine."

Murph took a deep breath, blew it out forcefully, and counted to ten, something his wife had taught him to try to control his temper in such situations. It worked this time. He nodded his thanks to Johnson for his intervention, although his headache had returned with his near-anger flare.

Johnson smiled at Murph's quick response to his warning.

Barbara watched the exchange between the detectives with interest, but said nothing.

"Did you ever hear from the man involved with Miss St. Marie?" Murph asked, the calmness back in his voice.

"No," she said after a brief pause, "never."

"Do you know his name, or where we can reach him?" Murph asked.

"Usually we don't give out such information," she said, after pausing for a few seconds to collect her thoughts, and rubbing her chin thoughtfully, "but since she's been murdered, and it's a police matter now, I don't think HIPAA rules apply any more. Even if they do, I don't see how our clinic could be held at fault for helping the police." She paused again, looking first at Murph, and then at Johnson, who waited to jot down the man's name by tapping his pen on his notebook.

After about thirty-seconds of an uneasy silence, she closed the chart, and slammed her open hand down onto it. "Okay, his name is Robert Kilmore. As you probably noticed, his name isn't in the chart. Unless the male is actively involved in the case, we don't record it, but Eve talked about him constantly. She held no grudge against him. It made no sense to me, but that was her position. I have no idea where he lives, but she said she met him at Kilmore's bar. That's why I remember his name. He has nothing to do with the bar, except that his name's the same as the owner's. I thought it a great coincidence. I pass that bar every day on my way to work.

It's on the corner of Third Avenue and Main Street." She chuckled, and then became somber. "Eve's boyfriend's first name is the same as my father's. It made the name really stick in my mind." She pointed toward the picture on the wall. "That's my father. He was a police officer in Rochester, New York. I lost both of my parents in a car accident two years ago. I miss them dearly. Anyway, Eve's partner's a regular at that bar. You can probably track him down with the help of the bartender there. If I remember right, Robert Kilmore is a nurse who works the three-to-eleven shift at the hospital."

"Thank you Ms. Schine," Murph said. "We appreciate your cooperation. We'll try to catch him before he leaves for work."

"Oh, please call me Barbara. There's no need for formality."

"Okay, Barbara," Murph said, "I'd like to get back to Miss St. Marie's phone call yesterday. Your note in her chart indicates she was very upset. Is that common among your clients?"

"Actually, no, most are very happy to end the pregnancy, and to get their normal lives back. It's extremely rare that we get this kind of negative emotion associated with a termination."

"Do you have any statistics in that regard?" Johnson asked.

"Well, statistics like that are hard to get. If some woman is unhappy, she may not want to come back to us to complain. Most realize we can't do anything to undo what's already been done anyway. Of course, we do schedule a two-week post operative check up as a matter of routine, and offer all who keep that appointment a chance for further counseling, if they want it." She leaned back in her chair. "But, to be honest, most who do keep that follow up visit don't seek any additional counseling. As I said, they're happy to have had the termination. As to the ones who don't keep the appointment, and are having any psychological problems, I still think they would call us as Eve did, but it's simply impossible to give you statistics on those who don't bother making that call. Believe me, we do all we can to help any who ask for it. Our clinic offers the best service in this state." She slammed her hand down hard on the desk again for emphasis.

"Of course," Murph said. "Do you know anyone who might want to hurt her? Did she mention anyone who had threatened her, or that she feared? How about this Robert Kilmore you mentioned?"

"Eve?" she asked, almost before Murph had finished his last question. "No, definitely not! I can't imagine anyone wanting to hurt her. Besides being pretty, she was sweet and very polite, at least while here. She must have had a harder side, however, because I understand she had become very successful in the corporate world for a woman of her age and experience. There may have been someone in her business life that had it in for her, but, if there had been, she never mentioned it to me, and nothing about Robert Kilmore threatening her either. No, the only people she talked about during our phone call were the Pro-Lifers. It sounded to me like they were the cause of her problems, and that's what I wanted our counselor to discuss with her on her next visit."

"You didn't want to discuss her problems over the phone?" Johnson asked.

"Oh, no, that would be inappropriate. Besides the fact that someone could be listening on an extension, the client's facial expression and her body language can give one great insight into how serious their problem is, or more correctly, their perceived problem really is. No, we never council over the phone except in dire circumstances, and this, I'm afraid, didn't sound all that serious…just some meddling 'do-gooders' messing around with her mind at a very critical and vulnerable time in her life."

"Do you think these Pro-Lifers are capable of murder?" Murph asked.

Barbara took a long time to answer, again consulting the great book of answers in the ceiling before speaking. "I wouldn't think so, especially with the name 'Pro-Life League,' but similar groups have actually been responsible for bombing other clinics, killing the innocent doctors, nurses and ancillary personnel who worked there. So, as a group, no, they wouldn't kill just one woman, but I guess one of them could be deranged enough to commit a murder if the circumstances dictated it." Her eyes returned to Murph. "Besides, why would they pick on Eve? What could possibly be their motivation?"

"We're just investigating all the possibilities in the case," Murph pointed out, ignoring her question. "Do you know of any other clients who have been assaulted, murdered, or killed? For that matter, have any reported being threatened by the local Pro-Life group, or any other group, or individual?"

Bill Rockwell

"Not to my knowledge, and I would be the one to know since anything that could affect the clinic, or a client's health, or welfare is filtered through my office."

CHAPTER 12

"Is there anything else you can think of at the moment that could possibly help us in our investigation?" Murph asked, fully expecting her to consult the oracle in the ceiling for the answer.

As if trying to fulfill Murph's expectation, she leaned back farther in the chair, and stared at the ceiling before answering. This time both Murph and Johnson looked up, half expecting to find a TV monitor with a teleprompter built into the ceiling. Only the white ceiling stood above them.

"No," she said, looking down, and shifting her eyes back and forth between the two detectives, as if trying to guess which would ask the next question.

"If you think of anything, Barbara," Murph said, "please call us."

Johnson placed a business card on her desk that contained both the Station's number with their extensions and their cell phone numbers. She retrieved the card, glanced at its contents and said, "Certainly, and I will ask our other employees if they might know anything else. We have four physicians, six nurses and three counselors. So, every day there are some who have the day off. It keeps us fresh that way."

"Could you give us your address and phone numbers in case we need to contact you?" Johnson asked, handing her another card.

"Sure," she said, as she began writing.

"Could you also include Dr. Svensen's address and phone numbers, if you know them?" Murph asked. "We may need to contact him, and we forgot to ask him for the information."

"Okay," she said after only a brief pause. "I'm sure he wouldn't object. It's not secret information anyway."

She flipped through a stack of cards in a cardholder on her desk, wrote down the information beneath hers on the back of

Johnson's card, and handed it back to him. She stood quickly, never taking her eyes from the two detectives, and headed for the door with them following her. "Let me show you the way out," she said, opening the door.

"That won't be necessary," Murph said. "We can find our way."

As they stepped into the hallway, Dr. Svensen ran toward them. Breathless, he said, "Gentlemen, I'm glad I caught you. I've got counselor Janet Robertson's contact information that you said you needed." He diverted his gaze to the floor. "I also have a small favor to ask."

Both detectives stopped, standing before the doctor without moving. Johnson accepted the small paper with Janet Robertson's contact information, placing it within the pages of his notebook for later reference.

"And what might that be?" Murph asked, his eyes narrowing again, as he tried to read the doctor's facial expression, with its partially closed eyes, slight frown, and reddened cheeks, accompanied by a few beads of sweat, now appearing on his forehead.

"We have a back entrance that leads to the parking lot in the rear. Could you please use that exit? There's a client in our waiting room, and, for her privacy, I would prefer that you leave by the back. Please."

"Privacy?" Murph asked, his face reddening, mirroring the doctor's. "Unless you're waiting client has a criminal record, and is currently on our wanted list, I can't see how two detectives, dressed in suits, could possibly invade her privacy in any way."

"But it's the policy of our clinic to have people enter by the front, and leave by the back when there's another client in the waiting room," Dr. Svensen insisted. He tilted his head, and placed his hands, palms up, in front of him in a pleading manner. "Besides, you know what they say, 'what you don't know won't hurt you.'"

"And won't hurt your clinic, I'm sure," Murph said, the sarcasm growing in his voice, "but in police work it often works out that what you don't know can get you killed, or, at least, let some criminal go free."

Barbara now joined the doctor so the two blocked the hallway that led to the front of the clinic. "Please, Gentlemen, I'm sure Dr. Svensen's small request would be best, and will in no way hinder your investigation. After all, we've been very cooperative with you, and would appreciate the same cooperation in return. So, please, come this way." She started to lead them down the rear hallway.

"I'm not sure it is such a small matter," Murph said, not moving an inch, but turning to face Johnson. "I think my partner should accompany you to the back entrance just to experience your rear entrance and parking lot, but our car is out front, and I fully intend to go out the way I came in. It sounds like there's something or someone you're trying to hide from us, despite your alleged cooperation, and I want to know what or who's out there. I would be shunning my duty if I didn't follow *my* instincts." Murph tapped his thumb against his chest twice to emphasize his determination.

Murph's mind returned to a case where the lead detective had been encouraged to leave an apartment before completing his questioning and search of the apartment to help an elderly neighbor who had fallen in her bathtub. It later turned out that the killer had been hiding in a back room, and fled down the fire escape when the detective went on his false alarm to the elderly neighbor, who turned out to be the mother of the killer. Luckily, the detective's partner had gone to check the back alley, and apprehended the suspect. The lead detective, however, received a reprimand from his superiors for not calling for backup to help the woman so he could continue his search of the apartment. Murph never forgot the lesson: Don't let suspects control what you do in an investigation, and always, always do what they don't want you to do, or, at a minimum, do what they least expect you to do. It had served him well and this time, he fully intended to find out who, or what had caused the doctor to lose his composure, and make the unusual request so adamantly.

"Barbara," Murph said, "if you will show my partner to the rear entrance, the good doctor and I will go out the front."

"Please," Dr. Svensen begged, "you don't know what you're risking."

"Maybe not," Murph said, placing his hand on the weapon in his belt holster, "but curiosity's got the better of me. Lead the way."

Now!" Murph left no room for compromise in his voice, only a determination that could not be altered.

"Are you sure you don't want me with you, Murph?" Johnson asked, shifting his jacket to catch it behind his holster.

"No, I can handle this. Meet me out front, but come running if I don't come out quickly."

The doctor shrugged, and then shook his head slowly. He let out a deep sigh. "If you insist, Detective Murphy, but let me at least explain what's going on. It'll avoid a lot of misunderstanding on your part."

"Too late for that, Doctor," Murph said. "No more discussion! Lead the way."

Dr. Svensen glanced at Barbara, and said, "Do what he says."

Barbara hesitated, and then walked down the rear hallway with Johnson in close pursuit.

Turning to Murph, Doctor Svensen shook his head. "This way, Detective Murphy."

Doctor Svensen walked down the hallway toward the waiting room with his head lowered, like a condemned man being led to the electric chair. He paused at the door, taking a deep breath before opening it. He closed his eyes, and held his breath as he pushed on the door.

Murph rushed into the waiting room, pushing the doctor ahead of him. He stood with his back to the partially opened door, scanning the room. The receptionist sat, head down, filing her nails, not even looking up when the door opened. The front door remained closed.

Murph remembered a couch and a few lamps that stood against the other wall, currently blocked from his view by the doctor and the half-opened door. He gently pushed the doctor farther into the room, bringing the couch into full view.

Murph froze, all his years of police training and experience disappearing in an instant. His hand loosened on his weapon, his face turned as white and cold as the first snow of winter. His arms and body began to tremble. His eyes sprung open. His jaw fell as the scene before him blurred into a surreal Dali painting. His knees became weak and numb. They buckled beneath him, causing him to stumble. He fought to remain standing. Sweat from his temples soaked the sides of his face, and poured into his eyes, burning them.

His vision blurred, the Dali-inspired image becoming more bizarre, more extraordinary, more unbelievable. His insides turned to jelly. He choked on his own saliva. His stomach churned, giving him the worst heartburn he had ever experienced. He felt like retching. He swallowed hard, forcing the acid back down into his stomach, but the feeling persisted. He tried to speak, but couldn't, his breathing had ceased, his vocal cords becoming paralyzed in that instant. He became light-headed. *Oh, God! No! This can't be happening! It just can't!*

In a squeaky voice, a startled teenager, seated alone on the couch, ringing her delicate hands together, screamed, "Dad?"

CHAPTER 13

The teenager leapt from the couch with the grace of a gazelle. She wore a short sleeved, white blouse, unbuttoned at the neck, revealing a gold cross, suspended from a thin gold chain. Her blue skirt ended two inches above her knees.

Murph stared at the freckled face of his only daughter. Her long, naturally curly flaming red hair bounced with her bound from the couch. Her thin lips were accented with pink lipstick, her eyelids tinted a light blue. Murph had so strongly disapproved of a young teenager using eye shadow that this had become the focus of countless family arguments at multiple breakfasts. Those arguments seemed trivial and unimportant at the moment. He could only muster: "Molly?" *My daughter…sitting in the waiting room of an abortion clinic? No! It can't be! Seeing this is worse than any of the disgustingly gory murders I've seen in the line of duty. Nothing could have prepared me for this. Nothing!*

His face contorted into a grotesque mask, lips deformed with failed attempts at speech, eyes staring blindly and gushing tears, those eyes now totally devoid of any signs of life. He felt numb, dead. His heart pounded as he tried to remain conscious. He barely succeeded.

"No, Dad," Molly screamed, as she dropped a tissue from her trembling hands. "No!"

Having circled the building from the rear parking lot uneventfully, Johnson heard Molly's scream coming from within the clinic. He pulled his gun, and rushed through the front door. He assumed a shooting stance with feet shoulder-width apart, gun held with both hands, his finger on the trigger. He pointed it in the direction he saw Murph looking.

Johnson fully expected to be confronting a weapon. Instead, he recognized Molly, whose complexion, in stark contrast to her father's, was crimson, and getting brighter by the second.

The receptionist finally looked up, saw and heard the initial, brief confrontation between father and daughter, and saw Johnson's gun that to her looked more like a cannon than a 9 mm automatic. She screamed, and ducked under her desk, the motion causing her chair to fly across the floor on its well-oiled wheels. The chair bounced off the wall with a loud "bang," and tumbled to its side, its wheels spinning and whirring.

Johnson raised his weapon toward the ceiling, his eyes searching the room to assure there were no real threats. He turned just in time to see the receptionist disappear behind her desk, and to see the chair's acrobatics. He stood from his crouch, and holstered his weapon.

"Are you all right, Murph?" he asked, circling, and approaching Murph from the front so as not to startle him.

Before Murph could answer, Dr. Svensen rushed to Johnson's side, both men forming a wall between Murph and his daughter.

"Please, let me explain, Detective Murphy," Doctor Svensen said.

Murph pushed Johnson aside as easily as if he were a rag doll instead of his one hundred and eighty pound partner, and walked past Dr. Svensen as if he didn't exist. The color began returning to Murph's face. He still felt nauseated, however, and could both feel and hear his heart, racing as never before.

"Dad, please, no," Molly screamed. She took a few tentative steps toward the father she loved. Her knees trembled almost as much as her lips. "Dad, calm down. This is not what it seems."

Murph's head throbbed in concert with the beating of his heart. His hands trembled almost as much as his daughter's. Without thinking, he grabbed both of her shoulders, squeezing much too hard for her delicate frame. "What the hell are you doing here?" Murph said, finally conquering his vocal cords, his voice much louder than necessary. He then took a deep breath, the first breath, he realized, he had taken since he had initially recognized his daughter, the only person he loved as much as his wife. "You're supposed to be at softball practice." He began shaking her, but much harder than he had intended. Before his bulging eyes, her head snapped back and forth. Tears began to streak down her face, many being thrown from daughter to father with each snap of her head.

"Murph, stop it," Johnson yelled, grabbing his arm. "You're hurting her."

Murph's grip loosened. He closed his eyes, hoping that the awful scene playing out before him would simply disappear; however, he knew it would not. He released Molly, letting his arms drop to his side. One lonely tear tried to force its way out from behind his closed eyelids. When he opened them, that tear blurred his vision further, and began a slow journey down his cheek. He blinked, but didn't bother to wipe it away. Instead, he reached up, wiped the tears from Molly's face, and then examined them in his palm, hoping they contained some magical answer to this macabre situation. They didn't.

Molly tried to speak, but, instead, choked, the words lost in her throat forever. Her father looked crushed, in worse pain than she had ever seen him. His normally strong persona of the upright detective, capable of handling any situation, melted before her tearful eyes, his projected invulnerability exposed as simply a façade, his imperviousness dashed into non-existence, and she had been the cause. *If only I can explain it to him, I know I can make it all go away...I hope!*

Dr. Svensen seized the moment to step closer to Murph's side and, just above a whisper, said, "Detective Murphy, this scene is accomplishing nothing. Your daughter is right. This is not what it appears. Please, let's go back to my office so we can talk this whole affair over. Please."

By now, Barbara Schine stood next to the doctor. "Please, Detective Murphy, before either of you say something you may later regret, let's do as the doctor says."

"Come on, Murph," Johnson said. "They're right. This isn't the place to hold a family discussion. Let's go inside to the doctor's office. Please!"

Murph couldn't wrench his gaze from his daughter's blue eyes that were clouded with tears like his.

Molly again tried to speak, but gagged again, her words buried in a noisy cough.

Murph sympathized with her. He couldn't utter a word either. Finally, in silence, he stepped forward, and hugged her. Tears burst from his eyes. The two sobbed in unison.

After a short time that felt like hours to both, Molly gained enough composure to whisper in his ear, "I'm sorry. I'm so sorry."

Murph didn't answer. He couldn't answer. He hoped she would understand later that speech had left him. He didn't know when it might ever return. He vaguely felt his partner guiding the two of them, frozen in an embrace, toward the door to the interior of the clinic, their gait unsteady, their vision still impaired.

As the group approached, the receptionist peeked over the top of her desk. "Is it safe to come out now?"

"Yes, Linda," Dr. Svensen said, "you can come up now."

Before following the others through the door, Johnson rushed to the receptionist's area, and offered his hand.

Trembling, she accepted his help, and stood. She leaned against the desk, steadying herself until assured she could stand with no problem. "Thank you," Linda said, brushing off her outfit as if every inch had been stained with dirt.

Johnson righted the overturned chair, and rolled it back toward the desk. Assured that she had not been injured, Johnson turned to leave, glancing at her computer screen as he passed. It displayed the clinic's appointment calendar for that day with Molly's name highlighted in the 10 AM slot. Next to hers, separated by a slash, was a name he didn't recognize, Betty Ann Larson. He read the other names in the schedule for the rest of the day, but didn't recognize any. At the top of the page were the words, "On-Call: Schine." Listed below were the phone numbers of all the clinic employees.

"Thank you, Detective," Linda said, resuming her seat, "this is much too much excitement for me."

"Oh, it's just a normal day in my life," Johnson said, smiling, as he rushed to catch the others.

CHAPTER 14

As he walked down the hallway, Johnson wrote Betty Ann Larson's name into his notebook. Without knocking, he entered the doctor's office to find Murph and Molly still in each other's arms. Both accepted tissues from Barbara. Doctor Svensen sat in his chair, hands extended in front of him. Johnson closed the door as quietly as he could, and leaned against it. He placed his notebook in his jacket pocket, and patted it a few times.

"Please, take a seat," Dr. Svensen said, "and let's discuss this as the adults we are."

"Adults?" Murph snapped, making no effort to move toward the couch. "She's only fourteen years old. She's not an adult yet, and has no business being here."

"On the contrary, Detective Murphy," Dr. Svensen said, "according to Connecticut law, she has every right to be here, and we don't even have to report the visit to you as her parent."

"Is all that true, Tom?" Murph asked, turning to Johnson. Murph shook his head, trying to clear his thoughts. *I should know the answer to that. I do know the answer to that. I just can't think of it. Why not?*

"I'm afraid it is," Johnson said, "at least in this state. Some states require parental consent, but not here. Young teenagers like Molly are treated as if they're adults when it comes to abortion. It's their choice. The clinic counselor involved must inform the girl that she is allowed to inform her parents, if she so desires, but parental consent is not mandatory." He suddenly jumped. He slammed his hand against his coat pocket. "Oops, my cell phone is vibrating." He took the phone out, checked the caller ID. "It's the Station. I'll take it in the hallway. Please excuse me." He exited the room with the cell phone against his ear.

Murph and Molly stared at each other as they moved in unison toward the couch, each guiding the other more than actually necessary. They sat, and continued their concerned stares. The couch groaned, accepting their combined weight as if all their troubles had increased their mass as much as it had their emotional stress.

"It's not what you think, Dad," Molly said, finally finding her voice, although it had become weak and child-like, sounding to Murph like the playful, innocent six-year old he remembered so well. The voice and the memory made him shiver.

Molly felt her throat constricting again. She coughed a few times, and swallowed hard. It didn't help.

Murph braced for what he feared Molly would say next by clenching his fists. He closed his eyes to block out the whole scene, wishing he could turn off his ears the same way. *I can't believe this is happening. When this case led to an abortion clinic, I never, ever, thought I would find my own daughter here. I thought my wife and I had taught her stronger family, moral, and religious values. We don't believe in killing innocent, unborn babies. We had hoped she didn't either.* Murph slammed his fist against the back of the couch, startling Molly, who then leaned away from her father, trying to escape his wrath, afraid to speak.

Opening his eyes, he allowed his gaze to drift down to her abdomen. *She's my daughter, and, if she's pregnant, that's my grandchild. No! What am I thinking? This can't be happening. It just can't be.* He shook his head, trying to clear it. Again, it didn't help. His head pounded. He still felt nauseated and lightheaded. He closed his eyes again, and clinched his fists so tight that his fingernails dug deep into the palms of his hands. *I don't care if they do bleed.* He prayed harder than he had prayed in a long, long time: *God help me! Please!*

"Dad," Molly said, lowering her head, half expecting her furious father to strike her, something he had never done, "I'm not pregnant."

Murph's sighed audibly, and followed this with a huge inrush of air. He opened his eyes, then his hands, not bothering to look at his palms, despite the pain. *I don't care if I am bleeding. I really don't care about anything right now except what Molly said.*

Nothing else matters. "If you're not pregnant, then why in God's name are you here? Don't you know what this place is?"

She looked at him, and smiled. "Of course I do, but I'm not here for myself. I'm here to do a favor for a friend."

"What friend, and what favor?"

"I'd rather not say." Molly lowered her head.

"Maybe I can straighten this out," Barbara said. She turned to Dr. Svensen. "It should be all right, Doctor, because Molly here *isn't* the patient, and Detective Murphy *is* her father. So, HIPAA rules don't really apply. Am I right?"

"I guess so," Dr. Svensen said, "but let's be careful about crossing any HIPAA lines, shall we? There may be an enormous financial penalty if we do."

"Of course," Barbara said, circling the desk to stand behind the Doctor. "You see, Detective Murphy, I know what's going on because we had discussed your daughter's visit at this morning's clinic meeting. She called a few days ago for the appointment, and spoke to our receptionist."

The door opened, and Johnson entered, returning his phone to his pocket. He leaned against the door. "Sorry, it wasn't an emergency. I'll tell you about it later, Murph. Please, continue. Again I apologize for the interruption." He pulled out his notebook.

"Anyway," Barbara said, frowning at the interruption, "it seems that one of your daughter's friends *is* pregnant, and had questions about her pregnancy, but is afraid to come in to discuss her options. She picked up one of our brochures somewhere...they're all over town...and wondered if termination might be the best for her. She asked your daughter to come here to find out what her options might be. Linda called me with Molly's unusual request...unusual because we usually don't discuss a woman's pregnancy with anyone except the client. After I talked with Molly on the phone, I cleared the proposed meeting with Dr. Svensen to ensure he would talk to her, and then set up an appointment, never dreaming she'd run into her father here."

Molly looked up, nodding to her father's questioning stare, enough to say: "It's true."

"We didn't realize she was your daughter," Doctor Svensen said, "until she filled out our intake form this morning. When you showed up here asking questions about a murder, we decided to try to keep you two apart. We obviously failed."

A "ring, ring," reminiscent of the sound produced by Barbara's cell phone interrupted the doctor. He reached into his jacket's breast pocket. "Sorry, I don't recognize the number. Let me check it in case it's an emergency. Hello, hello. No one there! It must have been a wrong number. Again, I apologize for the interruption."

As Doctor Svensen returned the phone to his pocket, Molly turned to her father, and said, "You mean you came here on a murder investigation, not to trap me?"

"I had no idea you were going to be here. We were just following some leads on a murder. No trap intended, honest." The corners of his lips turned up in the beginning of a minute smile; however, the rest of his face remained locked in a stern, wrinkled, lopsided frown.

"Our receptionist," Doctor Svensen said, "asked Molly about her father, and learned that you were a detective. Linda realized we faced a conflict if the two of you met. Apparently, Molly had noticed your police car, but didn't recognize it as yours. She almost ran out of the clinic when she found out you were really here. She only stayed because Linda assured her we would keep you two from meeting." He nodded toward Molly. "I must extend my personal apology to you, Molly, for not succeeding in keeping that promise. Anyway, your daughter said you would kill her if you found out she was here."

"Not quite true," Murph said with a larger hint of a smile, "but pretty close."

CHAPTER 15

Molly returned Murph's smile.

"I recognized your last name as being the same as my new client," Dr. Svensen said, "but wasn't sure you two were related, of course. Our receptionist confirmed the conflict after you left my office to interview Barbara. By then, I had gone into another room to perform a procedure. When I finished, I tried my best to avert any confrontation by having you leave by the back, unsuccessfully, of course."

"Is all that true, Molly?" Murph didn't know whether to be relieved Molly wasn't pregnant, or angry with her for getting involved, and giving him the scare of his life. "I mean the part about your friend, and why you're here."

Molly nodded as tears began flowing again. She had never cried so much, her eyes producing more tears then she thought possible. Her eye make-up ran down her face. She began to sob louder.

Murph put one arm around Molly, drawing her to him. She buried her face in his chest. He ran his fingers through her thick hair, remembering the bald infant she had been so long ago, and how proud she had been of her long tresses when she had entered kindergarten.

"Who's your friend?" Murph asked.

Molly sat bolt upright. "Please don't ask me, Daddy." She hadn't called him "Daddy" since she turned nine years old. She remembered telling her father that she had become a grownup, and would refer to him only as "Dad."

Murph looked toward Barbara, hoping to get the girl's name from her. She shook her head.

"I'm afraid," Doctor Svensen said, "that information is confidential. You really don't need to know that now, do you,

Detective? You know that your daughter's not pregnant, and that she came here merely to obtain information for a poor, unfortunate girl who is afraid to come in by herself. That should be enough. Be proud of your daughter for what she did for a friend. It shouldn't matter who that friend is, now, should it?"

Murph simply nodded his understanding. When he turned toward Molly, she had slumped into the couch, totally spent.

"We have a lot to discuss later tonight, Young Lady," Murph said. "I'm sure your mother is not going to be proud of your behavior, despite what the people in this clinic think."

Murph stood, almost carrying his daughter's dead weight with him. Her knees still felt wobbly. She leaned against him, thankful for the support. He wrapped his arm around her, and led her toward the door.

After letting them out, Johnson held his hand up to Dr. Svensen and Barbara. "I have some questions for you two before we leave. Where were you last night around midnight? Doctor, let's start with you."

"Oh, was that the time of poor Miss St. Marie's untimely death? I attended a medical conference in Massachusetts. As a matter of fact, I still have the brochure for the conference right here in my jacket." He removed a colorful brochure that advertised the yearly conference. He handed it to Johnson.

"Convenient," Johnson said.

"Not really, you see, it's a yearly conference that I must attend. I drove up to Massachusetts on Wednesday night because there were some committee meetings early Thursday morning I had to attend. They were voting on some important issues before the conference started on Friday; however, I couldn't stay for the whole conference because two of my partners from the clinic also attended. The conference goes on through Sunday."

Johnson read the brochure to confirm the timeline. It matched.

"So, I stayed through the dinner conference on Friday night, but decided I had become too tired to drive home even though it's only about a three hour drive. I checked out around five AM this morning, and got here a few minutes before you gentlemen arrived. That's why I still have the brochure in my pocket. I haven't even been home yet today. You can check with both my wife and the hotel. I stayed at the hotel that's advertised on the back of the brochure. My partners also saw me there on Friday right through the dinner meeting that broke up around 10:30. So, there's no way I could have driven home in time to kill Miss St. Marie at midnight." His smile grew wider, as did Barbara's.

"I'll be sure to check that out, Doctor," Johnson said, as he handed the brochure back to him. "Please write down the names of those partners, along with their cell phone numbers. I'll start with them. How about you, Ms. Schine?"

"Oh, please, remember, the name's Barbara. Let's see, at home alone, I'm afraid. We expected a very busy day today, not that we could have ever foreseen the turmoil your visit has caused, of course." She smiled, awaiting Johnson's smile in return.

Johnson ignored her, and continued to write, refusing to raise his head, or to smile. When she didn't say anything, he raised his eyebrows, and stared at her, irritated that she saw humor in their visit, especially after the emotional uproar experienced by both Molly and Murph.

"Anyway," she continued, "I knew I had to be at my best, so, I decided to make it an early evening. I stayed home, made myself an early dinner, and read a book until about 10:30, and then went to sleep. I got to the clinic a little before Dr. Svensen. So, I'm afraid I really don't have a good alibi, do I?"

"Hopefully, you won't need one, Ms. Schine…Barbara," he said, correcting himself, and taking the brochure back from Dr. Svensen. The names were just barely legible, but the numbers were written with precision. "Dr. Tim Aronson, and Dr. Quan Xi." He pronounced "Xi" as "Zi."

"Your pronunciation is correct," Dr. Svensen said. "Now, if you'll permit us, we *will* see you out this time."

"Thank you" Johnson said, holding his hand up again to prevent them from following him through the door, "but no, you two stay here. We'll see ourselves out for real this time. You and your clinic have done enough harm already…believe me." He closed the door before either could object, hurrying to catch up with his partner and Molly.

As they walked down the hallway, Murph whispered to Molly, "How did you get down here anyway, by bus?"

A very long pause ensued. "No, a friend drove me. I'm supposed to call him on my cell when I'm ready to get picked up." Her voice felt stronger, but still didn't sound totally normal to Murph, or to her.

"Is he the one who got your girlfriend pregnant?"

"Don't ask, Daddy. Please."

"I'll take that as a 'yes,'" Murph said, picking up their pace.

Murph threw open the door and, with Molly in tow, entered the empty waiting room. This time he had his arm firmly on his daughter's upper arm, and not on his weapon.

The receptionist had her ear to the phone, eyes glued to the doorway. She nodded at them and, with a wave, called them over. "The call," Linda said, pointing to the phone, "is for you, Miss Murphy."

CHAPTER 16

Molly started to head for the desk, despite her shaking knees. Murph pulled her back to his side, squeezing her arm like a criminal he had just collared.

"Ouch. You're hurting me."

"Who knows you're here?" Murph loosened his grip, but refused to release her, or to apologize.

"No one!"

Murph glared at Linda. "Who is it?"

"It's Barbara Schine. She wishes to speak to Miss Murphy before she leaves."

"She does, does she?" Murph released Molly's arm, and stepped to the desk. He wrenched the phone from Linda's hand before she could object.

"Hello," Murph said in his most official voice, "this is Detective Murphy. Exactly what did you wish to say to my fourteen-year old daughter, Assistant Director Schine?"

"Oh," Barbara said in a startled voice, "hello, Detective Murphy. I just wanted to assure Molly that we are still interested in helping her friend in any way we can. Could you please tell her that, and have her friend give us a call directly?"

Murph slammed the phone down so hard that the receptionist jumped at the sound, covered her mouth with her hands, and rolled her chair all the way back to the wall, fully expecting further reprisals from the angry detective. Murph scowled at the frightened receptionist, then turned, giving the same piercing look to Molly who had jumped in unison with the receptionist, and had stepped backward, away from the desk and her father.

Miraculously, Molly's trembling knees did not collapse under her, but their weakness forced her to add three small, awkward, corrective steps to maintain her balance. *I've never seen my father this angry. I thought I had dodged the bullet of dad's anger, that he had become calm and rational, but now, I realize his anger has only been suppressed in that six-foot, muscular frame, and could be brought out now by anything that even mildly upsets him. I dread being alone with him, and am terrified at the thought of both of my parents verbally assaulting me when I get home...if I don't die of fright before then.*

"The assistant clinic director," Murph said, resuming his position alongside his daughter, and grabbing her arm again, "wants your friend to call her." He pulled her closer until their two faces were only inches apart. "No phone calls to anyone unless I tell you to call. You got that, Young Lady?"

"Ye, ye, yes." Molly's lips trembled. As she nodded her head twice for emphasis, the tears began to flow again. She never realized she could fear her own father. He had never sounded this angry at anything she had ever done. *Of course, I've never done anything like this before, and gotten caught. He and mom are going to kill me.*

Murph closed his eyes as tight as he could, realizing all too late, that he had hurt his daughter more than he had intended...again. He had taken his anger at the clinic out on Molly. He instantly regretted his actions. When he opened his eyes again, the innocent daughter he had raised so tenderly since infancy stood before him like the vulnerable, young teenager she had become, but that he hadn't known existed until now.

"I'm so sorry, Molly. Please forgive me. I'm angry at the clinic. I'm angry at the whole situation, but I'm not angry with you...well, not as angry as I'm behaving anyway. Can you forgive me?"

Molly smiled, but still couldn't find her voice, or stop crying.

"Of course," Murph said, trying to lighten the situation and, at the same time, regain his stature as her father, "that doesn't mean you're totally off the hook. We're still going to have a family discussion about this whole affair when we get home. I'm afraid keeping your mother's blood pressure from blasting the roof off our house is going to be almost impossible." He smiled, then hugged her, trying hard not to start crying again. "Just remember, we love you, no matter what. Okay?"

Molly forced another smile, and nodded. With the second nod, the color drained from her face. Her eyes closed, and her chin fell to her chest. Her body went limp, as the whole experience finally overwhelmed all of her body's defense mechanisms, her knees finally losing their valiant battle against gravity. She wilted in her father's arms, and began to slump toward the floor. Murph held her tight.

Seeing Molly collapse, Johnson, who had been standing by the Clinic's front door, ran to Murph's side, and grabbed Molly's legs.

"Over to the couch, Murph," Johnson directed. "Get the doctor here, now," he yelled to the receptionist who had already dialed the emergency number, designed to get help into the waiting room as quickly as possible. A loud ear piercing, buzzing alarm sounded.

They laid Molly on the couch, raising her feet onto the couch's arm. Murph stroked his daughter's face. "Come on, Molly, stay with us."

Barbara blasted through the door, and rushed to the couch, kneeling by Molly's side. She grabbed Molly's wrist. "Her pulse is weak and slow. What happened?"

"I yelled again," Murph admitted, "and she suddenly went limp."

The doctor rushed into the room. "Shut that alarm," he yelled, changing direction, and heading for the group at the couch. "What've we got, Barbara?"

"The sensitive detective here yelled at his young daughter again, and she fainted. Pulse is thready and weak. We've elevated her feet, and her pulse is improving."

Doctor Svensen felt the pulse in Molly's neck with his index and middle fingers. "I agree. Her skin is clammy, but her pulse is definitely improving in both volume and tempo. She's obviously fainted. She should be fine, and should be awakening any moment now."

"I'll get her a glass of water," Linda said, jumping to her feet, and heading to the door to the inner office.

Molly's eyelids fluttered as her pale skin became, at first, mottled, then red. "What happened?"

"You fainted," Dr. Svensen said. "You'll be fine in a minute or two. Just lay there for a while, and when you try to get up, do so very slowly."

"I have a headache," Molly said, placing her hand on her forehead.

"You've been through a lot, Molly," Dr. Svensen said. "Between the stress of today, and fainting, it's not surprising that you'd get a headache. It'll go away once you've fully recovered. If it doesn't, a couple of acetaminophen tablets should take care of it."

Linda returned with a glass of ice water.

"Try sitting up now, Dear," Barbara said, "but do it as the doctor said, very slowly."

They let her feet down to the seat cushions, watching her for any returning symptoms. Nothing changed. In a few seconds, she swung her legs off the couch, and sat up, placing both feet firmly on the floor, making sure it remained solid and not wobbly under her. She looked around at the group, standing over her like nervous watchdogs.

"I feel a little better," Molly said, reaching for the glass of water with both hands from Linda, and bringing it to her lips with care, afraid she might spill it, producing further embarrassment.

"Only sips at first," the doctor warned.

She did as ordered. The water felt good in her cotton-dry mouth, but actually made her throat, chest and stomach grow cold. She shivered.

"I think that's enough for now," Molly said, handing the glass back to the receptionist. "Thank you."

"Do you think you can stand?" Murph asked.

"I think so. Let's give it a try."

Everyone stood, all eyes fixed on Molly, not knowing if she would collapse again, but she stood rock steady.

She pulled her blouse down, pressing it flat with both hands, trying to remove any wrinkles and hoping, at the same time, to wipe away her embarrassment. "Could we leave now, Dad? Please?"

"Sure," Murph said, grabbing her arm, this time being very careful not to squeeze too hard, and leading her toward the door. As he passed the smiling Doctor and Barbara, he frowned. *If you think I'm going to say, "Thank You," to you and your staff, you're wrong.*

Bill Rockwell

It's your fault this whole episode, including my confrontation with Molly, happened in the first place. I'll pay you no thanks...ever.

Without looking back, Murph, Molly and Johnson exited the clinic, closing the door, and, with it, the entire episode...they hoped.

CHAPTER 17

As they entered the sidewalk area, Officer Martinelli approached on his bicycle. "Everything Okay? One of the neighbors thought she heard some loud voices, and saw someone run into the clinic brandishing a gun."

"Everything's fine," Johnson said. "I had the gun. I thought there might have been a problem inside, but it turned out to be just, shall we say, a domestic disturbance."

"This is my daughter, Molly," Murph said as he directed his daughter into the back seat.

"Ah," Martinelli said, guessing the domestic disturbance involved Detective Murphy and his daughter. He thought it best not to pursue the issue any further unless Murph volunteered the information. He set the kickstand on his bicycle, and put both hands on his hips. "Is there anything further I can help you with here?"

"Maybe," Murph said. "Stick around for a few minutes." He leaned into the car. "How were you supposed to get home after your clinic visit, Molly?"

Molly patted the cell phone in its holster at her side. "I'm supposed to call my girlfriend, and then she and her boyfriend were going to pick me up. He's old enough to drive."

Murph stood, and scanned the area. Only a few cars went by. "Officer Martinelli, I need you in the alley where you won't be seen by a car that is going to be approaching the clinic. I'm going to have Molly call her friends to pick her up. When the car arrives, I'll signal you from across the street to pull out in front of them. Johnson, I want you to pull the car around the corner, and when I call you, pull the car behind their vehicle. I'll come across the street to confront the driver. They're not criminals, so I don't expect any problems, but if they panic, and run, I want no heroics, and no weapons drawn, or used. If they're stupid enough to run, we'll just

get the plate number, and have the patrol cars pick them up later."
He looked toward Martinelli. "If they do run, make sure you get out
of their way. I don't want you getting run over by some panicking
teenager."

Martinelli smiled. "Don't worry, I can move real fast when
it's necessary. I'll notify the patrol cars in the area via my radio so
they know the specifics of the operation ahead of time. That way we
won't have any tragic mistakes."

"Good," Murph said. "Thanks, Officer Martinelli."

Murph watched Martinelli get into position, and then bent
down to address Molly, no longer the father figure, but the police
detective directing a sting operation. "Call your girlfriend."

"Do I have to, Dad? Can't we just go home, and forget this
whole thing ever happened? I promise I won't get involved with her
pregnancy again."

"You shouldn't make promises you probably won't keep,
Daughter-Of-Mine." Murph shook his head, and smiling, resumed
his role as the father figure. "You're very much like your mother in
that respect, always willing to help a friend in need no matter what
the personal cost. I love you both for your selflessness, but, right
now, you have to call your friends. I'm not going to arrest them, but
I want to give your girlfriend and that boy a piece of my mind. They
should never have gotten you involved in the first place. So, call
them, but don't give them any hint that anything went wrong with
your visit. Remember, I'm listening."

Molly unclipped her phone, and speed-dialed her girlfriend.
"Hi, you can pick me up now." She said no more before
disconnecting. "They're coming. Please, Dad, don't make another
scene. Please!" She lowered her head, and closed her eyes. *After
his last outburst, I can only imagine how he's going to react when he
corners my friends like common criminals. He'll probably behave
like a maniac. How can I ever look them in the eyes again? How
can I ever show my face in school again? I'll be an outcast. No one
will ever want to date me, the girl with the trigger-happy, angry
detective father. I can hear the rumor mill now: "Talk to her, and
risk the wrath of the whole police force." God, help me! I think my
problems are just beginning, and are about to be compounded
greatly by my loving father.*

"Now, give me your cell phone," Murph ordered, holding out his hand.

Molly placed the pink cell phone into her father's shaking hand. She kept her eyes focused on it as it traveled the short distance to her father's pocket. *I wonder if I will ever see it again.* She cradled her face in both hands, and fell sideways onto the seat. *I wish I could make myself disappear.* She began to sob, at first softly, then louder until she couldn't control the crying any longer. She soaked the seat with her tears.

"Okay, " Murph said, "everyone take your position." He checked his daughter, observing her slow collapse onto the seat. By the movement of her chest, he realized she had begun sobbing again. He could feel his face redden as anger began to well up inside him once more. He turned and headed across the street.

Over his shoulder, Murph yelled, "Let's teach these kids a lesson they won't soon forget."

CHAPTER 18

Betty Ann and her boyfriend, Doug, huddled together in the front seat. They had found a parking space three blocks from the clinic, the space easier to find than conversation. All their previous discussion of the pregnancy had ended in fights that neither won, and both hated.

Doug had tried to act sophisticated and strong, but he felt neither. *I have no idea what to do. Should I insist on an abortion, or insist on letting the baby live, but then what? I don't make enough money at my part-time job to support a wife and child...and where would we live, with my parents or hers? Neither works well. In the end, I've got no choice: I'm going to have to leave the decision about the baby to Betty Ann, and live with it. I'm not strong enough to make the decision alone. Hopefully, she is, and can.*

Betty Ann felt long past tears of regret, or dialogue. *No one except Molly even knows I'm pregnant. I wish it could stay that way. I can't trust anyone else with that information. I don't even know how to tell my parents. I even had to ask Molly to gather information from the clinic; I couldn't face them in there, but I need the information...and direction. I hope it will make my decision easier...or at least more palatable. Maybe the clinic holds the answer; I don't know. I don't know.* She couldn't even bring herself to verbalize the thought.

Both jumped when Molly's call shattered the silence.

The brevity of the call worried Betty Ann. She had expected Molly to rant on about all her possibilities. When she didn't, Betty Ann's hope faded. *Maybe Molly failed to find a workable solution, or, worse, maybe she had become so fearful of what I asked her to do, that she didn't even enter the clinic. I hope not.* She looked to Doug with mournful eyes. "Molly's ready to be picked up."

Murph's trap only had to wait five minutes to be sprung. An older, green sedan with many fist sized dents rolled to the curb in front of the clinic. In a doorway across the street, Murph watched through eyes that were still puffy from crying. He tried to focus on the dark haired girl in the passenger seat who stared at the clinic door. Murph could only see the back of her head, making identification impossible. The male driver stared straight ahead, occasionally checking the rear-view mirror. Murph could see him clearly, but didn't recognize him.

When no one exited, Betty Ann placed her small hand against the window, and pressed her face against it. *Come on, we've got to leave before someone spots us here.*

Murph stepped out from the doorway, and signaled Martinelli by waving his arm. "Move in, Johnson."

Pocketing his phone, he began a slow transit of the street. He stared at the driver as if the young man were a suspect who might produce a weapon.

Doug noticed the officer on his bicycle as soon as he left the alley. He hoped the officer would simply warn him to leave the no parking zone. He rolled down his window. Instead of steering around the car, however, the officer stopped directly in front, dismounted the bicycle, and stood alongside it with his hand on his holstered weapon. Doug frowned. He checked his rear-view mirror to see a car with flashing red lights on its dashboard pull up behind him. The driver of the police car opened his door, and stood behind it. A movement to Doug's left caught his attention. Another man approached his car, displaying a shiny, silver badge.

Doug leaned his head against the steering wheel. "I think we're in trouble." He squeezed his thighs with both hands and rubbed his forehead against the steering wheel. Finally sitting back, he turned toward the approaching police officer, and attempted to look composed and confident. He failed.

"Can I see your license, registration and insurance card, please?" Murph held his shield much closer than necessary to the young man's face.

"What's wrong officer?" Doug asked with a tremulous voice.

"Just give me the license, registration and insurance card." Murph deliberately returned his shield to his pocket.

Doug pulled his wallet from his back pocket, and pointed to the glove box. "Quick, get me my dad's registration. It's in there. I know it is." *I hope he's just checking for valid paperwork, or my dad will kill me.*

Betty Ann opened the glove box with shaking hands, and shuffled through the contents until she came across a white envelope marked, "Registration and Insurance." She handed the contents to Doug who handed the requested documents to Murph. They were all valid.

"You're Doug Reilly, and the car is registered to a George Reilly. Your father, I presume?"

"Hello, Mr. Murphy," Betty Ann said, slumping down in her seat. A few tears began to stream down her cheeks. She wiped them off as quickly as they formed.

Murph recognized the voice, but couldn't believe his ears. He leaned down to get a better look. Betty Ann turned slowly toward him.

Murph's mouth fell open. *Oh, no, I can't believe this. This gets weirder and weirder by the minute. What's next? God help us!* "Hello, Betty Ann," Murph said, shaking his head, and blinking his eyes, hoping to improve his vision. It didn't help. "Why are you crying? Is this man bothering you?"

Betty Ann rolled her eyes, and leaned against the headrest. She clenched her eyelids shut, and shook her head. "No, of course not. You know why we're here. Molly called us to pick her up. No one is bothering anyone here except you. Please, let us leave."

"Afraid I can't do that. You see, Molly told me you're pregnant." Before Murph could say anything more, Betty Ann burst into loud wailing, leaned forward, and began banging her head on the dashboard. "Since you're under age, I may have to arrest this young man for raping you."

Her cries stopped in an instant. She snapped her head toward Murph, and began yelling. "It wasn't rape! We had consensual sex. That means we both wanted to do it, if you're too dumb to know the meaning of the word 'consensual.' We're consenting adults. So, you can't arrest him. I won't press charges." She pointed through the front windshield. "Now, get him out of our way before we run him down."

82

Martinelli retreated two steps, increasing the distance between his bike and the car.

Murph's voice remained calm. "I could now add threatening an officer to the charges." He leaned farther into the car.

Doug leaned back to avoid contacting the fuming detective.

"Now, why don't we just all calm down, and discuss this like the neighbors and adults you claim to be. Maybe we can get around all the laws you two have broken. This is a difficult situation already without complicating it any further." He paused, and then yelled as he pointed toward the pavement. "So, both of you, out of the car. Now!"

CHAPTER 19

Molly had been watching her father's antics with disbelief. When his anger erupted, and he ordered her friends to exit their car, she bolted from her father's car, rushing to aid her friends. She banged on Betty Ann's window, the sudden pounding reverberating throughout the car.

Betty Ann, who had not seen Molly's approach, jumped, and screamed in surprise. Doug jumped as well, striking Murph's face with his shoulder, and scrapping the edge of the shoulder restraint against Murph's chin. Murph's head pounded against the thinly padded roof. He stepped back, yanking his head out of the car, and banging it again on the window frame in the process.

"Ouch," Murph yelled, rubbing the top of his head with one hand, while the other brushed his chin, checking for blood: none. He looked up to see Molly energetically banging on the car's window.

Both Martinelli and Johnson ran to Murph's side, neither removing their hand from their holstered weapon as they approached. As Johnson checked his partner, Martinelli kept his attention on Doug, who had his face buried in his hands, trying to block from his mind the terrible vision of the injured officer with all its implications.

"Are you okay?" Johnson asked.

"Oh, no," Doug cried, shaking his head. "I hit him. I hit a cop. I'm as good as dead."

"Molly," Betty Ann screamed, "what the heck is going on?"

"Open the window," Molly screamed, continuing to bang. "I'm so sorry, Betty Ann. I'm so sorry." Her tears reappeared, and rushed down her cheeks, washing away the final remnants of her makeup.

Betty Ann opened the window, and the two girls hugged as if they hadn't seen each other in years. Betty Ann soon joined her friend in uncontrollable crying. Their combined sobs filled the air, attracting passersby, who stopped to observe the clamor.

"All right, everyone, calm down," Murph said, removing his hand from his head, again checking his hand for any bleeding; still none. "Molly, move away from the car. You, Mr. Reilly, step out of the vehicle. Follow me."

Doug did as he had been ordered. Shorter than Murph by at least six inches, he wore an old pair of distressed, faded jeans and a white pullover shirt. Murph returned his documents, and lead him to the sidewalk where several passersby had now gathered, watching the police action with interest. One reached for her cell phone.

"Don't even think of recording anything, Miss," Murph said. "This is an official police investigation, and if you snap a picture, we'll have to seize your phone as part of the investigation. You'll get it back in a few days. Do you want that?"

The woman, dressed in a smart-looking green pants suit, didn't respond, but returned her phone to her pocket without snapping any photos.

"Thank you for your cooperation," Murph said, turning to see Molly helping Betty Ann from the car.

Drawn by the clamor, Dr. Svensen, Barbara and Linda emerged from the clinic. Leary of Murph's angry outbursts, they trudged toward the participants, the group willing to give aid, but ready to retreat at a moment's notice.

"Okay, Folks," Martinelli said to the gathering crowd, "show's over. We've got the situation under control. Please go about your own business, and leave these young people alone. Go ahead, now. Move along."

The crowd slowly dispersed, all of them keeping their heads turned toward the action in hopes of seeing something interesting before they were out of sight. All left disappointed, as Murph and Johnson waited for them to be at a good distance before again addressing the teenagers.

"Now," Murph said, "enough hysterical behavior from you two! We'll all need level heads to figure out what we're going to do next."

"Level heads?" Molly snapped, continuing to hug Betty Ann. Her voice grew in volume as her anger increased. "You're the one who needs to get a level head. You should go back into the clinic, arrest your murderer, and let us innocent people go. You know your trumped-up charges of rape, assault, and whatever else you accused my friends of are simply your way of getting back at me for being here. Go on! Go arrest your murderer, and leave us alone. Can't you do that, Dad?" She turned toward Doug. "Come on. Let's leave."

"Wait a minute," Murph said, grabbing Doug's shoulder. "We're all going to leave peacefully, but I'll decide who goes with whom, and when."

Molly and Betty Ann, who had headed back to the car, stopped, and turned toward Murph.

"We have an audience," Molly said, pointing at the clinic staff slowly approaching. "Better be on your best behavior, Dad. We have witnesses."

Murph's head snapped toward the group. He growled, "Get back in your clinic. We've got this under control. Martinelli, please see them back inside."

"That won't be necessary," Barbara said, pulling on the sleeves of both the doctor and the receptionist. "We can see ourselves back. We simply wanted to make sure the girls are okay, that's all."

"They're fine!" Murph turned toward the girls. "Now, Mr. Reilly can leave, and we won't charge him with anything. I really don't want to arrest him...yet, but, Mr. Reilly, I would recommend you go directly home to tell your parents about your current situation so they can help you in an adult manner, rather than the childish way you've acted so far. Got it?"

Doug simply nodded, and headed for the car, head lowered.

"As for you two," Murph said, "both of you get into the rear of our car." He saw Molly open her mouth to object. "No arguments," he added in such a loud voice that, even if Molly had gotten the words out, his would have drowned hers out. "Get in the car! We're going to take Betty Ann home, then drop you home. Let's go!"

Before complying with her father's order, Molly glanced at both her friends. Through tearful eyes, Betty Ann stared at Doug as he climbed into his car. Before closing the door, he blew a loving kiss in Betty Ann's direction. She returned the kiss, and then buried her face against Molly's shoulder, sobbing in silence.

Murph put his arms around both girls as they plodded toward the car. Molly thought about shaking off her father's hug, but decided it would only add to her problems. Instead, she settled for staring into her father's eyes in hopes of finding the gentle being she knew lived in there. The squinted stare told her he wasn't home at the moment.

"No talking until we're home," Murph warned.

After Johnson got into the driver's seat, he glanced in the rear view mirror to find Molly stroking Betty Ann's hair. Molly's expression radiated pure love and compassion, her lips barely moving as she comforted her friend with, "Shhhh, it'll be all right."

Johnson hoped she was right.

CHAPTER 20

The ride to Betty Ann's house was the quietest, most awkward ride any of the passengers had ever experienced. No one spoke. Both Johnson and Murph never deviated their attention from traffic. Betty Ann had actually fallen asleep in the comforting arms of Molly who continually stroked her hair while keeping her gaze riveted to the back of her father's head.

I pray to God that I can change your opinion of this whole situation, Dad...and of my decision to help Betty Ann. Of course, I know that praying alone isn't going to get me out of this dilemma, at least not without confronting you alone, face-to-face. That terrifies me more than facing mom, who I'm sure will understand my motive better than you. She wanted to cry again, but her eyes were dry, unable to produce even one more tear.

With directions provided by Murph, they pulled into the driveway of a large, cape-style house. Murph jumped out of the car, afraid Betty Ann would rush into her home. He didn't have to worry. Betty Ann had just awoken. Molly helped her sleepy friend out of the back seat. Murph gripped one of Betty Ann's arms while Molly kept her arm around Betty Ann's waist.

"You'd better stay here, Molly. You can't help Betty Ann or the situation by coming."

"Please, Dad. Let me help her."

"No! You stay here."

"I'm sorry," Molly whispered into Betty Ann's ear. She gave her a kiss on her cheek, and climbed back into the car, watching her father and her best friend head for a confrontation she wished could be avoided.

Murph rang the bell before Betty Ann could retrieve her keys from her pocketbook. They waited only a few seconds before a woman dressed in off-white pants and a blue smock over an orange top opened the door.

The woman's jaw dropped when she saw the duo. She tilted her head, leaned against the doorframe, and frowned deeply, her brain suddenly recognizing the significance of the duo standing before her. "Bill?" she sputtered, pushing off the doorframe, and staring at her daughter. "Betty Ann? Oh, My God! What's wrong? What happened?" She reached for her daughter.

Without uttering a word, Betty Ann ducked under her mother's outstretched arms, and stormed into the home.

Her mother turned to watch Betty Ann run up the stairs toward her bedroom. "Bill, please, tell me what's going on."

"I'm sorry, Carol." The story he had prepared about Betty Ann's pregnancy had disappeared. He couldn't think of one word from the speech. He shook his head, but still couldn't think of the right thing to say. *I really hate to be the bearer of this news.*

"Bill?"

"I'm so sorry."

"Now, you're scarring me," Carol said, returning to her leaning position, preparing for devastating news. "What did Betty Ann do? Drugs? Shoplifting?"

"No, no!" Murph waved his hand in front of her, trying to stop her from any further conjecturing. "Betty Ann didn't do anything illegal; she didn't break any laws. It's just...it's just that, well, I came across Molly and Betty Ann during an investigation we're conducting, and I decided their interests were best served by bringing them both home personally."

Carol opened her mouth to say something, but Murph held up his hand again to stop her. He wanted to finish his story without interruption, at least what he could now remember of it, and to give his message as accurately, concisely, and as sympathetically as he possibly could.

"They weren't doing anything illegal, believe me." Murph shook his head. "I really had no right to force them to come with me. I'm sure Betty Ann will tell you that, and she's right, but once you have all the details, you'll hopefully see why I didn't want to risk having them get home on their own." He lowered his head.

"Carol, I value our friendship very much. We've been neighbors and friends for over ten years. I want that relationship to continue, but I forced Betty Ann to come with me, and I'm afraid that may jeopardize that friendship. I did what I felt I had to. I wanted the best for her. So, no matter how mad you may get at me, even if you hate me…"

"I could never hate you, Bill," Carol interrupted. "Just tell me what's going on before my imagination takes me somewhere I don't want to go."

"Okay. All I ask is that once things settle down we discuss this like friends, but I can't tell you the whole story. I don't think it's the right thing to do. I think Betty Ann should tell you. I'm going to take Molly home now. If Betty Ann's too upset to tell you, or flatly refuses, then come over, and I *will* tell you the everything. I really think that's the best way. I'm sorry."

Carol looked up the empty staircase, then back at Murph. Her mind raced, not knowing where to begin, or what path to journey down. *I want answers…I need answers, and I need them now!* "You've got me terrified, but I respect your opinion. I'll do it your way." She backed into the house, closing the door, but never taking her eyes off Murph, trying to read anything she could from Murph's expression. Sadness filled his eyes. It wasn't what she wanted to see.

CHAPTER 21

Murph had delivered an ambiguous message to his neighbor, totally aware that he had lacked the nerve to tell her of her daughter's pregnancy and planned abortion. *I've failed.* When the door closed, Murph stood staring at the Claddagh doorknocker for several seconds. He then began a slow journey down the footpath toward the car.

Molly watched as he approached, a forlorn expression now shared by both.

Halfway down the walkway, Carol's loud scream, "What?" resounded from Betty Ann's open bedroom window.

Without turning, Murph quickened his step, and jumped into the front seat as if the car had already been in motion. He took a deep breath, echoed by Molly as the car began to move, traveling the one hundred feet to his driveway in a matter of seconds.

Johnson parked at the front door of the blue-shingled colonial.

"Want to come in?" Murph asked, turning to Johnson who maintained his death grip on the steering wheel.

Johnson gave Murph a quick glance. "Not on your life! I'll wait here, and make a few phone calls. I've got some leads I want to check. Take your time. I'll grab a soda from the trunk if I get thirsty."

"Coward," Murph said with a small smile. "Let's go, Molly. It's time to upset your mother."

A movement across the street drew Murph's gaze to one of his neighbors. The sixty-year old man lived alone since his wife died five years earlier. He spent every day in a white, whicker rocker on his front porch. Owen waved. Murph returned the gesture. *Great! Owen, the "Mayor of Pearl Street," now knows something is amiss at both the Larson and Murphy homes. The whole street will know within an hour!*

"He really does catch everything that happens on this street," Johnson said. "Doesn't he?"

"He watches the street all day since his wife died. I think he expects her to come walking down the street again someday," Murph said. "It's his self-assigned neighborhood-watch job. He's retired Navy, and keeps a daily lookout, as if enemy submarines were in the area. There are no secrets on this street, thanks to him. None!"

Murph led Molly to the front steps. Neither made an attempt to touch the other, or to speak. Before they could finish their climb to the porch, the door flew open, and Molly's mother rushed out.

"Bill, what's wrong?" Jennifer asked. She stopped at the top of the stairs when she spotted Molly rushing toward her with an expression that screamed, "panic." "Molly? Why aren't you at practice? Are you hurt? What's wrong? What's going on?"

Before Murph could answer, Molly ran by her mother's open arms, mimicking Betty Ann's tactic only moments before, and flew up the hallway stairs, hurtling two steps at a time. Jennifer turned to follow her daughter's escape.

As Molly disappeared, Jennifer snapped her attention back to Murph, now climbing the steps as if being lead to the gallows. His somber expression caused her light-headedness. Her mind raced with memories of every dreadful story Murph had ever brought home to share, attempting, through their subsequent discussions, to make some sense out of their senselessness. *None of those stories had ever involved our family before, couldn't involve our family now! Could this one? Oh, no, please!* She knew he would explain everything, but only when totally ready. "Bill?"

"Jen, I don't know where to begin." He mounted the final step, and reached for both of her hands. She obliged, noting his sweaty palms. "First, Molly's fine. We were investigating a murder today, and it lead us to an abortion clinic."

Jennifer's eyes widened, her jaw dropping at the word "abortion." She sucked in the warm summer air, tasting her sweet, beloved roses that she had planted on either side of the stairs. She choked on the flowery taste and on the saliva building in her mouth. The sweet air stuck in her throat, refusing to move. She didn't care.

Breathing isn't important right now. Information is! Oh, God! Talk to me, Bill. Please!

"No, no, Molly's not pregnant," Murph said, at almost the instant Jennifer's astonished breath had begun. "It's Betty Ann."

"Oh, no!" She squeezed Murph's hands, her jammed breath suddenly released through a great sigh. "Carol and Ted will be crushed. Do they know yet?"

"I just dropped Betty Ann home." He tilted his head in the direction of the Larson home. "I couldn't bring myself to tell Carol. I thought Betty Ann should do that. I agree though. They'll be devastated. There may be another problem though."

"What other problem?" *Oh, no! It involves Molly, doesn't it? God, help us!*

He lowered his head. "I overstepped my authority. We found the girls, along with Betty Ann's boyfriend, at the clinic. They hadn't done anything to break the law...still haven't. They claim they were there to gather information...using Molly as a go-between. I'm afraid I panicked. I forced the girls to come home with me, and not with the boyfriend. I had no right to do that. He could have driven them; he's old enough...probably should have driven them, at least Betty Ann, but I didn't trust any of them to do the right thing...to go home to face their parents...big mistake on my part."

She smiled, and shook her head. "Bill, you didn't overstep your authority at all; if anything, you protected them. Remember, the girls are both minors. You couldn't risk letting them drive off with someone you didn't even know, even if they both argued that they knew him. You did the right thing. I know I would rather have my teenage daughter driven home by a police officer than by some stranger who's only recommendation is that he's romantically involved with one of the girls."

"I'm afraid Carol and Ted may not see it that way, even if the courts might. I may be morally right, but I still think I shouldn't have abused my authority as an officer of the law, and that's what I feel I did. They did nothing wrong, but I treated them like criminals...even thought of handcuffing the boy. I...lost my temper...and my dignity, to say nothing of my training. I hope I didn't lose my daughter too." He sighed. "I've ruined our friendship with our neighbors...our friends. I told Carol that I value

93

their friendship, and to call us after they discuss the situation with Betty Ann. I've got a lot to apologize for, I guess."

"We'll worry about that relationship later. We have more important things to discuss. What about Molly? From the expression on her face, and the fact she ran past me like I didn't even exist, I gather she's also not too happy with you right now, and I represent a species to be avoided, namely her other parent. Am I right?"

Murph smiled for the first time since arriving home. "That's an understatement! I've been working this case all night, and haven't slept. I know that's not an excuse for my behavior, but it's the only one I can come up with at the moment. Listen, before you ask anything else, I need an enormous favor from you, Honey."

CHAPTER 22

Jennifer returned Murph's smile. "*Honey*? Oh, this should be good. What is it, Bill? Come on. Tell me! What did you do to Molly to upset her so much…besides almost arresting her and her 'BFF'? Is there more to this intrigue of yours?"

"I'm afraid I came down really hard on her, especially at first when I thought she had gone there for an abortion." He lowered his head. "It turned out she went there only to get information for Betty Ann in case they decided to terminate the pregnancy. I guess that's what they call it instead of an abortion. I guess Betty Ann and her boyfriend are afraid to go there themselves." He looked up, hoping to see a supportive wife, but instead, saw a nervous mother. "Anyway, when I lost my temper, I yelled so much she actually fainted."

"Fainted?" She threw him a worried glance. "She's never done that before."

"The doctor at the clinic examined her, thought she was fine. He felt she had reacted to my…" he searched for the right word…"… attack…on her even before I had all the facts."

"You mean you acted like a scared father, shooting from the hip."

"I guess so." Murph lowered his head again, even lower this time. "I really blew it."

"And now you want me to mend the fences you destroyed by loosing your temper, right?"

"That and more, I'm afraid. I need you to go light on her. One of us has to play the good cop and, since I've already been the bad cop, it's up to you to come to her rescue. The clinic staff said we should be proud of her effort to get the information her friends needed. You know, I think they were right." He looked into her eyes, and took a small, cautious step toward her. "Jen, I really blew

95

it. I need you to treat her respectfully, unlike the way I did, and tell her you're proud of what she did. Above all, be a loving mother to her. Whatever happens, whatever she says about me, you can't lose your temper. Don't defend me. You have to keep your cool, no matter what. Do you think you can do all that?"

"So, unlike you," Jennifer said, with just the hint of a smile and a twinkle in her deep blue eyes, "I'm supposed to treat our daughter with the respect and love she deserves, praise her for trying to help a friend in need, and, on top of all that, save the image of you as her father, even though you treated her terribly, and at that time I'm supposed to stay calm and reserved. Is that everything?"

"Yeah." Murph placed his chin on his chest. He felt spent, mentally and emotionally. *If Jen fails, I have no idea how I'll ever approach, or even apologize to Molly. I'm an idiot.* "I guess so."

"Sure, I can do that. I'm a mommy, after all, but remember, you now owe me big time for at least the next twenty years." The smile grew on her face. "And, in the future, you'll have to not only treat your daughter with respect for those twenty years, but treat me like royalty too. Got it?"

"Sure, twenty years, I'll probably let her begin dating by then."

"Seriously," Jennifer said, releasing his hands, and gripping both his shoulders, giving him one gentle shake, "you know I've asked this before, Bill, but I really think it's time for you to go for anger management counseling. It's time for you to get that temper under control for your own good, to say nothing about Molly, me, and all your coworkers who would benefit. We all *need* that. Agreed?"

Murph kept his chin against his chest. "I'll really consider it this time, Jen, I promise."

"Please consider it very seriously. You need help." She glanced up the stairs. "Getting back to Molly, you totally forgot Molly signed a chastity agreement with the Church youth group and with God, didn't you?"

"No, but I thought she had broken that agreement, and went to the clinic to get an abortion, that's all."

"Bill, if she had, we'd deal with the problem the same way that Carol and Ted are going to deal with Betty Ann, with love, concern, and the hope that God would guide us. I want you to remember that your daughter takes that agreement seriously, and I love her for it.

"I will admit I also love her for her attempt to get the information Betty Ann needed. I may not agree with what that information contained, or where she went to get it, but I can't fault her for trying to help her best friend. I do wish she had asked us first, though. We could have directed both of them more appropriately, but it doesn't change the fact that she had the proper motive. That will definitely come across in my discussions with her."

"I knew it would. She's very much like you. I love you both for it."

Jen looked toward Murph's car, still parked in the driveway. "So, is your partner coming in for lunch, or are you going to leave him in the car to roast with this heat?"

"We can't stay. We've got leads to pursue that can't wait. We'll grab some lunch at the diner. I'll try to be home for dinner, but I can't promise. It all depends on how the investigation goes. We've got some people we may have to interview tonight, but I promise I'll try." He reached into his pocket, retrieving Molly's cell phone. "Here's Molly's phone. I told her she couldn't call anyone until I gave her permission." He closed his eyes. "I know. I know. I overreacted again. I'm sorry." He opened his eyes to find his wife, staring in disbelief, only the hint of a smile evident in one upturned corner of her lipstick-free, full lips that he enjoyed kissing so much.

"No wonder she's mad at you. You took her lifeline to the world away from her. I'm surprised you didn't take away all her video games, TV and lock her up with all the other hardened criminals like her in that jail of yours."

"The thought had crossed my mind." Murph tried as hard as he could to smile at his wife's attempt to both understand, and cheer him at the same time. He failed. "Please, if it's at all possible, let me be the one to give it back to her. Maybe it'll mean something to her if it's returned by me with both a huge apology and maybe some kind of reasonable explanation."

"Okay. You've given me enough to do to reclaim our daughter. Now, go catch your murderer, and tell Johnson I said, 'Hello.'" She reached up, pulled his head toward hers, closed her eyes long before their lips met, and kissed him, a long, deep kiss.

97

"Now, get out of here while I do some damage control." She kissed him hard on his lips again, eyes open this time, and with a loud "smack" when they separated. "Husbands!" She shook her head, eyes glued on Murph. "What a strange species!"

"Thanks. I love you too." He turned, and jogged to the car, feeling his wife's loving gaze, burning a hole in his back the entire way. *She really knows me after all these years. I truly am the luckiest man in the world.*

"Everything okay?" Johnson said, as Murph resumed his seat.

"It will be as soon as Jen talks to Molly," Murph said, watching Jennifer close the door. "She'll take care of everything."

"She always does." Johnson threw Murph a crooked smile, accompanied by a quick wink. "She always does."

CHAPTER 23

They drove to the diner with almost no conversation, reminding Murph of the quietness of their drive from the clinic. He still fumed over the events of the day, had little to say, and much to think about, both personal and professional.

Murph and Johnson took their usual seats in a booth close to the door. After they joked with the same waitress that had waited on them for breakfast, they ordered their lunch, two luncheon specials of triple-decker turkey with chips and two coffees.

After a few large gulps of the weak, but hot, coffee, Murph finally felt in control enough to discuss business. "Okay, what have we got so far?"

"Well, before we left the clinic, I asked Dr. Svensen and Barbara Schine where they were last night. Barbara has no alibi. She claims she spent the night home alone, went to bed early in anticipation of a busy day today. The doctor claims to have been at a medical meeting in Boston. He said he arrived Wednesday, attended some meetings on Thursday and Friday, and arrived in Adams early this morning. He claims he went directly to the clinic, and didn't even stop home. While you were with Jen, I called the hotel and they confirmed that he checked in Wednesday at 5:25 PM and checked out Saturday morning at 5:10 AM using their in-room, computerized check out system. So, he could have driven directly to the clinic, and arrived just before we did, as he claims. Of course, he could have driven to Adams Saturday, killed Miss St. Marie, and driven back in time to check out at 5:10 A.M. He did say he spent Friday night with two other physicians from the clinic who arrived in Boston on Friday afternoon. If they confirm he was there until after 10 P.M as he claims, then he couldn't have been at the St. Marie apartment to kill her. The doctors he mentioned are still at the conference. I left messages to call us at their first opportunity.

Didn't tell them what it was about, but I'm guessing someone from the clinic might call to warn them. I assume they have their cell phones turned off during lectures, and not because they know we're calling about a murder. Hopefully, we'll hear from them soon.

"By the way, on our trip out the back door, Barbara stated that the doctor drives a blue Lexus sedan. So, he's moved up on my list of suspects. That is, if you believe Mrs. Hanabee's story of the sound of the departing auto being a luxury vehicle. Anyway, the doctor's Lexus is parked behind the clinic next to hers…an older, yellow Toyota sedan. I've got the plate numbers of both."

"I *do* believe Mrs. Hanabee's story, but I'm afraid her ears aren't discriminating enough to positively identify the make as a Lexus. What else have we got?"

"More on the good doctor." Johnson smiled widely. "Remember when I left the doctor's office to answer my phone?"

Murph frowned. *Did I miss something important?* "Yeah, I remember being surprised because I've never known you to set the darned thing to vibrate. What about it?"

"I didn't receive any call. I pretended to so I could get into the hallway. I called the Station, and had them call the doctor's phone. I got the idea after hearing the ring from Barbara Schine's phone. I had really hoped we would hear Frank Sinatra, singing 'America the Beautiful,' the way your Mrs. Hanabee described. That would have made our job a whole lot easier. It didn't, of course…very disappointing."

"Resourceful, if not fruitful, and for the record, she's not *my* Mrs. Hanabee. She's just our only witness to the murder even though she only heard something. I won't write her story off until it's proven false. Okay, anything else?"

"Let's see. I tried calling Linda Robertson, the counselor from the clinic…no answer at her apartment, and her cell phone must be turned off because I keep getting her voice mail. I left her a message to call us back too, again with no details. I tell you, Murph, it's like no one wants to talk to me. It's a good thing I'm not paranoid."

"Maybe she just doesn't want to be disturbed on her day off, and has nothing to do with your paranoia."

"Maybe, but I'll keep trying. It would be nice to interview her face-to-face today, though."

Murph nodded his agreement as their second round of coffee arrived.

"I did get in touch with Katherine McDonahue of the Pro-Life League. I told her we were conducting an investigation, but not the details. She assumed it concerned her Pro-Life organization. She'll be home all day with her husband, working in her yard. She said we could stop by any time."

Murph smiled. "See, at least the Pro-Lifers aren't afraid to talk to you. Maybe only the Pro-Choice people are avoiding you. Be happy with what you can get, Detective Johnson." He took a large swig of his coffee. "What about the victim's boyfriend?"

Johnson flipped to the next page of his notebook. "One Mr. Robert Kilmore. I tracked him down through the hospital, talked to his supervisor. He works on the cardiac floor, takes care of heart attack victims, people having heart surgery, that sort of thing. He's highly respected as a nurse...been working there over eight years. Married once. Wife died of ovarian cancer a few years ago. He works the three to eleven shift, but has tonight off. Lives on the East side, not too far from that bar that bears his last name. No answer at his apartment either. I left the same generic message to call me back."

"Anything else?" Murph asked, finishing his coffee, and pointing to the empty cup as the waitress brought their food.

"Let's see, I also made some notes in case I ever find a bride." Starving, Johnson took a large bite of his sandwich almost the same instant the waitress placed the platter in front of him. "I intend to order a chastity belt for my future teenage daughter, and to lock my teenage son in a closet until he reaches twenty-one. I only hope I can find the note on my wedding day to remind me."

As Johnson had hoped, Murph relaxed, and laughed. He then also took a large bite of his sandwich. Between chews, he shook his head. "In your case, it won't help. If your children take after you, there's no hope for any of them in the love department, despite the chastity belt and locked closet."

They both enjoyed the first good, deep laugh they had experienced all day.

"I need a drink. What do you say we hit a bar after lunch?"

"Ha!" Johnson rolled his head back against the booth's padding. "This from the great, never-took-a-drink-in-his-life

101

Detective Murphy." He leaned forward and whispered, "I suppose you'd like to visit Kilmore's bar. I hear the owner, who shares his name with our victim's boyfriend, has a special interest for you."

"That is correct." Murph gave an exaggerated nod. "I don't drink, but both Mr. Kilmores are of interest to me. Maybe the bar-owner Mr. Kilmore has some insights into Eve St. Marie's relationship to her boyfriend, the other Mr. Kilmore. I really would like to interview him next. After that, assuming you can still walk straight after visiting the bar, we'll interview Katherine McDonahue." Murph leaned forward, mimicking what Johnson had done. "Do you think you can keep your hands off the whisky and rum while we're there?"

"It'll be very, very difficult, and a great personal sacrifice on my part for the department." Johnson placed a hand over his heart. "I think I can manage it. I warn you though, if they have our victim's Rockson beer, I'm taking one home to have tonight with dinner. Any problems with that, Detective Murphy?"

Murph gave him a huge smile. "None, as long as you pay for it. Now, let's finish eating, and head toward Kilmore's bar to get you that beer."

CHAPTER 24

·They arrived at the bar a little after two that afternoon. A neon sign announced: "Kilmore's Bar," in flashing red letters above its large picture window. Smaller, matching neon letters advertised two brand-name beers. A small outdoor patio with two picnic tables sporting green patio umbrellas stood on second floor above the bar. To the right of the front door stood a man and woman, talking between hurried puffs of their cigarettes.

"I guess the law banning smoking in bars has chased the smokers into the streets," Johnson said, as he pulled into a parking place a half block from the bar.

"Yeah, instead of polluting the air inside bars, now they're allowed to pollute it outside."

"Better hold your breath as we pass then," Johnson said, heading toward the bar with Murph on his heals, "or those clean lungs that you're always exercising will get a taste of those noxious fumes you're always telling me cigarettes produce."

The couple stared at Murph and Johnson with suspicion as they passed. They knew the look of police when they saw them. Johnson smiled, nodded a, "Good Afternoon," to them, and opened the bar's door. "Cigarette tax inspectors," Johnson said, as he disappeared into the bar behind Murph.

The bar had several hanging ceiling fixtures along with a highly polished wood floor that reflected the light, increasing the brightness of the establishment. A dark brown, curved bar with pedestal seating along its length covered the entire left wall of the room. One of two muted TV's suspended from the ceiling at both ends of the bar broadcasted a Boston Red Sox game, the other a mid-day news program. The dark haired bartender busied himself cleaning the mirror behind the bar, and didn't turn toward the detectives when they entered. Neither did any of the three men sitting at the bar, or the two couples occupying two of the five booths against the wall. They simply continued eating, drinking, and talking softly.

Murph and Johnson sat on the bar stools that sported red-leather, padded seats. Johnson knocked on the highly polished bar three times.

"Be with you in a minute," the bartender said. He swiped the mirror four more times, flicked off a small piece of fuzz that he had missed, and tossed the rag next to the cash register.

"What can I get for you, Gentlemen?"

"I'll take a Rockson beer," Johnson said, as he joined Murph in showing the bartender his shield.

The bartender smiled widely. "You've got to be friends of Eve. The name's Paul Kilmore. We don't carry Rockson yet, but if Eve is right, it'll be the number one seller in just a few months. You may have to come back then for a taste of what she calls, 'The Midwest's Best Tasting Beer.'"

"You haven't ordered any yet from her then?" Johnson asked.

"Oh, yes, I did. She brought in a few bottles, and my customers seemed to like it. I thought it tasted good, and it really is different from any of the big name beers, and the Connecticut microbrewery products we normally serve. It's got a bold, full-bodied taste that really quenches the thirst. I gave her a hard time at first, but she wouldn't be deterred, the epitome of a persistent saleslady. I thought Eve would threaten to kill me a couple of times while I made up my mind. In the end, I placed a big order with her a few weeks ago. Haven't seen her since come to think of it. Is she okay?"

"I'm afraid Miss St. Marie has been murdered," Murph said.

"Murdered?" Kilmore whispered as he grabbed the edge of the bar for support. "Oh, no!" He leaned across the bar, and continued his whispering. "I can't believe it. She is such a nice lady, fun to joke around with, but a strong businesswoman nonetheless. It's a rare combination in my experience. What a shame! Do you have any idea who did it?"

"That's why we're here, Mr. Kilmore," Murph said. "We're hoping you could give us some insight into who she hung around with, and any problems she may have had with them."

"She actually became a regular here about four or five months ago. I guess she came to town from Cincinnati. Wasn't here but a few times when one of our other Saturday night regulars went over to her in that booth over there, and introduced himself." He pointed to the second booth from the door presently occupied by a couple munching on hamburgers. "She enjoyed our burgers like those folks over there. The food's pretty good here for bar food. Anyway, they hit it off right away. Met here every Saturday night after Bob got out of work. That's his name by the way, Bob Kilmore...no relation to me though...pure coincidence. He works the night shift at the hospital as a nurse, I think."

"Had he been a regular here for long?" Murph asked.

"Oh, yeah, he came in about eight months after his wife died with a really sad story. His wife's cancer got really bad during her pregnancy. She desperately wanted to get far enough along so the baby had a chance to survive. It didn't happen. She went downhill fast, the baby had to be delivered very premature, and, unfortunately, didn't survive. Baby died just before she did. Bob took it hard. He has some brothers and sisters who gave him plenty of support, though. He happened to pass by one night on his way to the hospital when an accident forced him off his regular route. He stopped in the next night. Found out I'm a real good listener. He became a regular after that."

"Was he a heavy drinker?" Johnson asked.

"No, not really...never saw him to the point I'd have to cut him off. He'd have a few beers, sit and talk to me, or anyone else who'd listen for that matter. Never discussed his wife or her death with anyone but me as far as I could tell."

"Did he have other women he got involved with?" Murph asked.

"No way! He swore to me he would never get involved with another woman. He really loved his wife. He insisted there would never be another woman, or any other children for that matter. He said it would crush him to lose someone who had become a part of him again. However, he's very good-looking and very sociable. Being unattached, he attracted plenty of women, but he never showed any interest in them at all."

"Was he ever nasty to them?" Johnson asked.

"Oh, no," Kilmore said, picking up a clean cloth from under the bar, and rubbing his hands with it, as if they needed drying. "He always got rid of them politely, like a gentleman. I think it made him even more attractive to the women."

"But it was different with Miss St. Marie?" Murph asked.

"Definitely! Those two hit it off from the start. They were made for each other. She turned out to be great medicine for him. I really enjoyed seeing him genuine laughing. "

"Did you ever see them fight?" Johnson asked.

"Not really, but the last time they were here together, things seemed a little different, a little strained. That had to be about the time I placed the order." He pointed to another booth, presently unoccupied. "They sat over there, but had none of their usual laughter that night. They held hands across the table, but something had changed between them. I could actually feel the tension in the air. Neither touched their food. Drank a few more beers than usual. Then they left together." He paused, inspecting his hands and the rag before continuing. "But you can't possibly suspect Bob of murdering her. He's one of the gentlest men I've ever known. Besides, with all he's been through, I can't imagine him hurting any woman, especially Eve. As to killing her, no way! He couldn't do it. No, you gentlemen have the wrong man. I'd bet my bar on it."

"Did she have trouble with anyone else?" Murph asked. "Another woman maybe?"

Kilmore began cleaning the top of the spotless bar as if Murph and Johnson had just dirtied it. He made large, sweeping circles with the cloth. Both detectives had to lift their arms to avoid being hit.

Kilmore shook his head. "None that I noticed. As I said, Eve is a true businesswoman first. Her number one goal had been setting up her sales network. She wouldn't let her personal life, or any personal conflict get in the way of that goal. Besides, all the women who met her liked her almost as much as the men. Most of the people in here now are my Saturday night regulars. You're welcome to ask them, but they're going to tell you the same thing, 'Eve is a quiet, lovely girl.' I can't see anyone wanting to hurt her for any reason."

"The other women didn't see her as competition then," Murph said.

"No, never," Kilmore said, finishing his polishing before tossing the rag on top of the one next to the cash register. "As I said, they all liked her. She acted friendly to all of them, and treated them with respect."

"Do you know the names of any of the other bars she was attempted to get her beer into?" Johnson asked.

Paul shook his head. "Afraid not, but she did promise me I'd have an exclusive in the downtown area. So, if you're looking for other bars, you'd better check uptown. She also said she wanted to eventually cover Fairfield, Hartford and New Haven counties." He smiled. "I told you she had more ambition than most of my other suppliers, both men and women. That's a lot of territory to cover. Why she picked my bar to start with in Adams has always been a mystery to me. She wouldn't even give me a clue. I figured fate, or God, or something like that, put her here to meet Bob, so both of them could be happy, and I profited with an exclusive offering. Maybe I am wrong, though." He glanced at one of the TVs. "Oh, My God! Eve was pregnant?" He pointed to the TV. "It's on the news."

Everyone in the bar rushed to crowd around the area of the bar by the TV, their eyes glued to the broadcast.

Murph's snapped his head toward the TV. "What? Oh, no!"

CHAPTER 25

The young blond reporter had long hair worn in a flip. She wore a green blouse and a long gold necklace with a lopsided heart studded with diamond chips. As she mouthed the words, print streamed across the bottom of the screen: "Breaking News: A Channel 14 Exclusive: Sheryl Fontaine reporting live. We have breaking news: Channel 14's investigative reporter has discovered that Eve St. Marie, a beer distributor from Cincinnati, has been found brutally murdered early this morning in her East Side Apartment. Neighbors say police arrived after several 911 calls during the early hours to find her body just inside her apartment. She had been shot twice in the chest."

"Turn on the sound, quick," Murph said.

The report blared from the set. "Again, this is Sheryl Fontaine reporting for Channel 14 News. We're here at the East Side Apartments where twenty-six year old Eve St. Marie has been brutally murdered. It has been reported that she underwent an abortion at the Adams' Women's' Medical Clinic recently, and had been harassed by the Adams Pro-Life League. Neither group has made themselves available for comment, but we have it on good authority that both the director of the clinic, Dr. Elliot Svensen and the head of the local Pro-Life organization, Katherine McDonahue, are the chief suspects in the case, and are being investigated by the police. There has been a conflict between these two groups ever since Dr. Svensen opened the clinic fifteen years ago. The Pro-Life group often pickets in front of the clinic, attempting to prevent the women from entering to get their much-needed abortions. We've obtained some of their literature which claims the women who get these abortions often suffer from psychological and religious repercussions afterwards.

"On the other side of the issue, the literature and advertisements from the clinic and other Pro-Choice groups state that the abortions are necessary for these women to maintain their lifestyles, and that the procedure is safe. The Center for Disease Control in Atlanta reports that around a million abortions are performed yearly in the United States, and a total of nearly sixty-million have been performed since the Supreme Court's landmark decision of Roe v. Wade in 1973 that gave the right of abortion to women.

"How Miss St. Marie's abortion ties in with her murder today is unknown. We'll be talking to the detective in charge of the case, Detective William Murphy, later today, and will have a full report on the six o'clock news when we'll be broadcasting from Kilmore's bar, a place the victim frequented.

"Summarizing what we know about this case, we are told the police are actively pursuing clues in the murder of Eve St. Marie, and we're assured an arrest will be coming very soon. Channel 14 will keep investigating on our own, and will have breaking news as soon as it occurs. This is Sheryl Fontaine reporting from the East Side Apartments. Back to you, Ted,"

The picture of Miss Fontaine faded out, replaced by a young man with a mustache who began speaking immediately. "Thanks, Sheryl. On the national front, the President..."

"Turn it off," Murph said, burying his face in both hands. His face flushed. He took a deep breath, and blew it out in one, prolonged puff. He turned to Johnson, who still stared at the TV in disbelief. "How?"

"I have no idea," Johnson said. "No one at the Station would release sensitive information like that."

"Unless there's a leak somewhere," Murph said, grabbing his throbbing head, and pressing his palms into his temples. It didn't help. "The Chief is going to have a fit. I can see her opening a full-scale investigation...with us at the top of her list. Boy! I need a couple of aspirin, fast."

"That report paints both the clinic and the Pro-Lifers as bad guys," Johnson said, pointing at the TV even though the report of the murder had long finished. "I can't imagine who would release a report like that. Maybe one of the neighbors called them, but they wouldn't have the victim's personal information, or the facts about her abortion, or this bar." Johnson looked at Murph, who now massaged his temples with both hands. He sympathized with Murph. His own head had begun pounding also. "Before you ask, none of the messages I left on the voice mails gave any details at all. I'm at a loss."

"So am I. Gosh darn it!" Murph slammed his fist on the bar. "I wanted to get all our interviews finished today before the news got out. Now, the Pro-Lifers will have their backs up when we get there. I'm sure Dr. Svensen will have a different attitude on our next visit there too. Our day just got a whole lot harder."

Without saying a word, Kilmore grabbed a clean cloth, wiping the area that Murph had just struck. He then reached under the bar, and brought out a bottle of aspirin, placing it in front of Murph who shook out two white tablets, and handed the bottle to Johnson. The bartender provided two glasses of water. Murph and Johnson downed their entire drinks with their painkillers, as if the extra water would make the aspirin work faster.

"Thanks," both said in unison.

Murph's cell phone rang with a ring reminiscent of an antique, wall-mounted, crank phone. He retrieved the device, checking the caller ID. "It's the Chief. Let's go outside. I wish I had some answers for her." He flipped open the phone. "Hold on one minute, please, Chief." He glanced at Kilmore. "If you want to help us catch Eve's killer, don't say anything to the reporters when they arrive. Understood?"

"Don't worry! Everyone here will keep quiet. We owe it to Eve." He looked to the gathering crowd. "Everyone agree with that?" The gathered customers all nodded, and began murmuring among themselves.

After Murph and Johnson passed the smokers outside the bar, Murph took a deep breath, and put the phone to his ear. "Hi, Chief."

Chief Martha Stone held the distinction of being both the first female and the first African American to reach the prominent position of the highest-ranking officer in Adams. She had proven to be a tough leader, but demonstrated steadfast loyalty and consistency in supporting the officers in her charge. Everyone liked her, including the press, who appreciated her straightforwardness and honesty. Murph trusted her without question.

"Did you see the Channel 14 report on your case?" Chief Stone asked.

"I'm afraid we just saw it, but we have no idea who tipped them, or gave them the information on our victim."

"You know who the reporter is, don't you?" Her normally silky voice assumed a gravely quality.

"Of course, Sheryl Fontaine and I have a long history. She's a publicity seeking liberal. She'll do anything for a good story, including making up facts as she goes along. She won't give up her sources either, so we may never find out who tipped her."

"Any real suspects yet? The other reporters will be bugging me all day."

"Not really, Chief, but we haven't finished all our interviewing yet, and I haven't gotten any reports from the ME or the CSI team. I'm hoping they give us some leads."

Chief Stone's voice returned to normal. "Listen, Murph, you know I trust your judgment. You keep going with your investigation, and I'll try to get you the reports you need as soon as possible. I'll run interference with Miss Fontaine at the same time. Just keep me informed and, if you get anything I can release to the media, call me right away…and, please, do *try* to stay out of Miss Fontaine's way. I need you to concentrate on the case, and not on your differences with our Channel 14 friend. Can you do that?"

"Yes, Chief, don't worry, Johnson will keep me on track."

Johnson looked Heavenward. *God help me!*

"Let's get out of here," Murph said. He ran toward their car with Johnson at his side. His head still throbbed. "I'm beginning to hate this day."

CHAPTER 26

Minutes after they pulled from the curb, Murph's cell phone rang again. He answered it without checking the caller ID, not really caring who had called. "Hello, Detective Murphy here."

"Hello, Detective Murphy," a voice he immediately recognized said. "This is your wife, Jennifer. Remember me, or were you expecting a call from your *girlfriend*, Sheryl?" Murph also recognized the unmistakable light-heartedness in her voice.

"Just what I need," Murph said, smirking as if she could see him, "a harassing phone call to make my day even harder."

"Then, you must have seen the news. That's why I called. I wanted to make sure you knew you were being stalked by your archenemy again."

"Humph! She's not really my archenemy, Jen. You know her. Over the years, I've watched her develop into a reporter who's too aggressive and far too ambitious, but she's not really an enemy. In any case, we can't figure out where she got her information."

"She has her sources," Jennifer said. "That's for sure! She's proven that any number of times."

"Yes, she has. Thanks for the heads up. If you see anything on the news concerning this case that is earth shattering, give me a call. Who knows? She may find something before we do. We're going to be busy running around, interviewing suspects, and trying to stay one step ahead of my *girlfriend*, as you called her."

"Will do. Let me know if you're going to make it home for supper. I know a teenager who'd like a word with you, and would like the use of her cell phone returned."

"Oh, My God, I forgot," Murph said, hitting his forehead with the palm of his hand. It made his headache worse. He immediately regretted the action. "With everything that's happened, I truly forgot."

112

"Don't worry! *We* won't let you forget. See you tonight. Love you."

"Love you too. Tell Molly I love her. See you tonight."

Murph glanced at Johnson who stared at the traffic, pretending he hadn't heard Murph's call. Before he could say anything, his phone rang again. "Hello, Detective Murphy here."

"Hi, Murph, Doc Rebak here."

"Hey, Doc, you got something for us?"

"The Chief called, and asked me to give you some preliminary findings. I had planned to do it in a little while anyway. We all saw the TV report, so, I guess you could use some help with the case."

"At this point, I'll settle for the smallest information that the media doesn't have. I'm desperate for anything to give us the advantage. I'm going to put you on speakerphone so Johnson can hear. Okay?"

"Okay. I'll start with my autopsy findings. She hadn't been raped, but definitely had an abortion."

"Yeah, we knew that already. We've already interviewed the doctor."

"Well, you can tell him for me that he's a good surgical technician. He performed a first class operation. He definitely knows what he's doing."

"After that TV report, the doctor won't be in any mood to talk to me even if I am passing on a compliment. He'll probably kick me out of his clinic, unless I can prove he's the murderer."

"You mean the doctor that Sheryl Fontaine mentioned is the same one who performed Miss St. Marie's operation?"

"Yup, the same."

"Oh, no! No wonder you need some useful news. She's complicated your investigation, hasn't she?"

"More than you know. What else have you got?"

"Some good news, I think, but first let me give you the rest of her autopsy results."

Murph covered his eyes. *Come on, Doc! Don't bore me with all the details. Just give me the pertinent facts, and make them good.*

Picking up on Murph's frustration, Johnson whispered, "Relax, Murph. You know Doc. He likes to expound on his findings. Let him spout. We've got the time. It's a long way yet to the Kilmore home."

Murph nodded his understanding, and leaned his head against the headrest, wishing he had time for a power-nap, but knowing he didn't, and probably wouldn't for some time to come.

"She had been very healthy and apparently athletic, judging by her muscular development. No systemic diseases that I could find on gross exam. If that TV report is correct, and she worked as a beer distributor, her liver showed no evidence of her imbibing much. She must have drunk alcohol only in moderation. I've sent off samples of tissue and blood, but I really don't expect to find much.

"The two bullets were fired from a .38 caliber weapon. Both entered her chest cavity, as you know. The first went through her sternum or breastbone, through a small portion of lung, then through her heart at the level of her left ventricle, then through another portion of her lung, lodging in her spinal column at T4, that's the fourth thoracic vertebra. I'm afraid going through the bones has deformed it so it can't be used for ballistic identification."

"Great news," Murph said, the sarcasm in his voice thick. He frowned in frustration, and rubbed his eyes so hard he saw stars. "Got anything else, Doc?"

"Don't panic, Murph. I do, and it gets better for you, I think. The second bullet penetrated her chest just to the left of the first bullet. It passed between the fifth and sixth rib, also went through the lungs and heart like its comrade, but it got wedged in the muscles of her back after it passed between the ribs. The gods must be smiling on you. It's perfectly intact."

Murph sat upright at the hint of some good forensic findings. "Great! Any matches from ballistics?"

"That's why I had been waiting to call you. The report got faxed to me right before the Chief called. She wanted me to pass it on to you as soon as possible. Our Chief is most persuasive, you know."

"Doc," Murphy said, the tension in his voice building with each word, "please don't keep us in suspense. What'd they find?"

"Nothing, I'm afraid. It didn't match anything in our computer files here locally, or with the FBI nationally."

Murph slumped. He felt like he had just experienced an emotional roller coaster ride, and, unfortunately, had been on the downhill side of the tracks most of the time.

"But," Rebak said, "the CSI team said if you find the gun used in the murder, they should be able to match it exactly. I thought that might please you."

"I had been hoping we'd get a hit," Murph said. "One of our suspects has a father who served as a policeman. It would have been nice if the bullet matched his service weapon."

"Afraid not, Murph, that would be too easy. Maybe the officer carried a second weapon. If he served a long time ago, we may not even have ballistics on his gun, especially if he didn't fire it in the line of duty. Times change, Murph."

"True. How about fingerprints?"

"As you already know, they found many fingerprints at her apartment. Most were our victim's. There were a few different ones, and many with full prints, but no hits from IAFIS." He pronounced the term "A Fiss." It stood for the Integrated Automated Fingerprint Identification System used by police to match fingerprints with known felons. "The CSI team asked that when you interview the boyfriend you get his prints so they can at least identify which prints are his. They're assuming he has been in the apartment, and at least some prints are his, whether he committed the murder, or not. CSI found nothing to check DNA against in the apartment that they didn't think belonged to the victim, but they're still checking. That's all we've got for now. Sorry, Murph, hope the intact bullet works out for you eventually."

"Thanks, " Murph said. "If anything else turns up, let us know. Bye."

"Not much help," Johnson said, as he negotiated a tight corner. "Did you really think that clinic assistant, Barbara, would be stupid enough to use her father's gun in a murder, especially if its ballistics were on file?"

"I hoped she didn't know they were on file. How long until we get there? I haven't been paying that much attention to the traffic"

"With this traffic, it could be a while. Must be an accident up ahead. I saw some red flashing lights a few minutes ago." His cell phone rang. He handed it to Murph. "If it's one of my girlfriends, tell her I'm interviewing that reporter, and can't be disturbed."

"Your girlfriends never call when we're on a case. I guess you've got them afraid to disturb you." He pushed the speakerphone button. "Hello, this is Detective Murphy, answering for Detective Johnson."

"Hello, Detective Murphy," a male voice said with no accent. "This is Doctor Quan Xi. Detective Johnson left us a message to call him. I'm here in Boston with my colleague, Dr. Aronson."

CHAPTER 27

"Thank you for returning our call, Doctor," Murph said. "We're homicide detectives, investigating the murder of a patient who recently had an abortion at the clinic where you work."

"Yes, we know," Dr. Xi said. "We talked to Dr. Svensen. He called to tell us you'd be calling. You both left messages. His message said to call him before talking to you. So, we did."

"Oh," Murph said, glancing at Johnson who had shot him a quick glance. "Why did Dr. Svensen say to call him?"

A long pause ensued.

Murph smiled. *I imagine you two are now whispering to each other, trying to decide what to tell us about Dr. Svensen's call, or exactly how much to tell us, or whether to lie for your boss altogether...all bad choices. Okay, that's long enough!* "Are you there, Doctor?"

"Oh, yes, we're still here. It's just that...well..."

"Come on, Doctor," Murph said in the sternest voice he could muster. "This is a murder investigation. If Dr. Svensen told you to lie, you'd better think twice before passing that lie along to us. Don't let him put words into your mouth. Don't cover for him. You could be placing yourselves in jeopardy, and be found to be interfering with an official police investigation. That could mean jail time, and maybe even loss of your medical licenses."

"He didn't exactly tell us to lie, though. That's the whole point. He told us to tell you the truth."

"Now, I'm really confused," Murph said. "Were you planning to lie to us?"

"No, no, Detective," Dr. Xi said, so fast Murph could imagine him waving his hand frantically to emphasize his statement while sweating profusely. "It's just, well, let me start at the beginning. Maybe it'll all make sense then."

117

"Okay, Doctor, we're listening."

"You see, Dr. Svensen is, well, having an affair with someone at the clinic." He paused as if that explained it all.

That doesn't explain anything! I still don't get it. "So, what does that have to do with our murder investigation?"

"Nothing, and that's the whole point. You see, whenever we go to a local conference like this, Dr. Svensen drives up, signs in, and then heads back home to be with his girlfriend. At the end of the conference, we check him out at the appropriate time using the hotel in-room check out system, and turn in his key at the front desk, or leave it in the room."

"Okay, so, he's cheating on his wife. What's that got to do with you?"

"He asked us to lie to his wife if she ever called looking for him. We're supposed to say he's with us at the conference, but is in a different meeting with his cell phone off. We're then supposed to contact Dr. Svensen so he could call his wife as if he finally got the message to call her. He's asked us to do this at many conferences before this one, but she's never bothered calling to check on him. I guess she trusts him."

"I guess he's a better surgeon than husband," Johnson said, turning up one corner of his mouth in a disgusted snarl.

"That's probably true," Dr. Xi said. "He's working on his third wife. Janet will probably be number four."

"Janet?" Murph asked.

"Oh, sorry, Janet Robertson is one of our counselors. She started going with him right after he and Barbara broke up."

"You mean the clinic assistant, Barbara?" Murph asked. "She used to date Dr. Svensen?"

"Afraid so."

"Is there anyone there he hasn't dated?" Johnson asked.

"A few, I guess. He never dated any of our clients as far as we know. That's actually against medical ethics. He could lose his license for that." He paused. "Actually, come to think of it, the only other woman we know he dated for sure before Barbara was Georgi Clay, one of our other counselors. She left the clinic suddenly about three or four months ago. She just left a note on her desk stating she had to go home to Tucson because of some kind of family emergency. No one ever heard from her again. I tell you, talk about a tough break for Dr. Svensen. He really thought they were headed for marriage. He even talked about breaking up with his wife. Maybe Georgi decided she didn't want to contribute to the breakup of their marriage. Don't know for sure. Anyway, he took it very hard, and starting drinking heavily for a while. Then, he and Barbara starting dating, and that seemed to straighten him right out. Never heard him mention breaking up with his wife again." Another short pause occurred. "All that occurred a while ago. So, it can't have any relevance here, can it?"

"I don't know," Murph said. "Let's get back to Dr. Svensen's phone call. If I have this right, he originally told you to lie about his being in Boston, then, after our visit to the clinic, he called, and told you to tell the truth?"

"That about sums it up. He told us he had informed Detective Johnson he had been here with us on Friday night, but he didn't think you would follow up on his story. I gather that when Detective Johnson asked for our cell phone numbers, he started to worry about that lie, and told us to tell the truth. So, you see, the truth is he left right after his meeting on Thursday. He usually leaves his car in back of the clinic so his wife doesn't see him driving around town. Janet usually picks him up there, and they spend the rest of what should have been conference time together. I'm sure she'll tell you that's the way it happened this time. They would have spent Thursday and Friday together; so, Dr. Svensen wasn't here as he told Detective Johnson."

"Don't worry," Murph said, "we'll be asking her questions later today. Do you happen to know where she might be hanging out today? She's got the day off."

"When she has a Saturday off, and isn't with Dr. Svensen, she usually spends it shopping, even if she doesn't buy anything. She just enjoys being in the malls with the crowds, window-shopping, so to speak. She usually eats dinner out, and then heads home. So, you can probably catch her at home later tonight."

"You seem to know a lot about her daily activities," Johnson said.

"We have to, in case Dr. Svensen's wife checks in. Never know when we might have to track the two of them down, but I know for sure they're not together today. She took the day off, and Dr. Svensen is working at the clinic, covering us."

"Thank you for your information, Doctors," Murph said. "Please keep your cell phones at least on vibrate while you're in meetings. We may need to get in touch with you later, and I'd like to not have to wait for a return call."

"Certainly, Dr. Aronson and I will do all we can to cooperate."

The accident had finally been cleared, and traveling became much easier.

"I think I'll call the Station," Murph said, "and have them track down Georgi Clay in Tucson. Maybe she can shed some more light on Dr. Svensen."

"Doctor Svensen may be a good surgeon, but he's a scum bag if you ask me," Johnson said.

"Scum bag, or not, we have to seriously move him up on our list of possible suspects. We now know he had opportunity by being in the city Friday night, and the means to drive to and away from the murder in that luxury car of his. Being here probably explains his wet raincoat from last night. Wonder if he owns any guns." He chuckled. "I had predicted he would be mad at us for that news report. Now, I don't care how mad he is. He lied to us. He's got a lot of explaining to do, and he better have an airtight alibi with his current girlfriend, Janet."

"As long as she doesn't lie too. She and Dr. Svensen could also be in on this together." Johnson paused, and shrugged. "I know you hate my conspiracy theories, but they could have planned it together."

"Possible, and I suppose all of Dr. Svensen affairs could tie in with Miss St. Marie's murder somehow." He leaned back against the headrest, and then glanced at Johnson. "What do you think?"

"I'm not sure. Even with my conspiracy theory, I can't figure how Eve St. Marie's murder fits into all this. She didn't work at the clinic and, as far as we know, she wasn't seeing Dr. Svensen socially. So, why kill her?"

"I don't know how she fits in either. I just don't know. Maybe her boyfriend can make that connection for us."

<u>CHAPTER 28</u>

As Johnson parked in Robert Kilmore's driveway, Murph surveyed the area. A large flowerbed abutted the ranch style home, its multicolored flowers attracting bees that buzzed with delight at their nectar. Bright yellow birds chirped in the giant oak tree that shot up forty feet above their heads, its magnificent canopy providing cooling shade to the yard. The meticulously cut lawn appeared weed free. *He takes pride in the appearance of his yard. At least there are no reporters or photographers waiting in ambush.*

"I guess we beat that reporter here," Johnson said, reading Murph's thoughts.

"Thank God for that, but how long can our luck hold out?"

They listened to the musical chimes of the doorbell, sounding from within like a distant concert. After a few moments, the door opened to reveal a young man who wore a dazed expression. Tears streamed down his face. His expressionless face seemingly stared right through them. Murph thought about passing his hand in front of the man's eyes to see if he would notice. Instead, Murph just tilted his head, moving in front of the man so their eyes met: still no recognition.

Robert Kilmore needed a shave, his stubble sopping with tears, his lips cracked and swollen. Barefoot, he wore dirty, khaki pants with no belt that hung low on his hips. His white tee shirt, tattered at the neck, appeared wet and stained down the front where something purple had been spilled recently. He began rocking side-to-side as he blocked the entrance. He remained silent. He held the ornate door, with its multicolored glass inserts, loosely with one hand for support. It moved in time with his rhythm. In the other hand hung a bottle of wine that he gripped loosely by its long, thin neck.

"Mr. Kilmore?" Johnson asked, attempting the same maneuver with his face as Murph, trying to get a response from the zombie that stood before them. He had the same success: none.

"We're Detectives Murphy and Johnson," Murph said, holding his badge before Kilmore's face. His X-Ray vision continued, as he seemed to stare right through both the badge and Murph. "Mr. Kilmore, you are Mr. Kilmore, right?" Nothing. "We're here about the murder of your girlfriend, Eve St. Marie. Have you seen it on the news?"

He nodded; however, his eyes remained fixed on a point somewhere behind Murph. "She said you'd be coming," Bob Kilmore said, his voice harsh, but less slurred than Murph would have predicted.

"She?" Murph said, his voice dropping in intensity. "You can't mean that reporter, Sheryl Fontaine."

He nodded again. His eyes tried to focus on Murph's face. Finally, he tilted his head to one side, like a dog trying to understand its master. "That's the one." The intensity of his voice matched Murph's almost exactly. "She said you'd be stopping by right after she left."

"She left recently?" Johnson asked.

"Kilmore shifted his glazed eyes to Johnson. "Yup. You just missed her. You probably passed her van on the way up my street."

"If I had seen her," Murph said, "I'd have pulled her over, given her a piece of my mind, and maybe arrested her for interfering with a police investigation."

"Yeah, she said you two didn't get along. Don't worry, I didn't tell her anything. I really don't feel like talking to anyone to tell you the truth."

"We'd really appreciate it if you could see your way to talk to us briefly, Mr. Kilmore," Murph said. "It may help us catch Miss St. Marie's killer. May we come in, please?" Murph put his foot on the doorjamb in anticipation of entering, with, or without the zombie's permission.

"What?" Kilmore asked, as if it was the first question he had heard. "Oh, sure, come in." He stepped back, and then staggered to a large, overstuffed lounge chair in the living room. He plopped down on its brown, upholstered seat. "Come join me. Who did you arrest, Dr. Svensen from that terrible clinic, or that do-gooder from the Pro-Lifers?"

"Neither. We haven't been able to prove who did it yet. You shouldn't believe anything that Miss Fontaine tells you. She's not very well informed about the real facts of the case. She tends to speculate a lot."

The living room appeared neater than its owner at the moment. A blue couch faced the chair that Mr. Kilmore had chosen to occupy. The two windows had shades that were fully opened, and had only blue valances across the top for decoration. Through the doorway, Murph could see the kitchen counter with multiple empty bottles of rum, gin, vodka and at least two bottles of wine, red by the dark look of the glass.

"I'd offer you a drink," Kilmore said, "but I'm fresh out."

"We were told at Kilmore's bar," Johnson said, "that you weren't much of a drinker."

"I'm not usually," he said, looking at the empty bottle in his hand, and then placing it on the hardwood floor with a loud "clink," "but I needed a few today and, guess what, almost every bottle I had had been opened, and contained less than ten percent of its original content. I've had them for years...probably why." He rocked back and forth as he leaned over the empty bottle.

"I guess Miss St. Marie's death drove you to empty them, right?" Johnson asked, leaning forward, ready to catch Kilmore, who appeared ready to collapse on top of the bottle.

"I killed her," he said, leaning back hard in the chair, and nodding. "It's all my fault. It's all my fault." He finally bent forward, burying his face in his hands. "I killed her. It's all my fault."

CHAPTER 29

"Mr. Kilmore," Murph said in a firm voice. "Are you really confessing to her murder?" Murph had seen such outbursts from relatives and friends of victims so often in the past that he almost expected them. They rarely turned out to be the true perpetrators of the crimes, however. Murph had come to learn that, in most cases, grief, not remorse, drove the emotions of those who responded this way.

Kilmore raised his head, sat upright, and stared at Murph. "No, I'm not. I didn't shoot her. I couldn't ever hurt her, but I caused her death anyway, as if I had pulled that trigger myself."

"Care to explain?" Johnson asked, not looking up from his notebook, but continuing to write down every word Kilmore said, while, at the same time, keeping him in his peripheral vision, his weight shifted in Kilmore's direction, prepared to catch the falling man should it become necessary.

"Sure! Sounds like you've been to Kilmore's bar already, so you probably know we met there. God, her beauty overwhelmed me that first day. I had sworn never to look romantically at another woman...ever. Boy, did she prove me wrong. There she sat in her business suit, looking to all the world like the consummate business woman." He slurred the word "consummate." "But I saw her as the most beautiful woman I had ever seen, and I include my dead wife in that very elite group. Don't get me wrong, my wife was beautiful." He slurred "Don't" and "beautiful." He shook his head, swallowing with a large upward motion of his head.

I wonder if you're going to be able to finish the story, or will you become incoherent before you finish. I'll bet on the former. "Please go on, Mr. Kilmore," Murph said.

"Anyway," Kilmore said, looking down at the bottle, and frowning with disappointment that some invisible liquor-maid hadn't filled it with alcohol, "we hit it off right away. One thing led to another, as they say, and one day, she tells me she's pregnant with my baby. I went berserk." "Berserk" became his next slurred word. "We argued over what to do…our first argument, as crazy as that sounds."

"It doesn't sound crazy," Murph said. "Then, what happened?"

Kilmore again buried his face in his hands. "I forced her to go to that clinic. Oh, how I wish I hadn't. She didn't want to go, but I forced her."

"How, exactly, did you force her?" Johnson asked.

"I didn't get physical, if that's what you're asking. Didn't have to. I think she may have really wanted to go, but wouldn't admit it. She had to go; she had no other choice if she wanted to save her job and…me…our relationship. An abortion was her…*our*…only hope. Can you believe it, *our* only hope! As if *I* mattered in *her* life…I'm so stupid! That's what I told her, anyway…save our love by destroying the baby. My deranged logic worked, and I dropped her off the first time at that miserable clinic. She could have had the abortion that day, but chose to wait a week. Proves she had second thoughts. My fault, her death is my fault…totally!"

Murph frowned. *Are you trying to remove your guilt by confessing, or are you trying to divert our attention while you're covering your murderous tracks with made-up tales. Which is it? We've got to know.*

"In the end, I insisted on the abortion, so I guess I killed both the baby and her. So, you see, I'm guilty of two murders. Arrest me. Lock me up. Put me away. I deserve it."

"Maybe," Murph said, "but not just yet. When Eve finally went to the clinic to have the abortion, was she upset? Did she cry?"

"Not really," Kilmore said. "I wasn't with her for that appointment…the one where she had the…abortion. She told me not to come. Maybe she thought we'd change our minds if I did. Maybe she realized how weak I truly am. She knew getting rid of the baby would be best for her job, though. She was setting up a distribution network for her beer. It's great stuff. I wish I had a few cases here now. I'd salute her life, not her death. I'm sure she'd appreciate that."

"I'm sure she would," Murph said. "Can you tell me where you were after your shift ended on Friday night?"

"You mean when Eve died, don't you?" He shook his head. "I don't have an alibi, I'm afraid. I finished my shift at the hospital, on time for a change. Clocked out at eleven that night, but I felt very tired from a long day of really ill patients. So, I came right home. I usually go to the bar on Saturday night when I'm off, and after my shifts on other nights, if I'm not too tired. I like the owner, Paul, and the people who hang out there even more than the booze. Oh, how I wish I had taken her there Friday night. She'd be alive now. I couldn't go get her, though…too tired. Not sure she would have come with me…not after what I did to her and…our baby." He tried to get up but fell back. He frowned, tears appearing in both eyes as he sniffled. "Did I tell you I killed her? Might as well have shot all four of them."

"Four?" Johnson asked.

"Yeah, four." Kilmore counted them off on his fingers. "My wife, her unborn baby, Eve and her unborn baby. They all died because they knew me. I'm a one-man plague. Everyone I get close to dies, and it's my fault."

Johnson looked at Murph.

Murph shook his head. *We won't get much more out of him tonight.* Murph made the first move to stand up. Johnson followed suit.

"Would you like to see some photos of Eve before you leave? Did I tell you she was beautiful? Here, let me show you." He rolled out of the chair, catching himself before he fell, and then stood, rocking side-to-side a few times, using his arms for balance like a tightrope walker. "Guess I can't drink as much as I thought, huh?"

"Guess not," Johnson said. He moved to Kilmore's side to be of assistance. "Maybe we'll pass on those pictures for now. We have a lot to do the rest of today."

"Yes, yes," Kilmore said. "It'll only take a few minutes. Let me think." He rubbed the stubble on his chin. "Oh, yes, the pictures are in here." He moved to a cabinet against the wall. He yanked the top-drawer open. He reached in, found several pieces of paper, some paid bills, and a yellow legal pad. He tossed these over his shoulder as he continued his search.

Johnson ducked to avoid the flying debris, managing to catch the legal pad before it hit him. Murph moved to Kilmore's side, but remained silent.

"Please, Mr. Kilmore," Johnson begged. "Don't bother. We really have to leave now."

"No, no, please stay. I'm sure they're in here. Ah, here they are." He spun around, handing Johnson and Murph each a stack of about five color photos. In them Eve wore a bright smile and various outfits, ranging from a long gown to a purple, one-piece bathing suit.

"These are all of Eve," Murph said. "Aren't there any pictures of both of you?"

"Oh, those," Kilmore said, his eyes the brightest they had been since he had opened the door. "They're on my laptop. I didn't print out any of them. I just printed the ones of Eve. I didn't need to look at me, just her. Come on, I'll show you those."

Johnson threw a disgusted look at Murph for mentioning the other photos. *We have to leave, continue our investigation where it might prove more productive, and not waste time looking at family photos with this drunk.* "We should be leaving, Murph."

"Okay," Murph said to Kilmore, "but only a few, please. My partner's right; we really do have to get going."

Kilmore didn't answer. He headed toward the kitchen.

Murph squinted. *He's walking awfully well for a man who had almost fallen over a few minutes ago. Maybe it's the adrenalin from the anticipation of showing us his photos. Maybe, or maybe he's not as drunk as he's making out...a show for us? We'll see.*

Kilmore stopped at the kitchen counter, staring at the lineup of empty bottles. "Sorry, I didn't get a chance to clean up out here."

"No problem," Murph said. "Where are those photos?"

"Right here," Kilmore said, retrieving his laptop from a kitchen chair where it had been plugged into the wall, recharging.

Kilmore opened it, and pressed the "on" key. They watched as the computer booted and, in less than two minutes that lasted hours in Johnson's mind, it came to life. Kilmore moved the cursor using the touch pad, and opened a folder labeled, "Photos," and then an album labeled, "Eve." He clicked "slide show," and the first photo appeared, a photo of the two of them on a beach. She wore the same bathing suit they had already seen in the print now held by

Murph. Kilmore wore green swimming trunks, but no shirt. He had a muscular chest and arms with a flat abdomen, although the well-defined "washboard" muscles, so admired by many, were absent. In another, the couple stood on a boardwalk at some amusement park that could have been Atlantic City or Myrtle Beach. Murph didn't recognize the location, and Kilmore did not provide any narration. Murph checked Kilmore's face. His eyes were glued to the screen, his face once more expressionless.

As the next photo appeared, Murph's eyes widened. "Stop the slide show," Murph screamed. "Stop the slide show, now!"

CHAPTER 30

Murph's yell caused Johnson to jump, and take a closer look at the photo on the screen to see what had caught Murph's eye.

Eve St. Marie and Bob Kilmore stood by a bar, their drinks untouched on that bar. Both wore smiles, but small and forced. Although they held hands, they leaned away from each other, body language that broadcast mutual hostility. The curved bar, as well as the easily recognized owner behind it, made the locale easily identifiable: Kilmore's Bar. In the background stood a man familiar to both Johnson and Murph. He sat in a booth and held hands across the table with a woman with short brown hair.

"Isn't that Dr. Svensen?" Murph asked, his voice only slightly lower this time. "Right there, in the booth in the background." He pointed to the couple in case Kilmore had problems focusing.

"Sure," Kilmore said, pointing at the couple in imitation of Murph, "and that's Janet Robertson. They work together at his clinic."

"How do you know them?" Johnson asked, opening up his notebook again, having suddenly become very interested in Kilmore's computer-stored photos.

"Oh, I'll never forget them, or that night." Then, in silence, Kilmore stared at the photo, as if waiting for it to suddenly change into a video of the woman he loved.

"What happened that night," Murph asked, prodding him to continue, "and when was that photo taken?"

"Let me think. Oh yeah, now I remember. We were there at the end of April this year. That night Eve told me she had become pregnant. That's when I started her on the road to her death." He lowered his head, now trying to block out both the image of the photo, and the night it represented.

"Please concentrate, Mr. Kilmore," Murph said. *I know you're in pain, but I need to know exactly what happened that night. Hold on a little longer, and then you can go into a catatonic state to block out all these awful memories.* "What were the doctor and Janet doing there that night?"

Kilmore chuckled, more to himself than to the detectives. "Celebrating, that's what! Eve and I argued, and had become depressed over what to do about her pregnancy, and there they sat, celebrating! They celebrated while we suffered. It isn't fair." He shook his head, and tears filled his eyes.

"What were they celebrating?" Murph asked. "What could they possibly be celebrating at that bar?"

Kilmore looked at Murph, then closed his eyes, but said nothing. His hands moved from the keyboard to his stomach, the pain he experienced reminiscent of his bout of appendicitis three years earlier.

"Mr. Kilmore?" Johnson said. "Are you all right? Would you like a glass of water?"

"No, I don't want anything. I'm sorry, but it hurts to think about that night. Oh, how I wish I had more booze in the house."

"No more booze," Murph said, "at least not until you tell us about that night."

"No more booze," Kilmore echoed. "It doesn't matter anyway. I don't want any more booze. My stomach's killing me. I need antacids, not booze. They're in the bathroom medicine cabinet."

"I'll get them," Johnson said, getting up to look for the bathroom and the medicine he hoped would help.

"Okay, Mr. Kilmore," Murph said. "I know this is painful, but it may be very important to our case. Why were the doctor and Janet there that night, and what were they celebrating?"

"They were celebrating her pregnancy, that's what," Kilmore yelled. "We were planning to kill our baby, and they were celebrating their future baby, that's what." He started sobbing loudly. "It's not fair. I killed her, and the doctor helped."

"You're confusing me," Murph said. *The alcohol is clouding your mind. Come on! Concentrate a little longer.* "What did the doctor have to do with Eve's murder?"

"He overheard us discussing Eve's pregnancy when we sat in the booth behind him right after that photo was taken. I guess I got too loud. Anyway, he introduced himself as head of that clinic, and gave us his card. He told us to make an appointment. He said he would take care of everything. Eve remained skeptical, but I had become totally convinced he represented one of God's angels of mercy, sent to get me...to get us...out of our situation." He shook his head, and lowered his voice. "I couldn't go through loosing another woman I loved. I knew she would leave me for getting her pregnant. I also knew what her job meant to her. If she delivered that baby, she'd have to quit her traveling to stay home to care for the child. She didn't want that, at least not yet. I knew she would hate me if all that happened.

"I should never have fallen for her. I broke my own rule. Now, I realize that God punished me for getting her pregnant, and forcing me to choose between losing another child, or risk losing another lover...and now I've lost both. I should have let her have the baby. The heck with her job! She had enough talent to get another one locally, and maybe one just as important as the one she had, or I could have moved to Ohio with her." He paused, looking downward. "She'd be alive now if I had let her deliver. She would never have gotten involved at all with that clinic, if I had married her, and she had the baby. No, I became so fearful of losing her love, of her losing her job, and blaming me for it, of *my* not being able to handle the baby, that I panicked. I never really listened to what she wanted. I thought I knew best for both of us. I wouldn't let her make any decision about the baby...her baby...our baby. I forced her to listen to Dr. Svensen...to agree to have the abortion, and now, somehow, that led to someone murdering her. I'm sure of it, and it's my fault. It's all my fault. I tell you, *I* killed her." His tears intensified as he pressed his stomach harder.

Johnson returned with some chewable antacid tablets. He handed the opened bottle to Kilmore who shook four tablets into his palm, tossed them into his mouth, and chewed on all four at once.

"Thanks," Kilmore said between chews of the chalky tablets.

"So, Dr. Svensen gave you his card," Murph said. "Was that the first time you saw him there?"

Kilmore nodded.

"Can you print out a copy of that photo for us?" Murph asked.

Kilmore nodded again. He hit the print key. A wirelessly connected printer began printing the picture on plain white paper.

"There's another of the four of us," Kilmore said. "I'll print that one out too."

Kilmore printed the second picture of the two couples, standing to the right of the bar. He then hit the slide show key again, and they watched the remaining pictures in silence, except for the growling of Kilmore's stomach. None contained anything useful or interesting to Murph or Johnson. The pictures were all of the couple in happier days, presumably before the photo taken with Dr. Svensen and Janet, and the discussion of Eve's pregnancy.

When the show finished, Kilmore closed the laptop. He turned to face Murph. "If you will forgive me, I'm going to bed. I don't feel so good."

"One final thing," Murph said. "We found multiple fingerprints in Eve's apartment. Could we get your fingerprints so we know which ones are yours, and then we can concentrate on the others as possible suspects?"

"Sure," Kilmore said. He picked up one of the photos of Eve that Murph had carried in from the living room. He laid it face down on the table, and pressed his fingers against its back, first with his right hand, and then his left, spinning the picture on the table without lifting, being careful not to overlap the two areas. He lifted the photo by one corner.

"Will that do, or should I go to your police Station to get fingerprinted?"

"We'll let you know," Murph said, motioning for Johnson to take the photo.

Johnson placed a clear plastic evidence bag beneath the photo. "Okay, drop it into the bag."

Kilmore complied. His complexion had paled, and now had a green tint to it, adding to his zombie facade.

Johnson then retrieved the photos from the printer.

"Mr. Kilmore," Murph said, "do you have anyone who can stay with you during this difficult time? You don't look very well."

"I don't feel very well either," Kilmore said, pressing his stomach harder. "My brother and his wife are on the way." He glanced at the clock on the wall. "They should be here any minute now. Don't worry about me. I'll be fine. If I get too sick before they arrive, I'll call my neighbor. He's already been here once today. He'll help me, if needed."

As if on cue, a car door slammed, and the front door opened in rapid succession.

"Bob?" a male voice yelled. "Where are you, Bob?"

"In here, Earl," Kilmore said, the hint of a smile flashing briefly across his face.

Murph and Johnson rose, and walked toward the front door to intercept the new arrival. They met the man in the living room. He froze when he saw the strangers.

Murph quickly produced his badge. "I'm Detective Murphy, and this is Detective Johnson. We were just interviewing Mr. Kilmore. Are you his brother, or his neighbor?"

"I'm his brother. Is he okay?"

"He's not feeling too well, I'm afraid," Murph said. "He's in the kitchen, complaining of stomach pains. It may just be stress; he's been through a lot today, but you better keep an eye on him, and if he gets worse, get a doctor to see him." Murph handed him one of his business cards. "Should you need anything, or if your brother remembers anything he feels could help us in our investigation, please call us."

"Sure, don't worry about him. He's always had a nervous stomach. When he lost his wife and child, I thought he had developed an ulcer. He hadn't. He's really strong, although he doesn't think so. My wife and I'll keep an eye on him. She's a nurse. She'll pull rank on him to get him to do what is best for him, even if he doesn't want to. Thanks for your concern."

Earl headed for the kitchen. His wife charged through the room without saying anything to the detectives.

Murph checked his watch, and reached for his phone as he and Johnson exited the house.

Bill Rockwell

"Hi, Jen. Just wanted to let you know there's no way I'm going to make dinner tonight. Tell Molly how sorry I am, and that we'll talk tomorrow, I promise. We've got too much to do on this case now."

"I understand, Bill, and Molly will too, believe me. We know you're busy. Sheryl made another appearance on the news, saying their next stop is the head of the Pro-Life League. I can't remember her name, Katherine something, I think."

Murph's back stiffened. He stopped in his tracks by the car. "When did she broadcast that little piece of information?"

"About five minutes ago. She said she had already interviewed your victim's boyfriend, but he hadn't been very talkative, that he was just too upset. I wouldn't be very talkative in the same situation, if it were me, I tell you."

"Have to run, Jen," Murph said as he climbed into the car. "If Sheryl is already on her way to the Pro Life League, she may poison their president, Katherine McDonahue, that's her name, by the way, toward us. We may never get any useful information from her."

Johnson placed a red flashing light on the dashboard, and tore out of the driveway before Murph had even latched his seatbelt.

"Make sure I don't kill my supposed friend, Sheryl," Murph said without looking at Johnson and with no hint of a smile.

"At this point, I think I'd probably help you commit that felony."

The ride to Katherine McDonahue's house was as quiet as the ride earlier in the day.

CHAPTER 31

As Murph and Johnson approached Katherine McDonahue's street, Murph turned off the emergency siren and light. "Let's not advertise our arrival, or we'll have every neighbor out there with us."

"Too late, I'm afraid," Johnson said as they made the corner. A group of people congregating around a Channel 14 van stood before them. "I presume that's our destination."

"That'd be my guess." Murph closed his eyes, and shook his head. *I can't believe this is happening. Oh, how I wish I could erase this scene, this day...as I tried earlier with Molly. Didn't work then; probably won't work now.* It didn't. He opened his eyes slowly.

Eight curious people surrounded the white van that had a large, blue "14" painted on its side. Its satellite antenna sat on the roof, pointed toward the West, ready to transmit its signals to the studios.

Murph slowly shook his head. *I wish it could beam the whole van up, taking Sheryl Fontaine with it!*

They parked behind the van, and started a brisk walk toward the house. The crowd split as they approached, forming a tight corridor. No one said anything as they passed, but all stared at the officers.

As Murph and Johnson started up the walk to the large Dutch Colonial, the front door opened, and Sheryl Fontaine, accompanied by a man carrying a large TV camera on his shoulder, emerged. She smiled at the site of the approaching detectives.

"Well, hello, Detective Murphy. How's your investigation going?"

"Pretty good," Murph said, trying hard not to let his anger show. "You do know that you're interfering with an official police investigation, don't you?"

"Interfering?" Sheryl asked with a large smirk that broadcasted her contempt for any official investigation. "Whatever do you mean? We're only exercising our right to broadcast the news as we see it. We're not interfering. As a matter of fact, this is the first time we've run into each other on your '*official investigation.*'" She turned to her cameraman. "Jim, turn that thing on, and let's get an interview with the good detective."

"You turn that camera on, and we'll impound it as evidence," Murph warned.

"You can't do that," Sheryl said, the indignation in her voice emphasized by a large snarl and the placement of her fists on her hips. "We have every right to interview anyone connected to this case. Impounding the camera would be illegal."

"I disagree," Murph said, taking a step toward the cameraman, who took a step back, but said nothing. "You used that camera to interview the people in that home. We're interested in what they said. I'm sure you'd love to cooperate with your police department, and allow us to see your interview. After all, it may contain vital information on the murder. So, we'll just take the camera. We'll make a duplicate of the recording, and give it to you…in due time."

"Okay, Murph," Sheryl said, stepping between the two men, replacing her snarl with a deep frown, and putting her hands up in front of her to block Murph, "let's stop all this nonsense. We won't interview you, and you can let us pass…with the camera. We'll give you a copy…after the broadcast tonight, of course." She turned toward her cameraman. "Don't take any more videos." She turned toward Murph. "How's that for cooperating with the police?" She threw Murph an exaggerated grin, more forced smirk than happy smile.

"Glad you see it my way," Murph said, forcing a smirk that mimicked hers. "I thought your civic pride would come through in the end. Now, let's get serious, Sheryl. This case has been made much more difficult by your broadcasts, and probably by whatever you told the McDonahues. My only concern is to catch the murderer. You know that. You also know I'm serious about my investigations, and try to do a thorough job with each case. You're making that harder for me. How about we cooperate, stay out of each other's way, and share information at the same time?"

"I like the part about staying out of each other's way," Sheryl said, shaking her head, "but you wouldn't be totally forthcoming with your information now, would you? So, how can you expect me to give you the information I find?"

"Yeah," Murph said, "I can see how that could be a problem. Listen, Sheryl, how about some kind of compromise. We've got to find a way to cooperate. I can't keep finding you interviewing our suspects before we do. They may clam up, and not give us anything."

Sheryl turned her head toward the McDonahue's home. *Murph may have a point, but maybe I can turn it to my advantage.* "Well, you may be right there. Katherine McDonahue's not going to be very happy to see you right now. I can assure you of that, and I think my interview took a lot out of her. She looked exhausted when we left, but why should I care how hard your job is, or becomes? Mine is no easier, trying to follow you, having to drum up my own sources, and getting little, or no information from you, or your Chief."

"That's exactly what I mean, Sheryl. You're interfering by turning my witnesses against us. You're preventing us from collecting the very information both of us need. So, how can we pass it on to you if our witnesses won't cooperate, won't talk to us because you've turned them against us before we even get to them? It's got to stop."

"I'll tell you what, Murph," Sheryl said, walking by Murph, and signaling Jim to follow her with a wave of her hand, "you tell me who I can interview, and I'll tell you who I've already interviewed." She walked away as fast as she could. "You'd better check your knowledge of the law, though," she added over her shoulder, "because you don't have the right to interfere with *my* investigation, *my* broadcasts, or to seize any of *my* equipment without a court order. We still have the first amendment right of freedom of speech, and there's still a free press in this country."

Murph raised one side of his mouth in a giant sneer. "Grrrrrr." He turned toward Johnson. "I think I lost that battle."

"I don't know why you even try anymore. She's as slippery as a wet bar of soap, and you know she always gets her way. You should have impounded the camera, and let the courts give it back with an apology later, much later. I would have loved to take it away from that cameraman of hers. With any luck, he would have resisted, and we could have arrested them both for assault, resisting arrest and interfering with our investigation."

"I thought about it, but I feared Sheryl would attack you," Murph said, slapping his partner on the back, "and I'm afraid that's a fight you couldn't win."

"Maybe not, but it would have been fun to try."

"Now, let's go see what kind of damage she's done to our chances of getting any useful information from Mr. and Mrs. McDonahue."

CHAPTER 32

Murph trudged the remaining distance to the McDonahue's front door. *I know this interview is going to be the toughest of the day thanks to Sheryl, Reporter Extraordinaire. Oh, how I wish we had seized the camera just to see what she had recorded.* He shrugged. *I guess it doesn't really matter all that much. I'm sure I'll be seeing the footage on the eleven o'clock news tonight anyway, and I'll bet I turn out to be the bad guy. There's no winning with her. I guess there's just no winning at all today.*

Murph grabbed his badge as Johnson rang the doorbell. After a full minute with seemingly no response, Murph pushed the button twice in quick succession.

"Hang on, I'm coming," a distant female voice said.

After another full minute, a woman dressed in jeans and a green-buttoned blouse opened the door. She wore a work glove on her left hand, stained with soil, and in which she held the right glove.

"We're Detectives Murphy and Johnson," Murph said before the woman could speak. "Mrs. McDonahue?"

"Yes," she said, removing the other glove, gripping them both as tightly as she could in her right hand. "Are you here to arrest me? Do you mind if I finish my planting before you put the handcuffs on me?" She folded her arms across her chest, wrinkled her face into a frown, and stood in front of the two detectives like a roadblock, ready to repel any attempt at entry. Her eyes burned deep into Murph's, daring him to trespass on her territory.

"Mrs. McDonahue," Murph said, lowering his head, "I know what Sheryl Fontaine said in her report earlier today, but what she reported didn't come from us. She made it up. We just met her on your walkway. I don't know what she told you, but please believe me, we're just collecting information at this point in our investigation. We haven't even interviewed you yet, so, there's no way that we suspect you of anything. We do, however, need to talk to you because your name *did* come up during our investigation. That's why we're here, simply to talk, and gather information, nothing more at this point." *I'm going to make you pay someday, Sheryl, if you keep making me have to snivel to get people to even talk to me.*

"Should I have my lawyer present? I don't know who to trust, or who to believe at this point."

"You're not under arrest, Mrs. McDonahue," Murph said, turning to see if the Channel 14 news truck had left. It hadn't. Instead, Sheryl Fontaine stood beside her cameraman who aimed the camera directly at them. "Could we come in, please? Channel 14 is filming this little confrontation we're having, and I'm sure it'll air on tonight's news with whatever slant Miss Fontaine decides suits her broadcast. Neither of us wants that, I'm sure."

She leaned forward to check the validity of Murph's statement, and then stepped back, unfolding her arms to hold the door. "Come in, please. You'll have to forgive me, but I'm a little upset with all this attention, especially since it involves the unfortunate death of a young woman. I've been receiving phone calls all day from members of our Pro-Life group asking questions, and offering their support. We've also been receiving disturbing calls from people who think I'm guilty. I guess I'm not used to being accused of murder by people I don't even know, including you, Detective Murphy. If you believe Miss Fontaine and her TV crew, I'm your number one suspect"

"We have no idea where she got that notion," Murph said, watching her close, and lock the front door. "As I said, she simply made it up. It didn't come from us, I assure you."

"Let's go into the kitchen, and join my husband."

They followed her to the back of the house. Her husband wasn't there. She rushed to the back door, and yelled through the screen, "Mike, come in for a minute. There are some detectives here to speak to us."

Within a few seconds, her husband entered, wearing jeans and a dirty blue pullover shirt.

"These are the detectives that Sheryl Fontaine told us about," Mrs. McDonahue said, placing herself between her husband and the detectives, as if she expected him to charge. "They've explained that the Channel 14 report didn't come from them. They've assured me I'm not really suspected of anything. They just need to get some information since my name came up somewhere in their investigation."

"Is that right?" Mike rinsed his hands in the sink, dried them, and reached into the adjacent cabinet, retrieving four drinking glasses. "Where did that report come from then? Can I offer you gentlemen some water?"

"No thanks to the water," Murph said. "As to that report, it came from the imagination of Sheryl Fontaine. I guess she needed something to report, and you and Dr. Svensen became the easiest targets. She and I have a history. A couple of years ago, she used her knowledge of me to make up a plausible story connecting me to three murders. It made quite a fuss in the department, but an investigation found it to be all fabrication. It's as if she's repeatedly applying for a job at one of those national expose newspapers that's always reporting stories of alien abductions. You can't always believe them, either."

"Plausible?" Katherine asked. "In my case, do you think it's really plausible for the head of the Pro-Life League to be guilty of murder, the very thing I'm fighting against in abortions? It is murder in the eyes of God, you know."

"As long as you brought it up, let's start with some background questions," Murph said, as Johnson took out his notebook. "You imply it's unthinkable for someone involved in a Pro-Life movement to commit murder; however, in the past, there have been bomb attacks on abortion clinics that have killed doctors, nurses and even patients, perpetrated by antiabortionists. A doctor died recently during a Church service, assassinated because he performed such abortions. So, why is suspecting a member of the Pro-Life organization of murder so outrageous?"

"There haven't been many attacks like that," Katherine said. "They are extremely rare, and those who carry out such attacks are fanatics who misunderstand the message of God." She slammed her fist down on the table to emphasize her point, but she barely touched the table, making almost no sound.

Murph stared at the fist. *You either have full control of your emotions, or you've practiced explaining such attacks.*

"They assume the end justifies the means," Katherine said. "It doesn't, and it never will."

"That may be true," Johnson said, "but you can understand how we had to include you in our suspect list until proven otherwise. You had connections to both the Pro-Life League and the Adams' Women's Medical Clinic. To top that off, the victim had a Pro-Life brochure and a card with your name on it in her hand."

After a brief pause, Murph said, "We're not exactly sure how that reporter got so much personal information on the case, though, including your name and our victim's connection with that clinic. We suspect there is a leak somewhere in our department. Our Chief is trying to find it to plug it permanently, but we would never have released your name, Dr. Svensen's, or even the victim's name before interviewing everyone, and notifying the victim's family. That's standard police policy."

"So, that's how my name got mixed up in a murder investigation."

"We were about ready to lynch you guys," Mike said, placing four glasses of ice water on the table. "I got the water anyway in case you change your mind. Please, sit down."

"Thanks," Murph said. "Now, could you tell us if you knew the victim, Eve St. Marie?"

Johnson handed his cell phone picture of Eve St. Marie to Katherine.

"No," Katherine said after studying the picture, and handing the phone to Mike, "but if she had our brochure, she either was a supporter of our cause, or received one with the card from one of our members when she approached that abortion clinic."

"We think she got it the day she first visited the clinic as a client," Murph said. "That would have been on June 1st of this year."

"I don't recognize her either," Mike said. "Let me check the calendar." He walked over to a wall calendar. "We did have a prayer service that day, but Kate didn't feel well, and missed the whole thing. I remember the bright and sunny day vividly. I even got a little sunburned." He returned to the table, and studied the photo again. "I don't remember seeing her, though. I could have even been the one who handed her a brochure, and still wouldn't remember her. I'm not very good with faces or names for that matter. Sorry."

"We're going to check the brochure for fingerprints," Murph said, knowing already the CSI team had checked it, and found no usable prints. "So, we need to fingerprint you both, just in case you handled the brochure before the victim touched it."

"Fine with me," Mike said.

"Me, too," Katherine said. "Since you said she got it on her first visit to the clinic, I have to assume she returned to the clinic a second time, and underwent an abortion. That is unfortunate indeed." She took a large drink of the ice water, placed the glass on the table with a shaky hand, and stared into the swirling ice. She shook her head again, the motion just barely visible and much slower than before.

It reminds me of Mrs. Hanabee, who stared into her cup of coffee at the start of this very long day. I wonder if she's covering up something like Mrs. Hanabee. We'll see. "One of the things we're trying to determine," Murph finally said, addressing the top of Katherine's head, "is whether she also felt it to be unfortunate."

"Whatever do you mean?" Katherine raised her head to meet Murph's gaze. It seemed like an enormous effort on her part. Her eyes had become glazed over, as if she hadn't slept in days. "I'm sure only she could tell you that."

"Probably true," Murph said, remembering Sheryl's comment about how tired her interview had made Mrs. McDonahue, and now believing it to be very true, "but we're trying to establish a motive in this case. We have reason to believe she very much regretted having the abortion. If so, how would she be treated if she contacted your organization either before, or after the procedure?"

"With dignity and concern," Katherine said. "Everyone in the Pro-Life League has pity on any woman who contemplates having an abortion, or suffered having one, whether they regret it, or not afterwards. We pray for them daily." Her tone assumed an angry quality. "Certainly, if they have remorse, God will forgive them. As for our members, we offer them friendship, guidance and, when necessary, counseling."

"Do you do the counseling too?" Murph asked.

"If the problem is deemed minor," Katherine said. "Most of our members are volunteers, but all are required to have some training in order to counsel the women, especially the post-abortive ones. If we think that the problem is more deep seated, we refer them to professional counselors, psychologists or psychiatrists in the area."

"Do many post-abortion women seek such counseling?" Johnson asked, reaching for one of the waters.

"Many do, but many don't even realize they need counseling. That grief you mention can be experienced on all levels of the woman's personality, and may affect her in any number of ways. Many suffer from depression, anxiety, or bouts of anger without even knowing what the real cause is. Many are subconsciously looking to punish themselves for what they did. They can develop sleep disorders, including disturbing dreams about the aborted baby. Some women dream that the baby is talking to them, or calling to them from Heaven. It can be really disturbing, and, sometimes, drive them, well, almost insane. We've seen some who even considered suicide. Unfortunately, we've also heard of some who succeeded." She shook her head, and closed her eyes for several seconds.

Murph leaned forward, elbows on the table. *Are you going to be able to finish before collapsing? What's wrong with you anyway, something physical, or is the emotional strain of this interview draining you, as Sheryl suggested earlier? If so, why? Does it have anything to do with Miss St. Marie's murder?*

CHAPTER 33

When Katherine McDonahue restarted her story, her cadence slowed, her voice deepened. She raised her head, tilted it to the side as she began. "It's a sin what happens to these women. Most don't know where to turn for help. That's one of the things we offer them, hopefully before any permanent damage occurs. If we get to a woman before she opts for an abortion, we show them the abundance of resources available to them from family, friends, church groups and even the government's social service agencies to help them cope with raising a new baby. Some mothers opt for giving the baby up for adoption, which can really make the adopting couple extremely happy.

"If they undergo an abortion, many of those same agencies can still offer help. One example is Project Rachel, the Catholic Church's official post-abortive ministry and outreach program for anyone who has suffered from being involved with abortion. Have you ever heard of them?"

"No, not really," Murph said, searching his mind to find only a hint of the organization, but he couldn't remember where, or when he had heard of it.

"Not surprising," Katherine said. "I'm always amazed by the number of people unaware of their existence or their good work. Anyway, they also offer Rachel's Vineyard, which is a weekend retreat for the same purpose. Both offer confidential counseling and care to women and men who have suffered the trauma of abortion. As a matter of fact, its need has grown so much that Rachel's Vineyard Retreats are now offered not only all over America, but in over seventeen other countries as well. These retreats have had great success in helping people to heal. It's probably the best known of that type of resource. The Respect Life Ministry, The Gospel of Life Society, and The Sisters of Life, all in Connecticut, are a few others

145

I'm familiar with; I'm sure there are many others in this state and beyond, but many women have no idea where to begin the search for what they need. We offer that beginning."

Katherine glanced toward her husband. He reached across the table, took her hands into his and smiled, a smile filled with understanding, one that spoke love sonnets without the use of a single word. Katherine returned the smile, her eyes twinkling like a newlywed.

"They're the best at helping the ones who do get to her organization, before, or after the abortion," Mike said, his eyes glued to his wife's. "You should see her and her group in action. They know how to talk to these poor women, and how to get them the help they need. They really know how to guide them." He paused, nodding his head in admiration. "Believe me, I've seen them perform, well, miracles. I don't know how they do it, except through their love for the men and women involved. If only more women could take advantage of Adams' Pro-Life League and all their resources, this planet...well, at least Connecticut...would be a better place."

"Professional counseling is the best way to go, however," Katherine said, smiling at her husband's exuberance. "Don't get us wrong, though. We don't have the training or knowledge of those new reproductive psychiatrists. That's a field that's been spawned by all the problems women can get into psychologically during any stage of reproduction, not just abortion. Those psychiatrists can offer a lot more than we could ever hope to. What we offer is hope, the hope that comes with the knowledge that the problems these women are having aren't unique to them, that other women have suffered them also and, unfortunately, continue to suffer them daily. We teach them that God is waiting to forgive them, and help them forgive themselves, if they only seek His guidance. We ensure they realize there's no sin that God won't forgive...none!

"We try to guide them to the help they need. Mike is right. We're pretty good at what we do. We only regret we have to do it at all. We'd much prefer to have no abortions performed anywhere in the country...no abortions, no subsequent psychological illnesses to deal with, and no need for our organization. Everyone would be a winner."

***

In the Channel 14 newsroom, Sheryl Fontaine's phone rang only once before she pounced on the receiver. It had been a very long day. She felt tired, and had begun to develop, in the last few minutes, the signs of one of her classical, excruciating migraines. Recognizing her early symptoms, she had taken her medications, a combination of a strong, anti-inflammatory painkiller and a powerful, prescription migraine-stopping medication. She knew the combination would effectively diminish her symptoms within the next two hours, and would begin taking effect within a few minutes, but, until then, bright lights or loud sounds caused her head to pound, as if an evil gnome kept trying to bore through her skull with a hammer and chisel.

"Hello," she said, laying her forehead on her desk.

"Front desk here. Is Miss Fontaine available?" The high-pitched female voice cut into Sheryl's head like a stiletto. "I have a very important phone call for her."

"This is Sheryl."

"There's a frantic woman on line-two who says she has to talk to you." As well as being too high pitched, the voice sounded too loud also. It made Sheryl's head pound harder, the hammer and chisel morphing into a jackhammer. "She says it has something to do with that murder you're investigating."

Sheryl sat upright, making the motion as slow as possible to avoid shaking her head. She picked up a pencil, and wrote the date and time at the top of a yellow legal pad, pressing the button for line two at the same time. "Hello. This is Sheryl Fontaine. Before we begin, may I ask who you are?"

"Th, Th, This is Ja, Ja, Janet Robertson. I work at the Woman's Medical Clinic. I know who killed Eve St. Marie. I'll give you the details if you'll come here right away."

"Where are you, Miss Robertson?"

"I'm.... at home. My address is 4538 Highland Avenue. It's in the North end."

"We'll find it. Can't you tell me over the phone?"

"No, no!" The words were spoken very rapidly. "I have to show you the proof. You won't believe who it is, and, please, come alone."

147

"Alone? Why can't I bring my cameraman? We could record your proof for the whole world to see." She signaled the cameraman over to her desk with a frenzied wave of her arm.

"No, co...come alone, or I'll...I'll call Channel 6, and make them the same offer. I know they'll come. I called you first because you're already investigating the murder. I saw your broadcast earlier today, so, I knew you'd want the information first. Pl...Please, believe me. I have my reasons for the secrecy."

"Okay, Miss Robertson, but I'm going to have my video crew standing by at the TV station. If I think it's necessary to video your evidence, I'm going to send for them pronto. Agreed?"

A brief paused followed. Sheryl crossed her fingers. *A little cooperation will go a long way to get me my exclusive, Miss Robertson.*

"Agreed. Please come right away."

"It'll take me about twenty minutes to get there. Give me your number in case I need to call you."

Janet complied, repeating the number twice to ensure its accuracy.

"Goodbye," Sheryl said. "Jim, that was Janet Robertson, the counselor from the Women's clinic. I've been trying to reach her all day. I wanted to interview her tomorrow morning. She claims she has proof of the identity of the murderer, but will only show me if I go alone to her house now."

"Okay, I'll follow you in the van, and wait around the corner where she can't see me. Just give me a call, and I'll be there in two minutes to get our Emmy-award-winning footage."

"Exactly what I was thinking," Sheryl said standing up, still holding her head as steady as possible with one hand while using the other to brace against her desk. "Let's go get that Emmy."

CHAPTER 34

As Janet Robertson returned the phone to its cradle, the thrust of the gun against her temple decreased. She took a deep breath, the first full one she had experienced since the intruder had entered her home ten minutes earlier, and forced her to make the call. She sat back in the couch, unable to take her eyes off the gun. She had never been this close to a real weapon before. It glistened like a well-polished surgical instrument.

The killer stood before her, picked up a throw pillow and placed it against Janet's chest.

Janet remembered purchasing the crimson pillow at a tag sale. She bought it only because it matched her new couch. She tilted her head to one side. She had seen pillows used as silencers in many movies, but had never imagined her own shopping-spree find would become part of the instrument of her death.

"No," Janet pleaded. "Please. I won't tell anyone. I've always looked up to you. You know that."

Without a word, the killer pushed the barrel of the gun into the thickest part of the pillow, and pulled the trigger. The gun discharged, the pillow converting its blast to a barely audible "Puff." Janet's head snapped forward from the sudden pain, and then fell back against the couch, her eyes closed, her mouth open, as if still begging for her life. The killer went to the front door, opened it a few inches, checking for anyone who may have heard the muffled shot, and had come to investigate. The street appeared empty. Having left the door ajar, the killer then went into the adjoining room to await the arrival of Sheryl Fontaine, who would then join the late Janet Robertson, in becoming the latest star in Channel 14's next breaking news segment concerning local murders.

Thirty-five minutes later, Sheryl Fontaine pulled into Janet's driveway, a long straightaway paralleling the side of the blue ranch style home with complementing, light-blue shutters. The garage at the end of the driveway had its white door closed.

A car had followed Sheryl down the tree-lined street. It pulled into the driveway directly across from the Robertson house, its garage door opening as the car approached. Its occupant, a middle aged man with thick, black, hair noted Sheryl's arrival. As soon as he emerged from his car, he memorized Sheryl's license plate, a skill he prided himself on since he began the neighborhood watch program under the auspices of the local police several years prior.

Sheryl waved at the man, giving him a wide smile. *Have to keep my fans happy. Never know when I might need them, or the information they possess, for some news segment.*

She walked briskly toward the house, her migraine a thing of the past. *Thank God for migraine medication!* She climbed the three steps, and paused, noting the partially open door. She peered through the opening, but could see nothing except the foyer and a small portion of the living room, a large Abraham Lincoln rocker blocking the rest.

"Miss Robertson?" Sheryl pushed open the door. "Miss Robertson, it's Sheryl Fontaine."

She took a few tentative steps into the room, the horrific scene of Janet's body unfolding before her. At the ghastly sight, Sheryl's head began pounding again, as if she had taken no migraine medications at all. Her sudden inhalation of air caught in her throat, leaving her unable to scream. As she turned to flee, she caught a glimpse of a gun creeping around the doorframe across the room.

"No," she yelled, as she turned, and ran through the front door, catching the doorknob so the door would close behind her, hoping it would provide some semblance of protection. It didn't.

The first bullet blasted through the wooden door, splintering the hard wood into hundreds of sharp shards on its short journey to the soft flesh of Sheryl's upper back. It hit her with the force of a canon, driving her forward on the upper landing toward the steps and walkway far below. The second bullet whizzed by her ear, missing

150

only by inches, on its screeching journey across the street where it buried itself deep into the trunk of a large oak tree with a thud and the production of more wood shards.

Sheryl lost all feeling in her body. Her legs collapsed under her, sending her face first down the stairs. As her chest struck the sharp edges of the steps, her ability to breathe left her for the second time. She tumbled down the remaining concrete steps like a broken doll, rolling over and over, her left arm snapping loudly in her ear. A flood of nausea swept over her, as she laid on her side in shock, unable to move her legs or body, frothy blood oozing from the corner of her mouth. Breathing became almost impossible, the little air she could move becoming mixed with, and acquiring the nauseating, metallic taste of blood.

Across the street, the man who had memorized Sheryl's license had been removing a box of toys from his trunk when the bullets exploded through the door. He ducked his head, watching in horror as the woman he had just seen entering his neighbor's house fell headlong down the front steps. He started running toward the woman. He wasn't trained in first aid, but wouldn't be able to live with himself if he simply turned his back on a fellow human being in need of assistance. Halfway across the street, that all changed.

Inside Janet's house, the killer ran to the front door, peaking to find Sheryl, unmoving at the bottom of the stairs. Spotting the man running toward the house, the killer had no way of checking Sheryl's condition, or shooting her again without being seen. Swearing, the killer closed the door, threw the dead bolt to delay any entry, and walked back to Janet's lifeless body. The killer stared at Janet for only a brief moment before placing the barrel of the gun into Janet's mouth, and firing. Blood and gray matter burst through the top of her skull, the mixture further staining the already ruined carpeting. The killer then fired two bullets into Janet's lower abdomen, causing her body to jerk twice, then become still, oozing the last of Janet's blood.

Taking one, last, satisfying look at Janet Robertson, and a fleeting look at the sealed door, beyond which lay that meddling news reporter, the killer smiled, then ran out the back door, across

Bill Rockwell

the rear lawn, and into the car parked in the next street. *Everything's working out fine. It couldn't be better!*

CHAPTER 35

Sheryl had come to rest on the bottom landing. Although lightheaded, she longed to flee, to save her life. She tried moving her legs. They didn't respond. Her left arm screamed with pain, and refused to move. She knew immediately the fall had broken it. She moved her right arm, even that motion bringing excruciating pain to her left arm. She spotted the man across the street as he began running toward her. She reached for her pocketbook, finally snatching the shoulder straps. As she pulled it closer through a monumental effort, her brain began to shut down, the solace and blackness of unconsciousness slowly overcoming her. She fought to stay awake a few more seconds. She reached into her pocketbook, feeling for her cell phone, finding the thin instrument with difficulty among all her possessions. Her vision failed. She could no longer read the blurred keypad. She felt for, finally found, and pushed the speed dial for her cameraman.

Jim answered on the first ring. "Hello, Sheryl, are you ready for our big scene?"

Sheryl tried to speak, but couldn't generate any sound, the overwhelming darkness descending over her consciousness faster and faster.

"Sheryl?" He raised his voice, as if talking loudly into the device would make Sheryl hear clearer. It didn't. "Sheryl, are you okay?" He listened and, at first heard nothing, not even static. Then he heard three bangs. "Were those shots? Sheryl, answer me! Are you okay? I'm coming, Sheryl. Hang on! I'm coming."

The last three shots fired by the killer into Janet Robertson echoed in the would-be Good Samaritan's ears like machine gun fire. Terrified, he held his breath, and froze, fully expecting to feel the slam of the bullets. When he felt no pain, he regained his composure, and began running, although on wobbly knees, from his position in the street to the protection offered by Sheryl's car. Achieving his goal before his legs failed him, he squatted behind the car. His eyes remained glued on the unconscious woman at the foot of the stairs. He grabbed his cell phone, forcing his shaky fingers to push the correct buttons.

"911 operator," a calm female voice said, "what is the nature of your emergency?"

"This is Christopher Winslow. I live at...4541...Highland Avenue. A woman's been shot, and the killer's still inside my neighbor's home. He's still shooting! He's still shooting! Please send the police. Hurry, hurry, and send an ambulance. Hurry, please!"

Without fastening his seat belt, Jim started the van, the engine roaring to life on the first turn of the key. He put it in gear, and floored the accelerator, the tires screaming, and propelling the vehicle down the street. Keeping only a fleeting eye on the road, he dialed 911.

"911 operator," a calm female voice said. "What is the nature of your emergency?"

"This is Jim Deitz. I'm a photographer for Channel 14 news. Shots have been fired at 4538 Highland Avenue. Send the police and an ambulance." He hung up before the operator had a chance to tell him to stay on the line. He then speed dialed the TV station.

"Channel 14 news desk. Peggy speaking. How can I direct your call?"

"It's Jim. This is an emergency. Tell the boss to send another video crew to 4538 Highland Avenue. Sheryl may have been shot. I'll be there in a couple of minutes, and will call with an update, but I have a gnawing feeling that I'm going to be too busy to do any Emmy-winning videoing. Please, tell them to hurry." Not waiting for a reply, he disconnected, and threw the phone onto the passenger seat. *Oh God, Sheryl can't be dead. I'm so sorry, Sheryl.*

154

I made a huge mistake, probably the biggest mistake of my career...probably in my life...in letting you go into a trap alone. If I've gotten you killed, I'll never forgive myself. He held his breath the rest of the short trip, hoping that what he feared hadn't really happened. He sucked in a large gulp of air, his hopes dashed when he skidded to a stop in front of Janet Robertson's house, and spotted Sheryl, lying motionless on the front walk.

CHAPTER 36

Katherine McDonahue sat back, closed her eyes, and took several deep breaths.

Murph studied her. *She looks totally exhausted. I guess Sheryl's interview did take a lot out of her, and that speech she just gave drained the rest of her. She does know the issues well, though. I'll bet she's probably spoken those very words to many people, clubs, and organizations, anyone willing to listen, but the sheer effort has taxed her to her limit. Unfortunately, I have to continue to press you to get the information I need. You still have questions to answer. I'm sorry if you're tired, but no breaks, I'm afraid. I have to continue.* "You mentioned psychological problems, but can they suffer any physical consequences as well?"

"Sure," Katherine said, nodding her head, and forcing her weary eyes open. "Complications during surgery can lead to many physical consequences. Of course, death can occur, as it can for any surgery. In other cases, there might be the need for removal of the uterus, or the surgery could cause scarring that can lead to infertility. Those are only a few of the problems that can occur.

"After an abortion, some women suffer physical disorders, several with psychological overtones, such as eating disorders, or post-traumatic stress disorder, or PTSD, as it is often abbreviated. These physical consequences add more distress to the psychological ones."

"Is that the same PTSD suffered by returning veterans from a war?" Johnson asked.

"Exactly the same," Katherine said. "Of course, not everyone who has had an abortion suffers from a post-traumatic stress disorder, but it can hit these women hard. Are you familiar with the disorder?"

"Basically," Johnson said. "I've actually seen it in a few friends. The stress of battle kind of overwhelms their normal defense mechanisms. They become, I guess you'd say sick, disconnected from reality, and the cause is the stress of battle, even though it can occur long after the battle is over."

"Good explanation," Katherine said, "except here the trauma is the abortion, not any life-threatening battle. They can experience fear, helplessness and even horror. They may not even be able to pinpoint the abortion as the cause of their feelings, since friends and society have told them that having the abortion is what is best for them. Best for them...can you imagine being told that? It's an outright lie! Some women even feel like they've been surgically raped."

Katherine's agitation became more obvious as the water and ice vibrated against the side of her glass. She squeezed her drink so hard that her hands became white, and Murph feared that the implement might burst at any moment.

"You think society is adding to the some of these problems?" Murph asked.

"Definitely," Katherine said. "By legalizing abortion, society has made it seem it's just like having an appendectomy, a simple surgical procedure with no consequences afterwards, but it's not that simple. It's just the opposite. Abortion puts a drain on society."

"A drain?" Murph asked. "What do you mean?"

"There have been nearly sixty-million legal abortions in this country alone," Katherine said, her weary eyes worsening. "There may have been a Michelangelo, a Galileo, an Einstein, or maybe an Edison that we've prevented from being born. Our society could be totally different, better, or at least, improved. We may have killed the scientist who would have discovered a cure for cancer, or the inventor of a flying car that travels on brain wave energy. You never know what wonderful ideas we prevented from becoming reality. We've systematically destroyed the children who could have created those ideas before they even had the chance to breathe life into their own creations. So, we killed the ideas along with the child. Don't you see? We're killing our future." She paused and took a deep, rattling breath. "If nothing else, we've decreased our working population who could be contributing right now to society in general. So, yes, abortion is a drain on society. It's legalized murder. It's a license to kill innocent and defenseless children. The babies are victims that aren't even considered when someone chooses an abortion. They're just waste products to be disposed of, that's all!"

"Collateral damage," Johnson said.

"Collateral damage? What do you mean?" Katherine asked.

"Well," Johnson said, "in our business, when someone is hurt during the commission of a crime, and that person had no connection with the crime itself, that person is considered 'collateral damage.' They weren't supposed to be injured, but they were in the wrong place at the wrong time, as the saying goes. That's the image I got when you spoke of someone having an abortion for whatever reason. The unborn child just happens to be in the way of clearing the pregnancy, and it becomes 'collateral damage,' the end result of the abortion."

"I suppose," Katherine said, returning her gaze to her glass, "except in your example of crime, the injured individual wasn't an intended victim by whoever planned the crime. In the case of the abortion, there's no way to end the pregnancy without killing the child." She shrugged, the effort recording a grimace on her face. "I guess if you stretch your definition a little, you could say the child was 'collateral damage,' but it's still wrong in the eyes of God, if not in society's."

Murph studied Katherine's demeanor, squinting at her as if that would help him understand her. *You don't look right, but I can't put my finger on why. What's wrong with you? You look terrible, drawn. Can you really be that tired from just two interviews? Are you really ill, or acting, and actually hiding something?*

She glared at Murph.

Murph's eyes widened. *You actually remind me of my grandmother about to scold me for some childish behavior. Am I that easy to read? Scary!*

"Now, Detective Murphy," Katherine said without removing her gaze from him, "most of these questions have nothing to do with your investigation. Am I right? You haven't even asked us where we were at the time of the murder. Yet, you've been pumping me for information about abortions and my organization, and I really want to know why before I answer any more questions. Do you have a pregnant girlfriend, or is it your daughter who needs guidance?"

Johnson suppressed a laugh, but couldn't help but chuckle aloud. He tried to keep his gaze on Katherine's face because, if he glanced at Murph, he knew he would break out laughing, something Murph would definitely not appreciate under these circumstances.

"Guilty of deceiving you, Your Honor," Murph said, chuckling through a wry smile. "I *have* been pumping you for information, and I do apologize for doing it in this manner, and not being upfront with you. Some of my questions may relate to our murder investigation. I just don't know which right now, and, since I'm happily married, and don't have a girlfriend, it's someone else. So, you're partially right, but it's not my daughter. It's her girlfriend. We just found out today that she is pregnant, and sought counseling at the Adams' Women's clinic. I wanted to find out what she should expect if she opted for an abortion, and, to be honest, how you would handle a pregnant teenager before I referred her to you, that's all."

"Apology accepted," Katherine said, returning her stare to her drink, "but unnecessary. I would have given you the information even if you didn't have an ulterior motive. The correct treatment of women under these unique circumstances is my passion, after all. I hope you learned what you needed."

"I did. I also admire how easily you saw through my questions. Now, I just have to get the information to my daughter's friend and her parents."

"That's simple," Katherine said, looking toward Mike, "give them one of our new, expanded brochures before they leave." She slowly glanced at Murph. "It has more information than those we used to hand out at our prayer rallies. Mike can give you a stack of them if you want. Now, do you have any other questions? I'm getting very tired. I'd like to rap this up soon, if you don't mind."

CHAPTER 37

Murph squirmed in his chair. *You do look tired, but I still need to get more information from you…and I need to restore my credibility with you, if that's at all possible at this point. So, I'm afraid you're going to have to endure a few more questions.*

Mike placed his hand on Katherine's wrist, trying to give her strength, and, at the same time, calm her. It worked, as her hands steadied almost immediately.

"If our victim did have an abortion," Murph said, "and then suffered from any of the physical or mental problems you've so efficiently outlined, why would she choose to call the Women's Medical Clinic instead of your organization? Could she have feared your organization for some reason?"

Katherine's head snapped in Murph's direction. She glared at him. "Haven't you heard anything I said?" She screamed the words through gritted teeth. "If you think she turned to the League, and we put pressure on her, or killed her for some insane reason, you're wrong!" She leaned toward him, eyes ablaze. "Do you hear me? You're wrong!"

"I wasn't implying that at all, Mrs. McDonahue." *I wish I had phrased the question differently, and not incurred her wrath, nor put her on the defensive. I blew it! I need her cooperation, and instead of nurturing a good relationship with her, I've irritated her, making the situation worse, and my interview harder.* He shrugged. "After all you've said to us, I fully understand your organization as a whole wouldn't have hurt Miss St. Marie, however, it's the individual members I'm concerned about. Did Miss St. Marie contact your organization for advice, or any other reason, either before, or after her abortion." He paused, and when she didn't answer, he added, "Of course, we can check phone records, but I'd like to hear it from you first. So, did she call you?"

"Not as far as I know," Katherine said, smiling at her husband's support as he squeezed her hands harder, and blew her a kiss, "but I can check with our records, and let you know. Most of the phone calls are screened through me. So, I would think I should have taken her call, but she could have been directed to another member if I were unavailable. I will check for you, I promise, and I apologize for snapping at you. It's been a very long evening."

"Yes," Murph agreed, "it's been a long day all around. I'm sorry for upsetting you. Let me explain the reason behind my questions. We know Miss St. Marie called the Women's Medical Clinic yesterday afternoon, and spoke to someone there. She didn't make an appointment, but said she would call back. I was wondering if she realized she could get better counseling at your hands than at the clinic. I need to know if she followed up on that."

"Well, it's true she would have been better off with us, far better off," Katherine said, lifting her husband's hands to her lips for a gentle kiss, "but how would she know that unless someone told her. That clinic certainly wouldn't tell her. They don't want their clients talking to us under any circumstance. To those clinics, abortion is a business, an industry whose goal it is to do as many abortions as they can. There have been reports recently that they're selling the body parts of aborted babies. They even have quotas. Can you believe it? Abortion quotas! There have even been awards given to some clinics for the massive number of abortions they have performed. Outrageous!" She paused, and took several deep breaths before continuing. "As I said, I doubt if your victim called us. I would think if she had, I would have at least heard her name from whoever took her call. If you really want my opinion, if she had called, she'd probably still be alive."

"How do you figure that?" Johnson asked.

"Simple," Katherine said, never taking her gaze from her husband, "if she had called, we would have met with her immediately, and she wouldn't have been alone when death came calling."

"Unfortunately, if you had been there, death may have visited you too." Johnson said. "You might have become collateral damage yourself. Killers don't like to leave witnesses."

"Oh," Katherine said, turning to face Johnson, "you're probably right. I hadn't thought of that. I only wish we could have helped her."

"You couldn't have helped her by getting yourself shot," Johnson said. He shifted in his chair, his mind turning Eve St. Marie's murder over and over, trying to get a new view, a new idea, and, maybe, a new avenue to pursue. He came up empty. He decided to conclude his part of the questioning the way he always liked to...by establishing alibis. "Now that you have helped my partner and his daughter's girlfriend by answering all his questions about abortion, I need to ask you one more question before we leave. Where were you two last night between the hours of 10 PM and 1 AM?"

"Right here at home," Mike said, answering before his wife could speak. "Kate hasn't been feeling well, and we've been going to bed early because of it. Last night proved no exception. We went to bed by eight thirty. We learned about the murder while watching the morning news."

Murph's cell phone rang. He grabbed the phone, checked the caller ID, and stood, heading toward the front door. "Please excuse me. I've got to take this. It's important"

"Go out the back door, Detective," Mike said. "It's closer and more private back there. The TV cameras may be still be out front."

Murph changed direction mid step, and exited the back door, carefully closing it behind him so it made very little noise.

"I think we've finished with our questions," Johnson said, watching Murph, "but, as we said before, we may need to fingerprint both of you for elimination purposes only. Do you have any plans to leave the area in the next few days?"

"None," Mike said, shaking his head while maintaining his gaze upon Katherine. "We'll give you whatever you need to complete your investigation. We stay home a lot these days. Don't we, Kate?"

She smiled, and nodded, but said nothing.

Exiting the house, Murph stepped onto a redwood deck that lead to a yard enclosed by a chain link fence. In the neighbor's yard, two young children ran across their lawn, giggling as their Golden Retriever puppy chased them with its tail wagging excitedly. On the McDonahue's porch, balanced across the arms of a folding chair, were two wooden window planters, filled with rich, black soil. Several small plastic pots, containing bright colored flowers, sat on the floor waiting their turn to be transplanted into the window unit. At the bottom of the stairs, a shovel stood upright in a partially dug hole. Next to the hole stood a small bush with shiny green leaves that Murph recognized as a Boxwood shrub from the ones in his own yard. *This family work scene is what both Sheryl and I interrupted by our arrivals. I'm sure the flowers will get planted with love as soon as we depart...if Katherine regains her strength, and feels up to the task.*

"Hello," he had said before even closing the door fully.

"Murph? This is Jen. Did you see the news report?"

"News report?" Murph asked, bracing himself against the wooden railing. "No, what did it say?"

"They're repeating it now. Listen."

Murph could hear a distant voice become louder and more distinct. In his mind, he pictured his wife increasing the TV volume.

"We have breaking news," a female voice said. "In a Channel 14 exclusive, one of our cameramen on assignment with Sheryl Fontaine, our anchor here at Channel 14, has just reported that Janet Robertson, one of the counselors at the Adams' Women's Clinic here in town, has been shot, and killed in her home. Further, it has been reported that Miss Fontaine, who apparently walked in on the killer, and witnessed the murder, was herself shot in the back by the killer. We have no further details at this time on Miss Fontaine's condition, or whether the killer has been apprehended, as the police are interviewing our cameraman at this time, and he is unable to speak to us. As first reported on Channel 14, a murder last night of a young woman, Eve St. Marie, has also been connected to the clinic. We do not know if the two incidents are connected. Again, we have breaking news...."

"Did you hear that?" Jennifer asked as she decreased the TV volume.

"Oh, yes, I heard all too well. Thanks Jen. I've got to run. After that news, I can guarantee I won't make it home at all tonight. You understand?"

"Of course. Please try to get some sleep though."

"If I can, I'll come home to nap. If not, I'll grab some sleep at the Station. Thanks again for the tip. Love you." He disconnected without waiting for her reply.

Johnson stood as Murph returned.

"We have to leave, Johnson. Let's go."

"Another murder?" Katherine asked.

"How did you know?" Murph asked, stopping behind the seat he had vacated.

"Simple, I'd bet your blood pressure is rising by that brilliant red color developing in your face. Add that to the fact that you're already investigating a homicide, and it's not so hard to imagine you're probably rushing off to another murder." She smiled wider than she had since they arrived. "Oh, and by the way, I have the perfect alibi: I was being interviewed by the great Detective Murphy, one of Adams' finest, at the time of that murder."

"Brilliant deduction, My Dear Holmes," Murph said, returning the smile, "but I'll have to check on that Detective Murphy person to see if he can corroborate your alibi. By the way, do either of you know Janet Robertson?"

"No," Mike said, "can't say I've ever heard of her. How about you, Kate?"

"I think she works at that clinic as a counselor," Katherine said. "Am I right, Detective?"

"Yes," Murph said. "So, you do know her."

"Not personally," Katherine said, never lifting her gaze from her drink, "I just know the clinic's personnel. She's not a good counselor from what I hear. Is she your latest victim?"

"Afraid so, I guess it's all over the news. So, you'll have to excuse us. We really have to leave."

"I'll see you to the door," Mike said, "and get that brochure for your daughter's friend."

"We'll keep her in our prayers tonight," Katherine said, raising her head to meet Murph's eyes. She attempted a smile, but failed. "It's the least we can do for her."

CHAPTER 38

While Murph, Johnson and Mike rose, Katherine made no attempt to move.

Mike led them through the living room, stopping to retrieve a brochure from an end table drawer. He motioned the detectives to follow him outside where he handed the brochure to Murph. "I have to apologize for my wife. She's very ill. She's undergoing chemo and radiation for breast cancer following the necessary surgery. The treatments really take a lot out of her, as I'm sure you noticed."

"Oh, I'm so sorry," Murph said. "Why didn't either of you say something? We could have abbreviated our visit, and kept the questioning to the bare necessities until she felt better. You probably could have answered most of our questions anyway."

Mike smirked. "Katherine would have been furious with me if I had said anything. She's not ashamed of her diagnosis or treatment, mind you, but she won't give in to it either. She doesn't want to be treated as an invalid by anyone, especially me." He chuckled, and shook his head, imagining his wife balling him out the way she had at the beginning of her treatments for what she referred to as his "babying" her. "Of course, it has slowed her down a bit, especially right after her treatments. She feels horrendous then, but won't admit it. We're sure she's going to beat it. She does poop out quickly though. Believe me, she would have thrown you out if she got too tired. She'll feel a whole lot better tomorrow after another good night's sleep."

"Hopefully, she will," Murph said, "and I have no doubt that she could have tossed us out whenever she wanted. She's a very strong woman."

"Stronger than you will ever know, Detective, a lot stronger."

"Please tell her I'll keep her in my prayers," Murph said.

"She'll really appreciate that…more than anything else you've said to her today. We really believe in the power of prayer. Thank you."

"We may have to come back to question you two again. If so, I'll make it a point to thank her again for all the information she gave me that's not in this brochure," Murph waved it in the air once, and then placed it in his inside jacket pocket. "She's really passionate about the subject."

"She sure is. That's because she lived it as a teenager herself. She's not proud of her lifestyle back then, or of her decision to have the abortion, but she's not afraid to talk about it, and doesn't care who knows about it either. She's been healed through counseling and through the Church. She knows God forgives her and, although it took a long time, she's finally forgiven herself." He shook his head. "It happened long before we met. She was one of those that had been lied to, and suffered for it afterwards with anger and depression. She also became one of the rare cases where surgical and infectious complications occurred. Those made her both unable to have children and very fervent about the subject."

Murph stood motionless, his mouth agape. He pointed to a wooden plaque with the names Kate, Mike, George and April printed on it in white letters.

"Yes," Mike said with a huge grin, "that's our family. We adopted two children. We went through the usual channels, and it took forever, but we finally got two beautiful children. God has been very good to us, and we thank Him every day that their natural parents decided to have them, and put them up for adoption. They're both out with friends, or you would have met them. They've taken after Kate in a lot of their mannerisms."

"I couldn't think of anyone better to imitate," Murph said, "except maybe you. Tell your wife I really appreciate her putting up with my antics, and thank her for the brochure."

Murph ran the final few yards to the car, finding Johnson already in the driver's seat with the motor running. They took off before Murph had a chance to buckle his seat belt again, the chiming alarm insistent until he had.

"So, Janet Robertson's our killer's next victim," Johnson said, as he turned on the siren and lights.

"Yes," Murph said, slamming his hand against the dash, "murdered at her home. Maybe we should have gone to see her before the McDonahues. The killer outsmarted us again. I really blew it this time."

"Listen, I've been calling her phone all day with no luck. Our going there may not have prevented her death, and you know it. The killer may have been waiting for her, planning to kill her as soon as she came home. If we had gone there earlier, and no one answered, we would have left to go to the McDonahue's anyway. It would have been the same end result, her murder. Can't second-guess, Bill. You know that."

Murph remained unconvinced. "I suppose, but maybe we should have followed up on Doctor Svensen once we found he had lied to us. If he's the murderer, he couldn't have killed Miss Robertson while we talked to him."

"No, but, if we didn't arrest him, he simply would have waited until the opportunity presented itself. In any case, I think we should make his house our next stop after the murder scene. I want a minute-by-minute account of where he's been since early yesterday afternoon. He's still on the top of my list of suspects."

"Don't forget he does have a wife who's also on our list. An unfaithful husband with a pregnant girlfriend could be a good motive for murder."

Johnson shook his head. "I haven't forgotten the wife, and I suppose if she's the killer, the doctor could actually become her next victim. It sure will be interesting if we can catch them both together for our interview. The sparks would surely fly high then. Seriously, though, why would she want to kill Eve St. Marie? As far as we know, Eve wasn't fooling around with our hyper-sexed doctor."

"She sounds like she's one of the few women in this town who wasn't, but I can't figure out a motive there either. Maybe the Doc's wife suspected Miss St. Marie of having an affair with him. We'll just have to keep her in our sights too while we're ducking those sparks you mentioned."

Murph's cell phone rang again. The caller ID read, "Chief Stone." Wincing, he pressed the speakerphone button.

CHAPTER 39

With both the killer and Sheryl ahead of him at every turn, the last thing Murph needed were questions from his boss. His heart dropped, as did the tempo and timbre of his voice. "Murph here, Chief."

"Did you see the TV report?"

"No, but my wife called, and I heard it over the phone. We're rushing over to Janet Robertson's right now. What happened?"

"Don't bother rushing. Our patrol cars have the area cordoned off. CSI and Doc are on the way. All we know for sure is that the counselor from the clinic has been killed. Your old nemesis stumbled upon the scene, and got herself shot for her effort."

"Is Sheryl okay?" Murph asked.

"Haven't gotten a report. Maybe Doc will have more on her by the time you get there. He has a lot more pull at the hospital than I do." Murph could hear the shuffle of papers during the slight pause that followed. "If her cameraman is correct, she may have indeed walked in on the murderer. Maybe she can give us a description…if she survives." She paused. "She's been ahead of you during this whole affair."

Murph rolled his eyes upward. *Tell me about it!*

"Her enthusiasm may have cost her dearly this time," the Chief said.

"Collateral damage," Johnson said, just loud enough for only Murph to hear.

"Let's hope not," Murph said, answering both the Chief and Johnson.

"Can't tell you any more than that," the Chief said. "Neighbors called in the shooting. Maybe you'll get lucky with one of them."

"Maybe," Murph said. "It would be nice to catch a break for a change, and not feel like we're being manipulated and outpaced by the killer. When did those calls come in, Chief?"

"They were logged in at six-forty-eight this evening."

Murph checked his watch: 7:10.

"I lost track of time. It's later than I thought."

"It always is, Murph. Did you learn anything from the head of that Pro-Life League?"

"Not that relates to our case. There's no evidence that our victim contacted them. We can't figure a motive for them to have wanted her dead in any case. We're more interested in Dr. Svensen. He lied to us about his whereabouts during the time of the murder. He got Janet Robertson pregnant. It's too big a coincidence that she is suddenly murdered. It's very convenient for him, especially since she was supposed to provide his alibi for the St. Marie murder."

"How does the St. Marie murder relate to Dr. Svensen?"

"We don't know yet, but we're going to track him down right after we finish at the Robertson place to see if we can make that connection."

"Okay, let me know what you find."

"Okay, Chief." Murph disconnected. He turned off the siren and lights. "Slow down. There's no rush. The patrol cars have got the murder scene secured."

"Which patrol cars?" Johnson asked, slowing the car to match the speed of the others on the busy road. "Anyone we know?"

"The Chief didn't say."

"Great," Johnson said with a worried look. "I hope it's not one of the rookie cars that started today."

"Don't worry, we've got a good crew of officers starting this year. They may surprise you."

"I don't like surprises. Besides, today has had too many surprises in it for me already."

"Give me the phone numbers you got at the clinic today. I want to check on all our suspects."

"What do you hope to learn?" He handed his notebook to Murph. "Do you think they'll confess over the phone?"

"You never know, Detective Johnson. I can be very persuasive, you know."

"Right! I think you're hypoglycemic, Detective Murphy. Remind me to pick up some pizza after we leave the murder scene. You'll see things a lot more lucid then. I promise."

Smiling, Murph dialed the doctor's home. It rang four times, and then switched over to an answering machine. He disconnected

169

without leaving a message. Next, he tried the doctor's cell phone. It immediately went to voice mail.

"I guess he has his cell phone turned off," Murph said.

"Maybe after it rang during the first murder, he learned to turn it off during the second."

"Maybe." Murph dialed Assistant Director Barbara Schine's home. It rang twice

"Hello," Barbara said.

"This is Detective Murphy. Just checking if you were home."

"I've been home cleaning house. I'm tired now to tell you the truth. It's been a very long and stressful day. I think I'm going to quit, eat some leftovers, and watch TV."

"You haven't been watching the TV news at all then?"

"No, I usually watch the six o'clock news, but I've been vacuuming. You can't hear TV over the vacuum. Why? Did I miss something?"

Murph looked toward Johnson who looked skeptical.

"I'm afraid you did, and I have some bad news for you. Janet Robertson has been shot at her home."

"What? That's terrible! Is she all right?"

"The initial reports are that she's been killed, but we're on our way there to find out what happened. Do you know where Doctor Svensen is? I've tried his home and cell phone, but he's not answering."

"No, I have no idea. I'll make a few calls. Maybe he's with one of our other doctors, or at his club having dinner with his wife. I'll try to track him down for you. If I find him, I'll have him give you a call. I'm sure if he had seen the report, he would have called me already. He and Janet were, well, close."

"We really appreciate your help. We may have some more questions for you later this evening."

"I'll be here all night. Stop by anytime. Tomorrow, I have some errands to run. I'll be in and out all day, but you can reach me by cell. Give me a call if I'm not at home."

"Okay. Thanks."

"Goodbye, Detective Murphy."

Johnson glanced at Murph wide-eyed. "The doctor was *close* to Janet Robertson?" Is she kidding? It sounds like she didn't know Janet was pregnant by him."

"Maybe she didn't. Maybe Doctor Svensen didn't tell the others at the clinic."

"He wouldn't if he intended to kill her."

"True," Murph agreed, as he handed Johnson's notebook back to him, "but I wonder why Janet didn't confide in Barbara. Would she really have kept it a secret from her?"

"We'll have to check that one with Barbara when we see her again," Johnson said, as he made the final turn into Janet Robertson's neighborhood.

Murph closed his eyes, lowered his head, and said a silent prayer for both murder victims, whom he considered innocents in the eyes of God, and who may also have been collateral damage as professed by his partner. He said a separate prayer for Sheryl Fontaine and Katherine McDonahue. *I'm sure they are innocents, one an over-zealous reporter who definitely fits Johnson's definition of collateral damage, and the other who definitely fits my definition of innocent.*

Forgive me, God, for causing further distress to Katherine McDonahue. Murph shook his head. *She's suffered much in her life, and now functions as God's helper to many women. I'm sorry I used her to get the information I plan to pass on to Betty Ann and her parents, but I felt I had no choice. Maybe, just maybe, God used my interaction with Katherine McDonahue to teach me a lesson in humility.* He glanced Heavenward. *It worked, God. Thank you.*

171

CHAPTER 40

Murph and Johnson slipped under the yellow crime tape in front of Janet Robertson's home after showing their badges to a uniformed officer at the foot of the driveway. Three black and white patrol cars flanked the two Channel 14 news trucks.

Murph took a quick look into Sheryl's car, and then stood perfectly still, starring at the splotch of blood on the ground. Alongside the blood, a small, yellow plastic evidence triangle stood upright with the number "1" printed on it. He estimated she had 8 feet to run to reach the safety of the car. *It might as well have been 800 feet!* He inhaled and exhaled audibly. He stepped around the blood, his gaze lingering on the splotch, as if it would speak to him of some hidden secrets about the shooting. It didn't.

He climbed the steps, stopped at the top landing, and stared at the two splintered holes in the door. *Exit marks from the bullets on their journey to Sheryl's back.*

He donned rubber evidence gloves, and entered the house. Using one finger, he closed the door. The bullet holes inside were much smaller and distinct. *Entrance holes where the bullets bored their way through.*

After allowing Johnson to enter, he closed the door fully, and looked through the holes, imagining the line traveled by the bullets as they made their journey from the killer's gun, through the door and into Sheryl. "Assuming she ran after observing the murder, she must have pulled the door closed behind her as the killer fired. My guess is that she tried to hide her body from the killer's sights."

"It didn't work well," Johnson said. "The bullets probably hit her while she ran on the landing at the top of the stairs, and she fell from there."

"The door must have been the only protection she could throw between the killer and her," Murph said, tearing his eyes away from the bullet holes. "She didn't have much choice. If the killer had missed her, we'd probably all be applauding her ingenuity. She always could keep her wits about her in stressful situations."

"But why didn't the killer simply go over to the door, open it, and then shoot her again? He wouldn't have had to expose himself by going outside, or even open the door the whole way. All he had to do was thrust the gun out through the partially open doorway, aim, and fire." Johnson used his thumb and forefinger to demonstrate the technique to Murph, although he didn't bother opening the door. "Firing through the door isn't very effective, and is highly inaccurate. If Sheryl recognized the killer, I would think the killer would want to make sure he had killed her. That's the way I would have done it. Makes more sense than shooting through the door, and then not finishing her off."

"Maybe she didn't recognize the killer, or didn't get a good look at his face. Then, it wouldn't matter if she died. Warning shots through the door might have been enough to scare her away in that case. Maybe he didn't care if he killed her."

"So, you think he hit her by accident, then?"

"It's a distinct possibility," Murph said, walking farther into the house.

He stopped when he saw the top of Janet Robertson's head. It had a gaping hole in it that oozed blood and gray matter. The green Berber carpet had a seemingly endless supply of the gruesome mixture. He walked around the couch, and found Doc Rebak, kneeling in front of the victim, examining her wounds, and mumbling. Murph checked the angle to the front door. It didn't match what he predicted would be the line of fire through the door and into Sheryl's back. He moved until he felt he had found that line. He turned, and found himself between the front door and a doorway into the next room.

He hurried to the doorway, and entered the dining room. He peaked around the doorway's molding until he could see the front door. He stepped back into the living room, and aimed at the front door with his index finger. *CSI will have to confirm it with their laser indicators, but I think I know how the shooting went down.* He nodded to Johnson who returned the gesture.

Murph hurried back to Rebak. "Hi, Doc, you enjoy talking to yourself?"

"Oh, hi, Murph," Rebak said, looking back over his shoulder. "Didn't hear you come in…too absorbed with our victim. I was asking Miss Robertson here how anyone could do such a thing to her. Afraid she didn't give me a clue." He shook his head. "Two murders in one day is a little much for this little bedroom community, don't you think, Murph?"

"That's for sure! We were supposed to interview her later tonight about the St. Marie murder. I wonder if she had some information on the murder, or whether her murder has nothing to do with our planned visit."

"You'll have to figure that one out for yourself. All I can tell you is that this murder is different from Miss St. Marie's."

"How so?" Johnson asked, taking out his notebook and pen.

"The first killing seems like an execution: two shots through the heart, efficient and clean, maybe even a professional hit. This one is personal."

"Personal?" Murph asked. "What do you mean?"

"Unless I miss my guess, and I usually don't, the first shot killed her. The killer fired through this foam-filled pillow to deaden the sound." He picked up a blood soaked pillow from the victim's lap, and placed it in a large evidence bag. A gaping hole filled its center. "My guess is that no one heard that shot and, if they did, it might sound to them like a distant car backfiring." He handed Murph the evidence bag, and waited while both detectives examined it for a few seconds. "Sometime after that, the killer shot her three more times."

"I think I can confirm those three shots," a uniformed officer, who entered through the dining room, said. "I'm Officer Jacob Campbell. My partner and I were the first on the scene. We've got the neighbor, Christopher Winslow and Sheryl Fontaine's photographer, Jim Deitz, sequestered in the kitchen. The neighbor says he heard two shots, and saw that reporter woman fall down the stairs. He then heard three more shots. That's when he took cover, and called 911."

"I'm Detective Murphy. This is my partner, Detective Johnson. Did the photographer see, or hear anything else?"

"He said he had parked around the corner in the TV van, waiting for a call from Miss Fontaine, who had come here to interview the victim alone. He claims he received a call from the wounded reporter's cell phone. Apparently, she didn't say anything. He then heard three pops that he thought might be shots. When he couldn't get any response from her, he drove here. He said he called 911 on the way. We arrived a few minutes after that, and found him kneeling over the wounded woman and the neighbor hiding behind the car parked in the driveway."

"Are both of them in the kitchen?" Johnson asked.

"Yes, Sir, they're with my partner."

"They shouldn't be together," Johnson said. "Witnesses can change their stories to match other witnesses' accounts, if they hear them."

"Sorry," Campbell said, a reddish tint filling both cheeks. "I know that. I don't know what we were thinking. I'll separate them now."

"Is there a back door from the kitchen to the yard?" Murph asked.

"Why, yes," Campbell said, as he retreated toward the kitchen. "Why?"

"Presumably, that's how the killer got out after the murder. Go help your partner keep an eye on our witnesses while we finish here. Separate them, and keep them away from that door until the CSI team checks it for prints. We'll want to interview them separately."

"Sure, be glad to," Campbell said, disappearing into the dining room.

"Rookie mistake," Johnson said. "No real harm done, I suspect, though."

"Let's hope not."

"Doc? Got anything else for us?"

"As I said, there were three other shots. Can't tell you which came first for sure, but my guess is the first was fired through her mouth. It blasted through her skull, burying itself in the wall over there." He pointed to a beige wall, splattered with blood and bits of brain. "The next two entered her lower abdomen. Not much bleeding from either wound there. That's how I know they were post mortem wounds. I'm guessing on which came first but my money's on the head. Was she pregnant by any chance?"

"Yes," Murph said, "how'd you know that?"

"Educated guess. I told you I thought this was personal. Whoever killed her took the time to shoot her again after firing at your reporter. The killer probably put the gun barrel into her mouth, fired it, and then fired at her lower abdomen. Why blow off the top of her head *after* shooting her in the chest? There had to be something personal between them. Maybe the killer hated her, but, at a minimum, I think the killer knew her. Then, he shot her in the lower abdomen. There's not too much anatomically down there that would interest most people except her uterus. So, I concluded she must have been pregnant, and the killer knew it…and that pregnancy meant something to the killer. Maybe it's what caused the murder in the first place. Who knows? In my mind, when I put all of that together, it makes it personal, very, very personal. It's obviously much more violent than our first murder, and it's certainly not a simple execution. Anger must have been rushing through this killer's mind." He looked up to Murph. "I'll be able to confirm all of my speculations after the autopsy, of course."

"We'll await your results," Murph said, "but I think you're right on the mark as usual. I could see how anger could easily play into all this. We found out about her pregnancy earlier today. Now, we have to figure out how it relates to her death. Any help you can give us would be greatly appreciated. Anything else you can tell us about this murder right now?"

"No."

"Okay. Now, tell me about Sheryl. How bad is she?"

Rebak leapt to his feet. He spun around to stand face-to-face with Murph. "Oh, My God! How insensitive of me! I apologize. I should have known you'd want to know about your friend right away. I'm sorry. Please forgive me."

"Stop apologizing, Doc. We've both got jobs to do here. That comes first. Just tell me how she's doing."

"She had been transported to the hospital by the time I arrived. I called the hospital a few minutes ago, and spoke to both the EMT who transported her and the neurosurgeon who's going to operate. It's not good, Murph."

"How bad?" The back of Murph's throat tightened at Rebak's words.

Johnson took one step closer to Murph. *It's been a long, emotionally draining day. How much more bad news can Murph take before cracking, and loosing his temper again?*

"She's bad, Murph," Rebak said. "She's unconscious. She broke a rib in the fall that punctured her lung. She lost a lot of blood. They put a chest tube in to re-expand the lung, and stop the bleeding. She's got a compound fracture of her arm that'll have to be set. But those aren't her biggest problems. The bullet entered her spinal column at her upper back, and is lodged against her spinal cord. Right now, she's undoubtedly paralyzed from the chest down from the swelling in the area. The neurosurgeon is going to have to operate to relieve the pressure. She's not breathing on her own. They've got her on mechanical ventilation. We won't know how much damage is permanent, or how much movement she'll recover until after she awakens from the surgery, and the swelling decreases. There's no way to predict. I'm sorry."

"Doc, be honest with me. What are her chances?"

"Slim, but she has the best neurosurgeon in town, she's young, and she's got good recuperative powers. She's a fighter to boot. You know her. She won't give up easily. I'm sure she'll do everything she can to be back on the job to irritate you as much as possible, as soon as possible."

"You're right, she's a royal pain in my side, but I would miss her if she weren't there irritating us at every turn. Will you keep checking on her, and call me as soon as you know anything?"

"You can count on it. You'll know almost as soon as I do."

"Thanks. Come on, Johnson. We've got some witnesses to interrogate."

CHAPTER 41

As Murph and Johnson entered the dining room, a policewoman stood, and nodded to them.

"You must be Detectives Murphy and Johnson. I've heard a lot about you. It's a pleasure to meet you." She smiled, and then assumed a more serious expression. "I'm Officer Pat Stewart, Jacob's partner. He told me to stay here with...Mr. Christopher Winslow. He's very upset." She read his name from her notebook, pointing to him as she spoke.

She looked young, although Murph couldn't judge her age by the smoothness of her skin or her voice that had a deeper pitch than he would have predicted by her 5 foot 6 inch, thin frame. She had short-cropped, black hair and a small face with high cheekbones above a small mouth. She tried to speak like a seasoned veteran, but her voice cracked at her partner's name. It made Murph wonder if possibly some friction existed between them. He didn't know either officer, but he made a mental note to find out more about each. *The town of Adams needs effective teams on patrol, not dissonant individuals. Clashing partners could prove dangerous to both team members as well as other members of the Adams police force who have to work with them.*

"Please call me Chris. I live across the street." His voice quivered and cracked several times as he spoke. He took a few sips of water, and then stood, his color immediately turning pale.

"You'd better stay seated," Murph said, afraid he might faint. "We'll join you." Murph and Johnson sat while officer Stewart remained standing.

"You'll have to excuse me. I've never seen a dead body before...I mean a murdered body. Before today, the only dead bodies I've seen were in caskets. I guess I wasn't ready to see her like that. It was just too much for me."

"He's thrown up three times since we arrived," Officer Stewart said.

"My wife doesn't have to see Janet like that, does she?"

"No, " Murph said. "Where is your wife now?"

"She's at home. I called her on my cell phone after I saw Janet, and told her to stay there."

"Who let you in to view her body?" Johnson asked.

"I asked these two nice officers if I could come in to see if I could help Janet. After all, we were so close."

"That marks the first time he lost it," Officer Stewart said.

"He should never had been allowed near the body," Johnson said. "It's a crime scene. She is obviously dead. He couldn't have helped her in any way. Suppose he disturbed the evidence. It's hard enough investigating a crime without letting witnesses march through the room vomiting all over the scene." His voice slowed as he scowled at the officer. "He didn't vomit at the scene did he? Please tell me he made it to the bathroom."

"He didn't compromise the scene," Officer Stewart said, all the friendliness gone from both her voice and continence. She spoke into her notebook as if it were a recorder, refusing to make eye contact with either detective. "He made it to the bathroom. My partner went in with him to ensure he didn't touch anything there."

"That's the first thing you two did right, I'm afraid," Johnson said. "Who put the crime scene tape outside?"

"The team in the second unit. We secured in here. That's why we brought Mr. Winslow with us. Why? Did we screw that up too?"

"I don't know," Johnson said, trying to make eye contact so she would see his displeasure.

She refused to give him the satisfaction, and continued her love affair with her notebook.

"Easy, Johnson," Murph said. "Remember, no harm done." He turned to the officer. "Why don't you join your partner in the kitchen? We'll join you when we finish here."

"Fine," she said, as she left the room without ever lifting her eyes.

"Now, Mr. Winslow, Chris," Murph said, "please tell us what happened."

Winslow leaned back in the chair, and closed his eyes as if the scene would replay on the inside of his eyelids. "I had some errands to run late this afternoon. I got home around six thirty. I drove down the street behind that Channel 14 TV reporter. I watched her pull into Janet's driveway. Of course, at the time, I didn't know who she was. When I got out of my car, I memorized her license plate, and then wrote it down when inside my house. It's a part of our neighborhood watch program. I'm the leader. I never realized anything like this would happen, though. Believe me!" He paused, looking at Murph, waiting for some recognition for exercising his civic duty.

"You're supposed to watch and report," Johnson said, "not walk in on a crime scene."

Chris Winslow lowered his head.

"That's Okay, Mr. Winslow," Murph said, before Johnson could continue. "Ignore Johnson here. He's having a hard day." Murph formed the deepest frown he could, mouthing the words, "Stop it!"

Bill's right, though, I really am short tempered. What's wrong with me, lambasting a witness like that? That's not like me. He looked at his wristwatch, a departing gift from his last girlfriend. She had left him for someone who had a job with regular hours and less chance of being killed at work. She had told him she would miss him. He thought he would miss her, but after one month, he had forgotten almost everything they had done together. *Wow, I didn't realize it had gotten that late. Maybe I'm grouchy because I'm hungry. It's way past time for dinner. I've also been up for over sixteen hours. I'm exhausted. It's no wonder I'm a grouch. I guess I'm not as young and strong as I used to be. I'll apologize to Murph later, after we eat, and head home for some refreshing sleep, even if I don't have a good woman like Murph's wife waiting for me.*

"We need more people contributing like you," Murph said to Winslow. "We realize you're upset, and that none of this is your fault. You should never have been allowed into the house. None of this is your fault. Remember that. We need your information to catch your neighbor's killer. So, let's put all that behind us, and move on. Please, continue with your story. You wrote her plate number down and..."

Chris Winslow's skin began to return to its normal pink. His hands had stopped shaking. He stared at Murph. His words became more distinct, more regular, his voice clear, and strong. "I put her license plate number into a file. I came back out to get the packages from the trunk of my car. I had to make more than one trip because I couldn't carry them all. On the second trip, I heard this bang, bang from over here. I didn't know what the sounds were at the time. I looked over here, and saw the reporter, falling down the stairs. She bounced right onto her shoulder on the walkway. She didn't move. I had no idea what had happened. So, I started to cross the street to see if I could help her. The next thing I heard were three more bangs. By then I figured out they were shots."

"Were all three bangs bunched together," Murph asked, "or three separate, distinct shots with a pause between each shot?"

"Oh, no," Winslow said, "a brief pause followed the first shot, then came two more shots, closer together. Is that important?"

"It's all important," Murph said. "We're collecting all the facts we can now, and we'll sort them out later. You never know when something may be the thing that helps solve a case like this. What happened next?"

"I ran for cover behind the reporter's car. I called 911, and waited there for help to come. A couple of minutes later I heard the sirens, but it seemed like hours." He pointed toward the doorway that Officer Stewart had gone through. "Those first two officers arrived, followed by two more police cars. I stupidly asked to come in and, well, you know the rest."

"Did you see anything else," Murph asked, "maybe another car, someone running, anything at all?"

"No, I'm afraid once I heard those shots, I wouldn't have seen the killer if he had run right by me. I was too shaken up." He shook his head. "I still am."

"Okay," Murph said. "We want to thank you for your information, Mr. Winslow. I don't want to keep you here any longer. We may have some other questions for you later. Are you going to be home the rest of the weekend?"

"Yes, I'll be home tomorrow, and I think I'll take Monday off too. I'm in no shape to go to work. I'll answer any questions you have. Just call, or come over."

"What do you do for a living, Mr. Winslow, Chris?" Johnson asked.

"I'm a mechanical engineer at the Potter Tool and Die Institute here in Adams." He smiled for the first time since before he had witnessed Sheryl Fontaine's dive down the stairs. "I've been with them for the whole time we've lived here."

"If you think of anything else, please give us a call at this number," Murph said, as he handed Winslow a business card, "and again, thank you for your help."

"Oh, you're welcome," Winslow said. "Glad to be of help."

"Come on," Murph said. "We'll let you out the back door, so you don't have to go through the living room past the crime scene again."

"Thanks." As he stood, Winslow turned his head away from the living room, staring out one of the windows in the dining room. Later, however, he wouldn't be able to describe the view through that window, or really remember what he had told the detectives.

"Would you take him into the kitchen, Johnson?" Murph asked. "I'd like to check the area by the living room again."

"Sure," Johnson said. "Come on, Mr. Winslow. Let's go get you home."

"Fine by me, I can't wait to get there. I need a drink."

Johnson kept close to Winslow in case he showed any signs of returning queasiness. He didn't. Once in the kitchen, Winslow headed straight for the back door. The wooden door, with three rectangular windows rested open against the wall. A white, aluminum screen door remained closed, but not latched.

"Hold on, there, Mr. Winslow," Officer Campbell said.

Winslow froze, his hand inches from the door.

"Can't have you messing up evidence that might be on the screen door," Officer Campbell said. "Detective Murphy will have my badge for that. I'm already on his watch list."

"It's Okay," Johnson said, pushing passed Winslow, and opening the screen door with his glove-protected hand, making sure he only touched the edge of the metal where no obvious evidence of fingerprints or foreign matter existed. The door opened easily, but squeaked loudly. "Don't touch anything on the porch, and head right toward your home, next store, through that open path. Don't go anywhere near that gate outback." Johnson studied his face that again appeared green. "Are you sure you're going to be all right?"

"Fine," Winslow said as he rushed out the door. "I'll be even better when I get home."

"I'll bet the neighbors have become used to the noise of this screen door," Johnson said after Winslow bounded off the back steps. Johnson watched Winslow walk on the grass toward the side of the house closest to the squeaking door. As he staggered away, he covered his mouth with his hand, hoping to prevent a repeat of his vomiting.

"Think he'll make it home without being sick again?" Officer Stewart asked, peering through the back window at the retreating Winslow.

"The odds are against it," Johnson said.

"I guess you were right. We really upset him by letting him into the house. We're both sorry. We should have known better."

"Well, I shouldn't have come down on you so hard. So, I owe you an apology. I'm tired and hungry, but that's no excuse."

He turned to face her, releasing the door, and listening to the door scream its return to the closed position. She smiled at him, and nodded, but said nothing. Their gazes met, and lingered longer than Johnson thought necessary. He smiled, and then turned his attention to the noisy door. He opened, and closed it several times. The door screeched each time.

"I'll bet when the killer burst through this door, it made the same noise, and all the neighbors will swear they never heard it."

CHAPTER 42

Murph examined the floor and door molding at the doorway to the living room, finding nothing out of the ordinary. *Maybe the CSI team can find something microscopically.* He peeked around the edge of the molding again to line up the front door for an imaginary shot from his finger. *Why had the killer hidden here? Was the killer trying to draw Sheryl into the room? If so, why not move the body, and draw her farther into the house before shooting? Johnson asked the right question: Why hadn't the killer run over to the door to get a better chance at a kill shot? Did the killer panic? Did the killer even care if he hit Sheryl?* "We've got too many questions and not enough answers."

Murph walked into the kitchen just as Johnson turned his attention to the testing of the squeaking screen door. Officer Campbell stood near Jim Deitz.

Deitz shuffled toward Murph. "Boy, am I glad to see you! Any news about Sheryl?"

Murph shook his head. "I'm afraid I don't know any more than you. Doc Rebak said he'd keep me informed. I'll let you know if I hear anything. You do the same, please."

Jim leaned against the counter. "What do you think happened?"

"You tell me. Start at the beginning. Why did you two come here in the first place, and why did you come separately?"

"Sheryl got a phone call from Janet Robertson. She claimed she knew Eve's killer, but would only tell Sheryl, insisting Sheryl come alone. Sheryl and I agreed that she'd drive here, and I'd wait for her around the corner in the van." He lowered his head, and whispered, "I got a call with Sheryl's cell phone ID. She didn't say anything. Then I heard three shots, and I panicked. I drove here as fast as I could...found her lying on the front walk." A tear rolled down his cheek. He choked as he spoke. "Murph, she couldn't move. She had a broken arm. The bone stuck out through her skin." He paused and sniffled twice. He took two full breaths, expelling them forcefully through pursed lips. "She never said a word. These officers arrived a few minutes later. An ambulance came soon after that. They took her away quick. That's all I can remember. I'm sorry."

"Don't apologize, Jim. You did very well considering what happened. Did you notice anything else, like maybe a car speeding away?"

"No, can't say I did. Your Good Samaritan neighbor probably saw more than me."

"He's a lot more nervous than you, but his story does confirm yours."

Jim finally raised his head to find Murph smiling. He smiled in return. "Yeah, he did look like a little green man from Mars. First corpse?"

"Yes, and probably his last, if he has anything to say about it. I don't think he'll volunteer to help with a police investigation ever again, and it's probably just as well."

"Can I get out of here, Murph? I'd like to go to the hospital to check on Sheryl, maybe be there when she wakes up."

"Sure, Jim, I know how to reach you." Murph placed a hand on Deitz's shoulder. "Don't suppose it'd do any good to tell you not to talk to any reporters, would it?"

"Right!" Deitz laughed more at Murph's attempt to cheer him up than at what he had said. "I promise that if any reporters ask me what happened, I'll tell them that they have to clear it with Sheryl. I'm sure she'll allow me to give her Emmy-winning report to the first reporter from another station that approaches me."

Murph laughed loudly. "Get out of here before I decide to put you in protective custody to keep you from talking to anyone. Seriously, Jim, could we keep the gory details of the murder off the air for now? We'd like to have a chance to catch the killer before you broadcast every last detail. We need an edge. I'd like to hold some of those details away from the public for a few days. Do you think you can do that for us?"

"For you, no, but I can do it for Sheryl. I want her to be the first to report it, even if it has to be from her hospital bed. I'll tell her she really needs to clear the information with you first, though."

"Oh, great! If you tell her that, she's sure to blab everything you two know to the whole world the first chance she gets." Murph slapped Jim on the back as he pushed him toward the back door. "Now, get out of here before I lock you up."

Johnson again opened the door, listening to its annoying screech. "After the CSI team gets through, I'm going to oil this door's hinges to preserve my own sanity."

"Now, what should I do with you two?" Murph asked, turning to the two officers.

"We'll understand if you report us," Campbell said. "We got the neighbor sick, and that reporter saw everything in the room. He'll probably describe the gruesome scene to the world in their TV news program tonight."

"It's actually worse than that," Murph said. "Jim Deitz is probably the best photographer and videographer in the area. He undoubtedly took photos and videos with a small camera he always carries in his pocket."

"Oh, no," Officer Stewart said, "but you asked him not to give out any details. You mean he'd show actual videos of that poor woman's body?"

"You can count on it. He's part of a very liberal press, who think anything goes, and the more shocking, the better. Who knows? In their business, they're probably right. Sensationalism sure gets noticed more than conservative, accurate reporting. I've seen many awards given for photos and reports that were disgusting, and should have been destroyed, not published, and certainly should never have been broadcasted."

"Those pictures and videos will be all over the nightly news," Officer Stewart said, hanging her head. "We really blew it, didn't we?"

"Well, ordinarily I'd say yes; however, this time the conservative police are smarter than the liberal press. I think we can feel assured that Mr. Jim Deitz, photographer extraordinaire, will do exactly what I asked him, and will not release any photos or videos to his friends in the press." He reached into his pocket, removing a combination digital video and photo camera from his pocket, and held it up for all to see. "I believe you'll find some interesting pictures and videos of our crime scene on this camera, Detective Johnson. It must have jumped out of his pocket, and onto the kitchen counter as he left, or maybe he was playing with it nervously, and simply forgot it. I really don't know how it got there, but I'm sure the CSI team will have a ball checking its memory."

"You picked his pocket," Officer Campbell said, a look of surprise crossing her now raised face.

"Oh, no," Johnson said, "an Adams' detective would never do anything illegal like take a camera out of someone's pocket. I think I may have actually seen the camera levitate from the photographer's pocket, and fall onto the counter. Strangest thing I've ever seen." He turned to Officer Stewart. "You did see the same thing, *didn't you*, Officer Stewart?"

"Absolutely," she said, catching on to Johnson's implication, "and I can truly say that I never saw Detective Murphy's hand go anywhere near Mr. Deitz's pocket."

"You people are something else," Officer Campbell said. "You threaten to report us, then do something so outlandish and illegal that it makes what we did seem like great police work. I don't understand." He turned to his partner, a look of increasing surprise on his face. "Why are you joining in with them, Pat?"

"The alternative, Officer Campbell," Murph said, tilting his head in Campbell's direction while he fingered the camera, "is to report what you did to the Internal Affairs Division. They're sure to want to know which officers allowed unofficial photographs and videos to be taken at a crime scene. Which do you think is the better alternative, borrow his camera, or talk to IAD?"

"You know," Officer Campbell said, "I'm beginning to see what you're saying. I missed the point that you were just borrowing it, not stealing it. Besides, we get professional photos taken of our murder scene without even asking for them. Like the rest of you, I don't know how it got on the counter, but I can see how it may help our investigation." His smile grew larger. "I think it's a much better alternative than an IAD investigation. Thank you, Detectives."

"Just remember to learn from your mistakes, Both of You," Murph said, "and you'll improve every day as members of our police force."

"As I like to say," Johnson said, "no harm done. So, we just move forward with our investigation, as if nothing happened. It's like going to confession; your sins are not only forgiven, but forgotten forever. Agreed?"

"Agreed, agreed," the others said in unison, as if they had been practicing all day. They all laughed loudly.

"Forgotten forever," Officer Campbell said. "I like you guys."

"Don't like us too much," Johnson said. "We can be worse than an IAD investigation when we have to be. This isn't a cover-each-other's-behind, good-old-boy's club. If we thought you two deserved it, we'd report you without a second thought. We've done it to others who either abused their authority, were incompetent, or worse, dishonest. So, don't get us wrong. We like good officers. We train good officers. We detest bad ones. We're giving you two another chance. Let's just say we're hoping you're salvageable, and leave it at that."

Doc Rebak leaned his head into the kitchen from the dining room. "If these two detectives are giving you a second chance at something, you'd better take it. They don't give second chances to many young officers."

"Oh, we got the message," Officer Stewart said, smiling, and giving a wink to Johnson. "Didn't we, Officer Campbell?"

"Loud and clear."

"I've got to run, Murph," Rebak said. "I've got tons of work now, thanks to this case, and I do want to check on Sheryl. My assistant, Jerry, finally arrived. He'll hold things down here for now."

"Okay, Doc, let me know about all the angles, please."

"Don't worry, I'll give you a call as soon as I have any more on the case, or hear anything about Sheryl."

"Thanks," Murph said. He managed a weak wave, trying to read the last expression on the physician's face for any hint of encouragement about Sheryl, but found none.

"Is there anything else we can do to help in this investigation, Detectives?" Officer Stewart asked. "I promise we'll make you proud."

"Maybe," Murph said, turning to face the young officer. "Come with us. Let's go outside to see what the killer may have encountered as he rushed out the back door. Maybe he left us some clues."

Johnson carefully opened the screen door, again being treated to the door's serenade. It led to a wooden landing with two steps down to the grass. A chain-linked fence surrounded the yard. At the very back of the yard, a gate rested in the open position, leading to another street, currently devoid of traffic.

"The killer must have parked his car on that street, and ran across the lawn," Murph said. "The grass is wet from last night's rain, but I don't see any obvious footprints. Maybe the CSI team will have better luck. We'll let them do the traipsing across the yard, looking for evidence. Speaking of the CSI team, where are they? They usually beat us to the scene, and are all over the place, gathering evidence. I haven't see them since we arrived."

"I'll check," Johnson said as he pulled out his phone. "My guess is the killer either knew the victim and, or the layout of the house along with that escape route, or scoped out the layout before today. I know Doc says it's personal, but that makes it premeditated, not a crime of passion." He turned his back to the other officers when the Station finally answered. "Hello, this is Detective Johnson…"

"We're going to have to knock on all the doors on that street in back to see if anyone saw, or heard anything," Murph said. "If I can get you assigned to me temporarily, are you willing to spend tonight and maybe tomorrow morning canvassing the area?"

The two officers looked at each other, smiled and nodded their heads.

"We'd love to," Officer Stewart said, "and we really appreciate the opportunity."

"Make sure you coordinate with the CSI team, and, please, don't step on their toes," Murph said. "I don't want to hear any complaints about you two. Remember, they outrank you too."

"We understand," Campbell said.

"Check for any video surveillance cameras on the street," Murph said, "outside stores or banks that may get us a shot of the killer's car."

Murph nodded to Johnson who nodded his understanding, and called the Chief to ask her permission. She almost always granted Murph whatever he requested in an investigation because he had become very selective and careful to ask only for those things he knew would either improve his chances of solving a case, or improve Adams' police force. *In this case, maybe both!*

"Were either of the victim's immediate neighbors home during the murder?" Murph asked.

"No," Officer Campbell said. "The officers in the second unit checked after they set up the crime scene tape…no answer at any of the surrounding homes. Mr. Winslow said some are on vacation. Others, he thought, had either gone shopping, or visiting relatives or friends. In any case, the street was pretty deserted when all the action went down."

"Okay, Let's go back inside."

CHAPTER 43

"CSI's coming back to finish up now," Johnson said. "They were called to another scene across town right after they got here. This has been one busy day for our small force. The Chief says we can keep these two wayward officers, *if* we promise not to compromise their ethics too much. I think she figured out we have something on them." He raised his hand. "I swear I didn't even give her a hint that they did anything wrong."

"She's smart enough to know how we think," Murph said. "It's what makes her endearing to our hearts."

"It makes her scary to work for sometimes," Johnson said. "I think that instinct of hers is what makes her so tough, and probably earned her the position of Chief in the first place."

"That's the truth," Murph said, "better her than me, though. I would never want to be Chief. Never!"

"Okay, Detective Non-Chief," Johnson said, "why don't you give the newest members of our team their assignment so they can learn what it's really like to do detective work?"

"I already have. Haven't I, Officers?"

"Oh, yes," Officer Stewart said. "He told us exactly what he wants done. We'll get on it right away. We won't let you down."

"We'll call you as soon as we have something," Officer Campbell said.

The two officers headed toward their car.

"You don't really expect them to come up with anything, do you, Murph?"

Murph studied their patrol car, as it headed out to what he knew would become a tedious, door-to-door, information-gathering assignment with little hope of successful fruition. "No, not really, but it'll be good experience for them, and it truly is better than writing them up...both for them and us."

Johnson's phone rang. He signaled for Murph's attention. "You apparently missed a call. The doctor's wife left a message at the Station for you personally. She said it's very important that you call her right away. Here's her home number."

Murph re-entered the house as he dialed the number, and walked through the murder scene, searching for any overlooked clues, anything that the killer had touched, or changed. Nothing looked out of place or strange. *It's as if the killer came into the home, murdered the victim and left, having no interest in the rest of the house, no robbery motive, just murder. I'll have to check the bedroom later. Maybe the answer lies there.*

The phone rang only once.

"Hello?" a female voice said. "Is that you Elliot?"

"No, Mrs. Svensen, it's Detective Murphy. I got a message that you wanted to talk to me."

"Detective Murphy, I…I… I don't know where to begin." Her voice oozed fear.

Murph pictured the woman, gripping the phone with both hands, sweat accumulating on her brow. Her breathing sounded labored. "Take it easy, Mrs. Svensen, and tell me what happened. Start where you think something started to go wrong…the reason for calling me."

"It's Elliot. He saw the report on TV about Janet's murder…what a terrible thing…and he bolted out of the house. He didn't say where, or why. That reporter on TV said that you were looking for him as a suspect in the murder. That's ridiculous! In any case, I've never seen him act like this. He always tells me where he's going, always. Maybe he's worried about the police looking for him. I don't know. I'm so worried."

"Have you tried the other doctors and employees at the clinic?"

"As many as I could find. No one has heard from him. Do you think he went to Janet's house? She's one of his valued employees. He's very close to the people he works with…treats them like family. You know how it is when you spend so much time with someone, caring for the health of others."

"We're at Janet's house right now. Your husband isn't here. If he shows up, we'll let you know." Murph turned toward Johnson, his eyebrows raised. "I'll tell you what. My partner and I will come over to your house in a little while. We can try to figure out where he went together. We have a few questions for you anyway. We've got to finish up here first, but we'll be there as soon as we can. Don't worry too much about your husband. We'll find him for you. I'm sure he's all right."

"Thank you. I'll be waiting right here."

Doc Rebak stood by the front door, filling out some paperwork, while talking to his assistant. Janet's body had not yet been removed. Murph joined him in looking out the open door. The one remaining Channel 14 news truck stood in front of the neighbor's house. A reporter spoke in front of a camera with the murder victim's house and all the police activity as a background. Rebak finished with the paperwork, handed it to Jerry, threw Murph a quick glance, but didn't say anything, and hustled out the door.

"What was that all about?"

"Two things," Murph said to Johnson. "First, the report of her murder has hit the media. I expected that since Jim had already called his TV station, and the second truck they sent is videoing outside right now. They're reporting that we're looking for Doctor Svensen as our primary suspect."

"Where'd they get that information?"

"I'm not sure. Maybe our friend Jim became, shall we say, *a little upset,* when he noticed he no longer had his camera. He had to tell his Channel 14 buddies something to make up for the lost video footage. So, maybe he invented it. If it didn't come from him, I have no idea where it came from, but it may relate to Mrs. Svensen's call, and probably contributed to what's happened to Doctor Svensen. He bolted, as his wife put it, out of their house when he saw the report. She has no idea why, or where he went…thought it ridiculous that he's our chief suspect."

"Well, she can't blame us for suspecting him," Johnson said. "He certainly had a motive with his girlfriend being pregnant. Did it sound like the missus knew about the pregnancy?"

"No, but remember, we haven't ruled her out as a suspect either. She wouldn't be the first vengeful wife to kill a pregnant girlfriend. Which makes me wonder if she may have also finished off her husband. Again, she wouldn't be the first."

Johnson referred to his notebook, finding the card on which Barbara had written Dr. Svensen's cell phone number. He dialed. "Let's see if he answers this time."

The phone rang and immediately went to a voicemail.

"This is Doctor Svensen," a recording of his voice said. "I can't come to the phone…"

"He's probably still got his phone turned off," Johnson said. "I'll have the Station monitor his phone for any activity and for GPS positioning, in case he turns it on. On the assumption he's not dead, do you think he is making a run for it? Wouldn't be the first time for that either, right?"

"I guess not," Murph said. "Just in case he is running, you'd better get an APB out on him. You have the description of his car and plate. Have them cover the airport, train and bus stations in case he abandons the car. Get Martinelli, or whoever's on duty downtown right now to cover the clinic. He may go there. Have the APB mark him as a 'person of interest' in our investigation. I'm still not convinced he's our murderer."

"Okay, but my money's still on him. Not only does he have the kind of car our witness thinks she heard, but he also lied to us concerning his whereabouts at the time of the murder, and we found his raincoat, soaking wet. So, he was in last night's downpour, not with his girlfriend here."

"But he did finally admit to being in Adams at the time of the murder," Murph said. "So, maybe the raincoat got wet coming here with his girlfriend after they were out partying somewhere."

"Maybe, but it's a big coincidence that the woman who is both his pregnant girlfriend and his alibi is murdered, and then he disappears. No, I'm still betting on him."

"Just call it in, Johnson. We'll debate who's right on the way to dinner. I'm starved. What do you say to Chinese food on the way to Dr. Svensen's place?"

"Sounds great to me," Johnson said, dialing the Station once more to set up the APB, "but what about the missing doctor and his scared wife? Shouldn't we go there first?"

"After that news story, I'll bet he's running scared. Won't do any good to rush to talk to his wife. Let her wait a while. Maybe he'll think better of what he's done, and come home, or we'll get a lead with the APB. Let's give him the benefit of the doubt and the chance to redeem himself with his wife."

"Okay, but you'd better call your wife to tell her you're going to be really late tonight, if you make it home at all."

"Good idea! I warned her once already, but it wouldn't hurt to remind her again, and I should check on Molly, anyway. It's a good thing I have you for a conscience, and that they are *so* understanding."

"Oh, yeah," Johnson said, rolling his eyes, "like they're going to be *real* understanding. I wouldn't take that bet for anything in the world, not for anything in the world."

CHAPTER 44

"Is it true you're looking for Doctor Elliot Svensen for both of today's murders?" the Channel 14 news reporter asked as Murph and Johnson exited Janet Robertson's house, and walked toward their car.

The TV cameras were rolling, trying to capture a juicy response from Adams' leading detectives. They would get none. Murph didn't even give them a, "No comment," response. Instead, he remained steadfastly silent during his journey.

"Are they following us?" Murph asked as he pulled out his cell phone.

"Not that I can see," Johnson said, checking the rearview mirror.

"Good! It'll be nice to get to interview a suspect before they beat us to the punch." Murph pressed the speed dial button for his home once again, half hoping no one answered. *It would have been easier to just proceed with my job without telling Molly and Jen I'm going to disappoint them again. Thank God they usually understand.* The phone rang three long times.

"Hello," Jennifer said.

"Hi, Jen, I just wanted to tell you that I'm pretty sure that I won't be getting home tonight at all."

"What's happened now?"

Murph rubbed his eyes, trying to remove the sleep that was creeping into him. "It's complicated. How's Molly doing?"

"She's okay, I guess. She's upstairs in her room, waiting for you. I really hoped you'd find a way to come home to talk to her…even for a few minutes. No chance, huh?"

"Doesn't look like it. Do you think it'd be all right if I talked to her over the phone?"

"It's better than nothing. Let me yell up to her to pick up the extension."

"Wait, Jen," Murph said, glancing out the windshield without seeing the cars or pedestrians parading before them. "Do you still have Molly's cell phone?"

"Sure, right here in my pocket. Why?"

"Suppose we return her cell phone as a peace offering from her father. I can call her on that phone to talk to her...no, to apologize to her."

"I have no objection to returning her cell phone, but I don't think you should overdo the apology. I had a talk with her over dinner. She understands that you didn't do anything except behave like a loving father, and, by the way, it's exactly what I would have expected from you."

"But I treated her to too harshly, Jen, and I'm really feeling guilty about it."

"That's fine, Bill. Apologize for loosing your temper...again...but don't overdo the apology. Neither one of you did anything wrong. What she did may have been sneaky, but it wasn't immoral, and even you said it wasn't illegal. She tried to help a friend. That's all. We both agree she could have done it in a more straightforward manner, but that's an adult approach to solving a problem, not a teenager's. What you did was an adult response. It doesn't need a major apology, just a bruised-ego-fixing apology, and a promise to try to control your temper in the future. Make her feel that you understand why she did it, and that you approve of her motive, but not necessarily her means. Can you do that? That way you both keep some dignity and respect."

"Okay, I promise."

"In that case, I'll give her the phone as you suggested, but remember, you weren't totally wrong... she wasn't totally right. The truth is somewhere in the middle. I don't want you to undermine what she and I discussed."

"You underestimate me." Of course, you've never done that in our entire marriage. Why would I think you'd start now?

She chuckled. "Yeah, that'll be the day! Just keep it light and, no matter what happens during your talk, don't loose *your* temper, or your wife will make you regret it whenever you do get home. Do you understand?"

197

"Completely, Oh-Great-Wife-of-Divine-Wisdom! I hear, and obey. Now, go give my daughter her phone, and tell her someone who loves her very much wants to talk to her."

"Okay, I'll tell her the famous *Detective Johnson* wants to speak to her. Ha, ha!"

She disconnected the call before Murph could respond to her retort.

Smiling, Murph waited a few minutes, picturing in his mind's eye his wife's journey up the stairs to Molly's room, knocking on her door, and, finally, explaining his desire to talk to her. *Suppose she says she doesn't want to talk to me? Why am I so nervous? I'm the adult. I'm the father. No, I'm the frightened father, nervous...no, terrified, about talking to my only daughter. Hmmmm. Cool it, Murph! Relax! Relax! Who am I kidding? I can't!*

He pressed Molly's speed dial number so lightly he wondered if it would make a connection. It did. The phone rang once. He held his breath.

"Hello, Dad."

The melodic sound of her voice made Murph pause, become pensive and even more anxious. His breath caught in his throat, choking him again. *It wouldn't surprise me if she hung up, but I know she won't. We raised her better than that. Jen says don't overdo the apology, but that's exactly what I want to do, what I have to do. Get a hold of yourself, Murph! She's your daughter, not a threateningly dangerous criminal. Just talk to her. She'll understand...I hope.*

Murph finally cleared his throat. He tried to act as if the pause had been natural, planned, and purposeful. He wasn't sure it worked. "Hi, Molly, please, listen carefully. I have something important to say to you. First, I love you." He paused again, choking once more, and searching for the evasive, clarifying words he needed, as he had earlier that day during his stumbling speech to his neighbor. The initial words came out stilted, forced, and unnatural. *Can I explain myself, my actions, my love, and, ultimately, my apology to her when I can't even think of what to say, or how to say it? Is it too little, too late? Have I hurt her too much? Will she understand? I simply am not sure.* He cleared his throat. "It looks like these murders will have me tied up until very late tonight. I probably won't make it home until tomorrow. I wanted to talk to you so we both had a chance to understand the other, to clear the air as they say. I know I upset both you and your friends, but, when I first saw you at that clinic, I thought you were the pregnant one, and, after I found out you weren't, I thought that you were leading your friend down the wrong road. I overreacted, and lost my temper...as usual. I'm sorry."

"I understand all that, Dad. Mom and I talked about it. I told mom the whole story...about Betty Ann's failed attempt to get more information about abortion than she found on the internet. Betty Ann said it sounded so easy to get an abortion that she couldn't believe it, but didn't know if abortion represented the right choice for her and Doug, but she wanted all the information she could get before they made their decision, before their parents stepped in to stop them, whatever they decided. I tried to be her friend, her best friend, you know, her bff. She really needs one now, you know."

"I now understand all that, Molly, but when we were at the clinic, I was..." He paused, not knowing how to explain how he had felt. He stopped rubbing his now painful eyes, staring blindly ahead, unaware of the road, or anyone on it, waiting for the words to miraculously appear from his quivering lips.

Molly sat, crossed legged in her bed, two tears streaming down her cheeks, one for Betty Ann, and one for her father, trying in his crude way to reconcile his actions to her. *I love you and mom so much, but you're wasting your time, Dad; I already know what you're going to say. I told you, Mom and I discussed it. Please, simply keep your temper in control, tell me you made a mistake, and let me get on with my life. You have no idea how hard it is to be a teenager these days. You're so out of touch. So, get on with it, please, but if you can't say it, I'll say it for you.*

Outside Molly's room, her mother stood with her ear to the door and her fingers crossed. *I hope these two can find common ground, come to some agreement, and, maybe even understand the other better.*

Molly smiled. "You were acting like a scared father, frightened for both his daughter and his daughter's friend. Is that what you're trying to say?"

"Well, yes, and you put it very nicely, Young Lady."

"My parents taught me well. Listen, Dad, I know you're busy. I know you love me, and I know you would never do anything to really hurt any of my friends. Mom told me you were calling to apologize for upsetting me. Well, I'm the one who's sorry that I didn't come to you and mom for advice on how best to help Betty Ann. I'm sure Betty Ann and Doug will forgive you for any pain you caused them. If not, I'll get them to change their minds, so they will forgive you. Don't worry. I love you enough to cover for you. So, *I* apologize, and *I* accept your apology. So, incident over and forgotten, at least on this end! Now go catch some bad guys."

"You're a chip off your mother's block, Kid. You know that?"

"I could have done worse. I could have taken after *you*! Goodbye, Dad, we'll talk again when you're not so tired, rushed, and pressured to catch those bad guys. I do understand. Please believe me."

"Thanks, Molly. I love you."

He disconnected, and took several very deep breaths. He slumped in his seat, feeling totally spent.

"I guess I owe you an apology," Johnson said, as he pulled the car into the strip mall that contained the Chinese restaurant they both preferred for its food and quick service. "I also guess I lost the bet. Your family is one of the most complex, but understanding, families I've ever seen. They always surprise me."

"Yeah, they even surprise me sometimes. I'm a very lucky man, Johnson, a very, very lucky man. Now, let's eat quickly, and then go catch a murderer."

CHAPTER 45

The China House, a small storefront establishment located in a strip mall on lower Main Street had only six tables; however, it did a tremendous takeout business. They ordered their food, and took a seat near the large, plate glass window. The only other customer, a lone woman, sat at the table closest to the door, eating her Moo Shoo Pork. She never noticed the two detectives.

After their food arrived, the detectives began a discussion of their suspects.

"I still vote for Doctor Svensen," Johnson said, wolfing down his Beef and Broccoli as if he hadn't eaten in days. "I reiterate: first, he lied about being in town at the time of the murder. His car is a luxury car. His raincoat is wet. So, he lied about being out of town. He knew the first victim, even performed her abortion. He and his girlfriend met the first victim at Kilmore's bar, and even spoke to her, persuading her to have the abortion. That makes him an ambulance chaser in my book. Anyway, then, he claimed he and his girlfriend, one of dozens he apparently had by the way, were together at the time of the murder. When we're about to interview that pregnant girlfriend, she's murdered. When you tried calling him right after her murder, he wasn't home, and no answer on his cell phone. When he hears we're looking for him on a newscast, he bolts. There are just too many coincidences for me. He's our best suspect."

"What's his motive for killing Eve St. Marie?" Murph asked, as he enjoyed his General Tsao's Chicken, even though this batch was hotter than he preferred. "He certainly had motive for killing the pregnant girlfriend, but why kill Eve St. Marie?"

"I'm not sure. Maybe it has something to do with what they discussed while they were together at the bar. Maybe Eve St. Marie found out something about the doctor that he needed silenced. Who knows? Maybe she learned he had gotten his girlfriend pregnant, but has a wife. Maybe she blackmailed him. Maybe we'll find a large deposit to her bank account that matches a withdrawal from his."

Murph stared at Johnson. "That's a lot of *maybes*, but we have no evidence that proves any of that, and you know it. It's all supposition, and even if it's true, I can't picture the doctor killing over any of it, even blackmail."

"In the eye of the Pro-Lifers, he kills babies every day. He's used to killing."

"Yes, but in the eye of the law, he's doing nothing wrong. Destroying an unborn baby isn't the same as murdering a living, breathing human being, at least not in the eyes of the law and this sick society, but let's not get into a moral or religious discussion here. That won't help solve our case. Let's stick to the facts."

"Okay, in that case, I repeat what I said. The facts all point to the doctor as our killer."

Murph grinned. "I'm glad to see you're keeping an open mind, Detective Johnson. Let's look at our other suspects anyway. Who else is on our list?"

"Well, the wife has to also be under consideration even though we haven't interviewed her yet. She certainly had motive. Her husband is a philanderer who sleeps with any female who comes within striking distance. He even got at least one of them pregnant. However, we don't know the wife's whereabouts during either murder yet, or why she would kill Eve St. Marie. I'm afraid the case against her will have to wait until after we interview her."

"You just mentioned all the doctor's affairs. According to his partners, he's had several. What about that counselor who left? What's her name? I wonder if he got her pregnant, and that's why she left town with little, or no notice?"

Johnson flipped through his notes, took another big bite of his food, and said, "I've got it right here. Let's see, her name is Georgi Clay. Left three to four months ago for her home in Tucson due to some family emergency. You really think she may have been pregnant too?"

"Wouldn't surprise me." Murph sipped his Jasmine tea. "I haven't heard from the Station concerning my request for information on her. So, we may have to track her down ourselves tomorrow."

202

"I'll get on that first thing in the morning. You don't think she might have been murdered too, do you?"

"Actually hadn't thought of that." Murph sat back in his seat, placing his small tea cup down on the table so hard it clanged, almost spilling part of the tea. "Now there's an interesting supposition. Suppose she is dead. Who killed her? Would that increase our suspect list? Could we have more than one murderer? We have more questions than answers."

"That may be true, but I know which suspect I'd nominate for Miss Clay's murder: the good, or should I say the *bad* doctor. He gets her pregnant, and then decides to eliminate her when his new love shows up in the person of Barbara Schine. He gets Barbara to take care of the dead woman's affairs, and the story continues. It fits the facts nicely."

"Ah, a conspiracy theory," Murph said, holding up one finger, as if ordering more food. The owner, well known to them because of their frequent visits, raised her head, questioning his motion. Murph shook his head, and then gave the appreciative owner a thumbs up, pointing to the food on his plate, and mouthing, "Delicious." Murph smiled at Johnson. "I knew you'd come up with another one eventually in this case. Now we have a serial-killer physician knocking off anyone he happens to get pregnant, or anyone who finds out he's been cheating on his wife or, maybe, discovers that he's doing the killing. In any case, he then recruits his next love, and hires her as his assistant to erase all traces of his latest victim. So, now we have the doctor, his wife and the clinic assistant all involved. We might as well arrest them all. Case solved."

"Very funny, very, very funny, but some of what you just proposed might fit in the end. I'm just trying to keep an open mind as my partner told me to."

Murph dropped his smile. "I guess we'll have to wait to see if the absent counselor does fit in somehow, and make sure she is, indeed, still alive. Who's next on our short list?"

"The clinic assistant, Barbara Schine, who has no alibi for either murder. When we called her at home, she answered, but she could have call-forwarded her home phone to her cell phone, and been driving away from the murder as she talked to us."

"If she did, she's a cool customer, as they say. She didn't sound upset at all."

"Maybe the doctor coached her exactly what to say."

"Again the conspiracy? Okay, at least that's not as outlandish as your last theory. Go on."

"She also took care of the absent counselor's affairs, which may, or may not mean anything. She talked to Eve St. Marie before her murder, but, I didn't detect anything in her note, or what she told us, that would give her reason to want to kill the woman."

"That's true," Murph said, "but if Eve St. Marie said something that triggered Barbara Schine to want to kill her, Barbara wouldn't put it in her note, would she?"

"I suppose not, but if Eve did say something that inflamed Miss Schine, we won't be able to make any sense out of her murder until we find out what that something was. So, let's put that idea on hold for now. Let's see, what else do we know about her? She began her affair with the doctor right after she took care of the affairs of counselor Clay. We don't know if Miss Schine, or Barbara, as she prefers to be called, got pregnant, but no one has even suggested that."

"Dr. Svensen could have taken care of that one with a quiet abortion, without making a record of the operation."

"Easily," Johnson agreed, "but even without a pregnancy, Dr. Svensen next dumps Barbara for this new counselor, Janet Robertson. There's motive for Barbara to kill her since Janet stole the Doc from her, and got pregnant by him to boot. The doctor also considered leaving his wife for his new love, which he didn't do for Barbara. There's even more motive...anger, outrage, revenge."

"True, but remember, we've heard a couple of times that he had planned to leave his wife both for Miss Robertson and the missing Georgi Clay, but neither happened. I don't think he ever had any intention of following through on that, in either case. I wonder what hold the wife has over him?"

"Maybe we'll find out after we talk to her. One other thing that doesn't match any of our suspects is the murderer's cell phone ring, the Frank Sinatra tune. We heard both the Doctor's and Barbara's rings, both boring telephone sounds. Maybe there's someone we haven't even considered as a suspect yet, or maybe that old woman's hearing's not what it should be. Maybe she heard someone playing the Sinatra tune in another apartment."

"Maybe, but I still believe her. She's just so sincere. Is there anyone else we should consider?" Murph opened up his plastic encased fortune cookie. He didn't like the taste or consistency of the cookie, but always read the contents, never believing the fortune for a minute, instead, considering it part of the harmless ritual of a Chinese meal.

"Well, there's the boyfriend of the first victim. Most people are murdered by someone they know."

"I can't believe he did it. He looked so shaken up, and he didn't appear to be acting. He also was on his way out of town with his relatives at the time of the Robertson murder, but we should check on that. In your conspiratorial mind, that would bring two other suspects into this mix, but how his two relatives could possibly be involved I have no idea. We know the boyfriend did know the second victim because of their run-in at the bar, but unless you think he killed Janet Robertson because she and Dr. Svensen were *happy* about their pregnancy, and he and Eve were planning an abortion, he's not a good candidate."

"For once, we agree. I don't like him for either murder, but I'll leave him on our list for now until we check on his trip with his brother. I think that completes our list. Did I miss anyone?"

"I don't think so," Murph said, shaking his head at his fortune. He read it aloud. "Your plans will succeed in the near future."

"What plans, Murph?"

"Getting home and falling asleep for about ten hours in my own bed."

"Not likely in the near future," Johnson said, chuckling. "Mine says, 'A new relationship with someone influential will go well.'" Smiling, he placed the fortune in his shirt pocket for future use.

"Ha! Speaking of not likely in the near future! None of your relationships seem to do well. You need to find someone like my wife, Jen."

"Again, not likely! Unfortunately, there's not many like her around. I'll have to keep looking until I find one, I guess."

"Speaking of relationships," Murph said, staring at Johnson beneath raised eyebrows and with his head lowered, "did I sense something between you and Officer Stewart?"

"I certainly hope so." Johnson patted the pocket containing his fortune.

Murph let out a large sigh, shook his head a few times, and closed his eyes. When he opened them, Johnson sat bewildered, head tilted, and arms raised, palms up, in a "what's wrong with that?" posture.

"You have to realize that dating a rookie isn't a good idea, especially one we just did an enormous favor for. It might be taken the wrong way by Internal Affairs, and by the officer in question too. I can't see it leading anywhere except toward trouble. You've been there before…too many times, I might point out."

"Yes, Father," Johnson said, lowering his head, and folding his hands in prayer in front of his face. When he looked up again, Murph wore his normal, large smile. "I promise not to take advantage of the young officer's innocence or naivety."

"You better not," Murph warned, not for the first time. "You're her superior officer. Remember that at all times." He leaned across the table. "Please make sure you two don't compromise any investigations or evidence in this case. Understand?"

"Completely, Daddy! Who knows? Maybe my next girlfriend will influence me enough to get me wed? I'll make sure you and Jen get invited to the wedding."

"You're hopeless, Johnson." Murph piled all the empty plates on top of one another. "Let's get out of here, and see if we can wrap this investigation up, so at least *my* fortune might come true."

<u>CHAPTER 46</u>

Molly's cell phone rang. She grabbed the phone, checking the caller ID as quickly as she could, hoping to see Betty Ann's name. Instead, the caller ID read "blocked call." She couldn't imagine who would be calling her that way. She had already talked to her father. She had tried calling Betty Ann, but had been diverted to her voice mail. *Her parents probably haven't returned her cell phone yet. She doesn't have a guilt-ridden father, offering her the phone as a peace offering like mine. In any case, she wouldn't block her number.* "Hello," Molly said in such a low voice she wondered if the caller would be able to hear her.

"Molly, is that you?" a female voice that she didn't recognize asked.

"Yes, this is Molly. Who's this?"

"It's Barbara Schine from The Women's Clinic. I got your cell number from your chart at the clinic. We met earlier today."

"Oh, yes, I remember all too well. I'm sorry about fainting. It's the first time I've ever done that."

"Don't mention it, Molly. Under those circumstances, even a professional female soccer player might have fainted. I thought that your father might faint for a few minutes there."

They both shared a laugh, Molly's laughter forced and nervous.

"What can I do for you, Miss Schine?"

"Oh, please, call me Barbara. We don't have to be so formal. Are either of your parents with your, by any chance?"

"No, my father is busy working. My mom is downstairs. Do you want me to get her?"

"Oh, no, don't do that! Your dad became so upset yesterday that he wouldn't even give me the chance to talk to you before you left. Then I saw him almost arrest your girlfriend and her boyfriend. I assume she's the pregnant one, and you father ultimately didn't arrest them. Is that right?"

"That's right. He threatened to, but, in the end, he let Doug go, and took Betty Ann and me home. We've been grounded since."

"That's part of why I called, Molly. I think what you did was very brave, and you should be applauded for trying to help out a *friend-in-need.*"

"Yeah, tell that to my dad!"

"Unfortunately for your dad, in this case, what he thinks is less important than the fact that you were right in what you were attempting. I'll say it again. You should be applauded." She paused. "Anyway, your dad's opinion aside, yesterday, when your dad wouldn't let me speak to you, I wanted to offer some help to your friend. I'm sure she's getting an earful from both her parents and maybe some well-wishers, friends, or relatives who may force her to do something she's going to regret the rest of her life…without giving her any other choice."

"You mean like having the baby?"

"Yes, that's certainly one option for her. She could have the child, quit school, and stay at home to raise the child, no more social life, no more dating. She'd be on-call twenty-four hours for diaper changes and feedings. She wouldn't have time for friends like you, or going out anywhere. A baby really changes a teenager's life. They may also advise her to have the baby, and give it up for adoption. Imagine never knowing what happened to your own flesh and blood baby!"

"I don't see what you're getting at…" Molly paused, having difficulty calling an adult by her first name. "…Barbara."

"I'd like to meet with your friend, and discuss not only these choices, but also some others that our clinic can supply, including counseling to help her adjust to whatever final decision she makes."

"But her parents probably won't let her go anywhere near your clinic."

"That's true, and that's why you've got to keep this phone call a total secret between you, me and your friend. Do you think you can do that?"

"Sure, that's the easy part, but how do we get Betty Ann to your clinic?"

"I've been trying to figure that out, and I just came up with an idea. That's why I called you. Do you think you and Betty Ann could sneak out of your houses without your parents knowing? I could pick the two of you up, and we could discuss the matter. If you think it would be okay with Betty Ann, I do have a place that we could talk in private. Tomorrow is Sunday. Do your parents normally go to Church?"

"For sure! They'll be there, but they'll expect both of us to go with them. I'm not sure how we could get them to let us stay home."

"Does Betty Ann have any morning sickness?"

"No, at least none that she's told me about. Why?"

"See if you can get her to fake morning sickness tomorrow. Tell her not to make it so bad that her parents will want to call a doctor. Just a little stomach ache, enough to make her have to stay home. They may want to stay home with her. That's where you come in. You simply volunteer to stay with her while they go to Church. If you're persuasive enough, they will feel comfortable leaving you two alone. Then, our problems are solved. Tell them you'll call their cell phones if she gets worse. I'll come by to get you, and we can do the counseling she really needs and deserves, not something forced down her throat."

"We'll only have a short time before our parents come home, though. Is it going to be enough to get Betty Ann all the information you have for her?"

"It'll be plenty. Most of it I have in the form of brochures she can keep. The rest I have typed up from previous, satisfied clients. I think Betty Ann will really be pleasantly surprised at the wealth of information I can give her in that short period of time."

"But you can't pick us up in front of our house. Our neighbors will call my parents if they see us picked up by some stranger."

"Oops, I hadn't thought of that. You're right, Molly. Don't want to upset the neighbors or your parents. I'll tell you what you can do. As soon as your parents leave for Church, you two go for a walk around the block. That shouldn't arouse any suspicions. I'll meet you around the corner. What's the name of that street, Honey? I can find it using my GPS."

"Orchard Street. What kind of car do you drive?"

"A bright yellow Toyota. You can't miss it."

"How do I get in touch with you to let you know whether we'll be meeting you?"

"You can get it off your phone's recent calls, but I'll give you the number, just in case. It's not my regular phone. I bought it for just such emergencies. I pre-pay for a given number of minutes, and can throw the thing away when I'm done. I use it for situations like this when I don't want to be tracked down. No one has the number but you. So, call me when you've arranged things, and we'll meet as planned. You've made me very happy, Molly, by being a true friend to Betty Ann. I hope to do the same for you. I'm looking forward to seeing both of you tomorrow morning."

After writing down Barbara's phone number, Molly disconnected, and stared at the ceiling. *Now, I've got to figure a way to get mom to let me visit Betty Ann. I've got to do it without lying to them, or they really will kill me when they find out. That should be the easy part, though. I know how to manipulate my parents to get what I want. I've done it before. I'll play on mom's sympathy for Betty Ann and her parents. She'll let me visit if she thinks I'm very concerned about Betty Ann, which I really am anyway. The hard part of this deception will be up to Betty Ann. I hope she can pull it off for both her and her baby's sake, and I pray to God that Betty Ann makes the right decision for herself, her baby, her parents...and God Almighty.*

Molly closed her eyes and spent the next ten minutes praying to God for forgiveness for the deception she planned to perpetrate on her mother and Betty Ann's parents. *Will God forgive me? Can God forgive me? Will my parents and Betty Ann's parents ever forgive me? Will they understand I'm only doing what I think is right for my best friend? I hope so!* "May God help me!"

CHAPTER 47

Murph and Johnson arrived at Doctor Svensen's house twenty minutes later. The doctor lived in a typical colonial with an attached garage. The dark green shingles made the house blend with the green canopy of the surrounding trees. They found the screen door closed, and the front door, decorated with a colorful stained glass oval in its center, ajar. The doorbell chimed a series of musical notes announcing their arrival.

A woman with short, black, disheveled hair, clothed in black slacks and a dirty, red blouse, rushed the door. Breathing heavily, she pushed open the screen door. "Detective Murphy?" Her lips quivered between slurred words.

"Yes, and this is my partner, Detective Johnson."

"Have you found my husband yet?"

"No, I'm afraid not. Have you heard anything from him?"

"No, nothing! Come in." She walked down the hallway, staggering as she went, using the walls for support.

Murph rushed to support her as she missed the wall with her hand, and tumbled toward it. He caught her shoulder, righting her, releasing her only after she regained her balance, and continued her awkward journey. *I wonder if her drinking this evening is the result of the doctor's disappearance, or is a chronic drinking problem caused by his infidelity. Could her chronic drinking have driven him to seek companionship elsewhere? There could be a motive for murder mixed in all this, and could point to either of them.*

She led them into the kitchen, flopping down in a dark-stained, wooden dinette chair. She picked up an almost empty glass of a clear, amber liquid, took a sip, and motioned the detectives to the other chairs around the circular table. They did as directed.

"Can I get you gentlemen a drink?" she asked, holding the glass up. "Best whiskey on the planet."

"No thank you," Murph said. "We're still on duty. Please, tell me again what your husband did before he left today."

Her speech remained slow, slurred, and staccato. "Well, we had just come back from shopping. I wanted to look for new family room furniture, and Elliot wanted to look at a High Def TV. After he came home from work, we went to a few stores. I didn't find any furniture. Of course, Elliot found several sets that he would like to buy. He didn't buy any though. He wanted to go on-line to see if he could get a better price, and wanted to check out each set's performance record…or something like that."

She leaned so far to her left that she almost fell off the chair, catching herself at the last second, and then adjusting her seating to increase her stability. Her eyelids began to close, a slow trip down over her eyes that would ultimately lead to an alcohol-induced sleep.

"Mrs. Svensen," Murph said, "what happened when you got home?"

She jumped. "Oh!" The slurring of her voice increased with each word. "Sorry! Nearly fell asleep, didn't I? Sorry! It's all this stress of Elliot's disappearance. Let me think. Oh, yeah, I turned the TV on to catch some news. I like to have it on as background noise. Anyway, a breaking-news report came on, saying Janet had been murdered, and that you were looking for Elliot. He couldn't do anything like that. You should know that. He's a good doctor. He helps women all the time with their medical problems. He's very sympathetic with them. Murder? Never!" She threw up her hands, emphasizing her point. "Anyway, he didn't say a word to me. He ran out to the garage, and then drove down the street like a madman. That's when I called you. You know what you did by calling him your chief suspect, don't you? You've scared that poor man, my poor husband, out of his wits."

"It wasn't us, Mrs. Svensen," Johnson said. "The press made the announcement, not us."

"Oh!" Her eyelids drifted downward again. "It doesn't matter anyway. He's not here. So, where is he?"

"Does he have any places he likes to go to if he's having a problem," Murph asked, "maybe a bar or a friend's house, anywhere you can think of?"

"No," she said, shaking her head and body so hard that the little whiskey left in her glass sloshed back and forth, and overflowed the sides. "I called all our friends, even tried his partners. None of them heard from him."

"Was he home with you last night?" Murph asked.

"Last night?" She squinted her eyes, as if that would clear the alcohol from her mind. "Let me think. Oh, yes, now I remember. Elliot attended a medical conference in Boston. I'm sure his partners will confirm that. They were there with him. He came home early this morning to see his patients at the clinic."

"Okay," Murph said, glancing at Johnson, who busied himself writing an epic in his notebook. "We'll check with them later. Does Dr. Svensen go out of town like that often?"

"Oh, yes," she said, this time holding her glass steady while she nodded her head, sparing the little alcohol remaining. "He's a prominent doctor, you know that, right? He has to keep up in his field. There're some number of hours of…I think they're called CMEs…that he has to have to keep his medical license. He keeps right on top of those."

"I'm sure he does," Johnson said, rolling his eyes. "I'm sure he does."

Murph shot Johnson a warning glance that forced Johnson to again bury his head in his notebook. "How does your husband get along with the other personnel at his clinic? Does he have any problems with the doctors, nurses, his assistant, secretaries, or any of the counselors?"

She leaned back hard against the chair. "Problems? No, no problems; they all love him. He's really dedicated to the practice. He loves all his employees. You aren't going to find any problems, or hanky-panky going on at my husband's clinic. He wouldn't stand for it."

She leaned forward. Her eyes rolled up as her eyelids closed. Her head dropped the final three inches onto the back of her hand, resting on the table. She didn't move again, but began snoring rhythmically, loudly, and deeply, clear, foamy bubbles forming at the corner of her mouth with each breath.

"I guess that's all we're going to get out of her tonight," Murph said, removing the glass from Mrs. Svensen's flaccid hand, placing it farther away from her so she wouldn't accidentally knock it over when she awoke. "Let's let ourselves out."

"Wait a minute, Murph." Johnson leaned over the table. "Mrs. Svensen, we'd like to look around the house for clues that may lead us to your husband's whereabouts. Is that okay with you?"

The answer was a loud snore that rattled not only her body, but also the whole table.

"I'll take that as a *Yes*. Well, now that we have the owner's permission, and she's not in any shape to revoke it soon, let's look around."

Murph smiled while watching her deep breathing. "You're incorrigible, Johnson, but, technically, you're right. So, before the alcohol wears off, let's give the place a quick once-over."

CHAPTER 48

They did a fast inspection of the rooms downstairs, composed of a formal dining room, a formal living room, the kitchen and a large family room over the garage. Every room bore off-white paint. None of the areas had even a hint that the doctor lived there. Of all the pictures hanging in the family room, only a few contained the doctor's picture and, in those, he wasn't smiling.

Upstairs, the master bedroom looked like a minor battle had taken place. Clothes were strewn on the unmade bed, as well as the two chairs flanking it. Johnson checked the taller of the bureaus. On its surface were two novels, and one medical textbook. He moved some of the clothes on the chairs, but found nothing of interest.

"Where's his computer?" Johnson asked.

"Maybe he took it with him when he left." Murph checked both closets, but found nothing but clothes. "No signs of a hidden safe anywhere."

"Why would someone, who's so scared by a news report of the police looking for him, grab his computer, presumably a laptop or tablet, on the way out?"

"Maybe there's something incriminating on it that he doesn't want us to see."

"Like maybe a video of him committing both murders," Johnson said.

"I doubt that. The wife gives him an alibi for this afternoon's murder."

"She's so drunk, I'm surprised she could remember where she went today, or who she went with. You believe her then?"

"Yes, I don't think she knows anything about his affairs or, if she does, she doesn't care. In any case, drinking aside, if she sticks to her story, we've got to search for another killer. I don't think she's capable of killing anyone either."

"No, I'm not." The slurred voice of the doctor's wife resonated from the hallway leading to the bedroom. "You gentlemen finding what you're looking for?"

The detectives could hear her shoulder rub against the wall as she traversed the short hallway. She held onto the bedroom's doorframe when she arrived.

Murph began a slow walk toward her. *Without that support, I think you'll fall flat onto your face.* "Oh, Mrs. Svensen, we didn't hear you coming."

"We've been looking for clues to your husband's whereabouts," Johnson said, "as we told you before we came up here. Don't you remember?"

"No, but I usually don't remember much after I start drinking. I probably should give it up, but I never will. Elliot says I'm addicted to the booze. He's probably right, but I don't care. So, did you find any clues to his whereabouts?"

"We're not sure," Murph said. "Does your husband have a personal computer?"

"Of course! Doesn't everyone? I have my own. It's on the bed with Elliott's."

"On the bed?" Murph asked, glancing at the chaotic mound of clothes on the king-size bed.

"Sure, look under the clothes."

Johnson lifted a robe with two fingers and an expression on his face that indicated he thought the cloth had been contaminated with the plague.

"You don't have to worry, Detective," she said, laughing. "Those are clean clothes. I did one load of wash before we went out, and put another load in when those were ready. I didn't get a chance to fold them yet. So, I threw them on the bed. Our computers sort of got in the way. They're under there somewhere. Keep looking."

With Murph chuckling, Johnson picked up a pair of blue checked pajamas, and found two laptops.

"Which is your husband's?" Johnson asked.

"His is the PC. Mine is the MAC. I do a lot of artistic things, drawing and pictures, that sort of thing. He uses his mainly as a word processor, and to surf the net. There's not much on it. I should know; I check it almost daily."

"Does your husband know that?"

"Sure! He writes a lot of medical stuff, of course. That's all boring, but I like to read his poetry. He can be very romantic. Most of the stuff he writes is intended for me. It's real mushy."

Johnson turned his back, pretending to examine something on one of the computers, and rolled his eyes upward. *If she only knew!*

"Do you mind if we take both computers to check them?" Murph asked. "There may be something on one of them that will help us figure out where your husband went. We'll be very careful with all of the files, and won't break, or delete anything. I promise."

"I guess so," she said, staring at the machines. "Just don't put any of those love poems on the Internet the way those silly teenagers do. I wouldn't want the world to know all of our intimate thoughts. Those are *private*! You understand, don't you?"

"I guarantee we won't let anyone read them except our lab technicians," Murph said, "and they're trained to be very discrete about what they see on people's computers."

"Okay, then, take them, but have them back by Monday morning. Elliot is going to need his for work. I just need to check my email, so, mine can wait. Elliot always takes his to the clinic. He uses it there to write letters and reports. So, it's important he has it by Monday. Can you get them back by then?"

"No problem," Murph said. "One final thing, Mrs. Svensen, one of your husband's counselors named Georgi Clay left unexpectedly a few months ago. Do you have any idea why she left?"

"Well, I hate to say anything bad about one of Elliot's former employees, but the woman is a slut! She went out with the weirdest men I've ever seen. Some had long hair, and looked like they hadn't bathed in weeks. She had no shame about them, and would even bring them to office parties and out to dinner with us. Anyway, rumor had it that one of those guys got her pregnant, and she left to go home…somewhere out west. Don't ask me where. I can't remember."

Murph shot Johnson another knowing glance: both wore wry smiles.

Another girlfriend of Dr. Svensen who he had gotten pregnant is my guess. "Do you know if anyone has heard from her since?" Murph asked.

217

"Can't say I do," she said, slurring the words so severely that it became increasingly difficult to understanding her.

The soft, warm comfort of her bed finally won the tug-of-war between her desire to be a gracious hostess and the alcohol, making her want to sleep at any cost. She took three unsteady steps toward the bed, and fell face first into her laundry. She bounced once, settling with her face buried in a pink blouse, her loud snoring commencing again.

Murph picked up her robe, and covered her with it. "Let's get out of here. I don't think we're going to learn anything else here today."

As they walked downstairs, Johnson asked, "What do you think we're going to find on his computer besides love poems to all his girlfriends?"

"I'm not sure. Maybe nothing, but maybe it'll tell us the whereabouts of our missing counselor. If nothing else, you can copy his poetry to use on your girlfriends. His rhymes seem to work very well on them."

Johnson shot his right hand to cover his heart. He had a hint of surprise in his voice as he said, "How sweet of you to think of me! I'm sure Doctor Svensen wouldn't mind me borrowing some of his material. If it works that well, I'll have my pick of women." He patted his breast coat pocket. "Maybe his poetry will make my Chinese fortune come true, and get me that new relationship with an influential woman to fulfill all my wonderful dreams. I tell you, I hear wedding bells, Murph."

"Johnson, you inhaled too much alcohol off Mrs. Svensen. The fumes have made you inebriated. You're talking nonsense. When we get to the car, I'm going to administer a Breathalyzer to prove to you how drunk you really are."

Johnson laughed loudly as Murph pretended to check the trunk for a Breathalyzer to analyze his alcohol consumption. Adams' detective cars weren't equipped with such devices, and both detectives knew that all too well.

Murph made a big deal about not finding one, announcing his intention to inform the Chief of this terrible omission. Murph then pointed to the driver's door, as if he expected Johnson to have difficulty finding it. "You can drive, despite your condition,

Detective Johnson. I'm too tired to get behind the wheel. Let's head for the Station. I want to drop these computers off before we call it a night. Do try to drive carefully. I'd like to get there in one piece sometime before sunrise."

"Anything you say." Johnson imitated Murph's smile for a brief moment before becoming somber again. "Seriously, Murph, let me drop you off at home. You've got your family waiting for you, and a few, shall we say, issues to confront. I don't. I'll drop the computers at the Station, and make sure all of our inquiries are at least planned for first thing tomorrow morning, if they're not already underway. I'll pick you up at eight. Oh, wait a minute! Tomorrow is Sunday. Are you going to Mass tomorrow morning?"

"I'd better not. All day I've felt like we've been playing catch-up with this killer. I'd like to maybe get an early jump on him tomorrow. Pick me up at eight. We'll start the day collecting all we know at the Station. Make sure your new girlfriend is there with her partner too."

"She's not my new girlfriend...yet."

"Just have them there. In that case, I will accept your offer to drop me off. Maybe I can appease my daughter, and try to make my wife understand why I'm not going to Church with her tomorrow, but I think it'll be easier to explain to God than her."

"If I had my choice of whose wrath I'd rather have come down upon me, I think I'd choose God's. He's at least understanding, and willing to listen to a sincere confession. He's also more likely to administer absolution for your sins. Your wife, on the other hand, isn't so indulgent. If I find you sleeping on your front porch tomorrow morning, I'll understand completely."

"Just drive, Detective! Just drive!" Murph dialed Doc Rebak. "Hi, any news?"

"Sheryl's still awaiting surgery."

"What? What's delaying it? I thought you said she was critical."

"She is, Murph. Another case that needed the surgeon's attention first came in, a woman they had to extricate from her car following an accident on Route 7. Sheryl's under sedation, and appears to be stable. She is triggering the respirator on her own now, which is a good sign, but hasn't been able to communicate much, even using a hand signal to indicate how much she can feel, or move. I'm afraid the sedation isn't helping in that regard, even though they've lightened it a great deal. They'll get to her as soon as they can. I plan to stay here until after her surgery, but we really won't know much until tomorrow, probably late in the morning after the anesthesia wears off."

"So, swinging by the hospital on the way to the Station tomorrow morning won't accomplish much, right?"

"That is unfortunately true. You won't be allowed in to see her. Just go about your detective work. Let me keep an eye on her. If there's any major change either way, I'll let you know. I promise. What time will you be at the Station tomorrow?"

"We thought we'd get there early, between 8:30 and 9."

"Good. I may not have all the latest on Sheryl by then, but I should have some information for you on the murders. I'll plan to meet you then. Have to run. Bye."

Johnson dropped Murph at his front walkway without a word. A quick wave between the two ended what had become a very frustrating and exasperating day. Both hoped the next day would prove easier, and bring them closer to solving the murders.

Both the front porch lights, as well as those illuminating the first floor at the Murphy residence, welcomed Murph on his approach. *Maybe they both stayed up to have a family powwow. I'm exhausted. I'm not sure I'm up to it. Oh, well, into the valley of death...*

CHAPTER 49

As he approached the front door, it swung inward. His wife, still totally dressed, met him with a large smile, a hug, and a very wet kiss on his cheek, followed immediately by one on his lips.

"Mmmm, not the welcome I expected. What did I do to deserve such a warm homecoming?"

"You came home, period!" Jennifer smiled, and pecked him on the cheek again, this time so lightly he barely felt her touch.

"If I knew that was all it took to get you this lovey-dovey, I would have come home earlier."

"Carol and Ted are here."

Murph loosened his tie. "At this time of night? They must really be mad at me."

"You'd be surprised." Jennifer grabbed his jacket lapel, dragging him toward the living room. "Come on. I put out some cheese and crackers. We're all drinking ice water. You can have a glass too."

"Are you sure I can handle it?"

Smiling, Jennifer poured a glass for Murph, and put it on the marble-top coffee table.

"Murph," Ted said, as he rose from the antique couch, "we've been waiting for you."

Murph shook Ted's hand, and then bent down to kiss Carol on the cheek. Exhaustion finally overtook him. He hobbled over to the Abe Lincoln rocker, plopping down in its green, padded seat. Every part of his body either hurt, or felt fatigued to the point of near collapse. He grabbed a thick slice of the yellow, extra-sharp cheddar cheese, tossing the whole piece into his mouth. *Scrumptious!* The water felt even finer in his dry mouth, and tasted better. He savored it like the best California wine. He spoke between sips of water. "Listen, Guys. I'd like to explain what happened this morning, and apologize to you."

Carol held up both hands in front of her. "Stop right there, William Murphy! Betty Ann explained what happened. We came over to thank you, not to have you apologize. You did nothing wrong. We appreciate what you did, especially bringing her home safe to us."

"That's right," Ted said, gently pushing down Carol's arms, and smiling. "We're not mad at you. On the contrary, we consider ourselves lucky that you were there to help Betty Ann. The other person we appreciate is Molly. Betty Ann told us she is overwhelmed by everything she had read about pregnant teenagers. She became terrified of what could to happen to her. She desperately wanted help, and you and Molly were there for her like good friends and neighbors." He lowered his head and voice at the same time. "Betty Ann got herself into this predicament, but we're not going to let her face it alone. We're going to do all we can to help her work through it one way, or another. We thought we had taught her all she needed to know about sex and pregnancy in general, but it turns out we failed her. I guess we're not the great parents we thought we were."

"It wasn't all our fault, though," Carol said, placing a comforting hand on Ted's shoulder. "Betty Ann became so influenced by friends and this over-secularized society that she thought she could handle every aspect of her life without us, the Church...without even God. She felt she no longer needed any direction. She picked up some more crazy ideas from school friends that she looked up to, and some idiotic websites she had visited.

"After she became pregnant, she visited more of those crazy websites. Some had her terrorized about what occurred during childbirth. Can you believe it? Others told her the pregnancy would end her childhood, including all her friendships and dating possibilities. They mostly directed her toward pro-abortion sites that only gave one side of the unexpected-pregnancy issue, claiming abortion to be her best choice. Some claimed it was her *only* choice. The information she collected bordered on the ludicrous, and it's certainly not anything the Church, or we, believe, or taught her. The government should shut those sites down. They're preaching lies."

"It'll never happen, Carol," Ted said, covering Carol's hand with his, squeezing it tenderly, as if it were the very first time he had ever touched her. "It's one of the down sides of freedom of speech. They can say just about anything they want."

"Not wrong things, I hope," Carol said. "Anyway, we were hoping you'd get home in time for us to show our appreciation for protecting Betty Ann. You gave us a chance to counsel her on her pregnancy before she did something rash, something she might totally regret later on. Thank you, Murph. I'll say it again, we both really appreciate what you did."

"You're welcome," Murph said, taking another refreshing gulp of his drink. "I really expected to get lambasted by you two. I lost my temper, and really overstepped my bounds...I guess I yelled at all of them. I should have simply talked to them rationally, then done the same thing, but I'm glad you both understand." He paused, and when Ted and Carol simply smiled, he continued. "I know it's none of my business, but what's Betty Ann going to do?"

"Good question," Ted said. "We're going to set up a meeting, a counseling session with Father Jones at Church. I guess we'll take it from there."

"That's a great place to start," Murph said, reaching inside his jacket to retrieve the literature he had been given. "I got this today during an ongoing investigation. You may want to read it over. I met the woman who runs this Pro-Life organization. She's really sharp, and seems to have the pregnant women's best interest in mind. She really impressed me a lot. You may want to give her a call. I think it'd be good for Betty Ann to meet her too. It'll give her an entirely different perspective on the whole issue than those professed by the Pro-Choice people at that clinic, or those crazy web sites."

"Thanks," Carol said, taking the brochure from Murph, and opening it. "I think that's a good idea." She handed it to her husband who quickly skimmed its contents, and nodded his agreement.

Murph turned toward Jennifer. "Where's Molly? Is she asleep?"

"Not likely!" She motioned toward Ted and Carol. "She's actually over their house with Betty Ann."

"Did you send her with handcuffs and a ball and chain attached to her leg?"

"Very funny, Murph! I guess Betty Ann asked if she could come over. Right, Carol?"

"Oh, yes, it's been a tough day for her too. It's been a tough day for all of us, I guess."

"That's an understatement," Murph said, nodding his head, then finishing his drink.

"Molly actually initiated all this by asking me if she could call Betty Ann to check on her. You raised a good daughter, Murph."

"Oh, sure," Murph said, frowning his disagreement. "She's undoubtedly headed toward becoming both a philanthropist and a Saint. When she finally achieves both, I hope she bestows something other than indigestion on me."

"William Murphy! That's our daughter you're talking about. Behave yourself in front of company."

"I'm joking, Jen, and they know it. I am *very* proud of her and, if I ever see her in person again, I intend to tell her that very thing, but you got one thing wrong. Carol and Ted aren't company, they're friends."

"Here, here," Ted said, holding up his glass in an exaggerated toast. "I'll drink to that. Friends forever!"

They all raised their glasses, banging them in unison above the table.

"I gather that you're going to allow Molly to spend the night with Betty Ann," Murph said, devouring the cheese and crackers as if they were caviar. He had forgotten how hungry he really had become. He savored each bite, and the company that took his mind off the case even more.

"I think it'll be good for both of them," Jennifer said. "They both suffered a trauma today. It'll give them a chance to discuss all the issues, and maybe work through some of their problems together. There's a lot going on in both their lives. I think they'll be good for each other. Your full father-daughter family talk will have to wait until tomorrow on the way to Church."

Murph covered his eyes with one hand, allowing it to drift down his face, distorting his lower lip. He stared at Jennifer without saying a word, his facial expression saying a mouthful.

"You're not coming to Church?" Jennifer pronounced each word individually and distinctly. "What time is Tom picking you up?"

"Eight. We really have to get an early start. I'm sorry."

"Believe it or not, Bill, I kind of expected it," Jennifer said, refilling his drink. "Molly's going to be disappointed though."

"I know. At least we talked briefly on the phone. That's got to count for something. She said she understood. It seems that all I've done today is both hurt and disappoint her." He hung his head.

"No, you haven't," Jennifer said. "She understands your job is very important, and that, sometimes, it doesn't have regular hours like a typical desk job. She knows from experience that it can, and usually does, interfere with family plans. Trust me, Bill. She understands."

"We're all going to Church together," Carol said. "We'll pray for you, and for the swift completion of your case. We've been following it all day. It's terrible what happened to those women and to that reporter."

"Speaking of that," Jennifer said, "have you heard anything about Sheryl?"

"She's going to undergo surgery later tonight. That's all I know." Murph suddenly lost his appetite, and his desire for further conversation. He searched all three faces to find any hints of recognition that he had lied about his knowledge of the gravity of Sheryl's condition. He saw only their concern for the victims, including Sheryl. His lie had succeeded in protecting them from both worry and anxiety about something they could do nothing about. *Worrying is my job!*

"We'll pray for her too," Carol said, resting her hand on Murph's knee, and offering him a hopeful smile. "God will listen to us, I'm sure."

Next-door, Molly and Betty Ann banged their glasses of water together in a similar toast, celebrating, in advance, the success of the deception they were about to perpetrate on their unsuspecting parents.

CHAPTER 50

At precisely eight o'clock the following morning, Johnson pulled into Murph's driveway with a hot cup of strong, black coffee sitting in one of the cup holders.

"Good morning," Murph said. "Is this the good stuff?"

"Only the best that the Corner Deli makes is good enough for my understanding partner."

"*Your understanding partner?* Exactly what are you driving at? First it's a cup of the best coffee in town, and now I've suddenly become *your understanding partner*. What am I supposed to understand? What exactly have you done, Detective Johnson?"

Murph sipped the coffee. The coffee from the Corner Deli always proved strong, smooth and delicious, especially first thing in the morning. This cup proved to be no exception. He savored his first sip, and looked forward to the rest.

"I called Officer Stewart last night as you requested," Johnson said, trying very hard to keep from smiling too broadly, "and she and her partner will meet us at the Station this morning."

Murph sniffed the coffee as if it were Jennifer's homemade apple pie. It smelled almost as good, but had none of the calories. "That's good, but I still don't see anything I'm going to have to be understanding about, though."

"Well, if you must know, I asked the young lady out on a date, and she accepted."

Murph's head snapped toward his partner. He shook his head at Johnson's arrogance, and snarled. "She obviously missed the email I sent her telling her to avoid you like the plague." Murph glared at his partner who kept his eyes glued to the road, as if it was the first time he had driven on it. "Despite the fact that you said I would, I really don't understand your actions at all. I thought I told you it wasn't a good idea."

"Oh, you did. You did. You always do, and I always ignore what you say anyway."

Murph smiled. "You never learn. Do you? Every time you ignore my good advice, you always regret it in the end, and so do the women."

"Maybe this time will be different. You are understanding, aren't you?"

"For a cup of strong, Corner Deli coffee, I might be understanding, however, if IAD asks me, I never understood anything about you dating another officer, especially one you're working with on a case. Understood?"

"Yes, Mon Capitan," Johnson said with an exaggerated French salute.

Molly, still wearing her red pajamas, ran downstairs, and into the Larson kitchen where Carol Larson, wearing a pink robe, prepared a breakfast of scrambled eggs for the family. Molly's white socks made no noise on the tiled foyer or the smooth, linoleum kitchen floor. She came to a sliding stop at the center island, almost hitting Carol, who busied herself whipping eggs in a large, yellow bowl.

"Betty Ann's got morning sickness," Molly said, gasping.

"Oh, my goodness!" Carol dropped the whisk into the partially beaten eggs. "How bad is she?"

Molly took a deep breath before answering. "She's thrown up twice this morning. She says she feels better now, but she still looks green to me."

"Let's go!" As she ran up the stairs, Carol yelled, "Ted, it's Betty Ann. She's sick."

Molly, smiling wryly, followed Betty Ann's mother up the stairs. Upon arrival, she switched to a put-on look of deep concern. *I hope I can stay in character.*

Betty Ann sat on the edge of her bed with an empty plastic pan on her lap. It appeared wet, as if it had been washed.

"How do you feel, Betty Ann?" Ted asked as he ran into the room. He wore black pants and a white tee shirt, and had shaving cream covering half his face.

"Better now," Betty Ann said through a small smile. "Much better since I threw up. I'll be all right."

"Does anything hurt…your stomach, your head, anything?" Ted asked.

"No, Dad, I've got no pain now. Believe me I feel much better."

Carol sat next to her. "You're not having any bleeding down below, are you? I'll call the doctor to have you checked out right away. We can meet him in the Emergency Room."

"No, Mom, I'm not bleeding. I don't even have any cramps, at least when I'm not vomiting anyway. Please, don't worry about me. It's just a little morning sickness. I hear it's a common thing. You don't need to call the doctor. I think I'll stay in bed a little while. No breakfast for me, please."

"You'd better skip Church," Ted said. "I guess we should all skip Mass. I'll call Jen to tell her what's happening. She can go without us."

"Oh, please don't do that, Dad," Betty Ann said. "I'll be fine. I'll stay home while the rest of you go to Church. I don't want to ruin your plans, especially over nothing, really."

"I'll stay with her," Molly said. "If she as much as blinks funny, I'll call you on your cell phone, Mr. Larson, and you can come home. Church isn't that far away."

"Are you sure?" Ted said, directing the question at Molly, but looking at Betty Ann through the eyes of a loving father, trying to suppress the suspicions running through his mind. *Can I trust you now? I always have before, but now, I'm not so sure you're the same little girl I raised so carefully, so lovingly. Are you really sick, or are you faking for some reason? I want to regain trust in you again, but I simply don't know. I guess…* He took a seat next to Betty Ann, placing one arm around her, pulling her close to him. She rested her head on his shoulder, and closed her eyes. He turned his head toward Molly, awaiting her reply.

"Sure," Molly said, patting Betty Ann's knee. "We'll stay here, and behave ourselves."

"Behave yourselves?" Carol asked, her face mimicking her husband's doubt. "That will be the day! Are you two sure this isn't put on. Are you two up to something?"

"Mom," Betty Ann said, staring at her mother with wide open eyes, "you're acting like a suspicious mother. I'm not a criminal. I'm just not feeling well, that's all. Molly is being a good friend, trying to make the best of the situation. She's concerned for me, and I love her for it."

"Okay," Carol said, "but it's hard to trust you two after what's happened. As we told you last night, Betty Ann, you've got to earn our trust all over again. We only have your best interest in mind...especially when we're overprotective. Don't disappoint us again."

"I understand all that, Mom," Betty Ann said, "but this is best for everyone involved. Please, get to Church before dad's shaving cream hardens on his face, and he has to go around looking like a Santa Claus reject."

They all laughed, as Ted and Carol headed for the door.

"I'll turn my cell phone to vibrate, and will sit at the rear of the Church," Ted said from the hallway. "So, don't hesitate to call if she gets worse, Molly, and I mean anything out of the ordinary. Her mom had some morning sickness, but mild and brief. Hopefully, Betty Ann's will be the same, but that doesn't mean she won't get worse. So, please, don't be a hero. Call if she needs anything. I'd rather miss Mass than find her sicker when we get home."

"You can trust me, Mr. Larson," Molly said, crossing her fingers behind her back, and putting the other, protective arm around Betty Ann, who lowered her head on cue, pretending to feel queasy again. "I won't let anything happen to your precious little girl."

CHAPTER 51

Murph and Johnson walked through the Adams Police Station as if they were strolling through a park on a beautiful Sunday morning. The leisurely pace allowed room for thought as well as time for the on-duty officers to hand Johnson reports that had been printed out in expectation of his arrival. A skeleton crew always worked on Sundays, and this should have been no exception; however, Murph noted almost all of the Adams officers worked at their desks. He glanced at the empty glass-encased cubical that housed the Chief. *My guess is she ordered the extra help.* He smiled at her diligence.

The main room of the Station occupied the entire first floor of the building with several, darkly tinted, bulletproof windows occupying the front wall. It showcased the street outside with its current light traffic and few pedestrians. A reception desk, behind its own bulletproof glass provided a buffer to any armed intruder. Every detective and officer had his or her own desk. Officers Campbell and Stewart, who were on temporary assignment to them, proved no exception, and sat at their desks. All of the desks were arranged in a random pattern. Murph had long ago stopped trying to deduce the purpose for such a layout. The randomness, however, did cause one to have to take a circuitous path toward one's work area, forcing everyone to at least acknowledge the passing officer. This, Murph figured, was another invention of the Chief to increase officer interaction and camaraderie…maybe. The Chief would never give Murph the satisfaction of a straight answer to his query.

As they followed their usual route, Johnson took memos from his fellow officers, scanned their content, and put them in order of importance.

Murph dialed Doc Rebak as he hurried to his own desk, cluttered with memos, reports requiring his signature, and sticky-notes that covered his desk phone with the names and phone numbers of people requesting a return call. Unless an emergency, or connected to the current case, these would all wait until the following week, when he hoped he would have more time to devote to his regular duties.

"Hi, Doc," Murph said, "any news?"

"Yes and no. Sheryl came out of surgery a little while ago. She hasn't awoken yet. It'll be a while before she's awake enough for us to know anything. Besides, even if she can't move her legs then, you have to remember there's been swelling around her spinal cord, so it may take a day or two for that to go down. Until then, we may not be able to tell anything for sure."

"Oh, I understand that. I wanted to make sure the surgery went well. The rest we'll put in the hands of God. My family is in Church right now praying for her."

"Good! Every little bit helps."

"What about the autopsy on our victims?"

"Your second victim was indeed pregnant. The shots went right into the uterus. The kill shot went through her heart. It passed clear through her, and embedded in the couch. According to the CSI team, it matches the bullets from the first victim, so you're dealing with the same killer, or at least, the same gun. I still insist, though, that this is much more personal, more angry than the first. The killer took his time to give the victim three post-mortem wounds, including blowing the top of her head off. You don't usually do that unless there's some anger involved.

"I sent off toxicology screens on both victims, but I really think those will be negative. There is nothing under their nails, so neither got their hands on their killer. Neither had been sexually assaulted, although the first, as I've said before, did undergo a recent abortion. That's about it for now. I'll have more when I get the tox and chemistry reports. I'll come to the Station later, if you don't mind, Murph. I'd like to be here when Sheryl wakes up. I'll give you a call then."

"How about you, Johnson? Got anything we can use?" Murph quickly rifled through the messages left for him. He stuck them back on the base of the phone, all being concerned with other, less urgent cases.

"Reports from the CSI team head the list," Johnson said. "More negatives than positives, I'm afraid. Those wet spots on the diary did turn out to be Eve's tears. Most of the prints at both scenes match the victims'. In St. Marie's apartment, they also found her boyfriend's. In the case of our second murder scene, they only found Doctor Svensen's. We expected those. There were a few partial non-matches, but none of them came from the areas we think the killer would have been touching anyway. They found nothing of interest in either of their bedrooms except some semen stains on the second victim's bed that matched the doctor's DNA…of course. You can thank Chief Stone for the quick turn around for the DNA, by the way. She made it a top priority."

Murph nodded, but said nothing.

"CSI found no trace evidence where the killer's car might have been parked in either case, unfortunately." Johnson sat on a corner of Murph's desk.

"We didn't come up with anything either," Officer Campbell said, as he and Officer Stewart approached, "when we canvassed the street behind the victim's house. Most people were not home, and those that were didn't notice any unusual cars parked on the street. Most didn't even hear the shots, and there are no surveillance cameras in the area."

"I'm not surprised," Murph said. "We're going over some of the evidence. Give a listen."

Johnson smiled at Officer Stewart, who returned the polite smile. Murph just shook his head, his penetrating eyes glaring at the young, female officer.

"The computers didn't show very much," Johnson said. "Mrs. Svensen's computer contained some artwork, family photos, and letters of correspondence to friends, but nothing incriminating that they could find. They have some printouts, and a copy of her hard drive if we want to read them individually later. She tended to visit websites of historic interest and on-line stores. She apparently liked to spend money.

"As predicted, poetry almost filled the Doctor's computer. They weren't labeled with names, so we can't tell which women got which poems, but I would think that might not matter. There were some letters and e-mails to other doctors, medical associations, and medical journals. He visited medical sites, those same medical journals, and several writing sites, including ones specializing in poetry and short stories. No porn or illegal sites that they could find. No reference to Georgi Clay's location either. The lab's still checking for any hidden files, but said not to get our hopes up."

Murph's desk phone rang, interrupting Johnson's rhetoric.

"Hi, Detective Murphy, this is Officer Martinelli. I've been patrolling the area around the Women's Clinic as ordered in our briefing this morning. Something has happened that I think will interest you."

"Oh," Murph said, pushing the speaker button on the phone. "I've put you on speaker so Detective Johnson and Officers Campbell and Stewart will be able to hear you. Go ahead."

"Good Morning, All," Martinelli said. "I passed the Women's Clinic this morning when I noticed several cars driving into their rear parking lot. One of them is the Lexus that's on this morning's APB. I believe it belongs to Dr. Svensen."

Murph bolted upright. "What? Did you see him go into the clinic?"

"No, when I went around back to observe the other cars, I saw his Lexus already there. It wasn't here when I passed the area a half hour ago, so he must have arrived between then and now. Do you want me to go in to speak to him?"

"No, I want you to stay in that back parking lot, and keep an eye out for Dr. Svensen. If he comes out, and tries to leave, arrest him on suspicion of murder."

"I thought you didn't think he was guilty," Johnson said.

"I don't think he is, but I want to hear his explanation of where he's been, and why he ran when he thought we were looking for him. So, I don't want him driving off, and I certainly don't want to lose track of him again."

"That's fine, Detective," Martinelli said, "but I can only cover the back. He could walk out the front, take a taxi, and I'd never know about it."

"Don't worry, Martinelli," Murph said, staring at the two rookie officers, "I'm sending you back-up. You Two, get down there pronto. I want one officer and your patrol car parked in front, watching that entrance. The other officer stays in the back with Martinelli. You're to do nothing but watch until Johnson and I get down there unless Dr. Svensen tries to leave. Understood?"

"Yes, sir," both officers said in unison.

"Good! Now, get out of here! I want you at that clinic pronto."

The two officers ran toward the exit, weaving and bobbing around the desks like downhill skiers on a slalom course.

"Martinelli," Murph said, "Officers Campbell and Stewart will be down there to back you up, but don't be afraid to call for any unit in your area, if he gives you any problems. Remember, we're looking for a killer who's probably armed. I don't think it's him, but I don't want anyone taking chances. Whoever this killer is, he's vicious, and plans well. I don't want his next victim to be one of our finest. Do you understand?"

"Completely," Martinelli said, the confidence in his voice more worrisome than reassuring to Murph. "I won't take any unnecessary chances, but I won't let him get away either, just in case you're wrong, and he is the killer."

"Okay," Murph said, with a smile that exceeded that of his partner's, "goodbye."

"In case you're wrong!" Johnson said, trying hard not to laugh. "I guess he missed the memo that the great Detective Murphy is *never* wrong, just misdirected at times."

"I think I missed that memo from the very beginning of this case," Murph said. "Let's go see what Dr. Svensen knows about these murders that he's not telling us."

CHAPTER 52

Murph had just completed his instructions to the young officers when another detective spoke. "Before you leave, Murph, you may want to hear this. You asked us to track down Georgi Clay, who supposedly left for Tucson. The local Police Department found her family there. They didn't know anything about her plans to move back, and there hasn't been any family emergency requiring her attention. As a matter of fact, they haven't seen her for almost a year. They weren't concerned because she was a very independent woman. Sometimes, she wouldn't check in with them for extended periods of time…and then there's the fact that they've been receiving emails from her on a monthly basis, saying how good she's doing here in Connecticut, including the last four months after she reportedly left Adams."

"They've been receiving emails!" Johnson exclaimed, the shocked expression on his face reminding Murph of Carol's the previous morning when she first opened her door to find he and Betty Ann bearing shocking news. "That doesn't jive with our information. We were told she's left the area. So, who's sending the emails?"

"Good question," the detective said. "The computer guys are trying to track that right now. Hopefully, they can give us a location for the computer. Meanwhile, her family has decided to put in a missing persons report with the Tucson police. We're doing the same here, just in case someone knows of her whereabouts. We checked with the DMV, and her car registration has expired. All her bank accounts were closed a few months ago too."

"We knew they were closed," Johnson said, thumbing through his notes. "Barbara Schine said the Clay woman asked her to help with her move. I'll bet she can tell us where Georgi Clay is, and why she hasn't surfaced anywhere…and maybe why she didn't tell us before." Johnson looked at Murph, as if Murph could read his mind.

"Now I really wonder," Murph said, "if she had been pregnant when she disappeared."

"We know she was dating Dr. Svensen at the time," Johnson said, "and with his record, I would be surprised if she wasn't. I wonder if she's a third victim in this set, and not simply in hiding."

"She may be," Murph said, "*if* we can prove she's been murdered, and not simply gone somewhere else to have an abortion, or maybe have the baby. Her family did describe her as an independent woman. Who knows what she might do?"

"Let's pretend she's been murdered," Johnson said, "just for the sake of discussion. What else do we know that might tie her to the other victims."

"Well, we also know that Barbara Schine began dating Doctor Svensen when the Clay woman disappeared," Murph said, "and that the doctor dumped her for Janet Robertson, our second victim. Could Barbara Schine be the connecting link between both murders and maybe a third?"

"She did do the intake on Eve St. Marie, and talked to her before she was murdered," Johnson said, "but Eve didn't have any personal relationship with the doctor, Georgi Clay or Barbara Schine that we know of, anyway. So, I can't connect her murder with the others. It's all supposition at this point. We don't have enough proof."

"See if this helps your case," another detective said. "We checked the cell phone numbers you gave us for calls around the time of the first killing. I guess one of your witnesses said she heard a cell phone play some music."

"That's right," Murph said, "she said it sounded like a recording of Frank Sinatra."

"The ring sound I can't help you with," the detective said, "and, unfortunately, this may only add to your confusion." His gaze jumped back and forth between Murph and Johnson. Neither said anything, both staring at the detective with quizzical eyes until he spoke again. "Two of the cell phone numbers were accessed around midnight on Friday night. The one belonging to Barbara Shine received a call first from the Emergency Department of Adams

Hospital. Two minutes later, she placed a call to the Doctor's number. So, your witness could have heard either one."

"But not both," Murph said. "That goes against your conspiracy theory, Johnson. Even if one of them is the killer of Eve St. Marie, they both weren't at the murder scene, or they wouldn't have had to use cell phones to communicate."

"No, but they could still be in on it together. The one who did the shooting was calling the other to report that the deed had been done, or the one not there, Dr. Svensen in my opinion, called from the ER to check on the killer's progress. Works either way for me."

"You never give up," Murph said, shaking his head, and chuckling at the same time.

"No reason to," Johnson said, closing his notebook, "until I'm proven wrong."

"Anything else, Detective?" Murph asked.

"Only that we called Mr. Robert Kilmore's cell phone last night. Someone who claimed to be his sister-in-law answered. We checked her position using the GPS chip in the phone, and she was where she claimed to be, Pittsburgh, Pennsylvania. According to her they were driving Mr. Kilmore to their home at the time of the Robertson murder."

"We thought that's what you'd find," Murph said. "I guess that takes him off our list of suspects. I don't think we should pursue that line of investigation any more. Anything else?"

"I'm afraid not. If anything else comes in, we'll give you a call."

"Thanks," Murph said, standing up, and checking the Chief's office: still no sign of her. "Let's go see if the doctor can connect the dots for us."

"If he can't, then Martinelli will learn to trust the memos that say Detective Murphy is always right."

"Not always," Murph said, as he ran his fingers through his thick hair, "almost always, but I have the 'almost' erased from any memo sent to a rookie. I look better that way. Now, let's go."

Jennifer walked over to the Larson house as Carol and Ted exited their front door. Molly and Betty Ann appeared behind them.

Jennifer waved at the girls. "Hope you're feeling better by the time we return. Keep a careful eye on Betty Ann, Molly. See you in a little while."

"Goodbye, You Two," Carol said through a worried expression. "We'll pray for you, Betty Ann. I *do* hope you're feeling better. See you after Church."

"Goodbye, Mrs. Murphy," Betty Ann said, holding her stomach, as if speaking increased the pain. "Bye Mom and Dad."

"Goodbye, Betty Ann," Ted said. "See you later. Remember to call me if you need us."

The three parents climbed into the car, driving off with Jennifer Murphy staring out the rear window with a look of concern, and an accompanying, unsettling sensation, burning within her, informing her she might never see the girls again. The feeling refused to subside, even after they made the corner, and could no longer see the children.

.

"Do you think they suspect anything?" Betty Ann asked, standing upright, adjusting her clothing, and turning to face Molly.

"Not a chance," Molly said with a broad smile. "We're too good at acting for them to catch on. Let's make that phone call."

"Are we doing the right thing?"

"Listen, Betty Ann, you want more information than your parents preached to you last night, and more accurate stuff than you found on the Internet, right? Even Doug wants more information before you decide anything. Barbara's got all that information for you. She works with it every day. She told me some is typed up, and that the rest is in the form of brochures. Some of it is probably a duplicate of what you already have, but she has experience in this type of problem. She can tell you stories about other pregnant teenagers, I'm sure. We can't pass up this opportunity. She said she'd have us back in plenty of time to beat our parents home. We've got nothing to loose. Okay?"

"Okay" Betty Ann said, the quivering in her voice increasing, as she agreed to all the aspects of Molly's plan. "Go call-forward the house phone to your cell phone in case my dad calls on that line to see how I'm doing. Then call Miss Schine. Tell her to meet us around the corner. Tell her to hurry, though, before I change my mind."

Not thirty-seconds later the two teenagers were walking down Pearl street, conversing about music, the newest reality TV shows, and anything else that jumped into their minds that had nothing to do with pregnancy, babies, or abortion.

Around the corner, a yellow Toyota had parked with its motor running, waiting to take them on a fateful one-way trip. Its driver smiled, fingering the gun in her handbag. It felt hard and cold like the dead bodies the girls would become before the end of this day.

CHAPTER 53

When Murph and Johnson arrived at the Women's Medical Clinic, they found Officer Campbell leaning on the rear fender of his black and white patrol car. They parked behind the car, leaving plenty of space between the two.

Campbell walked toward them, never taking his eyes off the front door of the clinic. "No one went in, or came out since we arrived. I tried the door. It's locked. What's next?"

"Call your partner. Tell her and Martinelli we're going in," Murph said. "We'll let them in once we're inside. Tell them to stay alert. No one is allowed to leave."

"Yes, sir," Campbell said, reaching for the microphone attached to his shirt.

"Call the doctor on his cell phone, Johnson," Murph said, "and let me talk to him if he answers."

"What are we going to do if his cell phone is still turned off? We don't have a search warrant, and we don't have enough to get one at this point."

"We'll make such a racket at that front door that they're sure to hear it inside and, if they don't, we may force our way in. We may not have enough to convince a judge yet, but we do think a murderer might be in there, and any others in there may be at risk. We have probable cause, but let's try the easy way first. Make the call."

Johnson consulted his notebook for the doctor's number. It rang three times.

"Hello, this is Doctor Svensen."

Johnson handed the phone to Murph, who cleared his throat before speaking.

"Doctor Svensen, this is Detective Murphy. We're out in front of the clinic. We know its Sunday, and your clinic is closed, but we know you're in there. We need to speak to you. Please open the door for us."

"Certainly, Detective Murphy, give me a minute."

Murph motioned to Johnson and Officer Campbell to station themselves on either side of the door. Murph stood directly in front of the door, but several feet back, his right hand on his holstered weapon.

The door opened slowly. Doctor Svensen emerged, and placed both hands at his side. As soon as he spotted Murph with his hand on his gun, and the two officers flanking him, he immediately raised his hands above his head with his fingers spread. "Please, Detective Murphy, I'm not armed. None of my staff is. What is the meaning of this?"

Murph relaxed, taking his hand from his weapon, and approached the doctor. "As I said, Doctor, we have some questions for you and your staff. Let's go inside. Shall we?"

The doctor lowered his arms as he led the three officers into the clinic. "This is an outrage," he said, turning to face Murph. "You could have just knocked. Someone would have let you in." He shook his head. "There was no need for theatrics."

"Listen, Doctor," Murph said, watching Johnson and Campbell walk to the door that led to the inner part of the clinic, "I'm not here to have you question my tactics. I'm here to ask you questions about two murders. So, you'd better start listening carefully, and answer truthfully, or we can do this at the Station. It's up to you."

"Okay, I'll answer any questions you have. I've got nothing to hide because I had nothing to do with any murder."

Being careful not to make a sound, Johnson reached for the door, and yanked it open in one fluid motion. On the other side stood Linda Summerset, dressed in black slacks and a loose fitting, green blouse. Her hands were empty.

"Oh," Linda said, startled at being discovered.

"Why don't you join us, Miss Summerset," Murph said, reading her name again from her nameplate on her desk. "You can hear better from this side of the door."

"I wasn't trying to hear anything." Her voice quivered with each word. "I was…I was…"

"You were eavesdropping," Murph said, "and when we get through with the doctor here, we're going to find out why."

Linda started to walk to her desk.

"No," Johnson said, jumping between her and her desk. "Stand by the doctor over there."

Johnson checked every drawer for a weapon. He found none, but decided he wouldn't let her return to her desk until they had finished their questioning, in case he had missed a hidden compartment in the area.

"I just wanted to sit down," Linda said.

"Sit over there on the couch where your clients sit," Johnson said. "Your desk is off limits until we're done here. Keep your hands where we can see them."

Linda collapsed onto the couch, folding her arms across her chest, the expression on her face radiating hate for Johnson. He could actually feel the stare, even when he wasn't looking at her.

"Officer Campbell," Johnson said, "please keep an eye on her for us." Johnson next checked the hallway: empty.

"Go let Martinelli and Stewart in," Murph said to Johnson. "Where are your other clinic employees, Doctor?"

"Room five, down the hall to the right."

"Have Officer Stewart stand guard outside that door, Johnson," Murph said. "No one comes out of that room until we say so. Have Martinelli join us out here. This is his territory. I'd like him to be in on this part of the investigation."

"Right." Johnson headed down the hallway with his hand still resting on his gun. He stopped at Room 5, listening with his ear pressed against the door. He could hear the low rumbling of people speaking, but couldn't make out any distinct words. He then rushed to the back door and the awaiting officers.

"Now, Doctor," Murph said, "your wife said you ran out the door when you heard we were looking for you. Where did you go, and why did you turn your cell phone off?"

Johnson returned with Martinelli on his heals. Murph nodded to Martinelli, but said nothing to the young officer, who went to stand next to Officer Campbell.

"Is that what this is all about?" Linda asked, dropping her hands to the edge of the couch to use to help stand. She walked to the doctor's side, continuing to throw angry looks at Johnson. "He was with me, if you must know."

"With you?" Murph asked in disbelief. "Why did he run to you?"

"He got very upset at the news of Janet's death, and needed consoling. His wife is not very good at that, to put it mildly. He called me to ask if he could come over to talk. Of course, when I heard what had happened, I told him to come right over. He sounded so upset."

"I suppose he was so upset that he had to spend the night," Murph said.

"Well, yes," Linda said, her face reddening, "but it was my idea. I couldn't let him drive home in that condition. I also told him to turn his phone off so he wouldn't be disturbed. He needed the sleep."

Murph shook his head. *Unbelievable! His pregnant girlfriend isn't dead a full day yet, and he's already working on his next conquest. He is truly unbelievable!*

"It's not what it looks like," Dr. Svensen said. "Linda is a kind soul who listened to an old man's grieving, that's all. Two fellow employees grieving together…"

"You left your wife grieving by herself," Murph said.

"That's between me and my wife. It's not police business."

"I hope you're right," Murph said. "We'll leave it as your business for now, but, if it turns out it does relate somehow to our case, you can be sure we'll be revisiting it. Now, how did this morning's soiree with the rest of your staff come about?"

"Actually, it's the same thing on a larger scale. I realized last night that our staff would be suffering the same grief and loss that I felt. So, I called everyone to arrange this meeting so we could talk about our loss, and they could get some grief counseling. The timing seemed perfect for such a meeting, since it *is* Sunday, and we had no patients scheduled."

"Is your full staff back there?" Murph asked.

"All except Barbara. Her cell phone must be turned off, and there's no answer at her apartment. I left a message with the reason I had called, and for her to call me, but I haven't heard from her. I have no idea where she might be now."

Murph turned to Johnson. "Get a patrol car out to her home now! If she's there, have them bring her. If not, put out an APB. Find her!"

CHAPTER 54

"What does Barbara have to do with all this?" Dr. Svensen asked.

"We were hoping you could tell us that," Murph said.

"As far as I know, nothing. We both had a professional relationship with Eve St. Marie and, of course, with Janet. Neither of us would have any reason to kill either one of them."

"A professional relationship, huh?" Murph waved Johnson to his side. "Do you still have the photo of our doctor and his girlfriend with you?"

"Of course. He handed the photo of the four of them, standing next to the bar, to the doctor."

"Does that professional relationship include meeting Eve St. Marie and her boyfriend at Kilmore's bar?" Murph asked. "It looks like the four of you were having a good time, and it doesn't look professional at all. Looks more like you were all good chums."

"Oh, yes, Janet and I happen to stop there for a drink. It's a clean bar, and relatively close to the clinic. Janet wanted to celebrate her pregnancy, that's all."

"Did you want to celebrate too, Doctor?" Johnson stared at Linda, hoping she would understand that the doctor was a user of women. She only shot back more angry looks.

"It was Janet's idea, not mine," Dr. Svensen said. "I had a couple of beers and, at my insistence, she had nothing stronger than a Ginger Ale. Eve and her boyfriend came in, and sat in the booth next to us. They were arguing over her pregnancy. I felt sorry for her. So, I approached them to offer the services of the clinic. I gave them my card, and told them to call to set up an appointment. I told them we could counsel them on their best option. They seemed appreciative. It wasn't a planned meeting, or a date, or anything personal, as you seem to be implying."

Johnson's cell phone rang. He walked over to the front door to take the call.

"Did you ever meet Eve again outside the clinic socially, whether those meetings were planned, or accidental?" Murph asked.

"No, never!"

"Barbara Schine is not at her apartment," Johnson said, returning to Murph's side. "The patrol unit had the Super let them in. They're going to stay there to see if she shows up."

"Good," Murph said, and then returned his attention to the doctor. "What about Barbara? Did she have any social interactions with Eve St. Marie outside the clinic?"

"Of course, who do you think took the picture?"

Murph took a swift step toward the doctor, causing the doctor to flinch. Murph then stood inches from him. "What? Do you mean to tell me Barbara Schine was at the bar that night?"

"Yes." Dr. Svensen backed away from Murph. *I've witnessed Detective Murph's uncontrolled anger once, and want no part of any recurrence of that rage.* "I was talking to Miss St. Marie and her boyfriend when Barbara walked into the bar. She said she happened to be driving by, noticed my car parked outside, and so decided to stop in to see if she could join us for a drink. She took some photos with her cell phone, and printed them out later. She also e-mailed a copy of a few of the photos to each of us. I deleted them before my wife found them. She's always going on my computer, looking for samples of my poetry. Anyway, to get back to Barbara, as far as I know, that was her only social interaction with Miss St. Marie, and that one only happened by accident."

"That means Barbara also lied to us when she said she hadn't met Eve's boyfriend. What else happened that night at Kilmore's? Did Miss St. Marie have a disagreement with anyone?"

"Not that I saw. It turned into a very quiet evening. We had a few drinks in one of the booths, posed for that photo, and then all went our separate ways. Barbara and I never even talked about it afterwards. I guess we both figured it was no big deal, unlike you, who are trying to make something more of it."

"Listen, Doctor," Murph said. "You both knew the victims here at the clinic, one, a client, and the other, an employee. You also had drinks at a local bar with both victims. That makes you and Barbara our top suspects."

"You've got to be kidding! Barbara and I are both dedicated to saving lives, not murdering them."

"Then answer this," Murph said, pounding one fist into the palm of the other, "around the time Eve St. Marie was shot, the two of you were conversing on your cell phones. What was the topic of that conversation, the murder?"

"No, of course not! Let me think. Oh, yes, now I remember. A doctor from the hospital called our answering service, and needed to speak to me about a patient...and, before you ask, it wasn't either of your victims. Barbara happened to be on-call that night."

"I can confirm that she was on-call, Murph," Johnson said, pointing to Linda's computer. "I saw their on-call schedule and cell phone numbers on that computer when we first came here."

"Nosy, aren't you," Linda said, the anger burned permanently onto her face.

"Go on, Doctor," Murph said, ignoring both interruptions.

"Well, the answering service called Barbara, who then called me to give me the message. She triages the calls, handling the easy ones herself, but calls me for more serious problems, or if I have to speak to another doctor the way I did that night. You can check the times and sequence of the calls with both our answering service and the hospital. I'll give you the doctor's name, so you can check with him. I'm sure he'll remember. There should be a note with the time we talked in the patient's chart. I'm sure Barbara will confirm what I just told you when she finally shows up."

"Where were you when you got the phone call?" Murph asked.

"I told you before that I was with Janet. She lives not too far from where Eve St. Marie's apartment is...was. It's a nice neighborhood. I left my car here at the clinic for Barbara to use for the weekend. Janet picked me up. I spent the night with her."

"Wait a minute! Why did you leave your Lexus for Barbara to use?"

"She told me her car needed some work, and that they could do it on Thursday, but they didn't have a loaner to give her for the couple of days they needed to fix her car. It had something to do with her transmission, I think. Anyway, she had the car until I came back to work on Saturday morning. When Janet drove me here, I found my car in its usual parking spot. Barbara's Toyota was parked alongside it. Barbara told me it had been an expensive repair, but she loves the car, and felt the money was worth it."

Murph looked at Johnson, who had a bewildered look on his face, as if the information had made him more confused rather than clearing up issues.

"That means Barbara had access to the right kind of luxury car that we suspect the killer used in the first murder," Johnson said, "and she did receive a call on her cell phone, but her cell phone ring doesn't match what our witness heard."

"Oh, Barbara's always changing her cell phone ring," Linda said, in a voice that hid the hate she felt toward Johnson. "As a matter of fact, she changed her ring while you were here yesterday."

"She did?" Murph asked.

"Sure, she came out here to tell me she wanted to demonstrate her new ring to you while you were with her in her office. She told me to wait a couple of minutes, and then call her. So, that's what I did. I presume you got the demonstration of the ring that she wanted you to hear."

Murph stood wide-eyed. "Oh, yeah, we got just the demonstration she wanted, and we fell for it."

"She acted like she hadn't expected the call," Johnson said. "She's apparently a good actress. Do you happen to know what her ring sounded like before her supposed demonstration of the new one?"

"Sure, the day before she had downloaded Frank Sinatra, singing *America the Beautiful*. It actually sounded pretty good to me considering how small the speakers must be in her phone."

"Oh, My God," Johnson said. "She must have killed Eve St. Marie!"

"That's crazy," Dr. Svensen said. "I don't care if she was driving the right car, and had the right cell phone ring. Why would she kill Eve St. Marie? There's no reason."

"We'll ask her when we find her," Johnson said.

Murph slowly turned toward the couch, recently vacated by the clinic receptionist. He stared in disbelief, remembering the day before more vividly than he really wanted, remembering his innocent daughter, sitting there, awaiting an appointment with Dr. Svensen. The color drained from his face.

"What's the matter, Murph?" Johnson asked.

"When Barbara came out to tell you to call her," Murph asked, pushing his face to within inches of Linda's, his voice wavering, his face now a bright red, "was my daughter sitting there by any chance?" He pointed toward the couch.

"She most certainly was. I remember because I explained Barbara's obsession with her cell phone ring to her. We shared a laugh about it. Why?"

"Oh, My God, Johnson!" Murph said, reaching for his cell phone. "Molly's a witness that could put Barbara's cell phone at the scene of the first murder. Molly could be her next target."

"Oh, God, no!" Johnson said. "I'll get a patrol car rushed to your house."

CHAPTER 55

"What about me?" Linda asked, her hand covering her mouth. "Am I a target because I witnessed the same thing as your daughter? Barbara called me last night. She told me she wanted a private meeting later tonight. I thought she was going to give me a promotion or maybe a special assignment. Was she really planning to kill me?"

"Yes," Murph said flatly, pressing the speed dial to Molly's cell phone. "Martinelli, no matter what happens, you stay with Linda here, and provide her protection."

"Yes, sir!" Martinelli hurried to stand next to Linda, and gave her a brief, small smile.

Murph's call immediately went to voice mail. "Molly, it's dad. Call me as soon as you get this message. It's an emergency. Stay away from Barbara Schine, the assistant clinic director you met yesterday. Don't believe anything she says. Call me on my cell."

Murph next dialed his wife's cell phone. It rang once.

"Hello, is that you, Molly?" Jennifer asked, so fast that Murph didn't get a chance to say anything.

Murph realized at once that Jen hadn't taken the time to check the caller ID, and that meant something was wrong, very, very wrong.

"No, Jen, it's Bill. Where's Molly?"

"I don't know, and we don't know where Betty Ann is either. They're both missing."

"Has Ted tried Betty Ann's cell phone?"

"Of course. There's no answer, and, for some reason, their home phone is being call-forwarded to Molly's cell phone. It makes no sense. What's going on?"

"We've got a patrol car on the way, Jen. First, tell me what happened."

"We left the two of them home when we went to Church this morning because Betty Ann had a stomach issue that we thought might be morning sickness. We left Molly with her with instructions to call us if she got worse. We didn't get any call, but when we got home they were gone, and we can't find them. Ted's calling the hospital now, but if they called 911, I would think Molly would have called us also, or left us a note. Carol is going door-to-door checking the neighbors to see if they saw them. Why would they call forward the house phone? It makes no sense. I'm really worried, Bill."

"Listen to me, Jen," Murph said, trying to speak in his official, calm, police voice that he used so often to talk to distraught family members. *The problem is I don't feel calm at all...just the opposite.* Over the phone, he heard the distant sound of a police siren. It didn't comfort him. "I need you to calm down. If Molly called-forwarded the house phone, they probably left voluntarily. Maybe they went for a walk, although I can't imagine both cell phones being turned off, or out of power at the same time."

"So, where are they?"

"I don't know. When the officers arrive I want you to go over the whole story again with them. Tom filled them in. So, they know who you are, and who we're looking for. Be patient, I have some ideas I'll need to follow up on." *Like finding the killer before she finds, kidnaps, and kills both girls.*

"Hold on a minute," Jennifer said, "here comes Carol. Maybe she's got some answers."

The longest minute in Murph's life, filled with images of deceased teenagers he had seen, occurred, followed by Jennifer's excited voice.

"Carol says the only one who saw anything was Owen. Here, you talk to her."

"Murph, Owen says he saw the girls leave right after we left for Church. He thought it unusual because we usually all go to Church together. They looked like they were going for a walk around the block. Bless his nosy soul. Owen decided to follow them to see where they were headed. He said they took the corner onto Orchard Street, and got into a yellow Toyota. He didn't get the plate number. We don't know anyone with that kind of car, Murph. What does it all mean?"

"Put Jen back on the phone, Carol, and don't worry. I think I know who owns that car. So, we should be able to track it down."

Only the briefest of delays occurred before Murph heard Jen's voice.

"I'm here, Bill," Jennifer said in the calmest voice she could muster, her quivering lips foiling the effort. "The officers just arrived."

"Listen, I think we know who owns that car. We're going to track it down, and get the girls back. I promise."

"Who is it, Bill? Who has our girls?"

Murph considered lying to her, but knew she would see right through him. She always did. They had been together so long, and had been through several bad times together. They knew each other very well. No, he couldn't get away with a lie, no matter how bad the truth sounded.

"Okay, but please don't panic in front of Carol and Ted. It's not as bad as it may sound. We think the assistant clinic director at that Women's Clinic owns the car. She may have something to do with our murder investigation."

"Oh, no!" Murph pictured his wife, covering her mouth with her hand. He also pictured Ted and Carol, panicking because of her reaction.

"Listen, Jen. If Molly and Betty Ann are meeting with the assistant director, it may have nothing to do with our murders. Remember, the girls never got the information they wanted from their clinic visit yesterday, thanks to me. Maybe she's just giving them that information, and it's taking longer than they thought. Maybe they lost track of time. In any case, tell Carol and Ted to stay put, just in case the kids call, or show up. That goes for you, too. I need you to stay calm, Jen, for our daughter's sake. Now, let me do my job. Please put one of the officers on the phone. Remember, Jen, I love you."

Murph could hear the muffled cries of his wife, followed by a deep male voice.

"Officer Kaylin here."

"Officer Kaylin, this is Detective Murphy. Please don't repeat anything that I'm going to tell you. I don't want my wife or our neighbors any more upset than they already are. I want you and your partner to get back on the road to join the search for a yellow

Toyota that picked up my daughter and her girlfriend. Detective Johnson will give you the car's plate number. If you spot it, do not stop it. Just call it in. The driver may be the murderer we're after. Have you got all that?"

"Yes, Detective Murphy. Okay. We'll get on it right away."

Murph handed the phone to Johnson, who read the Toyota's plate number to the officer.

"We've got every car looking," Johnson said. "She still hasn't shown at her apartment."

"She probably won't," Murph said. "She's too smart for that. Come on, let's search her office."

They all rushed to Barbara's office. Johnson rifled through the drawers of her desk, but found only stationary supplies and a few menus from local take-out restaurants.

"Where would she go, Doctor?" Murph asked.

"I don't know. I can't think straight right now. It's all too much for me."

Linda put her arm around the doctor's waist, and laid her head against his shoulder, offering him comfort.

Murph turned away from the sickening scene, his gaze falling upon the picture on the wall of Barbara fishing with her father. *Joe Smithson always said criminals leave clues whether they intended to, or not.* Maybe you were right, Joe. Maybe Barbara left us one. "Does Barbara still own that lake house?" He pointed to the picture, but stared at the doctor.

"Why, yes, she does, come to think of it. I had forgotten about it. It's on a small lake, about half-a-mile in diameter. They don't allow any motorboats, just rowboats and small sail boats. She's had the office staff up there for picnics. It's not far from here."

"Can you give us the address?" Murph asked.

"I can do better than that. I think I still have the directions printed out somewhere in my desk. Those directions will get you there faster than your GPS since it uses back roads with no signal lights and usually very little traffic. I'll get them for you."

"Go with him, Officer Stewart, and bring the directions back to us. Johnson, when we have the address, I want every available

253

unit converging on the place, silent mode, no sirens or lights. If Barbara Schine has the kids there, I don't want to spook her into shooting. No one goes in before we get there, unless shots are fired. If that happens, I want them to charge the place, and take her alive, if possible."

"You got it." Johnson pressed his quick dial number for the Station dispatcher.

"Let's go," Murph said as he began running to the car. "We've got a killer to catch."

To Murph, the run took place in slow motion and, the harder he ran, the farther away the car seemed to become. Exhausted and hyperventilating by the time he climbed into the passenger's seat, he started sweating profusely. His hands shook. *Control, control, control…it's not working! Please help me, God!*

Johnson joined him in seconds, bolting into the driver's seat. Officer Stewart passed the directions to Johnson through the car window, and ran to her patrol car. Johnson read the address and directions to the Station dispatcher, handed them to Murph, and floored the accelerator, burning rubber behind Officers Stewart and Campbell. They hugged the rear of the patrol car as they sailed through the streets of Adams, their lights flashing, and sirens blaring until they were within five blocks of the lake house. The ensuing silence felt both eerie and worrisome.

"Don't worry, Murph, we'll get there in time."

"We'd better!" Murph crumpled the paper containing the directions into a tiny ball, as if that alone would eliminate Molly's present predicament, crushing Barbara Shine into a small spitball. However, the crumpling didn't alleviate Murph's fear, although it did help Murph contain the harsh and uncontrollably loud scream of desperation he suppressed in his throat. *If I give in, and scream, it would mean I'm admitting failure, and that would mean I could lose my only daughter…forever. I can't let that happen! No, I won't let that happen!* He suppressed the scream further by swallowing the little saliva he could muster. "We'd better," he repeated, throwing the spitball onto the floor, "or else…"

CHAPTER 56

They found one patrol car parked alongside the road when they arrived at the lake. The two officers approached Murph as he exited the car.

"Detective Murphy, I'm Officer Kaylin. We talked on the phone from your neighbor's house a little while ago. We were the closest unit when we got the call. We've scouted the layout. The Toyota is parked at the top of the driveway, right next to the house. The driveway's about one hundred feet long. It's not paved, so we're going have to be careful about making noise on the gravel as we make our approach. There's no garage. There's no other way for anyone to get away except by boat on the lake. She's essentially trapped in there."

"Did you see any signs of the girls?" Murph asked.

"No, but we were afraid to get too close until you arrived. We found a place that gives a good view of the house. It's over here."

He led Murph and Johnson to a little hill alongside the road, about twenty feet in front of the cars. They climbed the six-foot, dirt hill, crouching when they reached the top. Kaylin separated the branches of a thick bush, allowing Murph a good view of a brown, ranch style house, standing majestically before a still, blue lake. There were three windows on the roadside.

"My guess is the window on the right is a bedroom," Murph said, "since it's the farthest from that entrance. The small window in the center must be the bathroom. The other is probably another bedroom, or maybe a family room. That's where we have to check for the girls first. There may be another entrance on the other side of the house that we'll have to cover."

Murph turned and climbed back down the incline. He knelt, picked up a stick about the length of a pencil, and motioned the others to join him.

"We can't wait for any more units," Murph said, drawing a rectangle to indicate the house in the dry, loose soil. "So, here's what we're going to do. Kaylin, I want you and your partner to work your way around to the front of the cottage to cover that other entrance." Murph placed an "X" in the presumed position of the lakeside entrance. Murph looked at Kaylin and his partner. "But I want you two to stay outside while we enter from the roadside. Don't do anything on your own. Listen for my orders. Understood?"

"Yes, Sir," Kaylin said.

"Stewart," Murph said, "you're with me. Campbell, you're with Johnson. The four of us will try to get in by the door on this side of the cottage." He drew another "X" to indicate the roadside entrance. "We move only on my say so. Remember, the girls' lives may depend on how quiet we can be, and on our working as one unit. Everyone, keep an eye on me for orders. Let's go."

Murph pulled his automatic, and started to walk toward the top of the driveway, being extra careful not to step on any large, loose stones that might cause him to lose his balance, or make noise when they skidded out from under his step. His approach was noiseless, his steps firm and sure.

"He's assuming the girls are still alive," Kaylin whispered, grabbing Johnson's arm to delay him. "Suppose he's wrong?"

"He's not wrong! Until we know differently, Officer, you assume the girls are alive. A negative attitude like yours could lead to the failure of this rescue. If you're going to be negative, you'd better stay here, and let the rest of us do our job."

Johnson shook off the officer's grip with an exaggerated pull of his arm, and ran after Murph and the others, watching where his feet landed as carefully as Murph.

As Johnson caught up to Murph, Kaylin overtook him. "Sorry, Detective," Kaylin whispered, "I didn't mean any disrespect or doubt. I'm in, fully."

"Good, now do your job, and do it right."

Reaching the front door, Murph gave Kaylin and his partner a full minute to circle the house, the second longest minute in his life. The two officers ducked under the windows to avoid detection, finding the lakeside door that Murph had predicted, closed. They took positions on either side of the door, and waited, guns at the ready by their heads, safeties off, their eyes glued to the door, ready to react at the first sign of movement or gunfire.

Murph peaked through the white, lace curtains that covered the lower half of the window that he thought might be to a living room. The girls were seated on a couch against the back wall, huddled together, their arms wrapped around each other. They were obviously crying, their bodies visibly shaking. Barbara stood in front of them with her gun held loosely at her side, pointing toward the floor. On the wall above the couch stood an enlargement of the photo she had taken at Kilmore's bar. The faces of Eve St. Marie and Janet Robertson had been crossed out with red "X"s. A red heart encircled Dr. Svensen's face. Murph spotted two entrances to the room, both behind Barbara's current position, one to her left, one to her right.

Murph re-joined Johnson at the door. He drew a picture, in the ground, of the room and the couch, indicating the two girls' position. He marked a large "X" in the ground, and mouthed, "Barbara," and then indicated the positions of the two entrances behind her with slanted lines. *I hope Johnson understands my cryptic message.* Johnson nodded his understanding. Murph then indicated he would take the entrance on the left, by pointing first to himself and then the left entrance, and Johnson should cover the other one by pointing to Johnson and th3e right entrance. Johnson nodded again. Murph reached for the doorknob of the screen door.

Johnson scrunched up his face. *I hope it opens quieter than the one at Janet Robertson's house. If it squeaks as loud at that one, Barbara will know we're there, and Murph's plan could change from a well-planned, quiet rescue into an all out attack, and a complex, deadly shootout with Barbara. That would greatly lessen the girls' chance of survival. Please, God, no noise!*

The doorknob turned silently, and when Murph pulled on the door, it opened without a sound.

Johnson looked Heavenward. *Thank you, God.*

The white, wood door with three, six-inch long by three-inch wide, rectangular windows, stood ajar. Murph pushed it. Like the screen door, it opened easily, and without any noisy protest. Murph signaled the officers to follow them as they entered the kitchen.

Bill Rockwell

Murph and Stewart headed to the left entrance to the living room, while Johnson and Campbell circled to the right. Neither team made a sound.

When Murph arrived at the doorway, he checked to see if Johnson had secured his position. Murph peaked around the corner. The situation hadn't changed. Barbara still stood with the gun pointing toward the floor.

CHAPTER 57

"Why are you doing this to us?" Molly asked. "You promised to get us back to our homes."

"My Dear Molly, I'm afraid you were in the wrong place at the wrong time, and your girlfriend, well, she knows too much now too."

"We won't tell anyone anything," Molly said. "We promise."

"I'm afraid it's not that easy. You'd eventually blab what you know to someone, and it would get back to your father. I have to prevent that. It's the only way I can be sure I'm absolutely safe. So, I'm afraid, Miss Molly and Friend, I have to make sure you won't be able to speak to anyone about anything...ever. It'll be all over in a few minutes." Her mouth morphed into a mean grin, as her hand began to tighten on the gun, still pointed at the floor.

The girls' crying became louder. They choked, and gasped for breath between bawling sessions.

Murph had heard enough. He stepped around the doorframe, and into the living room with his gun aimed at Barbara, ready to shoot if Barbara even moved her weapon in the girls' direction. His feet were spread shoulder width apart for maximum balance. He held the gun in both hands, aiming toward his target. His hands were steady, but he had to force himself to breathe smoothly and deeply as he had been trained; however, he found it difficult to avoid holding his breath. His emotions still ran high, driven by his personal involvement in the case. Luckily for him and all the participants of this raid, his training won out in the end, his breathing finally easing as he awaited Barbara's next move.

Officer Stewart came to his side silently, knelt on one knee, and assumed a shooting position with both hands holding the gun at arm's length, aimed at the suspect. Unlike Murph, however, her hands shook, and she found herself holding her breath. No one but she would notice, she knew, but it still bothered her.

"Police! Freeze, Barbara," Murph yelled.

Barbara slowly turned her head in Murph's direction.

"Dad," Molly said, her voice just above a whisper.

Murph's eyes remained fixed on Barbara. He knew he couldn't miss from this distance, but he had to remain focused, ignoring his daughter, her pleas, and, most of all, his inner rage. Johnson and Campbell stepped into the room to Barbara's right, assuming the same positions as Murph and Stewart, Campbell's hand, shaking as much as his partner's.

"Freeze, Barbara," Johnson said. "Do it. Now!"

Barbara's head snapped in Johnson's direction. She smiled at the officers, as if they were welcomed guests, and not armed policemen, determined to capture her.

"Drop the gun, Barbara," Murph said. "There's no reason for anyone else to die. Do it now, Barbara. Drop the gun."

"Hello, Detectives," Barbara said, without moving, and without dropping the gun. *I couldn't possibly turn fast enough to shoot all of them. They have me outnumbered four to one. I wouldn't even get one shot off before they killed me. I could shoot one of the girls, probably the detective's daughter. She deserves to die, but they would shoot me just as quickly. No, my only hope is to surrender, and explain myself, explain all my actions, explain why I'm the injured party here. That way, the world will know I'm right. It's the only way they'll ever learn the truth.*

"Come on, Barbara," Murph said when she didn't make any move to comply. "You gave us a big speech about how much you help people. Getting yourself killed now is going to help no one. Rest assured, Barbara, we *will* shoot if you don't drop the gun. Don't let my child have to see that, please."

Barbara's head fell back, her head bobbing slightly at full extension. She began laughing hysterically. "Okay, you win, Detective Murphy." She allowed the gun to slip from her hand. It bounced once, landing near her feet.

"Thank you, Barbara," Murph said, running into the room, keeping his gun trained on her. "Now put your hands on top of your head."

She complied, returning her gaze toward the children, still huddled on the couch, sighing deeply.

While leaning his upper body back away from Barbara, Murph swept his foot across the floor, kicking the gun toward Johnson. It slid in one fluid motion into the awaiting hand of Johnson who placed the weapon in his pocket. Like Murph, he approached Barbara with his gun trained on her.

The two rookie officers had stood like statues, keeping their guns trained on Barbara while the detectives had disarmed, and were preparing to handcuff her. Their rookie hands were now sweating as well as shaking, their breathing shallow and irregular. Later, they would discuss their nervousness during the rescue with each other in the privacy of their patrol car, but, for now, their self-presumed failings would remain their secret. They both hoped Detectives Murphy and Johnson would never discover that secret. In reality, neither detective had noticed anything unusual about the two officers behavior, nor did they care. Their focus had been on the alleged killer, their only concern the rapid and safe completion of her capture and the safety of the children.

Johnson took a pair of handcuffs from his belt and, having holstered his weapon, snapped them onto Barbara's left wrist. He grabbed that wrist, twisting it behind her back in one motion. He then grabbed her right wrist, joining the two hands behind her back, and locking the handcuffs around her right wrist also. The handcuffs clicked loudly as he latched them.

"You have the right to remain silent…" Johnson said, his mouth only inches from Barbara's right ear, his voice gruff and lacking sympathy.

"You Two Officers, check the rest of the house," Murph ordered, pointing to Stewart and Campbell. "Be careful, in case she has a partner lurking somewhere. Don't forget to check the basement and attic, if the place has them. Let Officer Kaylin and his partner in, so they can help."

The two young officers moved out of the room with their guns elevated by the side of their heads, and wearing serious expressions. Stewart went first into every room, followed by Campbell and then Officer Kaylin and his partner, each checking a different part of the room, including closets and behind every door.

"Clear," each officer shouted as they found a section free of hidden suspects.

Murph turned to the two girls on the couch, still frozen with anxiety and fear. He walked over to them, after holstering his weapon.

Molly tried to jump up to meet him, but her legs felt like liquid rubber, quivering underneath her. She collapsed back into Betty Ann's arm.

Murph sat next to Molly, and received a powerful hug and a large kiss on his cheek. Betty Ann's arms reached around Molly to try to hug him. He hugged the girls harder than they hugged him. He fought back the tears that started filling his eyes. He wanted to scream at them and, at the same time, he wanted to cover them with kisses. He now realized how afraid of losing Molly he really had been. *I hope I never experience anything like that again, never, ever again.*

"Oh, Daddy," Molly said, "I was so scared."

"Me too," Betty Ann added.

CHAPTER 58

"Now, what am I going to do with you two?" Murph gently broke free of their simultaneous embrace. "I'll have to decide later, I guess. Right now, we'd better let people know you're safe."

Jennifer answered on the first ring.

"Hi, Jen, the girls are fine. They're both safe. I'll tell you the whole story later. Here, you can talk to them now." He handed the phone to Molly, and stood.

"Hi, mom, we were so scared. Daddy was so brave."

Jennifer spoke quickly, her nerves exploding in her voice. "Molly? What happened? Where were you? Why didn't you call us? Why did you leave the house? Why didn't you leave a note? Are you really safe? You had us worried to death. You just wait until you get home..."

"Mom, mom," Molly said, trying to interrupt her mother's tirade, and, at the same time, trying to control the tears and sobbing that came from deep within her, "we'll explain it all later. I can't talk long now. Dad needs the phone. The important thing is we're both safe. Are Betty Ann's parents there? She'd like to talk to them."

Alongside Molly, Betty Ann shook her head. Terror covered her face. "No," she mouthed to Molly who ignored her friend's appeal, and handed her the phone. Betty Ann frowned, and closed her eyes as she brought the phone up to her ear, fully prepared for the yelling she expected to explode from her mom.

"Betty Ann," Carol said, her crying interrupting each syllable. "Are...you...all...right?"

"Fine, mom. Molly's dad saved us. We're fine."

"What happened, and why didn't you stay at home, or give us a call? You know better than that. You had me worried to death. Your dad's going to kill you, if I don't first. I want you home as soon as Detective Murphy is through with you. Do you hear me, Betty Ann? You better have a good explanation too."

"We'll tell you everything later, mom," Betty Ann said. "Mr. Murphy needs his phone right now. So, we'll have to keep this short. I promise we didn't do anything wrong. We were just in the wrong place. That's all that happened, but we're fine now. I love you both, but I really have to hang up now. Bye, Mom."

"We love you too. We'll talk later. You've got a lot of explaining to do. Put Detective Murphy back on the phone."

Betty Ann sighed, as she handed the phone to Murph, who stood above them bearing a deep frown. He sighed deeper than Betty Ann.

"Hi, Carol, the girls aren't really up to talking to their parents right now."

"Are they really all right, Murph? I mean *really.*"

"Yes, Carol, They really are fine. They don't have a scratch on them." Murph sent a questioning glance at his daughter by raising his eyebrows, and lowering his head. Molly nodded her agreement. Murph smiled, relieved he hadn't lied, no matter how unknowingly, to Carol. "They're a little shaken up by their ordeal, but otherwise, they're okay. I'll get them home to you as soon as I can. You can have a go at them with all your questions then. I'll debrief them here so they won't have to come downtown to file the report. I'll also talk to them so they don't try any more lies on us for a long, long time, if ever."

"Thanks, Murph. We owe you."

"No, you don't, Carol. Believe me, you don't."

"I need my cell phone, huh?" Murph stood with both fists on his hips, and wearing a deep frown.

Both girls responded by smiling wryly, and looking deep into each other's eyes, their foreheads touching, their arms again wrapped around each other.

"That will be the last lie you two are allowed in this lifetime. I think I can guess what happened. So, I'm going to have Johnson debrief you, because I'm afraid I might do something I might regret later. He'll be a lot easier on you than I would, but remember, Molly, he's known you a long time. You can't lie to him. He's your human lie detector. Then, he's going to give me your stories. It better be the truth, and it better match the ones you tell at home. Do both of you understand all that?"

They both nodded, releasing their embrace, and separating their foreheads, relaxing for the first time since being kidnapped.

"We're through with lying, Dad. Honest!"

"Yeah, for this week," Murph said with as much sarcasm as he could muster. "Just be honest with Detective Johnson and your parents, and you'll both get out of this with your bodies intact, and with a couple of bruised egos as your only injuries. You both should consider yourselves very lucky. It could have turned out a whole lot worse."

Murph glanced over to Barbara who gave the girls a huge smile. The look sent chills down both girls' spines. They jumped into each other's arms again, clamping their eyes shut to block out Barbara's malicious stare. Molly peaked with one eye to ensure that her father remained to protect them.

"Oh, I think we *totally* understand."

"You'd better," Murph warned. "Tonight, Molly, I want you to stay up until I get home, no matter how late that may be. After our family discussion of everything that's happened this weekend, you and I are going to have our own private talk. Understood?"

"Okay, Dad. I'll stay awake." She clamped her eyes shut in dread of the lecture she anticipated her father had planned for her. She already knew its content, volume, and her emotional reaction to it. Her dad loved her, she knew, and he would try to be gentle; however, she also had seen his temper in action many times before. *I hope he leaves his temper at work.*

"There's no one hiding anywhere in the house," Campbell reported, "or in the small, musty attic. There's no basement."

"Good," Murph said. "Thank you."

"Who'd you expect to find in my attic, Santa Claus?" Barbara asked with a chuckle. "I work alone. It's better that way."

"Do you understand your rights to have a lawyer present while we question you?" Johnson asked. He maintained a vise-grip on her arm to prevent any sudden movements.

"Of course I do. What do you think I am, stupid?"

"The thought had crossed my mind."

"Well, I'm not! I don't need any lawyer present either. Record anything you want. No jury will convict me. I'm in the right in everything I did."

"What about kidnapping the girls here?" Murph asked. "You think that was right?"

"I didn't kidnap them," Barbara said, glancing at the girls. "They came with me of their own volition. I didn't even have to force them to get into my car. Ask them."

Murph shot a glance at the girls who drew closer to each other, hiding their faces behind their hands, as if frightened by the ugly, wicked witch in a movie. Murph stepped between the girls and Barbara to shield them from her cruel stares.

"What were you doing with them here, then?" Murph asked. "You had a gun in your hand. It looked like you were planning on killing them like you killed Eve St. Marie."

"Oh, I was, I was. They were the first of today's scheduled victims. They're better off dead anyway. Look at them. One needs an abortion before she burdens society with her dirty offspring, and the other is a gullible friend, who'll probably end up in the same condition soon anyway. Society's better off without both of them."

The girls cried in anguish, loud and hard, harder than they had ever done before. Murph took a quick step toward the witch before him.

Johnson yelled, "No, Murph, no!"

Murph stopped, lowering his head, and gritting his teeth until they hurt, angry for not protecting the girls from Barbara's stupid, ego piercing remarks. *I'd like to kill you, You Bitch, but...control, control, control...*

"Officer Stewart," Murph finally said through the anger in his voice, "and you other officers, please escort the girls out of here before this suspect hurts them anymore...or before I do something I'm going to regret."

CHAPTER 59

"Sure, the great Detective Murphy moves to protect his daughter and her friend *now*," Barbara said, as the officers escorted the two girls out of the house, "when it's his fault they're here in the first place. You would have been responsible for their deaths, Detective Murphy, if you'd given me five more minutes, just five more minutes."

"How do you figure that?"

"Yesterday, after I realized that your daughter had seen me tell Linda to call me with my changed ring, I knew I had to do something to keep her from telling you what I had done. I thought I could persuade her to keep quiet about that little detail. So, I tried to talk to her before she left the clinic, but you wouldn't let her come to the phone. You yelled at me instead." She smiled. "I bet I could have convinced both her and Linda to keep quiet. I can be very convincing when I have to, but you wouldn't let me talk to Molly. No, the great, interfering Detective Murphy blocked my plans, and put his daughter at risk.

"Then, when you confronted Betty Ann and her boyfriend, Molly told you to go back into the clinic to arrest the murderer. I thought she had figured out I had killed Eve...smart detective just like her father, I guess. I realized then that she had to die. I also knew she would undoubtedly tell her girlfriend. I had to kill both of them before they told you anything, and I would have too, if you hadn't interfered again. So, if I had succeeded, Great Detective Murphy, you would have been the cause of their deaths...*should* have been that cause."

"But my interference, as you put it, also got them out of danger. Did you also plan to kill Linda for the same reason?"

"Yes," Barbara said with no hint of emotion, "that would have been scheduled for later tonight. By then, your daughter and her girlfriend would be in the lake out there with our old counselor, Georgi."

"You mean you did kill Georgi Clay?" Johnson asked.

"Fish her and her car out of the deep end of the lake, if you don't believe me. They would have made a happy threesome, two pregnant women and a naïve, policeman's daughter. It would have made a pretty picture."

Murph's eyes widened. He took a step toward Barbara, grunting loudly, and bunching his fists.

Johnson quickly jumped between the two, shaking his head. "No, Murph! So, Barbara, you were the one sending the emails to the Clay family in Arizona."

"Oh, yes, they didn't suspect anything, The Fools."

"Why did she have to die?" Murph asked, pushing Johnson aside, and nodding his assurance that he now had control of his emotions again. "Simply because she was pregnant?"

"No, no; I fell in love with Doctor Elliot Svensen the minute I met him. He is so handsome, so strong, so debonair, and so intelligent. I knew we were going to be a couple immediately, but Georgi had become pregnant by him first. So, she had to go. I didn't want to hurt Elliot by simply killing her, and having her body discovered somewhere. He was, after all, fond of her. I didn't want him to have to go through the ordeal of a funeral, of unnecessary grief. I decided it would be best if she simply disappeared after announcing, through me, that she had a family emergency. It hurt Elliot a little, but not too much." She winked. "I made him forget her real quick."

"I'll bet you did," Johnson whispered.

"Why did Eve St. Marie have to die?" Murph asked. "She didn't have anything to do with the Doctor's social life."

"Now, there you're wrong," Barbara said. "Look at that picture I took at Kilmore's bar. I was planning Janet's murder by then. I had followed them to the bar. I decided to be bold, and go in, so I could be close to Elliot. That's when I found out Janet had become pregnant by him. He had left me for that overbearing bitch. Can you believe it?"

"I don't understand," Murph said. "You started talking about Eve, and now are talking about Janet. If I understand right, you killed Janet because she had replaced you in the Doctor's heart, and had become pregnant by him, but I still don't understand why Eve became one of your victims."

"Don't you see? Look at that picture closely. She's looking at Elliot with those large, green eyes, and he's staring back at her. They're falling for each other."

The two detectives studied the picture. Janet and Eve's boyfriend were looking directly at the camera. Eve's eyes were looking to her right and Doctor Svensen's eyes to the left. They could have been looking at each other, or at something that caught their eyes in separate parts of the room, as the camera captured the picture.

Murph stepped closer to the picture, and studied it for a few more seconds. *I don't see how anyone but a paranoid person could interpret those eyes as anything but distracted. They don't look like the longing eyes Barbara is describing.*

"I know that look," Barbara continued, as if answering Murph's thoughts. "Eve would have had the abortion, dumped her boyfriend, and then come after my Elliot. My suspicions were confirmed when Eve made that bogus call to the clinic saying that she had problems after her abortion. There were no problems! She wanted another visit to the clinic to get close to *my* Elliot again. I know her type. She'd see our counselor, then request a meeting with the doctor who performed her abortion, and then she'd be in his life as a lover, and I'd be out.

"Next would come Eve's second pregnancy this year, this time by Elliot, and I'd have to kill her then. So, I decided to eliminate her as a problem even before she became one. I wasn't going to let her have Elliot. I ended up killing her first because Janet wasn't home when I went to her house. I didn't want to wait for her to return. So, I went to Miss St. Marie's apartment, and found her home. Shot her as soon as she opened the door.

"Then yesterday, after the clinic closed, I caught Janet home, and gave her what she deserved. Of course, I'd been in her house before for parties, and knew of the easy access from the quiet street in back. So, getting in and out of the yard proved to be no problem at all. You see, everyone opens the door for the assistant clinic director, no questions asked."

"Why did you shoot Sheryl Fontaine?" Murph asked. "Did she walk in on you while you were killing Janet?"

"Oh, no, I forced Janet to call that reporter. I told her to tell her she knew the name of the killer, and wanted to give her the information personally. The fool fell for it. Reporters will do anything for what they consider a big, exclusive story. I think they call it a 'scoop.' They don't care if there's any danger involved."

"Why did you want to kill her, though?" Murph asked. "She had nothing to do with the clinic or Dr. Svensen."

"I have to admit that I made a small error, a slight miscalculation, with that one. You see, I had been anonymously feeding information to the news media through her about the murder. I fed her personal information about Eve and her boyfriend, information she couldn't get from the police. I told her about Eve's abortion, and connection with the Pro-Life League. I even planted a card from the Pro-Life League in Miss St. Marie's hand after I shot her. I wanted to throw suspicion on the head of that Pro-Life League, but it backfired. That dumb reporter announced that Elliot had become the chief suspect. I never told her that. She made it up. I told her that Katherine McDonahue was the person you thought to be the most likely candidate, but, no, she had to name Elliot. Imagine suspecting Elliot of murder…ridiculous! The man's a saint! So, I decided she had to die for her lies. Unfortunately, she made it out the door before I could shoot her. I guess I hit her through the door though, but I feared going after her. So, I left without knowing if she had died."

"But not until you shot Janet three more times," Johnson said, his voice almost a growl.

"Oh, I couldn't resist it. She was lying there with her mouth open, asking for it. She still had that filthy baby inside her. So, I emptied the gun into her mouth and her belly. I would have shot both her and her baby a few more times, but I ran out of bullets."

"This may sound cruel," Johnson said, lowering his voice to a whisper, and shooting a quick glance at Murph, "and, believe me I don't mean it to be cruel, but it sounds like you're the only girlfriend of the doctor who didn't get pregnant. Why no pregnancy? Wouldn't that have sealed him to you?"

Barbara yelled and spat, as she spoke, "I didn't get pregnant because I can't get pregnant! The abortion I had in Rochester was botched by the butcher of a doctor I had. I bled like crazy. They couldn't stop the bleeding. They had to do a hysterectomy to save me. So, I'm sterile. That's why Elliot didn't stay with me. He wanted children. That wife of his is drunk all the time, and won't give him any. She was going to be the last one I eliminated, since there is no chance of her getting pregnant, The Damned Drunk." She spat on the floor to emphasize her statement.

"No spitting, You Crazy Loon!" Murph said.

CHAPTER 60

Johnson yanked on Barbara's arm. "Stop spitting, or I'll gag you."

Barbara defiantly stared at Johnson, ignoring his warning. "I decided I would eliminate all my fertile competition, and then move on to Elliot's wife. I planned to keep working on him to adopt a child...our child. I almost had him convinced when that other witch, Janet, moved in with that large smile and those long eyelashes. He fell for her almost as fast as he had fallen for me. He'll eventually come to my way of thinking, and we'll spend the rest of our lives together, with, or without children." She threw the same disgusted look at Murph. "You mark my words, Detective Murphy. No one is going to stop me, not you, nor anyone else in this world."

"A jury might think differently," Murph said.

"Are you kidding? You're the crazy one. They're going to sympathize with me. Every time I tried to make *wonderful* Elliot, happy, one of those other women moved in to take him away from me. Any jury is guaranteed to agree with me that I had no other choice. I had to do what I did. They'll understand completely...and a lot better than you. You'll see."

"What about your victims? You didn't give them a choice in the matter," Murph said. "Eve St. Marie was certainly innocent. She wasn't even after your precious doctor. I don't see any look of desire or longing in her, or in the doctor in that picture you're using as an excuse for her murder. You're reading too much into it."

Barbara shrugged her shoulders, smiled, but remaining silent. *It isn't worth arguing the obvious with the oblivious detective. He's definitely the crazy one.*

"Georgi Clay would have given the doctor the baby you claim he wanted," Murph said. "The same goes for Janet Robertson. I'm not condoning Doctor Svensen's extra-marital affairs, mind you, but none of those women deserved to die. None of them *had* to die. They were innocent. It's only in your warped mind that they did something to hurt you and your precious doctor. On top of that, you were about to compound your actions by killing two innocent young girls, who really had no idea how they got into this mess. Then, to top off all that, you now tell us you were planning to kill Linda and the doctor's wife. Don't you see what that makes you? You're a mass murderer, a crazy serial killer."

"No, Detective Murphy, it doesn't make me a mass murderer, crazy, or not. It makes me justified. All those women, including Elliot's wife and your precious little girls deserve to die. They're all better off dead. Besides, they all were becoming a burden on society. They had unplanned pregnancies. They were going about stealing a married man from his wife for the purpose of having more unwanted children, unlike me, who wanted to release him from his wife's drunken lifestyle, and provide him a happy, stable home instead. Don't you understand? They were stealing *my* man from *me*, and, worse, they were interfering with our love for each other. No! There's not a jury in America who would convict me. You'll see. The jury will totally agree with me. All those women are better off dead."

"You're better off behind bars," Johnson said, turning off his recorder, and leading her toward the door. "I'll put her in the car, Murph, while you finish in here."

"Keep her away from the girls. Get a search warrant for her place. We need her laptop for those emails she's been sending to the Clay family, and whatever else she has that we can use."

Murph shook his head. *Darn it! I almost lost it altogether there. I'm so glad Tom stopped me. I wanted to hit her so bad. I wanted to kill her...still want to kill her, but I shouldn't have lectured her, even though it helped get a confession from her. She's a psychologically sick woman. She is crazy. She probably didn't hear anything I said, anyway, but I shouldn't have been provoked by her, shouldn't have come close to losing my temper with a suspect, any suspect. I owe Tom more than he knows. Maybe I do need those anger management classes Jen has been trying to get me to attend. That would make her and Molly happy, that's for sure, to say nothing of my partner. He would be absolutely delighted.*

Murph walked over to the picture that had helped get two women killed. He wondered what they were really looking at. He tried to picture the bar, and where the picture placed the participants. *Eve would have been looking toward the bar, toward the owner and bartender. Maybe he had waved at her. Maybe she looked to him for help in getting away from the doctor, his pregnant girlfriend and Barbara. The doctor would have been looking toward the booths. Had he spotted someone he knew, a patient, a friend, or maybe a colleague? I'll have to go back to the bar and clinic to find the answers.*

"Murph?"

"In here, Chief!"

The Chief wore a loose-fitting, gray sweat suit, and white sneakers. "Congratulations on catching our alleged murderer. I saw Johnson helping her into the car."

"Thank you, Chief. What are you doing here on a Sunday?"

"Johnson called me when he sent out the general call for our forces to converge on this place. He told me about the kidnapping. I decided to supervise the raid...from a distance."

"Thanks for not interfering."

"You're welcome, Murph, but I came here for two reasons. First, I had been worried that your raid might not turn out as it did...with everyone safe."

"You mean with my daughter and her girlfriend alive, don't you?"

"Exactly! I drove here very, very slowly, praying the whole way. I didn't want to interfere with your raid because I trust you and your experience. If I got here before your raid, I would have been forced to pull you off. Having your daughter involved would have precluded you from participating. We both know that. There wasn't time to brief anyone else, including me, on all you knew about this case, especially about the suspect. I could have trusted Johnson, but I wanted you. You're the best we've got. So, I had to trust your judgment, and now I'm glad I did, but, if it didn't work out, I wanted to be here for you, Murph, and, of course, to gather information so I could explain to Internal Affairs why I hadn't taken you off the case as soon as we knew Molly had become involved. However, I have to be honest with you. I came because I wasn't sure how you would have reacted if the worst had happened."

"You mean angry, don't you? You were afraid I'd shoot her. To be honest, I thought about it, came close to doing it."

"I was more worried about how you would feel emotionally; I worried less about your anger than you might think. You wouldn't have killed her. You're too well trained, but, if Molly didn't make it, you would need more than Johnson to hold you together emotionally until Jen could get here to pick up the pieces. I wanted to be there for both of you in that circumstance. Jen's the best, you know. She really loves you. You should listen to her more than you do."

"Funny you should say that. I was just thinking the same thing. She's been encouraging me to attend anger management therapy for some time now. I think I'll take her up on that before I *really* do something I'll regret. Do you mind if I tell her you agree with that?"

"No, not at all, and if it makes it easier for you, tell her I ordered it."

"Thanks. You said there were two reasons you came. What was the second?"

"You said it yourself already, your anger. Although I knew you wouldn't kill her outright, I thought you might strangle, or beat her a little before Johnson could pull you off, and we had a chance to interrogate her. Not that I would blame you, but legally, it's a good idea *not* to be judge, jury and executioner, even if your daughter *had* been elevated to the alleged murderer's next victim. We'd like to prove she killed those women with a confession…without any brutality associated with obtaining it…holds up better in court."

"I almost did just what you said before you arrived, but Johnson stopped me. Is that why he called you, because he thought I'd kill her, or beat her a little, or maybe a lot?"

"He cares for you, Murph. He feared you losing your temper no matter how it came out. The suspect looks intact physically, no bruises, I presume. So, I guess he defused your anger. Please, don't blame him. He went by the book and beyond. He knew I'd trust your judgment about the raid, but, like me, feared the consequences afterwards. He feels the same way I do, but feared he might need someone who outranks you. So, I'm here. Are you happy, or angry with all that?"

Bill Rockwell

"Let's see. My daughter's safe, my partner kept me from strangling our alleged murderer, that alleged murderer is in handcuffs, my wife's going to be happy her husband is finally going to seek help for his anger problem, and my Chief is here to comfort and care for me, as well as protect my job. So, yes, I'm happy, very, very happy. Thanks again, Chief. I really do appreciate you're coming out here and, most of all, for understanding."

"Again, you're welcome. Now, let's get going. Remember, our story for everyone except Johnson, I came here to relieve you because of your daughter's involvement, but got here too late. I've got an image to maintain, you know."

Both Murph and the Chief laughed all the way to the door. They then both assumed serious expressions, as if they had been arguing over the Chief's arrival, and who had the ultimate authority to run the case. Neither really cared if they could pull it off.

CHAPTER 61

The next day, Murph, Jennifer, Molly and Johnson stood by Sheryl Fontaine's bed. Her arm had been casted, and stood bent at the elbow, hung above her by a series of ropes and pulleys. A clear, plastic chest tube could be seen emerging from the edge of the sheets that emptied into a large bottle, filled with water. Occasional bubbles forced their way from the end of the tube.

"I'm glad to hear your surgery went so well," Molly said, "and that you can move your legs."

"The surgeon said I'd be up walking in no time. I'll need rehab, of course, but then I'll be on your heals again, Murph. You can count on that."

"Don't you mean ahead of me, beating me to the next stop in my investigation?"

"Of course, just trying to be polite. You've been falling far behind me ever since the three of us were in high school together. I was always ahead of you. Remember all those school newspaper reports I did on the events at school. You were always playing catch up."

"Yes, Sheryl," Murph said, putting his arm around Jennifer, "that's true, but while you were so far in front of me, you never looked back to notice the woman who chased me…and eventually caught me, I might add." He gave Jennifer a light kiss on her cheek.

"That's her loss and my gain," Sheryl said with a big smile.

All three friends laughed.

Johnson shook his head. "You three are sick. Do you know that? You're all sick in your heads."

Murph slapped Johnson on his shoulder. "You'll understand someday, Johnson, if, and when you get married."

"I don't think I can stand any more of this sloppy friendship thing," Johnson said, "I think we should leave."

277

"I'd like to second that," a young doctor in a long, white lab coat said as he entered the room. "She needs her rest more than laughter. Now, get out of here. We said five minutes, and that's long past."

"One thing before we leave," Murph said. "I promised Jim that you could have all the details on the case so you could be the first to report them."

Johnson handed her a large, thick manila envelope.

"That's everything we have up to this morning," Murph said, "including some things no other newspaper, or TV news station could possibly have yet. There are a few details we're keeping to ourselves, but the information in there should heat up the air waves a great deal for you and your station."

Sheryl hugged the envelope. "Thanks, Murph."

"You're welcome. Get better as fast as you can. It felt awfully strange yesterday, capturing a criminal, and not having you standing in front of that van of yours reporting on the scene. I hate to admit it, but I didn't realize I'd miss you that much...but I did."

"You're an old softy. Now get out of here so I can read this stuff. Hey, Doc, how soon can I have a video crew in here to film the report?"

"Thanks, Detective," the doctor said with a large frown. He pointed to the door. "Now, out!"

As they walked through the lobby, Officers Stewart and Campbell approached them.

"The Station said you'd be here," Stewart said. "We've got some reports for you."

"Let's go outside," Johnson said.

"First," Campbell said, "scuba divers found Miss Clay's car at the bottom of the lake. Her badly decomposed remains were inside. Doctor Rebak is examining her now. We'll get the results on the bullet that killed her as soon as they find it."

"Ballistics does confirm, however," Stewart said, "that the weapon you took from Miss Schine killed both Miss St. Marie and Miss Robertson. The gun originally belonged to her father. It's his police weapon. We checked. He never had to use it while on duty, and, in those days, police weapons weren't routinely fired for identification purposes. That's why we couldn't find a match in any of our ballistic databases."

"The computer techs," Campbell said, "found all the letters and emails she had sent to the Clay family. She made it sound like Georgi Clay still lived here in Adams. It's no wonder they didn't suspect anything. They're going over it to find any hidden files, but when we left the Station, that's all they could confirm."

"Anything else?" Johnson asked.

"No," Campbell said, "but Officer Stewart and I would like to thank both of you for the experience you gave us, and for the understanding way you handled our errors yesterday."

"What errors?" Johnson asked, glancing at Murph.

"Don't look at me," Murph said. "Yesterday's one big blur."

"Thanks," both officers said in unison. "We'll never forget it."

"That's the whole idea," Murph said. "Now, get back on patrol before the Chief finds you dilly-dallying with us old timers."

"Old timers?" Johnson asked, watching the two officers walk to their car. "That hurt, Murph."

"No harm done," Murph said, with a broad smile, "unless you pursue her as your girlfriend. At least now she's been warned that you are a dirty *old* man."

"Pursue her," Johnson said, as he began running toward the officers, "That's a great idea, Murph. Thanks for suggesting it to me."

"No, that's not what I meant."

"Hey, Officers," Johnson yelled, "wait for me. I need a ride to the Station. See you later, Murph."

CHAPTER 62

"What do you think will happen to Barbara?" Jennifer asked, watching Johnson and the two officers climb into the patrol car. "Will she get the death penalty?"

"I really doubt it. The Chief told me her lawyer planned to plead her out as insane. I think that can be proven to a jury with very little effort. Her computer files will probably give increased credibility to that defense. She became insanely jealous of anyone who got close to Dr. Svensen. She's just not rational. No, I think Barbara lost her sanity a long time ago, maybe after her father died, or after her botched abortion. It escalated into an obsession with Dr. Svensen. She thought she had to kill anyone that she perceived as a threat to that relationship. To boot, we discovered that two of the female employees from the last clinic she worked at disappeared before she left. Can't prove she killed them unless she confesses, but they're looking for them in the surrounding bodies of water. My bet is that they'll find their remains, and that will seal her insanity defense. She's an insane serial killer."

From behind Murph came a familiar, female voice. "Hello, Detective." Unlike her appearance the day before, Katherine McDonahue looked bright and chipper. She wore a flowered, yellow dress with short sleeves and a curved neckline. Mike wore a blue shirt with "HAWAII" plastered all over it and khaki pants.

"Hello, Mr. and Mrs. McDonahue," Murph said. "This is my wife Jen and my daughter, Molly. We met Mr. and Mrs. McDonahue during our investigation. She's head of the Pro-Life League."

"Please call me Katherine. This is Mike."

"Nice to meet you," Jennifer said.

"Why are you here?" Murph asked. "Is there something wrong?"

"Just the opposite," Mike said through a broad smile. "She finally got the all clear from her oncologist. Friday's dose of chemo was her last, thank God. It looks like all the surgery, radiation and chemo did the trick. He thinks she's cancer free."

"We'll have to see about the cancer free part," Katherine said. "We can't say I'm a survivor for another five years, but I do feel good about it. More importantly for the moment, I feel good *now*."

"Congratulations," Murph said. *God, please let it be true!*

Jennifer and Molly quickly joined in expressing the same sentiment.

"There's another reason we're here though," Katherine said, "and, unless I miss my guess, here she comes now."

Betty Ann and her parents walked toward the group. Betty Ann ran ahead to hug Molly.

"Well," Jennifer said, "this is quite a surprise. Is Betty Ann all right?"

"I'm fine, Mrs. Murphy." Betty Ann released Molly, but gripped her hand in both of hers. "We're here to talk to Mrs. McDonahue about Pro-Life and my baby. Is that you, by any chance?"

"Yes," Katherine said, smiling and shaking the hands of everyone except Betty Ann, who refused to release her two-handed grip on Molly. Katherine then turned to Jennifer. "Your husband was kind enough to give Betty Ann one of our brochures. Her parents called us last night after her terrible ordeal. Betty Ann is still really eager to get some information about her pregnancy. So, I thought we could meet here this morning after my doctor visit. We're going to head somewhere private and neutral for some serious discussions."

"Yeah," Betty Ann said, "I want to learn all about the options Doug and I have, including having the baby, and maybe giving it to some nice family for adoption."

"That's only one option," Katherine said. "We've got many more to consider, though."

281

"I think this conversation should be kept personal and private," Jennifer said. "Let's move on, Murph, and leave these people alone."

"Can Molly come with us?" Betty Ann asked. "We've been through so much together. I'd really appreciate having her around. Besides, I'll probably forget half of what I'm told before I meet with Doug and his parents. Molly can help me with that. Please."

Jennifer looked to Carol and Ted for direction.

"It's Okay with us," Carol said, looking to Ted for confirmation. "*If* it's okay with you."

"Sure, if Molly wants to come," Ted said.

"What do you think?" Jennifer asked, looking to Murph, who nodded his approval even before she finished her question. "I guess it's all right with us, *if* Molly wants to go."

"Sure, I'll go. Besides, Betty Ann's got such a death grip on my hand, she'd drag me with her, even if I didn't want to go."

"Okay," Jennifer said. "That's settled. Where are you off to then?"

"My office isn't far from here," Ted said. "I took today off, but we can still use my place. It's private enough for what we need, and we shouldn't be disturbed. Is that all right with everyone? If so, let's go. My car is in the lot across the street."

"I'm glad you got them the information," Jennifer said, as they watched the group cross the busy street. "I'm sure they'll do the right thing."

"I'm not sure what the right thing for Betty Ann is," Murph said. "It's a terrible thing to say, but I'm glad we don't have to make that decision…at least not yet."

"I pray to God we never have to, but if we do, we do. Then, we'd be the ones calling Mrs. McDonahue for advice."

"Maybe Carol and Ted will come over later to tell us what they've decided," Murph said.

"Unless I miss my guess, that's exactly what they'll do. I'd also bet they won't let that unborn baby become just another statistic of the innocents who have been destroyed."

"You should have said killed," Murph said. "Unfortunately, this society can't tell the difference, and doesn't appreciate what a gift life truly is."

CHAPTER 63

Murph made two stops on the way to the Station. First, he stopped at the Women's Medical Clinic.

Officer Martinelli waited for him outside. "Good morning, Detective Murphy, I got a message from the Station that you wanted to meet me here."

"Yes, indeed, it is a good morning, isn't it?"

"Yes, you caught your murderer, saved the children, and probably prevented more murders by closing the case so quickly. I'd count that as more than a good day's work."

"That's the reason I asked to see you, Officer Martinelli. I wanted to thank you for your help in our investigation. I like your enthusiasm and style. It's fresh, and it's what this downtown needs. You're a credit to your uniform."

"Thank you, Detective Murphy." He smiled, and bowed slightly at the waist. "You don't know how much that means to me coming from you, Sir. My mother, father and grandfather were all police officers in New York. They're all gone now, but they'd be proud to hear what you said. They taught me to think of this as more than a job. It's a profession that, if done right, can improve this town. I guess I took my parents' teaching to heart. I'd like to thank you again for the experience I gained by helping you and for your gracious comments."

"You're welcome." Murph walked toward the front door of the clinic. He turned back before he opened the door to see Martinelli donning his helmet in preparation for mounting his bike. "Just so you're forewarned, I spoke to Chief Stone about your performance, and how it helped us solve the case and protect potential victims. I wouldn't be surprised if you hear from her very soon. It could mean a promotion."

"Well, thank you again, but, if it's all the same to her and you, I'd like to stay on patrol here a while longer before being transferred, or promoted. I've been studying hard, and I think I can pass the exam, but there's still some good I can do around here, and I need to learn more about police work through on-the-job training, so to speak. I hope you understand."

"I thought you'd say something like that. When you're ready for a change, or want to move up, give me a call."

Martinelli waved as he peddled away. Murph watched the young officer pedal down Main Street. *I see a lot of me in him. I think I'll follow his career. He'll make a great detective someday. Hope I'm around to see it.*

"I'm sorry about your assistant director," Murph said as he took a seat in Doctor Svensen's office.

"She must be truly insane," Dr. Svensen said in a monotone voice and without a smile, "to have killed three women over me."

I can't argue that one. "I came to follow up on something you might be able to straighten out for us. It's about this picture that Barbara snapped that night at Kilmore's bar. Your eyes seem to be focused over to the side. What were you looking at?"

He paused before speaking. "Oh, now I remember; I spotted a doctor I knew. He waved at me just as Barbara took the picture, I guess. I went over to him afterwards. I want to be truthful to you, Detective Murphy. I feared he would mention my being there with Janet. So, I asked him not to mention it to my wife. Of course, that doesn't matter any more, does it?"

"Excuse me, but I don't understand. Why do you say that?"

"A few minutes ago, that Channel 14 newswoman reported on all my affairs, and how Barbara murdered my pregnant girlfriends. I assume she got that information from you."

"You assume wrong. Our office gave her only the information about Barbara's murder victims, not why, or who got them pregnant, or whom you were dating. We were hoping to save that until the trial, and only intended to use it if we really had to. She obviously has another source. She is very good at her job, even from a hospital bed. We've been competitors for years, with her usually coming out on top. I didn't release that information, Doctor.

I would never do something like that to you, or anyone else. Whether I approve of what you do, or not, your life is your life to live. I'll try to find out how it leaked, and plug it."

"It's too late for that, I'm afraid. My wife has already screamed at me. It wouldn't surprise me if she divorces me."

I'll bet Johnson included that information in the packet we gave Sheryl. How could you, Johnson? How dare you release that information behind my back? You know better than that! You're trained better than that! "It really is none of my business, but maybe you should use the opportunity to talk to her about your differences. Maybe you both could benefit from marital counseling, a talk with your minister, rabbi, or priest, and, maybe even a trip to Alcoholics Anonymous."

"Ha! I'm the doctor, and you're giving me advice on how to save my marriage. You're a policeman. What do you know about counseling?"

"Probably less than you, but I'm a person who recently realized I could use some counseling myself. It's a humbling experience for me to admit it, but I've seen the consequences of not getting that counseling. It's a lot worse. You mentioned divorce. I've seen the other extreme, violence and murder. I'd rather not be at your home, investigating either your wife's murder…or yours."

"A little presumptuous aren't you, thinking that my wife and I are capable of murder?"

"Maybe, but who would have thought your clinic assistant would have turned into a serial killer? You and your wife both have a lot of issues that could erupt into violence also. They're different issues, of course, but they could lead to violence, nevertheless. Professional counseling may be the only way to save your marriage, but that's up to you. You're right, I'm not a priest or counselor. I'm just a concerned police officer, butting in where I think it might do some good, but I'll stop preaching. It's really not the main reason I stopped by today."

Doctor Svensen lowered his head, and spoke slowly. "Believe it or not, I've been considering exactly what you just suggested. I'm not sure it'll work, but you're right, it's the only chance my wife and I have of saving our marriage. It won't be easy, but I'm willing to give it a try." He leaned back and looked skyward. "Now, I have to get my wife sobered up and agreeable, before she takes the step you're afraid of, and divorces me, or shoots me."

"Good luck, Doctor, I hope it works out for both of you."

Murph never looked back. He still fumed as he entered his car. *You're definitely going to get chewed out, Johnson, even if it all works out well for the Svensens. You were still wrong, releasing that sensitive information. You knew Sheryl would broadcast every juicy detail. You wanted to hurt the doctor because you dislike his lifestyle. That's not an acceptable excuse…not by a long shot!*

For his second stop, Murph parked in front of Kilmore's Bar.

Paul Kilmore waved as he entered. "Detective Murphy, come join me. Congratulations on solving Eve's murder."

Murph took a seat, and slid the photo toward Kilmore. "Recognize this photo?"

Kilmore studied it for a few seconds, and then looked to the area where the photo had been snapped. His cheeks puffed, the corner of his lips turning upward as his face brightened. He pointed to the area adjacent to the bar, and then returned his gaze to the photo. "Sure! Eve wasn't very happy that night. I tried to cheer her up a little."

"Cheer her up? Is that why she's looking toward the bar area?"

"Exactly! I had just popped the top off one of her Rockson beers. I took a big gulp, and then gave her a thumbs up." He demonstrated by holding his thumb elevated far above his head. "That's why she's smiling in the photo. It turned out to be the first time she smiled that night, and the last time I ever saw her pretty smiling face."

"I'm sure she appreciated your effort." Murph pocketed the photo, deciding not to relate Barbara Schine's misguided interpretation of both the smile and the direction of Eve's gaze in the photo. *No need to make him feel guilty of contributing to Eve's death. No, that all falls on crazy Barbara Schine.*

"I've called her company, and ordered a continuous shipment of her beer." Kilmore grabbed a rag, and polished the bar that didn't need polishing. "Yup, I'm going to feature her beer as our customers' top choice, and going to put up a neon sign saying,

Bill Rockwell

'Home of Eve St. Marie's Rockson Beer!' It's the least I can do for such a nice lady."

As Paul Kilmore's eyes began to gloss over with tears, Murph pushed himself away from the bar, and silently headed for the door. As he passed through it, Murph waved his goodbye. He paused outside the bar, and looked Heavenward. *Rest in peace...in Heaven...with your unborn child, Eve. Your murderer has been brought to justice. I now vow to return to see your name up in lights!*

Outside the dogs,
the sorcerers, the unchaste,
the murderers, the idol-worshipers,
and all who love to practice deceit.

Revelation 22:15

Rachel mourns for her children;
she refuses to be consoled
because her children are no more.
Thus says the Lord,
Cease your cries of mourning,
wipe the tears from your eyes.
The sorrow you have shown
shall have its own reward...
There is hope for your future...

Jeremiah 31:15-17

ABOUT THE AUTHOR

Bill Rockwell is a retired physician who wrote many articles and a chapter on allergies in a medical textbook. Since retiring, he has taken to writing mystery and fantasy novels, listed elsewhere in this book. He lives in Connecticut with his wife.

NOTE FROM THE AUTHOR

Thank you for reading my novel. If you enjoyed this story, tell your friends, and consider reviewing it on amazon.com, goodreads.com, or any other website you frequent. For further information about my other novels, including their first chapters and summaries, as well as a preview of future novels, visit my website, http://billrockwell.net

My author E-Mail: billrockwell203@gmail.com

Rachel's Vineyard Contact Information:

1-877-467-3463 (1-877-HOPE-4-ME)
www.rachelsvinyard.org

Bill Rockwell

Made in the USA
Columbia, SC
06 May 2018